Fay Weldon

was born in England and raised in a family of women in New Zealand. She took degrees in Economics and Psychology at the University of St Andrews in Scotland and then, after a decade of odd jobs and hard times, began writing fiction. She is now well known as novelist, screenwriter and critic; her work is translated the world over. Her novels include, most famously, *The Life and Loves of a She-Devil* (a major movie starring Meryl Streep and Roseanne Barr), *Puffball*, *The Hearts and Lives of Men*, *The Cloning of Joanna May* and *Darcy's Utopia*. She is married, has four sons, and lives in London.

FAY WELDON

Growing Rich

Flamingo
An Imprint of HarperCollinsPublishers

Flamingo
An Imprint of HarperCollins*Publishers*
77–85 Fulham Palace Road,
Hammersmith, London w6 8jb

Published by Flamingo 1992

9 8 7 6 5 4 3 2 1

First published in Great Britain by
HarperCollins*Publishers* 1992

Photograph of Fay Weldon
© Mark Gerson FBIPP

ISBN 0 00 654495 9

Set in Baskerville

Printed in Great Britain by
HarperCollinsManufacturing Glasgow

The world is full of little towns that people want to leave, and scarcely know why. The hills crowd in too closely, they say, or the plains which stretch around are too featureless, or the freeway runs through, or doesn't run through: you can hardly put your finger on the source of their discontent, or indeed your own. There's a doctor, a school, good neighbours, kindness and even friends – it's just you know you have to get out of there or die: let the name of the place be Dullsville, Tennessee, or Borup, Denmark, or Newcastle, New South Wales, or El Ain in the United Arab Emirates, or Fenedge, East Anglia, a kind of sorrow creeps along the streets and drags you down; you can hardly lift your feet to shake it off. The shops in the High Street are forever closed for lunch, or would be better if they were: the houses in the centre may be old, veritable antiquities, but still lack resonance: a tuning fork that declines to twang, dead in the face of all expectation. And if nothing happens you know you'll soon be dead as well, or your soul will be. Some marriages are like this too, but that's another story.

Now it is dangerous to speak these thoughts aloud in case the Devil, in one of the many forms he takes, is flying by; and he often is, especially in such places, for it's here he locates his safe houses, which in its turn may be why you register the place as desolate. By 'a safe house', for those of you not familiar with thrillers, I mean a house maintained by our security services to offer immediate safe haven for anyone under threat or duress. Houses belonging to the Devil will be on the outskirts of town (though sometimes the town creeps up to engulf them); they will be large, ramshackle, damp and crowded by trees but nevertheless have a kind of seedy status. Woe betide anyone who buys such a house, and sometimes the nicest people do, but that too is another story.

Not so long ago three young girls were rash enough to have a dangerous conversation as they walked down a country road just outside Fenedge, East Anglia, England (The World, The Universe, Space, The Cosmos, etc.). They were on their way home from school. Their names were Carmen, Annie and Laura. All three were sixteen, all three had been born in the same week in the same small-town labour ward, all three were close friends, and restless, and all three were virgins. (I know because I know everything that goes on round here.) Not that I necessarily attribute their restlessness to their virgin state, but I do see it as a contributory factor. And the Devil scents restlessness as a dog with its head out of the car scents a rabbit in amongst a thousand other reeking aromas.

'This place is the pits,' said Carmen. She was their leader.

'Dullsville, Tennessee,' said Laura. She was the pretty one.

'We've got to get out of here,' said Annie, who was always desperate.

And on they walked, shuffling the white dust of the autumn road all over their shoes, because they were school shoes and who cared? And the Devil, who just happened to be driving by in his big black BMW, picked up the scent of discontent and entered it into his mind for reference. God may have eyes in the back of his head so everything you do is known to him, but I tell you the Devil is worse. He just observes and presses Enter and there you are, your weakness, your vices, sealed into his awareness for ever, available for instant recall any time he chooses. And he accepts no excuses; he offers no leniency for youth, inexperience or stress. That's you! Too bad!

The Devil, or this particular version of him, for indeed his name is legion, didn't hang around to hear what else the girls might have to say. He'd heard enough. He just stopped alongside them, as if to ask directions, startling them, and then accelerated away, with a throom, throom more evident in racing cars than in BMWs; he was an old-young man with startlingly blue eyes; he wore a navy blue military-style uniform and a chauffeur's cap which cast a shadow over a strong, bony face.

'That driver was a bit of all right,' said Laura. She had a sweet face and a gentle air, and was altogether unalarming. She felt it was her role and her duty to make the best of things.

'Well, that driver wasn't my type,' said Carmen, though she had little idea what her type was. She just felt like contradicting Laura, whose determination always to look on the bright side she saw as dangerous. Carmen had been born with a sense of the dark and terrible profundity of things. If the country roads were awash with men whom Laura thought a bit of all right, how were they ever to get out of Fenedge? Because Annie was right. They had to watch out for themselves and each other, because no one else would do it. The whole world, except for a teacher or two, conspired to keep them exactly where they were for ever, plus a baby or two or three.

'You're so picky,' said Laura, 'you'll cut yourself,' which meant Laura and Carmen weren't talking.

'What would someone like that want with one of us?' asked Annie. 'He took one look and just drove off. Why? Because we're small-time, small-town girls and it shows.' It was in Annie's nature to diminish herself if she possibly could, which was just fine, so long as she didn't include Carmen in her self-assessment.

'Speak for yourself,' said Carmen, and then Annie and Carmen weren't talking.

'You keep bumping me when you walk,' said Laura to Annie, and that was them gone too.

But that's what happens when the Devil passes by. He searches out discontent and then leaves a whole great surging wake of it behind to make things worse, so even friends feel friendship less, and become scratchy and disagreeable with one another.

The three girls walked in silence until they reached Landsfield Crescent, where they lived. Annie was the tallest: she had a long thin body, and knobbly knees and elbows, and a cross unpretty face and short straight brown hair which became greasy unless she washed it every day, and her mother Mavis not only controlled the hot water but maintained that hair should be washed only once a week: Annie looked, and was, a difficult girl. But she was not like anyone else, which was why Carmen kept her company. And Laura could confide in her and trust her to listen and keep secrets, and Carmen and Laura were best friends and thus the three of them combined to form their own special pact against the world.

Carmen was shorter than Annie but taller than Laura. Her legs were not as long as they could have been, her nose was too large for comfort, her brown eyes so large you could see the whites beneath the pupils, her hair dark and profuse, her complexion sallow, and her mouth sulky. This, at least, was what she saw when she stared at herself in the mirror, as she did a great deal, trying to relate the sense of herself as 'I' to the notion other people had of her as 'you', or, more remotely still, as 'she'. Others saw something different.

Bernard Bellamy did, as the black BMW, Driver at the wheel, Mr Bellamy in the back, returned along the road just as the girls, still in their sulky silence, turned into Landsfield Crescent.
'Hey, stop, Driver,' he said. 'Back up a bit.' And Driver did, the car obeying him like magic, smooth and silky even in reverse, and Bernard Bellamy looked straight into Carmen's eyes, and saw something there that made him think this is the girl I am going to marry, in spite of, or perhaps because of, his having been married three times already and being older than Carmen by God knows how many years.
'That's the girl for me,' said Bernard Bellamy, and Driver said, 'Oh yes? Well, there's one or two things we have to get straight first,' and they drove on.

They had a strange relationship, these two. If you see Driver as Mephistopheles and Bernard as Faust you're getting somewhere near it, though since the century is what it is, Bernard was not so much a man weary of intellectual achievement as bored with plain straightforward money-making, a talent which in the contemporary world is not as well regarded as you might think. Friends drink your champagne and sneer, and your soul shrivels up. To Driver, a shrivelling soul is as mad a waste as letting a £5 peach from Harrods wither forgotten on the shelf. Better gobble it up while it's soft and fresh and delicious.

4

It was dusk, and Driver switched on the headlights, and the back lights glowed red in the autumn air as the car departed, and seemed to hang around a long time, and crows, rising in flocks from the trees that lined the road as the car passed, flapped black wings edged with red.

Around here the land is flat and drained. The people of Fenedge – a place smaller than a town, larger than a village, altogether indeterminate, in fact – will say, 'The sea? A couple of miles away.' Or 'five miles away' or 'just down the road', depending on what they think you want to hear, and because they are themselves unsure. The margins between sea and land are unclear. Personally I prefer seas which crash and wallop against a high shore, so you can be absolutely certain where water and earth collide, and appreciate the tumultuousness of their meeting: beaches where the tides rush up and rush out again over rocks, leaving crabs scuttling for cover, and anemones battered but waving their applause. Not for us, not in Dullsville, Somewhere-Near-The-Sea.

2

Be all that as it may, Carmen was sixteen when Bernard Bellamy first set eyes on her where the road to the coast meets Landsfield Crescent. Driver had been working for him for four months. During that time Bernard had been divorced by a very disagreeable and unloving wife, and his disposable income had risen by twenty-six per cent, one per cent of which he gave to charity. The Bellamy soul was beginning to revive. Such things can take a long time, but Driver had all the time in the world. The Devil's central being takes many forms. If you can be everywhere at once all kinds of things are possible, and what's time anyway?

I ask myself this as I sit in my wheelchair at the window of 8 Landsfield Crescent and life ticks away, and come to the conclusion that what we mean by time is the measurement of change. I have sat here for seventeen years, as long as the Crescent has been in existence. I have watched trees grow from saplings set in mud, and climbing roses creep up concrete walls – that's the good news – and the skin on the back of my hand change from smooth to wrinkled – that's the bad. The Crescent is a short, curved road on the outskirts of Fenedge, central to a housing development which never really happened, apart from this one road which shoots unnaturally out of the town, as if one of a cloud of gnats had strayed too far from the centre and couldn't get back to its gestalt, no matter how it tried. The Crescent houses are detached, ticky-tacky boxes, all trim and no substance, each one with a small front garden, a larger back one, fenced off from the beet fields which surround us. We are without natural shelter: it is not a proper place for human habitation. The wind blows rough and hard up here, and sometimes you can smell the salt sea in it, and sometimes the slurry the farmers use to help the beet crops grow.

Carmen, Annie and Laura, as I say, were born in the same week. I watched the ambulances turn into Landsfield Crescent to take their labouring mothers to the hospital, watched them return, one, two, three. I blessed them in my mind, one, two, three, as if I were the Fairy Godmother, because, knowing their mothers, it seemed to me they needed all the help they could get. I looked forward to watching the babies grow and change, to see how time and event worked through them. The better to do it, I developed the art of seeing through walls, overhearing what could not be heard. I have nothing else to do but develop these arts. Sometimes I get taken out by my social worker, or friends; mostly I just sit here at the window and wait for Carmen, Annie and Laura to pass and wave and reanimate with their actual presence their continuing story in my mind. When you think you can see through your neighbours' walls what is fact and what is fiction is hard to distinguish.

Let me reassure you it was not coincidence – for readers hate coincidence – that led to the girls being born in the same week; rather a matter of housing policy. Compulsory Redevelopment had led to a generous relocation scheme in which heavily pregnant women received priority: Carmen's parents Raelene and Andy had been housed next door to Laura's parents Kim and Audrey, opposite Annie's mother and father Mavis and Alan; next door to me. I also received priority, not because I was pregnant, but as a consolation prize because I am so severely disabled as to need a miracle to become so. At least I have a pleasant window to look out of. The girls' families would normally not have granted two companionable words to one another, except that propinquity, and the nervousness endemic to enforced relocation, obliged them to, at least for a time. (As for me, I speak to whoever is prepared to speak to me: I'm not proud.) Now, sixteen years later, the three families are once again neighbours rather than friends: only their first-born remain attached to one another, bound together by common cause, common experience, sisters in their imagination. And they all still wave at me, but that might be habit, not kindliness.

Sometimes I wonder whether in fact it's I myself, sitting in my window, who control their lives, and not just fate; I who set Driver and Bernard Bellamy down the tree-lined road to encounter the girls as they walked home from the little station at Fenedge Halt. Perhaps it was I myself who, on a bored day, initiated the trouble between Kim and Audrey, the melding of Count Capinski into Mavis's mind, to Alan's distress, and rendered Andy unemployed and Raelene miserable and did it irresponsibly, and all just to liven things up a little down here on Landsfield Crescent: a Bad Fairy, after all, not in the least Good.

But then I remember that a sense of omnipotence can be a symptom of mental illness, and put the notion from my mind. I live in fear of going mad, just to add to my other troubles.

Look at it like this: on the day I summoned Driver out of the flat East Anglian landscape, set him uniformed and gaitered and bright-blue-eyed at the wheel of a black BMW, flickered hell fire through the evening sky to scare the crows, created Bernard Bellamy as both the tempter and the tempted, I did it in response to Carmen, Laura and Annie's desire just to get out of here. I was being helpful, honestly. Creating a window of opportunity for them to leap out of.

'But how do we get out of here?' asked Laura, before they parted. (Driver being a long way off, ill temper just evaporated.) 'Out of Dullsville, Tennessee? How does a girl ever get out?'

'You can work your way out, you can sleep your way out,' replied Carmen. 'You can sell your soul to the Devil.'

'Bags I work,' said Annie, who always believed that if it hurt it was good for you.

'Bags I sleep,' said Laura, but she kept her fingers crossed while she spoke. She believed in love, romance and fidelity, but hardly liked to say so.

'That leaves me,' said Carmen sadly, 'to sell my soul to the Devil.'

And they went into their respective homes, to face whatever there was to face.

Laura's fate waited for her outside the front gate. He was seventeen and had zits; he leaned against his motor scooter. He wore a leather jacket and he had soulful brown eyes and a dogged demeanour. Laura ignored him. She walked straight past him and into her house and Carmen and Annie watched and giggled, and Woodie pretended not to hear them.

Now although Laura accepted her fate she meant to fight it off as long as she could, at least until Woodie had grown out of his zits, had calmed down and could earn an honest living. He was studying technical drawing and carpentry at a college in Norwich, but could think only of Laura. He'd taken her outside at an end-of-term disco and kissed her under the moon, and some kind of yellowy light had pierced through to the marrow of his bones, so now, as he put it, 'She's in my system, for good or bad,' but alas he wasn't in hers, not yet. He knew he would be, one day.

Audrey, Laura's mother, opened the window and spoke to Woodie. She wore a flowered cotton dress, and her arms and her face were thin, but her voice was strong. Laura took after her father Kim, both of them being on the fleshy side, and soft-voiced. 'Woodie,' she said, 'do go away. It's unsettling.'
'I like to be near her,' he said.
'Woodie,' said Audrey, 'the way to get girls to run after you is to run away from them.'
Once she'd run away from Kim, who'd run after and made her pregnant with Laura, and when his divorce was through he'd married her, and moved into the house she'd shared with her mother, until the Town Hall tore it down and housed them here in Landsfield Crescent. She'd had asthma ever since. The climate didn't agree with her: the constant wind deranged her: she always had a pain here, an ache there: she, an inland person by nature, lived in fear that the tide would forget one day how to ebb and would simply rise and rise and drown them all in their beds. After Laura her stomach and bosom had drooped: Landsfield Crescent was not lucky for her. She taught General Science part-time in the local Further Education College. Her husband Kim taught English Literature and Business Studies, full-time, likewise. His classroom and his home smelt sweetly of marijuana, or perhaps it was herbal cigarettes. He had a beard, and wore sandals at the weekend for the health of his feet. He was an energetic lover.
'I don't like playing games,' said Woodie to Audrey. 'Laura either loves me or she doesn't.'
'Then she doesn't,' said Audrey briskly. It is not easy, even for

the most sensible and sensitive of mothers, to accept that their daughters are now of an age to receive love, and offer it. 'She's too young. She has to concentrate on her school work. She wants to go to college. She has to pass exams.'

'I don't care whether she passes her exams or not,' said Woodie. 'It makes no difference to me.'

He spoke with the lordliness of Alexander, Prince of Persia, for all he was seventeen and had zits, and it was at that moment that Audrey perceived that her daughter's fate was indeed to marry Woodie and have his children and there was no saving it. You give up your life for them, she thought, and they're never grateful, they take it all for granted, and then they grow up to give away their lives as well, in just the same way. Where's the point? This depressing thought, which she believed singular to herself, gave her a pain in her stomach, or perhaps it was the other way round and the pain led to the thought. Whatever it was, the pain never thereafter quite went away, nor the sadness.

'Woodie,' said Audrey, 'she's passing exams for her sake, not yours. If you can't understand that what can you understand? Go away.'

And still he stood there, leaning against his scooter, chewing a fingernail. He didn't believe a word of it, until Laura appeared at the front door, in her short white shorts and blue and white striped top.

'Woodie,' she said, 'this is getting embarrassing. Go away.'

So Woodie went away, at least for a time. And Laura went back to her room and stared at her homework. One year to her exams. And shouldn't her father be home from college by now? He was having an affair with a girl no older than her, and Laura knew and Audrey didn't, and should she tell or should she not? She thought perhaps she should but she didn't have the courage.

The moment that Woodie revved up and drove off was the moment that Count Capinski entered Annie's mother's head and took up his fitful residence there. Annie's mother Mavis Horner, you must understand, was a clairvoyant, and her husband Alan Horner a preacher in the Fenedge spiritualist church, so the event, which to others might seem strange, was well within Mavis and Alan's field of comprehension. Spirits of the departed, figments of the other world, flitted in and out of Mavis's head at the best of times; what was unusual was that on this occasion this one not only arrived unsummoned but stayed. Perhaps – to use the Horners' rather Victorian terminology – the ordinary borderlines between this vale of tears and the spirit world were breached by the shock of Driver's appearance in the neighbourhood, to take up residence in his Fenedge safe house, and Capinski managed to slip through and find a tenancy in Mavis's head. At any rate, there he was. This was how it happened.

Annie was upstairs in her small back bedroom doing her homework. Mavis and Alan Horner were inspecting the garage which Carmen's father Andy Wedmore had built for Alan, at no little cost. Alan, who worked for the local ambulance service, occasionally found it convenient to stop off with his ambulance at home on his way back from a call, just to recover from the trauma of his work. His was an accident vehicle; a particularly bad section of motorway ran nearby.

'He's made a bodge job of this,' said Alan, running a finger over a window ledge, getting a splinter as a result. 'I could have done it better myself.' The first part of this statement was true enough, and could be said of all work undertaken by Andy; the second not so.

'You don't have the time for DIY,' said Mavis. 'Each to his own. The cook to his wooden spoon, the bootmaker to his last.'

They eased their way round the side of the ambulance, between metal and concrete, noting a loose piece of wiring here, a wrongly placed shelf there, the general air of flung-together. Alan wore a suit which wrinkled round the crotch and under his arms, but a nice blue shirt and yellow tie, and Mavis wore a blue dress and a yellow cardy. They liked to echo one another in every way they could. They felt very close. She had the puffy face, stolid body and puzzled eyes of the habitual clairvoyant. Too much contact with the other world is bad for the appearance. It muddies the outlines of the self as it appears to the real world. Fudge and fuzz: half one thing, half another.

'What are those two funny black bags?' asked Mavis. 'On the shelf over there? Rolled up carpet, or what?'

'They're not important,' said Alan. 'I'll have them out by the morning. The morgue's taken to closing down at four. I never like to knock the staff up, when they're tired. It's easier for everyone to face nasty work in the morning.'

'You mean they're body bags?' asked Mavis. 'And they're full?'

'Full as I could manage,' said Alan. 'I hope I got them both properly sorted out.'

And Mavis started to moan, for all the world like someone in childbirth.

'It's only till morning,' said Alan. 'They'll be okay. It's not a warm night.' But it was, of course.

Mavis's moaning stopped and a particular look came over her face, one Alan was accustomed to seeing only on Sundays, and which alarmed him even more than the sound of her evident distress.

On Tuesday and Thursday evenings Mavis conducted private séances (eighteen pounds a head, minimum number of partici-pants four plus medium) and on these occasions, exhausted after a day in her surgery, made do with the tricks of the trade while in conversation with the recently dead. (That is to say, most people of a certain generation – and her clients were mostly elderly – know a Harry or have bad backs, or were known to the ambu-lance service and, besides, Mavis kept extensive files on local residents and had notice of who was coming along.) But some-times on Sunday afternoon at the Spiritualist Church service, when she was rested, she would be conscious of what she called the real thing. The fuzz and fudge of her normal appearance would sharpen and harden: her neck would seem longer, her cheeks more hollow, and when her mouth opened she spoke with someone else's voice. He could see her now begin to change.

'Oh my God,' said Mavis. 'It's much too strong. Make him go away.'

'It can't be coming from the body bags,' said Alan, 'because they were both female.'

Next time Mavis spoke it was in a guttural male voice with an Eastern European accent.

'Dear lady,' said the Count/Mavis, 'I am charmed to make your acquaintance at last. I am deeply indebted for your hospitality. May I introduce myself? Count Capinski at your service. And so this is your husband?'

'Shake hands with the Count, Alan,' said Mavis, stretching out a surprisingly male hand, which Alan, taken unawares, accepted and shook.

And that was how, by all accounts, Capinski arrived in Mavis's head, where he stayed on and off for some years. Since his alternative dwelling was a little dungeon in Cracow in the fourteenth century, where he was, or so he claimed, starving to death, Landsfield Crescent must have seemed agreeable enough while he waited for possible rescue in his own time.

Annie came down from her little back bedroom in search of a cup of tea and found her mother devouring an entire sliced loaf and the week's ration of cheese, and the hot water supply switched on, which was unusual mid-week. Everyone has their favourite economies, and Mavis's was not to waste hot water. But today she planned on a bath.

'So this,' said Count Capinski, from Mavis's bread-filled mouth, 'is your little daughter. But isn't she of an age to be married?'

'She's still at school,' explained Mavis, in her own voice, swallowing.

'But not for long,' observed the Count/Mavis. 'Soon she will meet a tall dark stranger from overseas, who will sweep her off her feet and carry her off to paradise. She will travel to the ends of the earth and back again. It will not be all happiness. I, Count Capinski, prophesy.'

'It's too bad,' said Annie. 'Your own mother ill-wishing you,' and, outraged, she went over with her homework to Laura's and knocked on the door.

'Please can I do my homework here?' asked Annie.

'Is there something the matter at home?' asked Audrey.

'No more than usual,' said Annie.

'You might as well go on up, since Carmen is there already. But try to concentrate on your homework,' said Audrey, who often talked like the back page of a women's magazine, 'and forget your personal problems.'

Annie went up to Laura's room, which had been especially decorated to Laura's taste in pink and white, not like her own room, which was so full of steel filing cabinets and card indexes she could scarcely find her way to bed.

'What now?' asked Laura of Annie.

'There's a strange man in my mother's head,' said Annie.

Carmen said, 'Will your father sue for divorce?' and Annie said, 'No such luck. It will turn him on.'

Now Carmen too had run into trouble on reaching home. Observing how often any one of the three girls, on returning from school, would stay home only briefly, to reconvene the group in either Laura or Carmen's house after a spat of door-slamming, I would comfort myself with the notion that though not to have children is a terrible fate, to have them can be worse.

Carmen came from a family of slobs. Everyone knew it, no one denied it, not even Carmen. The general belief was that she had been switched at birth. She had a fineness of feature which her alleged parents did not; a composure and a sense of wrong and right altogether alien to them, which they interpreted as the putting on of airs. Andy, Carmen's father, had a reputation throughout Fenedge as a bad if cheerful builder. His extensions fell down: his damp courses never worked: if he painted your window frames you could be sure those windows would never open again. It was nothing to him that his final bills would outstrip his estimates by more than a hundred per cent: his wife Raelene seldom dared answer the phone for fear of outraged and impatient clients; yet enough work came his way to keep him going. At least he sang, not swore, on top of his ladder, and if you failed to move the furniture before he arrived to paint the ceiling he would not pull a face but simply get on with the painting, and charge you extra for non-drip paint. He would take on work other builders would scorn to – the tarting up of premises between one tenant and the next: bodge jobs specifically asked for. His large beer belly flopped over his belt; he had little piggy jolly eyes, and on hot days he seldom left home with a shirt. His wife Raelene ate for comfort and suffered from depression: her chin and her neck were as one: she had once been on a shoplifting charge. Stephen, Carmen's younger brother, had been on two drug charges (though only for marijuana) by the time he was fourteen. They were not a hard or criminal family; on the contrary, Andy would stop whatever he was doing to mend your burst pipes in an emergency, and Raelene would feed the neighbour's cat if required. They were just slobs and everyone knew it, and pitied Carmen for being one of their number, and Carmen hated to be pitied. Who doesn't? At least anyone you care to talk to.

On this particular afternoon when Carmen let herself in, she found her father and her brother eating fish and chips for their tea, which Raelene had just finished cooking. The chips were dripping with oil, the way the family liked them: no tales of the desirability of polyunsaturated fats had come their way so far. Stephen was reading the morning's edition of the nation's favourite tabloid, *The Sun*. He always opened Page 3 first. In those days the nude girls always appeared towards the front of the newspaper; later, for some reason to do with I don't know what, except perhaps the fact that the owners of the most fabulous tits failed to live up to expectations of equally spectacular and lascivious lifestyle, they had drifted towards the back and become more to do with the sports pages than home news.

Carmen stood in the doorway to the kitchen and raised her eyebrows, as she was well accustomed to doing. The cat's food hardened, maggoty, in a saucer uncleaned for days; dirty dishes piled in the sink; the smell of frying fish lingered in the air; little dusty yellow globules of fat spotted the ceiling above the cooker. Raelene, her own plate of fish and chips keeping warm in the oven, attempted to save the cooking oil for reuse by pouring it through too small a sieve, so that it slopped over the draining board. Now, hopelessly, she squirted detergent into the slops. She had pretty little hands, which Carmen had inherited, but they were lost in the whole of her.
'So,' said Andy to Carmen, 'Madam honours us with her presence. Too late to help her mother with the tea.'
He wore no shirt. Stephen wore a T-shirt made of his nation's flag. Carmen raised her eyebrows further.
Raelene said, 'Carmen, will you put the garbage out? I've only got two hands,' and Carmen replied, 'Why did you call me Carmen if you only wanted me as a beast of burden?' But they all looked at her blankly, so she said, 'After tea, mum,' and took her plate from the warming oven and sat down at the table, carefully brushing the chair before she did so.
'No chips,' she said, and pushed them to one side of her plate,

and picked away at the fish, carefully removing the burnt batter to reach the almost raw white flesh inside.

'Carmen,' said her father, 'I don't know what it is with you. You're the great wet blanket of all times.'

And Stephen turned to the photograph of Peachey Penelope, whose bare bosom upthrust not just all over Page 3, but whose nipples extended back into Page 2, as a special exercise in energetic typographical ingenuity.

'Coo, Dad, look at that,' said Stephen. 'How about those?'

Raelene complained from the sink, where spilt oil and bargain-price detergent had just formed a kind of foamy cake, 'Don't look at it, Dad, I don't like it.'

Andy looked at Penelope's likeness and said to Raelene, 'Don't be such a prude. Everyone's got them.'

Carmen said, 'Men don't, only women,' and both Raelene and Andy said, 'No one asked your opinion, Car,' and Carmen said, 'Why did you call me Carmen if you meant to call me Car?'

Stephen said, 'How'd you like a handful of that, Dad?' and Andy, looking more closely, said, 'I don't know so much. I reckon that's silicone, not flesh.'

Carmen took off her navy school jumper and undid her tie and took that off too.

'Do you think that's silicone, Raelene?' asked Andy of his wife and Raelene refused to look but said, 'How would I know?'

'Feel the texture,' said her son, 'you'd tell soon enough. A bit of a squeeze and you'd know.'

Carmen took her shirt off and no one noticed. She sat there in her bra. Raelene stared at the draining board and the menfolk at the photograph.

'Silicone or not,' said Andy, 'I wouldn't complain and nor would you, Steve, if you're a chip off the old block.'

Carmen took off her bra and sat there naked from the waist up. She had a white skin, and a bosom smaller than Peachey Penelope's and discreet and rosy nipples. She pecked away at her fish.

'I'm a chip off the old block then, Dad,' said Steve, and then caught sight of Carmen and rose to his feet, spilling tea all over the newspaper, at the same time as Andy said to his daughter, 'You disgusting little bitch, cover yourself up at once.' Carmen just said, 'Don't be so prudish, Dad. We've all got them. Why don't you take out yours, Mum, and give the lads a treat?'

At which Andy and Stephen both left the room in a hurry, leaving their meal half finished. They were both upset.

'I'll get the social worker on to you,' said Andy as he left, 'for Unruly Behaviour. You're no daughter of mine. I blame you for this, Raelene.'

Raelene wept into the mess on the draining board.

'Carmen,' she said, 'cover yourself up. You let me down. What are we going to do with you?'

Carmen put on her bra, saying, 'I'm going to write and ask them to put men's privates on Page 4. Give the girls a treat.'

Raelene said, 'You're the Devil's own daughter,' and certainly in those days Carmen could be fiendish and Raelene would complain about her to me when she came over for a cup of tea. But I wasn't surprised. Landsfield Crescent was point eight of a mile nearer Driver's safe house, Sealord Mansion, than any other street in Fenedge, and the Wedmore home was on the outer curve of the Crescent, so it caught the full force of trouble, as some houses in a road will get the force of the prevailing wind, not others. You can tell by the way the trees in the garden lean. But I didn't tell Raelene all that. I'd just say adolescent girls were often difficult for a time but then grew out of it, which I would have thought self-evident, but it's surprising what people don't know. What is more, Bernard Bellamy had that day looked into her eyes and seen what he was looking for, so one way and another it's not surprising she took off a garment or so. Forget the provocation.

'If I'm the Devil's child,' said Carmen to her mother, 'then you must have had it off with the Devil.'

Raelene dropped the plastic bottle of detergent onto the floor. The red cap fell off and the liquid slunk towards the cat's saucer unnoticed.

'Or perhaps one night, seventeen years ago,' said Carmen, pressing home her advantage, 'you got lucky and a knight in shining armour came galloping up to you, and had his wicked way, and forgot to take you with him. I just can't believe I'm that man you call your husband's daughter,' and she put on her shirt and took her homework over to Laura's, and asked Audrey if she could put her school clothes through the wash, so she could be smart for school the next day. Audrey said of course. Audrey ran a one-woman rescue service for the benefit of her neighbours' children, but it didn't stop her getting a pain, which she put down to indigestion, caused by worry over her husband Kim's whereabouts; an unreasonable worry, she told herself, born of the guilt of having in her time been the other woman.

And of course Carmen, Annie and Laura talked and idled their days away instead of working at their lessons and when the time for their final examinations came a year later were even more hopelessly unprepared than could reasonably have been expected. Blame the parents if you like; personally I blame the Devil . . .

3

The very next day after Driver drove through Fenedge and Bernard Bellamy looked into Carmen's eyes, I received a letter. Now it's a known fact that where there are devils there are angels too, and vice versa, so I couldn't be sure whether the letter was sent by the agents of heaven or hell. It came from a transplant surgeon in a large Chicago hospital who offered to operate on me free of charge, in an attempt to reinstate the flow of blood to my spinal column – by either a kind of backbone bypass or, better still, the clearing of blocked veins by miniaturised balloons – and thus return to me the use of my legs. (Accounts of my condition get written up from time to time in the medical press.) I replied by return yes, of course he was welcome to try, rather to the discomfort of my own local Fenedge general practitioner, Dr Grafton, whose belief it is that his patients deserve whatever afflicts them, and that they shouldn't struggle too hard to be rid of it. This in turn may be why Mavis Horner has so many patients lining up to visit her. I flew off to Chicago within the week.

I shan't dwell upon the ins and outs of catheters, the fancy drugs and startling lasers that contributed to my treatment; indeed, I can't remember much of it, I swallowed so many rough large red forgetfulness pills. I only mention the event to explain that I was away from my window for six months or so, and that when I returned to my watching post, my legs no better and no worse, it became apparent that there had been an exciting development or so in my absence. Exciting, that is to say, in Fenedge terms, if not Chicago's.

Sealord Mansion had been bought by Bernard Bellamy, who was now Sir Bernard Bellamy, knighted for services to industry, struck on the shoulder by a sword wielded by the Queen herself. It is a fact that to be made a knight you have to be able both to kneel and to bend your neck, and that on occasion certain individuals, too old and stiff to do such things, have had to decline the offer on account of their infirmity, but Sir Bernard Bellamy had no such problem. He looked these days as Elizabeth Taylor looked after three months in a health hydro – younger, skinnier and fuller of future than ever – now that Driver drove him everywhere.

Sir Bernard, it appeared, had diversified out of catering – he made his initial fortune selling chicken patties in the Chick-A-Whizz franchise concern – into the hotel business. Sealord Mansion, that mecca of the naturalists, had at the stroke of a pen become Bellamy House, and the builders been moved in to strip both the inside and the outside of the building to make it look less like what it was, an admiral's folly, and more like an hotel, American style, and one fit for the rich and famous. A Save Sealord group, composed mostly of botanists and bird-watchers, had risen and fallen in my absence; been defeated in their struggle to permit the house, in whose attic bats bred, and in whose grounds rare heathers and ferns grew, to remain undisturbed.

'Can all these people be wrong?' Bernard had enquired of Driver, 'and only me be right?' That was when Driver was nudging his way through a crowd of some eighty placard-bearing people, whose hearts were clearly in the right place, and whose spelling was excellent, which is not necessarily the case with the protesting classes. 'Save the *Hippuris vulgaris*!' they read. 'Protect Our *Typha latifolia*!' 'Our Whinchat Is Precious To Us', 'The Wheatear Shall Not Perish', 'Long Live Sealord, Home To The Hooper Swan', and so on.

'Very easily,' Driver had replied. 'For every man who wants to achieve something, there are at least a hundred who try to hold him back. And just look at the Adam's apples of these particular folk; how they jerk up and down in their scrawny throats in rhythm as they chant! Hard to take them seriously.' And Sir Bernard Bellamy looked and laughed, for what Driver said was true. The Devil is often right about things: it helps explain his power over the hearts and minds of men.

And the other sad truth was that Sealord Mansion, built by an admiral for a child mistress a couple of centuries back, had in the first place been a bodge job dedicated to an unholy purpose, and had caused outrage when it was built, so that the outrage which attended its change of use, to use the planners' term, was thereby undermined.

And so when Driver drove over the foot of one young bird-watcher and lamed him for life, the protest fizzled out, instead of gaining force as could have been expected. But then again, though it is in the nature of bird-watchers to endure great discomfort in pursuit of their ends and think nothing of cold and damp and shortage of sleep, they perhaps see too much virtue in stillness and silence: they are simply not the kind to persist in aggro.

To get to Sealord Mansion in the days before it became the Bellamy House Hotel, the proper way, the walkers' way – or so I am told: I must rely upon others in this instance – you would scorn the main road. You would walk inland in a northerly direction from the sea wall at Winterwart, leaving behind you the tidal flats, where the waders and wildfowl abound; you would crunch across the shingle stretches where the yellow-horned poppy grows, and the hound's-tongue and the curled beet too; you would skirt the flooded gravel pits, which the sticklebacks so love, and where a bittern was once sighted, and so reach the heather-clad dune slacks, where the ling and the rare cross-leaved heath abound. A little further inland and you would pass the habitat of the rare natterjack toad – that strange burrowing creature with its unnaturally short back legs, whose habit it is to utter such eerie cries of a summer evening as to scare the unwary out of their wits – proceed further still, into the woodlands, down the banks of the reed-lined stream and then, finally, under the green arms of the willows, you would come to Sealord Mansion itself, shuttered, dilapidated, but beautiful enough in its disorder, its grounds so richly rewarding to the botanist – anyone searching for the rare royal fern, the *Osmunda regalis*, or the even more rare crested buckler – and an excellent and undisturbed breeding ground for the siskin, the redwing, the redpoll and the brambling and every warbler you can think of. What did they care if Sealord was the Devil's safe house; what do flora and fauna need to know about these things?

Some pleasures are no longer. Sealord Mansion is now Bellamy House Hotel, and a breeze-block wall bars the rambler's way from the sea, and bright green lawns roll neatly over the levelled high dune ridges; the gravel pits are filled the better to fashion a golf course, so the red-breasted merganser calls no more, and only the natterjacks remain, their voices, unloving and unloved, calling through the summer nights. But that's enough of all that nature talk. What's gone is gone.

I never saw any of it anyway.

While I was away in Chicago trying to grow a new backbone, Sir Bernard Bellamy spoke at Fenedge High School for Girls. Driver encouraged him so to do. The event was not a success. Perhaps Driver had his reasons for wishing it thus to turn out.

'But this really is the back of beyond,' complained Sir Bernard as the BMW took the road from the new improved Bellamy House Hotel, with its mock Tudor facade and grand new steps flanked with an imported palm tree or so to add a touch of the exotic. Workmen were still at work: the grand opening was yet to come. The helipad was being built where once a little colony of the rare pasque flower grew. 'Are you convinced it's ripe for development?' 'The back of beyond,' said Driver, 'normally provides a pool of cheap labour for men of vision such as yourself. That is to say, people content to be happy in their own way, which is not ours. Fenedge may not be sin city, but nor do we want it to be.' 'I've never spoken to schoolgirls before,' said Sir Bernard. 'Just deliver the speech we agreed upon,' said Driver, who seemed a little irritated. 'Say the lines and leave the stage; have your cup of tea afterwards, a piece of the cake baked by the Home Economics class, be pleasant to everyone, and they'll all be lining up for jobs at Bellamy House Hotel. You'll see.' 'I may throw away the prepared speech and speak from the soul,' warned Sir Bernard. 'It's what I usually do and it's always worked to date.' At the very mention of the word soul, Driver lifted his handsome head and sniffed the air, like a fox trying to pick out chicken. 'You have quite a snuffle there again,' said Sir Bernard, who knew that Driver was after his soul, but being unconvinced that he had one, felt that selling it was a risk well worth taking. Sir Bernard

22

was accustomed to selling things that did not exist – eternal youth, perfect health amongst them – having a strong financial interest in one of the nation's leading health food chains. There was a slight bump, as if the car had run something over.

'That wasn't a cat, I hope,' said Sir Bernard.

'Good Lord no,' said Driver. They drove on in silence.

By the time they reached the uncompromising square brick building which was Fenedge School for Girls it was raining: the kind of sweeping misty drizzle which so often affected the area, although no doubt it helped the wild flowers grow. (Plants can absorb moisture through their leaves as well as their roots.) A small group waited under umbrellas to greet Sir Bernard. Mrs Baker, Head of English, was there: a woman in late middle age with a beautiful Renaissance face perched on an overflowing body, which she had clothed in layer upon layer of dusty black, in a way that was almost Islamic. Sharing her umbrella were Carmen, Annie and Laura, the three of them making one of her.

'Welcome, Sir Bernard,' said Mrs Baker, 'to Fenedge School. We have been so looking forward to your visit. These days we depend so very much on the support of local enterprise.'

Driver stood to one side; he did not need an umbrella: the rain fell all around but not on him. He held his over Sir Bernard's silvery head, a model chauffeur, always there but never ostentatiously so.

Mrs Baker introduced Laura, Annie and Carmen to Sir Bernard. 'These are my best girls,' she said. Mrs Baker's best girls! By that she meant the girls least likely to succumb too soon to the local boys; girls who would go out into the world and show just what a woman could do, unburdened by domesticity; girls who would pass their exams without trouble. And the exams were only a month away. Annie was Head Girl; she meant to follow in her family's footsteps, and go into the healing arts, that is to say, nursing. Laura was Head Prefect; she planned to go to the University of East Anglia, and Carmen was to do Art & Design at the local Polytechnic. All this Mrs Baker told Sir Bernard, careless of the weather.

But no one was listening. It was raining too hard, and the wind blew the words back into her mouth, and as for Sir Bernard, he was staring hard at Carmen. Rain glistened on her eyelashes; she was, as my grandmother used to describe it, 'in good face' that day, and when she saw Sir Bernard staring she blushed, and looked more enchanting still.

'Shall we go inside?' suggested Driver, because he did not at that time include a chit of a girl like Carmen in his plans. She was not the Marguerite he had in mind for Sir Bernard. Her soul was far too firmly hers; and what's more it swam around in the sphere of Mrs Baker, a woman he disliked on sight, for all she wore layers of black. He could not abide a plump woman, and that was that; a plump good woman was anathema to him.

Sir Bernard stood on a platform in front of two hundred and fifty-three girls and listened to Mrs Baker's introductory talk, or half listened, because Carmen was standing at the very back of the hall, just by the back exit. He would rather she had sat in the very front, but at least he could see her. She is my Marguerite, he thought, and it's up to the Devil to provide her. Mrs Baker was speaking about the transition from the world of school to the world of work, and the usual guff about equal opportunities and women making their presence felt in business and politics, so he paid no attention to his notes and spoke from the soul.
'I reckon all your noses,' he said, 'are too pretty to be kept to the grindstone. I reckon too many people spend too much time telling the young what they ought to hear, and not what they need to hear. Which is this. What this nation needs, to solve its employment problems, is for women to return to the home; to stay out of the workforce once they are married. What's so bad about staying at home?'

Mrs Baker shuffled discontent and disapproval beside him, but he took no notice.

'It's our experience,' said Sir Bernard, 'that throughout the Bellamy Empire the most efficient executives are the ones with stay-at-home wives, the ones who create happy families, healthy children, and give a man something worth fighting for. A man's duty is to support a family; a woman's duty is to make a home he's happy to come back to –'

He could see Driver at the side of the stage. Driver was shaking his head at him. Sir Bernard carried on.

'Book-learning,' said Sir Bernard to the girls, 'is not much use to a girl, and don't let your teachers tell you otherwise. I left school at fourteen; I never passed an exam in my life –'

The stage was lined with curtains allegedly fireproofed. But now a little flicker of flame ran up them. Perhaps it was the fierce focusing of Driver's eyes that set it off, and it was then fanned by Mrs Baker's flush of outrage – though of course it might have been the caretaker's cigarette, discarded but not stubbed out as he entered a No Smoking Zone – but, whatever the cause, Carmen at the back of the hall was the first to see the flames. She shrieked, 'Fire! Don't panic!' and the whole audience rose as one girl and filed neatly from the hall, well drilled as they were in proper emergency procedure, while Laura, Annie and Carmen counted them through. They did not believe in the fire, but they trusted Carmen to get them out of a boring situation if she could.

Sir Bernard and Driver left by the side entrance, made hasty goodbyes and drove off.

'Why didn't you keep to the script?' said Driver.

'I was speaking from the soul,' said Sir Bernard, 'I was speaking the truth as I know it,' and Driver buried his head in his handkerchief and sneezed, and there was a bump as they ran over something.

'That was a dog,' said Sir Bernard.

'It shouldn't have been in the road,' said Driver. 'You must never swerve to avoid an animal: it can cost human lives.'

'Shouldn't we stop?' asked Sir Bernard, but he didn't press the matter, for his soul was so nearly not his any more, and the black BMW slithered on through the flatlands, where the alder trees abound, and ashes and the silver and downy birch, bowed low by bindweed, towards the oak woodlands of the heath.

'Tell you what,' said Sir Bernard, 'you get me that girl for a wife, and I'll follow whatever script you put in front of me.'

'For a *wife*?' asked Driver.

'For a wife,' said Sir Bernard. 'I want her body and soul. I am a man of swift decisions. She is my Marguerite.'

'Sir Bernard,' said Driver, 'Marguerites are in scarce supply these days. Busybodies like Mrs Baker put ideas in their heads. They pass exams, lose the knack of perfect love.'

'Then see to it,' said Sir Bernard, 'that they don't.'

If you treat the Devil like a servant, he tends to act like a servant, and do what he's told, at least for a time.

The fire caught the wood above the stage; the entire school was evacuated, and the Fire Brigade called. The engines came promptly, but water from their hoses, rather than fire, damaged the structure of the roof, and the school was closed for two weeks for emergency repairs.

'Annie, Carmen and Laura,' said Mrs Baker to her best girls, 'this couldn't have come at a worse time for your exams. Already you're falling behind with your studies. If you don't get your exams, what will become of you?'

Laura said, 'I'll get married and have kids.'

Annie said, 'Help my mother with her clairvoyance.'

Carmen said, 'Be a call girl.'

And they all said exams weren't the be-all and the end-all of life, look at Sir Bernard, who did well enough without, but they were only teasing Mrs Baker, or she hoped they were.

The local newspaper merely reported that a fire had broken out at Fenedge High during an address by Sir Bernard Bellamy, and the school had consequently been closed for structural repairs. It could not, said the Headmistress, have come at a worse time for girls now studying for public examinations.

4

As Mrs Baker observed to her friend Mr Bliss in the pub, over a glass of wine and a plate of mashed potato and sausage, 'I don't know what it is about parents! They wait for the weeks just before A levels, and then they divorce, or die, or break up the home, or sell the house, almost as if their sole intent is to blight their children's lives.'

To which Mr Bliss replied, 'I don't have children myself; I only have horses. But I've noticed how often they fall lame just before a race. They blight their own lives without any help from anyone.' Mr Bliss was in his late fifties. He ran a centre for ailing horses; he used natural herbs in their treatment, though, as he was the first to admit, it might merely be the passage of time which restored them to health, rather than comfrey, or feverfew, or borage. He had a puzzled, gentle air. Mrs Baker and he met in the pub from time to time. Mrs Baker was a widow, he a bachelor. He considered her wilder statements calmly, gave them due attention, and contributed to the discussion his own experience of the world, although that was on the whole limited, as he would explain, to horses. Mr Bliss visited me from time to time in Landsfield Crescent, and I always enjoyed his company. Sometimes he came on his horse, Snowy, and would tether it at the gatepost, which always created an agreeable flurry up and down the Crescent.

Now I am not arguing that Laura, unlike Carmen, was specifically singled out by the Devil to fail her exams; I am merely remarking that the more girls who failed to get through them the more staff would be available to chambermaid up at Bellamy House Hotel, and the more competition for the jobs there would be – which would lower wages. The Devil, unlike God, works in not so mysterious ways as you might think. When self-interest rules, motive is always apparent.

The very day that Fenedge High reopened after the fire, Laura came home from school to find her father on the landing, replacing the waterweed in the tropical fishtank which stood in the window, and sorting out the confusion of wires that service such tanks – a line each for heater, thermostat, airstone pump, filter, and two for its neon lights. In the tank swam a large black ornamental carp, its elaborate fins stirring gently, its big eyes goggling, backed into a corner by the intrusion of a human hand and arm into its home. 'Poor Kubrick,' said Laura. 'He hates change. Why are you home, Dad?'

Kim replied that he was home to make sure Kubrick was all right, and that he was entrusting the fish to Laura's care. She would find feeding instructions on the cork noticeboard in the kitchen. And he had something to tell Laura.

'Don't say it,' said Laura.

'I have to, puss,' said Kim, 'and I want you to remember that whatever happens between your mother and myself, we both love you very much.'

'Oh yes,' said Laura sourly. 'You love me so much you are going to get a divorce.'

'No one's saying anything about a divorce,' said Kim. 'That's just a piece of paper. Your mother and I are going to live apart for a while. Now don't make things difficult for me, puss.'

'Don't call me puss,' said Laura. 'And if you did get a divorce it would be a great relief. You're not invisible, you know. You've been seeing Poison Poppy for more than a year now, and the whole world knows it, especially my friends. It hasn't been very nice for me, I can tell you.'

'Your generation is too prudish,' complained Kim. 'The thing is, she's going to have a baby.'

'That is disgusting,' said Laura. 'She is my age. I went all through primary school with her, and she was poison then and she's poison now, and I don't see how a baby could survive inside her.'

'I know you're upset, puss, but I have to do what's right,' said Kim, putting his forefinger under Laura's jaw and lifting her head so he could look into her eyes, thus greatly embarrassing her. 'You do see that – it isn't a happy situation for me. I love your mother very much, but Poppy is having a baby.'

'Yuk,' said Laura. 'If you go off and live with her you just take Kubrick with you. Let Poison Poppy look after it.'

'Poppy doesn't believe in keeping pets,' said Kim, 'and that's a very silly and childish nickname you call her by,' and by the end of the evening he'd packed and left, leaving Audrey sitting at the kitchen table staring into space, and when Laura tried to focus on the reasons for the First World War her eyes blurred too and it all made a great deal less sense than usual, not that it ever made much.

As for Annie, she was so tired in class that on one or two occasions Mrs Baker actually had to shake her awake. Annie declined to give the reasons for her exhaustion; it was left to Carmen to explain that Annie lay awake at night, fearful of hearing the Count as a third party in the parental bedroom. And on occasion the Count tried to chat her, Annie, up: Mavis's mouth would open and instead of her mother's voice asking her to do the shopping, or make tea, or get her nose out of her book, which was bad enough, the Count would be telling her how long it was since he'd had a woman, and asking her to give him a little kiss. There had also been some poltergeist activity in the kitchen: Annie's favourite cup had hurled itself across the room and broken, and Alan had blamed Annie on the grounds that poltergeists were only ever active in the presence of neurotic teenage girls. Annie's claim that she was not the neurotic one in the family – on the contrary, wasn't she Head Girl of Fenedge High? – was taken by her parents as a personal affront. One way and another Annie's home life was not conducive to study.

Nor was Carmen's life tranquil. Andy, Raelene and Stephen all came down with food poisoning. Dr Grafton came and went at number 19, and the Borough Epidemiologist too. Raelene had purchased six chicken pies at half-price because they were a day past their sell-by date; she had put them straight away into her freezer. Alas, Andy had unplugged the cabinet in order to use his battery charger and forgotten to reconnect it for a day or two, and quite what had happened inside the freezer during that time Raelene didn't know; nevertheless she was convinced that the pies would be okay warmed up. Carmen, who declined to eat the pie her mother served her and was mocked for her prudence, was the only member of the family not affected. She was therefore the better able to nurse them through their illness, cleaning up after them as their bodies appeared to deliquesce, spooning water into their fevered mouths. Raelene, who had eaten the pie Carmen refused, was obliged to spend a couple of days in hospital. For some ten more days Carmen got no school work done, nor were her family grateful; rather they seemed to feel Carmen had somehow unjustly cheated fate.

Annie, Laura and Carmen, in the week before their exams began, bunked off school and went down to sit on the banks of Sealord Brook – the very same stream which ran through the grounds of Bellamy House Hotel (where it was being widened to provide a jet-ski pond – to lick their wounds, lament their fate, and wonder why they were all so suddenly thus afflicted. Down here the great hairy willowherb – *Epilobium hirsutium* – grows, and marsh valerian, and milk parsley, and sometimes – in the month of May – swallowtail butterflies hover and dance. It was a bright, bright afternoon and it was difficult to feel miserable, but they tried.

'We're not going to pass,' said Laura.

'We're going to let Mrs Baker down,' said Annie.

'We'll never get out of here,' said Carmen. 'We'll have to take local jobs and marry local boys.'

'That's if we're lucky. Who's ever going to marry me?' said Annie, and it was true that in those days, when other girls are at their prettiest, a kind of unbearable plainness suffused her, a muddiness of complexion, a puffiness of skin, a lankness of hair. Or perhaps it was just depression. Carmen and Annie stared at their friend and could see that she was indeed a worry.

'There's always someone for everyone,' said Laura comfortingly.

'You're okay,' said Annie. 'You've got Woodie.'

And so it seemed Laura had, one way or another. Woodie had returned not as suitor but as family friend, to be supportive in the bad times which followed her parents' separation. He was kind to Audrey, in the lordly charitable way of very young men who cannot understand what all the fuss is about, and brotherly to Laura. He even once persuaded Audrey to go to the cinema with him in spite of the stomach pains which made her think she'd just rather sit at home and suffer. Her doctor, Dr Grafton, the one who sees illness as God's punishment for lack of serenity, told her the pains were due to stress and she should pull herself together, eat more and cheer up.

'All I've got,' said Annie, 'is Count Capinski saying come here my little milkmaid and chasing me round the kitchen.'
'You're making it up,' said Carmen.
'He did it once,' said Annie. 'He did.'
'Your mother ought to see a counsellor,' said Carmen.
'She *is* the counsellor,' said Annie, and laughed, and looked better at once.
'We'll all get jobs and save up so you can have a nose job,' said Carmen.
'It's not how you look that matters in the world,' said Laura primly, 'it's your personality,' but they all knew it wasn't so: that was just the kind of thing people told them. Would Prince Charles have married Lady Di if she hadn't been pretty?

Annie said, 'The only good thing that happened all last week was that while Count Capinski was having yet another bath – he's the only one allowed to use all the hot water he wants, because of the dungeon – he had this kind of flash from heaven that a horse called Yellowhammer was going to win the three o'clock at Newmarket. So Mum leapt out of the bath and went to find Dad – she didn't even wrap herself in a towel – and told him to put a ten-pound bet to win. Dad doesn't believe in gambling, so I had to go all the way to the betting shop. And Yellowhammer won. And then I had to go all the way back again to pick up the winnings. Two hundred and twenty pounds. They only gave me two. The rest went to the Temple of Healing Light. That's the Wednesday afternoon do; it's half-price when the rich pay for the poor. Dad says no one should benefit from gambling.'
'If the Count can predict the future,' said Carmen, 'and if you asked him nicely, would he give us our exam questions? Then at least we'd know what to revise.'
'I expect he'd want to steal a kiss,' said Annie. 'I hate the way he puts things. I'm really glad I didn't live in the past, if that was what it was all like.'
'A kiss is a small price to pay,' said Carmen, 'for our key to a successful future. Look at it as a mother's kiss.' Annie just stared at her, so Carmen said, 'Well, we'll all go then, or at any rate we'll think about it.'
And they put their plan on ice for a whole twenty-four hours.

Now I had checked various Count Capinskis out with the help of the Fenedge Mobile Library, soon to be demobilised, and had indeed traced a fairly nasty specimen of Capinski back to fourteenth-century Cracow. This one seemed to be some kind of early Polish Rasputin, a man alleged to be both a practitioner in the black arts and the Queen's lover; he had led a general uprising against the King, burned alive a church full of people, and been thrown into a bottle dungeon and left there to languish, since the general belief was that to put a magician to death would merely increase his powers. It is perfectly possible – though not likely – that Mavis had read the same book – *Bad Men in History* – and absorbed its contents unconsciously, as those people are said to do who are regressed by hypnosis into remembering the lives they believe they lived before death. The history books and chronicles used to check out their stories turn out to be the very ones which initiated the fantasy in the first place: what is occurring is a kind of living plagiarism. I do not believe Mavis consciously deceived her family and clients when she spoke with the Count's voice; nor do I believe he was really in there with her; she just thought and acted as if he was. She and he had been over on occasion to try to heal my legs; she would lay on hands and I would feel the familiar healer's tingle, and the Count would invoke the Powers of Light in his guttural broken English, but nothing of a healing nature ever actually happened. But Mavis did it out of the goodness of her heart: she came over with the Count several times and didn't charge a penny for it. And at the time I for one, in spite of the Count's historic past, had quite grown to trust him. Mavis said he was company for her while Alan was away; Alan said he added class to the Temple of Light; and as for Annie's allegations, well, girls as plain as Annie are prone to sexual fantasy. And something had to be done. Matters were going from bad to worse. Mrs Baker summoned Annie, Carmen and Laura to her office. Their essays on Lady Macbeth were in front of her.

'What is the matter with you three?' Mrs Baker demanded. 'You use family trouble as an excuse for idleness. It's disgraceful. If you do that now, what chance have you got later on in life, when you have husbands and children? The brightest girls I have, and their heads emptied out of all sense, all information! You are on the road to self-destruction. If you do not get to college you will be dependent on a man forever, for the wage of an untrained female is never enough to keep her in dignity or comfort. So you will marry, and what is marriage, as George Bernard Shaw said, but legalised slavery? Unpaid work in return for your keep, attended by daily humiliations. Who gets the best piece of steak, the only egg in the fridge? He does! He's bigger than you and more powerful than you, and he allows you to wheedle and charm a little pleasure from him now and then, and the law offers you a little protection, it's true, but not much. All you have to bind him with are chains of love and duty, and they're pretty flimsy, believe you me.

'And don't tell me,' added Mrs Baker, 'that the world has changed since I was young, for it hasn't.'
The three girls stared at her, unconvinced. And Mrs Baker looked from one to another of them and picked at the layers of dusty black fabric she wore and said, 'I know what you're thinking. You're thinking if you pass exams you'll end up like me. I tell you this, you pass exams and end up like me if *you're lucky*.'
Still they stared.
'Life is *short*,' said Mrs Baker, 'and life is shit,' and stalked out of the room.

And that clinched it. The next day Annie, Carmen and Laura sat in Mavis's hall on the row of chairs kept for patients, and waited. On the door handle of the front room hung a notice which said 'TEMPLE OF HEALING – DO NOT DISTURB'.
'Fancy having to line up to see my own mother in my own house,' said Annie.
'Look at it this way,' said Carmen. 'It's not your mum you have to see, it's Count Capinski.'
'I want my mum back,' said Annie. She was near to tears, and Laura was not happy either.
'It feels like cheating to me,' she said. 'I expect this was what my dad felt like while waiting for an assignation with Poison Poppy.'
The others felt it would be unkind to contradict her.

The Temple door opened and an elderly man with a florid face limped out. He was smiling. 'She's a wonder,' he said to the girls. 'It's a miracle. I am completely cured. And that Count is such a gent. He adds real tone to Fenedge. He says you can go in now.'

And in they went and Mavis looked up from the hard chair in which she sat enthroned alone in the room, and said, 'Oh, it's you three. What do you want? We're doing Temple. It's very tiring,' and then the Count spoke from her lips: 'Never too busy for your daughter and her charming friends, dear lady. What can I do for you today? Warts, arthritis, colds in the nose? Puppy fat, a thing of the past! God sends his healing power through me, into this blissful age of plenty.'

'We just want a little glimpse of the future, Count,' said Carmen. 'We want to know what questions will come up in our exams.'

'The nerve of it!' said Mavis. 'That's cheating.'

'Nem problemi,' said the Count, in the same breath, quite crowding out Mavis's disapproval, and a voice which they recognised as Mrs Quaker's of the French department referred them to Flaubert and the justification or otherwise of Madame Bovary's suicide, and Tom Ellis (History) suggested they compare the Corn Law and the Poll Tax riots, and Mrs Baker (English) said forget Banquo and concentrate on Lady Macbeth, and so on throughout the range of their subjects while Carmen took notes.

Now we must remember Mavis had once or twice been to Open Evenings at the school and had encountered most of Annie's teachers at one time or another, so these revelations, this speaking in the living voice of others, may have been the real thing, a genuine exercise of clairvoyance, or it may have been a mixture of hysteria, exhaustion and mimicry. I will not say malice, for Mavis was not malicious, or only unconsciously so. I cannot answer for the Count. But incarceration in Eastern Europe in the fourteenth century can't have done much for his temperament.

After some twenty minutes the Count's voice seemed to run down; like a tape on a sticky spool, it became slower and slower and deeper and deeper and finally stopped, and Mavis slumped over the table. The girls filed out.

'I wish she were someone else's mother, not mine,' said Annie, but Laura and Carmen said they envied anyone whose mother could tell the future: Annie must not look a gift horse in the mouth. They were all elated. It seemed to them they had their ticket to leave, their escape route clean out of Dullsville, Tennessee.

So elated were they, so word-perfect by the end of the week in the questions suggested by their favourite man, the Count, but not so perfect as not to build in sufficient difference of phrase to avoid the charge of cheating, that the night before their first exam – in English Literature – they felt they could well afford to go to the disco.

I know that three girls going to a disco when they shouldn't is not the stuff of drama in Chicago, USA, but here in Fenedge it is of significance. And perhaps Fenedge is in some way pivotal to the great cosmic conflicts of good and evil – not for nothing did Driver patrol the flatlands in his big black silky car; for all he described himself as Sir Bernard Bellamy's chauffeur, I reckon that was just a front. A kind of idle occupation, to snaffle a soul or so, while thinking of other things. It is tempting to believe one is always at the heart of things, even in Fenedge, East Anglia, central to the drama – even creating it – when actually one is in all likelihood just some bit part player, at the very edges of the stage. I will be humble.

Be that as it may, Laura, Carmen and Annie went to the disco that night. Carmen and Annie's parents couldn't care what they did, or when and how, but Laura's mother did, for once.
'Don't go out,' begged Audrey of Laura, 'I feel really lonely; I think something terrible is going to happen. I have such a pain. And, besides, don't you have an exam tomorrow?'

It was the first mention in weeks Laura's mother had made of her exams. As for Kim, there'd been neither sight nor sound of him since the evening he left Kubrick in his daughter's care, and had packed and gone. Kubrick was flourishing: Laura dosed the tank from time to time and every white-spotted scale was now velvety black again, and pure.
'I'm going to the disco,' said Laura, 'and you can't stop me.'
But when she got there Woodie was waiting for her on his new, more powerful motor scooter, and all his zits had gone, and she drove off with him to the fenland, above which the yellow moon hung long and low, to a bed of mosses and red campion (*Silene dioica*) underneath a canopy of birch, sallow and willow, intertwined with reed mace (*Typha latifolia*) and hawthorn, and here

he and she made love. A willow warbler, misled by moonlight into believing it was day, began to sing.

Woodie said, 'I suppose you are on the pill or something?' and Laura said, 'Of course I'm not,' and they both fell silent, except that Laura, half hoping, half fearing, spoke to her mother and father in her head and said to them, 'Now look what you've done. You'll be sorry.' Laura wasn't at all. It hadn't even hurt. Her future in the natural world of love, delight and procreation was that night assured.

I stayed by my window till the early hours, watching the arc of the moon. I saw Carmen and Annie come home on the last bus, and hoped they'd get at least some sleep that night. And I waited and waited for Laura to come back, but she didn't, not until dawn was in the sky and the yellow moon turned little and uninteresting. And then I heard the putter-putter of Woodie's bike, and Carmen and Annie's doors opened and out they both came into the Crescent, Carmen in a T-shirt down to her knees, Annie in a nightgown buttoned at the wrists. And Woodie left Laura at her front door and waved at her friends and put-putted off into the dawn.

'Where have you *been*?' demanded Carmen.

'I couldn't sleep a wink,' complained Annie.

'I never need to sleep again,' said Laura, and went on into her house, and found Audrey waiting up for her, if you can call spending all night leaning over the kitchen table clutching your stomach waiting up.

'Make me some tea,' said Audrey to Laura.

'I ought to get some sleep,' said Laura. 'It's A level English today. I've been out all night, Mum.'

'You're old enough to look after yourself,' was all her mother said. 'The pain's getting worse. Ring the doctor.'

'It's too early in the morning,' said Laura, but her mother insisted, so she called Dr Grafton, and woke him from his sleep. He was quite kind to Laura, saying he understood what a hard time she had with her mother, and explained that the pain was not functional but neurotic, and had in itself been a contributory cause for Kim leaving home, and could he now go back to sleep? So Laura put the phone down and Audrey, so drained of colour that even the dawn light couldn't drain it any more, fell off her chair and under the table. Laura rang Dr Grafton back to describe what had happened and asked what she could do, and this time he was really angry and said Audrey no doubt had an alcohol problem too, so Laura called the ambulance service – who should only ever be called by a doctor – herself, and they came within five minutes since it was a call from Landsfield Crescent and Alan Horner was one of the duty crew that night. His uniform suited him. He looked, and was, kind and helpful. It was only Annie, and sometimes Count Capinski, he ever had problems with.

'Stomach cancer, most like,' he said to Laura. 'Takes a long time to get going, but when it does, pow! Collapse of thin party, if not stout.' And he laughed. 'Well,' said Alan apologetically, 'if you don't laugh you cry.' Laura laughed too. She assumed she was in a dream. The crew persuaded themselves that Audrey was still breathing. They rolled her onto a stretcher, and carried her out to the ambulance. Laura went along too. The siren sounded all the way, not just at traffic junctions, but Laura was so tired she fell asleep, propped in a corner as she was, which at least made the dream stop. I watched the ambulance arrive, and go, and listened to its sound fading into the Fenedge distance. Dramas happen everywhere, if only you hang around for long enough.

As for the questions in that year's exams, nothing the Count had predicted came true, not a single thing, almost as if the error was not accidental, but intended. No mention of Madame Bovary's death, not a breath of Lady Macbeth, or a hint of the Poll Tax riots. Laura turned up from the hospital halfway through the exam and, for all the sense they wrote, Annie and Carmen could have stayed home altogether.

Carmen left the examination hall early and decided to walk home to Landsfield Crescent, although 'home' seemed to her a place she had long ago grown out of. But where else could she go? The day was hot. The road was dusty. She was angry. She thought she would hitchhike but no cars came along the long ribbon of road she walked. Even the trees which lined its sides seemed indeterminate and without name, and the only birds around were the crows, which circled, and cawed, and yelled defiance and could only cooperate in anger, when they dive-bombed and forced out of their sky a little tremulous passing creature, some wretched peewit or blackcap that had strayed into their airspace by mistake.

Carmen began to feel nervous, as if the power of her anger had moved her out of one reality into another, dumped her and a flood of crows into an empty world.

So when she heard a car behind her she was relieved. When she turned and saw it was Driver coming up fast in the big BMW, she was pleased. He was someone she knew, if only vaguely, and she was still not old enough to understand that the danger to a woman comes mostly from someone vaguely known. Driver slowed down and stopped beside her and the window slid down without any effort from him at all.

'It isn't safe,' said Driver, 'for a young lady to hitch rides; it's asking for trouble.'

'I'll do what I want,' said Carmen. 'I'm not scared.'

'Who are you angry with?' asked Driver, and Carmen replied, 'God.'

Driver looked at her with interest, as well he might.

'Why are you staring at me?' Carmen asked.

'I'm wondering if you'd shriek and cry rape if I offered to give you a lift. A driver can't be too careful these days.'

So Carmen got in, of course she did, and he drove her to Landsfield Crescent.

Now it was the first time I'd actually seen the BMW, though I'd heard tell of it. The sight of the big black car, as it nosed round the bend that lunchtime, made my toes tingle, which was strange because I normally had no feeling in them at all – the state of my spine forbade it. I was eating my lunch – bread and cheese, pickle and apple, brought to me on a tray by my carer Alison. Alison is eighty-six, and a keen ornithologist, though her vision is not as acute as once it was. Whose is? The BMW stopped outside Mavis Horner's house and I watched while Carmen got out; and Driver got out too and bent his head and seemed to kiss her neck, though perhaps he bit it, because she jumped and squealed a little.

What really happened between the time Driver picked Carmen up and the time he dropped her off, who is to say? I know what Carmen told Laura and Annie, which was that she'd met the Devil on the way home from school, and he offered to buy her soul in return for wealth, success and soul-searing beauty, but she'd refused. And I know Laura and Annie had trouble accepting (a) that Sir Bernard Bellamy's chauffeur was Mephistopheles and (b), if he was, that she could have resisted him, but I was prepared to go along with Carmen's version. I heard with my own ears, I'm sure I did, what Driver called after Carmen as she marched up Mavis's front path to give Count Capinski what for. Nip, he went, with his sharp, even, handsome teeth, and then he said, 'All the joys that flesh is heir to, yours all yours, and all for such a small, small price. Something you don't even believe in.' And I'll swear I heard her reply, 'Oh go away and tempt someone else. I like to do things my own way.'

And Driver drove off in a silken fury – I could almost swear the BMW's wheels were an inch above the ground – and Carmen rubbed her shoulder where he had nipped it and continued unabashed in her mission. She knocked upon Mavis's door – bang, bang, bang – and Mavis answered it, and would have reprimanded Carmen for her noisy impertinence but Carmen got in first.

'Why did you let your friend the Count mislead us? It was spiteful and malicious.'

Carmen came into the little dismal hall, which always seemed smaller than those of the other houses in the road, though if you measured you'd find them all exactly the same size. Perhaps it was the row of chairs that did it, or the unframed New Age posters depicting mystic light sources, unicorns and so forth, all rather badly executed, stuck up on the walls with Blu-Tack. Mavis backed away from Carmen and the stamp of Count Capinski firmed and formed on her face.

'Is something wrong, dear lady?' Capinski asked Mavis. 'I feel your alarm.'

'She's brought in something nasty with her, Count,' complained Mavis, 'something really dreadful. Can't you feel it?'

'I do, I do,' and Mavis/the Count's teeth began to chatter. 'It's cold, so cold. Make your eyes clear for me, dear lady. There is black, there is wet. Oh, the stench! I am slipping back –' and he began to moan most terribly and roll his eyes and his hands clawed and shrivelled. 'You're just trying to get out of it,' said Carmen, though she was quite alarmed. 'You did a dreadful, spiteful thing.'

At which the Count/Mavis fell squirming and shrieking on the mat, waving his claws about, and Alan came running from the kitchen. He'd been back to the hospital to check on Laura's mother. They were operating immediately. She had stomach cancer, advanced but not, they thought, quite terminal: it's always good to have an instant diagnosis confirmed when, even though the news is not good, it's not as bad as it could be. It's pleasant to be right, even about tragedy.

The Count wailed from the floor, 'I'm going, I'm going, oh my darling, your soft sweet bed –'

'That's enough of that now,' said Alan, kneeling on the floor beside his wife. 'We won't have talk like that –' and he slapped her face, at which Mavis sat up, quite herself again.

'I really think he's gone,' said Mavis brightly. 'What a relief. It's been a nightmare. In bed, on the bog – and not even a spirit of the departed; someone still alive, if only just. My nails kept getting dirty, all by themselves. I must write it up for *Psychic News*.' Her face darkened as she turned to Carmen. 'As for you, miss, the sooner you're out of here the better. You bring trouble with you, always did. If Annie fails her exams, it will be all your fault. I told her so but she wouldn't listen.'

And those were the circumstances in which Annie, Carmen and Laura all failed their English exam, and most of their other papers thereafter – sufficient to make them ineligible for further education grants – and in which Mrs Baker was moved sideways to make room for a male head of department, and Laura became pregnant, or thought she was. But at least thereafter Annie slept more peacefully by night. For a time.

5

Alison, my voluntary carer, had been learning how to drive. She had been told she would need one lesson for every year of her life, but managed to pass her test after exactly half that number, that is to say, after forty-three. Since she could afford only one lesson every three weeks, the process of learning had taken just under three years. Her ambition – and I took it most kindly – was, in a car specially converted for that purpose, to be able to drive me in and out of Fenedge's pedestrian shopping precinct, where there was a centre for the handicapped. The Centre was shockingly underused, since public funds had not been made available for transport, and the disabled are seldom rich. It was, Alison maintained, each individual's responsibility to do their bit to help their neighbour. I only mention this because, although my problems are not part of this story, Alison's endeavour and determination so outstripped the problems of her own increasing infirmity as to deserve applause. I think she thought that if she could keep me going, she'd keep herself going.

So I now had two windows: one to look out upon the suburban serenity of Landsfield Crescent (serenity, that is to say, with a dollop of ambulances and body bags thrown in, not to mention clairvoyant phenomena, infidelity, loss of virginity, eruptions of Dark Forces, white-spot in the fish tank, and so on; but at least serenity was the avowed aspiration of the place) and a window in Fenedge Pedestrian Precinct, where from time to time, when Alison could get her car going, I could do much as I did in Landsfield Crescent – that is to say, sit and stare. I didn't wish to look Alison's gift horse in the mouth; I didn't like to say, 'Well really, Alison, more goes on in Landsfield Crescent than in Fenedge Centre and the journey is perhaps more effort than it's worth.' No. I just fell in with her plans, and watched the War

Memorial instead of the Crescent, and the steps around it on which the youngsters sat when there was nothing to do – that is to say most of the time – and presently things began to happen.

Let me draw you Fenedge's former market square, at that time a pedestrian-zone shopping centre, although most of the shops had already given up, since a hypermarket had opened five miles out of town, and everyone with cars – that is to say, everyone with any money – preferred the fresher, cheaper goods it offered, and hated the personal contact small shopkeepers, suffering from competition, like to say is so important. Only Boots the Chemist, the Welcome-In Café, the Post Office, a bank or so, the Handicapped Centre, a perfectly pointless florist and what was then called the Employment Exchange remained open, to create the markedly unbustling heart of Fenedge.

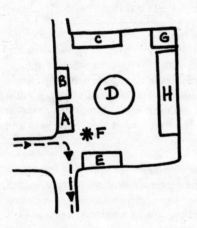

A. the Employment Exchange
B. the Chemist
C. the Welcome-In Café
D. the War Memorial
E. the florist
F. Alison's dropping-off point. Passers-by are asked by Alison to assist me over to H, since she doesn't like to stop her engine in case it doesn't start again.
G. the Post Office
H. the Handicapped Centre, now known as the Otherly Abled Centre

The dotted line marks a one-way traffic system with sleeping policemen every few yards, so it was seldom used by vehicles. Though Alison managed. Bump, bump, bump. Her driving instructor hadn't explained you're meant to slow down.

Alison liked to drive me into Fenedge before the traffic rush began. (Alison's idea of a rush is two vans and a stalled Citroën 2CV.) So it was remarkably early on a Monday morning in late August, at that time of year when you suddenly become conscious that the sun is beginning to rise later and set earlier, and there is a hint of autumnal mist in the air, when I saw Carmen, Annie and Laura stroll into the Centre, in their best one-for-all and all-for-one mode, and settle themselves on the steps of the War Memorial. This is how I imagine the conversation went:

Carmen said: So how do we get out of here?

Annie said : Not by education anyhow, we buggered that one up.

Laura said : Wherever I bring my baby into the world is paradise to me. I won't have a word said against Fenedge.

And Carmen and Annie said between them: 'You don't know if you're pregnant or not. Anyone can miss a period, or even two. Why don't you do a test? The chemist's opening up.'

To which Laura replied, 'Because it's so nasty and mechanical. I just trust my baby to be there.'

They were waiting for the Employment Exchange to open. They'd been waiting for one thing or another all summer, while the mock yellow irises (*Iris pseudacorus*) and the marsh marigolds (*Caltha palustris*) turned the fen woodland bright, and the dragonflies and the damselflies hatched (dragonflies are larger than damselflies, and don't fold their wings, which is how you tell the difference) and the skuas turned up on the beach to make the life of the common tern wretched for the season, and the slipper limpets changed sex, and on the saltings the glasswort (*Salicornia sp.*) and the sea campion (*Silene maritima*) sprouted – enough, enough! It's just that the Handicapped Centre had a shelf full of remaindered nature books, donated free, for good reason. The girls, as I was saying, had been waiting for one thing or another all summer; first for the end-of-term disco, then for Laura's menstrual period to start (it didn't: first not one, then not two) and for Audrey to be let out of hospital, and perhaps even for Kim to repent and come home to look after her, and for Woodie to come home from a carpentry YTS course in Shropshire; then for the letters through the post which would say they'd failed their exams (they came),

43

and to be in a mood to make proper life decisions (which never did arrive), until one day there could be no more waiting, if ever they were to get out of there, and there they all were, obliging their parents, finally waiting for the Employment Exchange to open. A queue was already forming outside it, but they felt above joining it. They would sit on the War Memorial steps until they were well and truly ready. They were in no hurry.

They were pleased to be further delayed by the approach of a bright young woman, with un-Fenedge-like high heels, and the kind of perfectly made-up face which was not often seen in these parts, and especially not first thing in the morning. In her hand she held a clipboard. She was engaged in market research. (She'd caught a glimpse of me in my open window, and craned in, but quickly uncraned again on seeing my wheelchair. Obviously her research was focused on those with working legs. I thought her manners rather bad.)

She introduced herself to the girls as Maureen; she smiled with perfect teeth; she said what a lovely day it was; she said when someone was in business, as she was, all days were lovely. The positive approach inspired confidence. That morning she was targeting females between sixteen and twenty, socio-economic group CDE, and look, good luck had come her way! Three of them in a row!

Laura said she was probably a B, but didn't mind being a CDE if that helped. Maureen asked her the number of taps there were in the house, and Laura said five, including the one in the garden; so Maureen wrote her down as borderline B/C, but on being told – Laura liked to tell everyone – that she might be pregnant marked her down at once to borderline D/E. She was talking about earning potential, she explained, to make Laura feel better, not disposable income or educational qualifications. And on hearing that none of them had A levels and that they were late school leavers with O levels but without training, and currently unemployed, she shook her head and said they fell into a nasty section of her curve: they shouldn't have taken the summer off; there was a seventy-two per cent chance of their all being pregnant within the year, a forty-two per cent chance out of that seventy-two per cent of their getting married before the birth of the baby, twelve per cent after, and forty-six per cent of not getting married at all. Twenty-six per cent of that forty-six per cent would cohabit, and seventy-four per cent would live off the State. There was an eighty-three per cent likelihood that they would still be living in Fenedge twenty years from now.

'What chance of us growing rich?' asked Annie.

'Zero,' said Maureen, without even pausing for thought.

Laura said plaintively that there was more than one kind of rich than money rich – there was rich in babies, in personality, in love, in virtue or experience – you could surely stay in Fenedge and still end up rich somehow? – but Carmen and Annie had given up listening. They were stricken. It is never very cheering to find yourself part of a statistic. Laura's voice faded away. Then she said, 'I suppose that's the kind of thing my mother's always saying, and look at her! I'd better shut up.' Then she brightened. 'If the baby's a girl I'll call her Polyanna.'

Maureen asked if by any chance Laura was in the first trimester and Laura said yes, and Carmen said not for long she wasn't, one thing taken with another Laura would just have to get rid of it; she couldn't ruin her whole life because of a night on the tiles with Woodie's zits; and Annie said that was a very wicked thing for Carmen to say, what about the transmigration of souls? Laura would be interfering; and Carmen said what a load of New Age junk, and Laura responded to another of Maureen's questions by saying she'd be washing the baby's nappies by hand to give it a proper start in life, so she wasn't interested in brands of washing machine. Maureen took herself and her clipboard off to Boots the Chemist, which was just opening its doors, saying, 'Don't play silly buggers with me', when what should I see but the black BMW nosing round the corner of the Employment Exchange into the precinct. Then the sudden uproar made sense. Obviously trouble went ahead of Driver as well as behind; nets were cast forward as well as trailed, to haul up and focus every scrap of dissent around.

Driver's window slid down and he said to Carmen, 'Tell you what, you can have a freebie – just to show you what I mean,' and off he drove. At least that's what Carmen said he said; to which Annie said Carmen was cheating: she, Annie, was the only one still a virgin, and Carmen hotly denied it. I thought I saw the BMW move backwards, like a film rewinding, back out of the square, but I may have been wrong and, what is more, I had a clear impression that Driver was waving at me, in a knowing kind of way, as if he knew more about me than I knew myself. I didn't like that. And my toes were tingling again. And I could see through walls, right into the Employment Exchange, where Carmen, Annie and Laura now sat. Spooky.

They sat on chairs welded into a convenient row – convenient, that is, for manufacturer, purchaser and whoever had to sweep the floor beneath them, but not for those who sat upon them – so that Carmen pressed into Annie and Annie into Laura, and they presented a kind of untidy wodge of unhealthy pale young female flesh topped by clouds of hair. They were not sufficiently differentiated to attract the lecherous looks that one by one they would have – even Annie, for youth is youth even though the clothes it wears, and the look in its eyes, mean it would rather not think about sex, or not yet.

Carmen began to wriggle, and Laura said, 'Do keep still, Carmen. You're driving me mad.'
Carmen said, 'My bra's too tight.'
Annie said, 'Lucky old you. I don't even need one.'
Carmen disengaged herself from the others and stood up, and all the male eyes in the waiting room went to her, and the hooks of her bra at the back where it fastened gave suddenly, and there were her breasts unconfined beneath her white sleeveless T-shirt, a tangle of untidy undone bra and bosom. Carmen went to the Ladies room and when she came out she said, 'Something's wrong with me. It must be hormonal. I reckon I've gone from an A cup to a C overnight. It's disgusting. I flop when I walk. And my waist's got small, so my hips poke out in a ridiculous way. And I swear my legs are longer, or somehow my skirt has got shorter,' and she squeezed herself in between Annie and Laura with her arms over her chest, and sat sulking.
'I expect you're still growing,' whispered Laura, for everyone was staring. 'They say you don't stop till you're twenty-three.'

'Yes,' whispered Annie, 'but people's legs don't suddenly grow longer. Carmen's right. Something's terribly wrong.'

When Carmen's name was called, and she had to stand up to go to Employment Officer Mr Prior's booth, a kind of sigh travelled around the room. Both men and women stared. Although there was a head-on robustness about her figure, clothed as it was in a far too tight T-shirt and a skirt on the short side even when she'd put it on and now shorter than ever, there was a fine-boned tranquillity about her face, as if she'd never had to give it a second thought from the day she first observed its perfection. She frowned a little because her feet were now too long for her shoes and growing and narrowing even as she stood there, so they hurt, but even the frown was delicate, and the skin on her brow smooth and perfect: that same facial expression which yesterday would have meant Carmen was in a sulk now made her seem charming, and in need of help.

Carmen pointed to her feet with a little moan of dismay, a fluttering of pale fingers, and Laura and Annie watched in fascination and alarm as soles and uppers parted to make room for her toes, no longer stubby but elegant. They all stared at her hands: the fingers had narrowed and lengthened; her nails were almond-shaped and pearly pink, and not their familiar flaky, rather dirty, bitten-down-to-the-quick selves.
'I expect we're dreaming this,' said Laura. 'It's a joint hallucination.'
'Miss Wedmore?' enquired the crackling loudspeaker in the corner once again. 'Miss Wedmore? To Mr Prior please.'
'You remind me of the Incredible Hulk,' said Annie. 'His clothes were always splitting as his true nature appeared.'
'Oh, thank you very much,' said Carmen, and went in to see Mr Prior, whose chronological age was twenty-eight but who liked to appear fifty. He seemed overwhelmed by Carmen's general appearance. He did not meet her eyes, but shuffled through papers with trembling hands. He apologised for there being so little work on his books: he would do his best. Of course Peckhams the chicken factory, the biggest employer around, was out of the question: Miss Wedmore wasn't the sort to work with frozen chickens; and he didn't think she would be happy doing domestic work at

Bellamy House Hotel. But there did happen to be one vacancy which had just come through. What luck! Bellamy Airspace, a new charter airline, was looking for a trainee stewardess. 'What a coincidence,' said Mr Prior. 'How seldom the ideal applicant and the ideal job turn up together!'

'I don't want to be a flying waitress,' said Carmen. The improvement in her looks had not softened her nature.

'But every girl dreams of being an air hostess,' said Mr Prior, rather offended. 'Flying the world, after all!'

Carmen almost made a rude joke, but the new configuration of her lips – perfectly moulded: a natural smooth line of clear rose around a cupid's bow of softer pink – somehow prevented her from saying words too upfront for comfort.

'I prefer to have my feet on the ground,' said Carmen instead. 'And if I'm going to be a waitress I'd rather do it at Bellamy House Hotel with my friends,' and even as she spoke she felt her bosom diminish and her waist widen, and either her skirt lengthened or her thighs shortened, and her shoes, so far as she could see, were now only fit to be thrown away. She felt sleepy. Mr Prior changed his mind about her and said quite sharply, 'If you feel the air hostess position is not for you, I respect your decision. It is foolish to take up a career which is beyond your capacity.'

Annie and Laura, offered a choice of up at Peckhams the chicken factory – piece work; although the plucking was done by machine, the gutting was hand done, and good money could be earned if you were fast and efficient and in good health – or Bellamy House Hotel, chose to apply to the latter. Such work was only, or so they told each other, until each could get her act together.

6

Annie, Carmen and Laura walked all the way from Fenedge to Bellamy House Hotel. The event is imprinted into their minds: the long straight road to Winterwart, the hot afternoon, the white dust, that day when they set out to meet their fate, or at least to have their interviews. Now, it's a good half hour's walk from Fenedge to Bellamy House Hotel (forty-five minutes to Winterwart) and many still walk it daily, there and back; for though these days the Bellamy House Courtesy Car is despatched to pick up guests who arrived at Kings Lynn or Norwich stations, or to meet the little Lear jets which fly into Bellamy Airspace outside Fakenham, its function is to oblige the leisured, not to transport staff. A courtesy car, Bellamy House bound, overtook Carmen, Laura and Annie that very afternoon but did not stop, and rendered them despondent. They feared this was the pattern of life to come. Some rode in carriages, others walked. And how did you get to be one of the privileged? How did you get from here to there?

The road from Fenedge to Winterwart runs parallel to the coast for a time, and then veers off towards it. It passes first through the beet fields, interrupting the long straight lines of low foliage which run sternly on either side to meet the horizon, allowing all the space in the world to the sky and the winds – painters love East Anglia because of the light – then crosses a patch of the old wood, where the oak, the ash, the maple and the beech stretch above the road to form a dappling canopy, before coming to the straight and boring conifers of the Forestry Commission – at least the crossbills love the conifers, if nobody else does. (Crossbills are small parrot-like finches; their presence anywhere excites bird-watchers very much.) Then the forest in its turn gives way to grassy fields, and the white paling fences of the 'Convalescent

Centre for Ailing Horses – Prop. Mr E. Bliss, Homoeopathic Remedies a Speciality'. And then, in time gone by, as reward and privilege, two thirds of the way to Winterwart, you would reach the high wrought-iron gates of Sealord Mansion, and peer through them to its wonderful formal garden, for so long in marvellous wrack and ruin: yew hedges falling into delphiniums, ivy creeping into the disused fountains, clematis and climbing roses fighting for space and light, and everywhere butterflies – the silver spotted skipper, the holly blue, the painted lady, the Duke of Burgundy (the latter if you were lucky) – attracted to the garden by the presence of nettles, St John's wort and lady's-smock (*Cardamine pratensis*) – plants that botanists agree deserve more than to be dismissed as weeds. And there, half-hidden by abundant foliage, you would see the great house with its glass rotunda – once home to one of the biggest telescopes in Europe – its curving glass panels (an architectural wonder) cracked and broken, the better for bats and barn owls to fly in and out. This was surely Driver's safe house – its facade cracked and crumbling, pulled to pieces by weather and ivy; the absurd cherubims weathered noseless, the bolts of the big black front door rusted through – a door which local legend said opened of its own accord on Halloween night to let out the year's batch of vampires, which would then fly howling and cackling over the fens and the forests and the marshes, bringing the next year's crop of trouble. All this, for the sake of Fenedge and environs, to bring prosperity and energy to the area, and offer opportunities for local employment – or so Sir Bernard suggested in his Change of Use application to the Planning Committee – was now to be swept away: cleaned up; tidied; brightly lit and unspooked; renamed Bellamy House as Windscale was renamed Sellafield, in a piece of potent magic.

And though Alison says to me, 'I always found the place perfectly pleasant and I'm very sensitive to atmospheres,' I thought if she could so misjudge herself, she could also misjudge the house. But what do I know? As I say, I never saw Sealord in its decay, which was also its prime. I was taken to its smart restaurant once, after Sir Bernard had got his hands on it, and found it very boring: the smoked salmon dry and the lamb cutlets overcooked and flaky, though of course I didn't like to say so.

As Carmen, Laura and Annie approached what was rapidly turning into the Bellamy House Hotel, workmen were taking down the old iron gates, and putting up a steel security barrier, which was to open by remote control. The girls were early for their three o'clock appointment with Mrs Haverill, the housekeeper, so they just sat down by the side of the road and watched. Carmen, Annie and Laura remarked to one another, with nudges and giggles, that the workmen were unusually skeletal; their expressions were dour; there was no opportunity here for banter, whistles or agreeable bridling. They were not local workmen, that was for sure. Annie wondered where Sir Bernard had dug them up, and that convulsed them again.

On the other side of the gate, tractors and diggers swept up and levelled the overgrown flowerbeds and the remnants of lawns, crunched up the ornamental lead border markers, turned up the little bones in the pets' cemetery, and made one mass, one mess, of a thousand different things, from the heath spotted orchid (*Dactylorhiza maculata*) to the dewberry to the dog rose to the *Digitalis purpurea* (or foxglove) to the paving slabs brought south (with great difficulty) from York, to the melon frames; shovelling soil so that the entrance to the underground ice house must remain forever hidden – but everything passes; everything that grows must die, everything that's built must crumble; it's just sad to be around when it does. Enough.

A whirr was heard and a wind arose, and a smart black and red helicopter came down over the row of beeches – fortunately, they were to stay – onto a make-do helipad behind, and out of the machine stepped Sir Bernard and Lady Rowena, whom Driver had been trying to palm off on Sir Bernard for some time. Lady Rowena had done Driver a favour or two in her day: he owed her something now, that is to say, marriage to someone as energetically rich and famous as Sir Bernard; and failing that, she could at least serve to make Carmen jealous, should the occasion arise, and she be Sir Bernard's final choice. Driver likes to keep all his options open as long as he can. Don't you? Who knows what's going to happen next?

Lady Rowena had a long, haughty face and upswept hair. She wore fine leather boots, britches and a crisp white shirt. She had a long back and a stylish very flat what the Americans refer to as ass and my grandmother as 'derrière'. Over her shoulder was flung an ugly leather bag, hand-stitched, of good quality. She had a loud plummy voice.

'Some things won't do,' said Lady Rowena to Sir Bernard, her voice carrying in the wind. 'Some things will and some things won't, and this is one of the things that won't.'

'What are you talking about?' asked Sir Bernard, who still remained socially insecure, at least just a little. His father, after all, had been a local farm boy, who later took to breeding boiling fowls.

'That, darling,' and she pointed to a swinging sign being carried past by workmen. It read 'Bellamy House Hotel. Old World Value, New World Comfort'. 'Whoever thought of that?'

'I did,' said Sir Bernard. 'What is more, darling, I think it's rather good.'

'I don't,' said Lady Rowena. 'Old World simply doesn't recognise the existence of New World. You'll get the dreadful helicopter set in for a while, but only till they realise Old World isn't in situ. Then they'll be off. Just "Bellamy House", dear, pure and simple.'

Oh, she was smart. Sir Bernard had spent hot nights with Lady Rowena, her long legs, still booted (for he rather liked that) wrapped round his strong neck (or he rather thought that was what was happening), or else lying more sedately, her plummy voice in his ear (she never whispered: the whole world could hear her bizarre suggestions. What did she care? Servants didn't count as other people anyhow, she'd told him so), so he thought it behoved him to call her darling. And Driver would nudge him by day and say, 'A bit of hot stuff I found you there. I told you the brave deserved the fair. And she's got so many contacts, that woman. The right lay is the best entrée!'

And because Driver's advice always seemed to work out, Sir Bernard listened, and slept with Lady Rowena, and dreamt of Carmen.

A catechism

Q: This is all very well, but what does the Devil do with souls once he's got them?

A: Pretty much what the tractors were doing that day at Sealord Mansion. That is to say, making one undifferentiated mass of a whole lot of originally rather nice if trivial things. Like an angry child churning up all his dinner on the plate before he eats it. The Devil seeks sameness. It's the Devil's plan to create a faceless, tractable, self-interested crowd out of the human race; a crowd whose behaviour is predictable, and therefore controllable. Self-interest is supremely predictable. It's the same for everyone everywhere, as morality is not.

Q: Can you hold out against the Devil?

A: Yes. You can trick him by word, and surprise him by deed, because the only thing he really understands is self-interest. He lacks imagination. So his deals often don't hold. They fail, like a Moscow coup.

Q: What sort of deal has Driver made with Sir Bernard?

A: In return for surrendering his soul to the Devil and not to God when he dies, so that the Devil gets a nice rich extra goblet for the mashing (or another ally in the war of Evil against Good, depending on which tradition you favour), Sir Bernard gets his wishes granted, his desires fulfilled, though this could sometimes be a problem for Driver. How can Driver square Sir Bernard's wish to have Carmen for a wife with his desire for social status? It's a problem. Driver, on the day the three girls went for their interview at Bellamy House, had been hoping that Sir Bernard would forget Carmen and fall in love with Lady Rowena and make life simpler all round. Carmen was meant to have gone after the air hostess job. But she didn't, so that was that. The Devil's only weapon against free will is self-interest. Now he just has to stand back and see what happens.

Q: How do I know when the Devil has got his eye on me?

A: You will hear a little voice in your ear saying, 'I have to look after myself; no one else will.'

Q: Then what do I do?

A: You think of your mother and try not to believe it.

Q: Does the Devil have rules he has to keep to?

A: Oddly enough, he has a sense of fair play. He doesn't move the goal posts.

Q: What is his hold over Sir Bernard?

A: Sir Bernard once said, while the Devil was passing, 'I'd give my very soul for enough capital, just for once,' and the Devil heard and now Sir Bernard goes from strength to strength and Driver is his chauffeur, his amanuensis, his Grey Eminence, the private whisperer in his ear, and those who knew him before and know him now marvel, so changed a man is he. The clumsy oaf, chicken farmer, drumstick maker, now a friend to celebrities, patron of popular causes, a man who leaps out of bed in the morning to do his press-ups. Who ever has enough capital? You can go on needing more, more, for ever. Driver's going to be around for a long time.

Many people, of course, put the improvement down to Sir Bernard's former nasty wife's being so unfaithful he at last found the courage to divorce her, but I know it's more than that. Fat had turned to muscle, meanness into lordliness, twenty years been taken from his life clock just like that. Mind you, Sir Bernard still had no taste. The Devil can give a man everything but taste. He has none himself, or very little. God is his brother. You know how it is in families: how the qualities are doled out by common consent. God was the one with taste; the serious one with an eye for a painting, an ear for a symphony; the Devil the one who knew how to have a good time, and who listened to Radio One, down-market to his leather boots.

Q: How do you know all this about the Devil? Stop, stop, or I'll call the vicar.

A: I *am* the vicar.

7

At ten to three Carmen, Laura and Annie tried to effect an entry through the barred steel gates of Bellamy House, now in place, only to find they couldn't be opened manually. The workmen had gone off to watch Sir Bernard's arrival; the girls rattled and shook and shouted, but to no avail.

And then the BMW, Driver at the wheel, came up beside them. 'What's the trouble?' Driver asked.
'We can't get in. First we were early, now we'll be late.'
'The mechanism's metal activated,' said Driver. 'Hop in and I'll get you through.'

And they did. The interior of the car was dark, warm and cosy: the leather seats soft and crinkly; the vehicle was far more spacious on the inside than the outside would allow you to believe – a car designer's dream come true. Carmen sat in the front: Annie and Laura in the back. Their thin white limbs glowed pinkly perfect: they could admire themselves.

Driver punched a button: the gates parted: the BMW slid through.
'So how was the gift of beauty?' he asked.
'It was a real drag,' Carmen replied.
'I simply don't understand,' said Driver, 'why any young woman whose avowed ambition is to get out of here would rather be a domestic than an air hostess.'
'I want to be with my friends,' said Carmen.
Driver swivelled his head to look at Laura and Annie in the back.
'Friends,' said Driver, 'can be an Achilles heel. And you have two of them. Ouch! Ouch!' He could steer the car perfectly well with his eyes altogether off the road, and his hands off the wheel as

well. The drive was lined with gracious oaks. A host of pollarders swarmed up them to remove as many lower branches as they could without actually killing the trees, which were protected by a court order so powerful not even Sir Bernard could gainsay it. They carried saws and rope; they scuttled, halfway between man and monkey, or Demon and Pict. Take your pick.

Driver said to Annie, 'I know your mother well, and her good friend the Count. I'm almost part of the family. I expect I'll be seeing quite a lot of you, so long as you stick close to Carmen.'

Then Driver said to Laura, 'Nice little baby you've got in there. I'll give him a silver christening spoon, when the time comes. Any friend of Carmen is a friend of mine.'

And then he turned his blue eyes back to Carmen. Oh, he was handsome! 'You weren't so wrong about your mother,' Driver said to her then, 'only it was the black knight not the white. As for you, if you don't do as I suggest, it will be the worse for you Chickedy-chick!'

And as the car doors opened to let them out Carmen felt a sharp sting on the side of her neck: she slapped the spot with her hand. 'A bee sting, I expect,' said Driver. 'A queen bee. Better get in the house quick before the whole swarm arrives.' And off he drove.

'What was he going on about?' asked Annie.

'You do know some weirdos, Carmen,' complained Laura.

'Queen bees don't sting,' said Carmen, 'so sucks to him.'

Nevertheless, whatever it was it hurt and made Carmen irritable, though Annie and Laura remained conscious for some time of being suffused by a kind of languorous bliss – perhaps it was the squelchy cushions of the BMW's spacious interior that did it.

As Sir Bernard and Lady Rowena climbed the steps to the big front door, its iron hinges now replaced by repro-Gothic steel, the dents in the wide steps made by the feet of the past first smoothed them marble-veneered, Carmen, Annie and Laura followed up behind. The door was opened – smoothly and easily, with an electrical device which was the interior designer's equivalent to power steering – by Mrs Haverill, a woman of indeterminate age, but of very determined temperament. She was a reincarnation, or so it seemed to the girls, of Daphne du Maurier's Mrs Danvers in the novel *Rebecca*, which Mrs Baker had last year obliged the class to read. Her pupils had of course hired a video of the film and made do with that, but never mind.

'Welcome, Sir Bernard,' Mrs Haverill said, 'welcome, Lady Rowena,' and she took one look at the girls and shut the door in their faces.

Once inside, Lady Rowena strode around the great hall, which for the sake of dignity and grandeur had been timbered and raftered in the Gothic style, and its rotunda squared off to facilitate the conversion of wasted space to more guest bedrooms.
'Not my taste, darling,' she said. 'In fact it's a monstrosity, but good taste never earned anyone a penny.' And she laughed; her laugh was always rather like a horse's neigh. She was one of a pair of partners who ran a firm of interior designers in Sloane Square, London. Her usual stamping ground was Chelsea and Kensington. She thought here was the back of beyond and she was right.

She ran to the top of the stairs and down again – Sir Bernard could only admire her stamina: she was well exercised; even he, from hours in the gym a week, couldn't match it.
'Why isn't the carpet on the top floor laid?' she demanded of Mrs Haverill. Sir Bernard marvelled. Of all the people he knew in the world, Mrs Haverill was the one who most scared him. She was a good friend of his chauffeur's: if it hadn't been an absurd notion he would have thought he and she were having it off.

Q: But doesn't Sir Bernard *know* Driver is Mephistopheles? Surely he's *aware* he's mortgaged his soul in advance of his death?

A: He does and he doesn't. In the same way as you can dream you got up and found a front tooth missing, and went to work, and it seemed perfectly real, if distressing, at the time, until the alarm goes and you wake up and have to do the same thing all over again, but at least you have the tooth. If you have someone like Driver (or, come to that, my carer Alison) around, reality and dream are easily confused. Was that real, or was that dream? Was

57

that in a book I read, or did it happen? Okay? Can we continue?

'We're opening within days, too!' said Lady Rowena to Mrs Haverill. 'I am accustomed to being let down, but seldom to this extent.'

Mrs Haverill's eyes snapped, in the same way Driver's could if you crossed him.

'The instructions issuing from your office,' said Mrs Haverill, 'were both confused and confusing, and perhaps Sir Bernard needs to be advised of that.'

'Now, now,' said Sir Bernard. 'No quarrelling in the ranks,' and if Lady Rowena hadn't wanted so badly to become Lady Bellamy that would have been that, but Ann & Rowena Interior Design was in some difficulty: orders had been falling off. A scandal had connected Lady Rowena to royalty in a rather unfortunate way – and though scandal amongst the titled is normally good for business, if it concerns royalty ranks quickly close. Lady Rowena needed Sir Bernard's robust good name, his reputation for straight talking and honest thinking, to see her through the next few years. She'd just have to put up with a quick dive down through layers of social strata. Anything she could get.

The front door bell rang: ding dong. A real bell, from an ocean liner, at the reception desk had been activated by an electric bell, set in the midst of a plaster rose on the front door. The sound echoed, as it would in a fog at sea: it startled everyone. A poor, lost, lonely bat, determined not to be driven out of its home, rose from a cornice and circled in its much-diminished habitat and sank again. It had no way out any more.

'I suppose that bloody thing's protected,' said Lady Rowena. 'No wonder this country is going to wrack and ruin. The wrong people are in control. I suppose we could turn bats into some kind of Olde-Worlde feature. Olde-Worlde Bats in the New Worlde Order.' You could tell she was in a bad temper. She rearranged her face and nuzzled Sir Bernard's strong neck. 'Darling,' she said.

'Darling,' he said.

Mrs Haverill opened the door to Carmen, Laura and Annie.

'We've come about the job,' said Carmen.

'Jobs,' said Laura.

'You have no business coming to the front,' said Mrs Haverill. 'Go round to the servants' entrance.' Lady Rowena had had the 'Staff Entrance – This Way' sign changed to 'Servants' Entrance' and an arrow. She liked changing signs. Her arrangement with Driver was on a purely reciprocal basis: you do me a favour, I do you one. It did not involve the selling of her soul: could not, for she never had one to begin with. Her mother had obviously noticed it when she was born, handing her over instantly to nannies for rearing. Who is ever to say what is cause, what is effect?

Carmen said to Mrs Haverill, 'I'm not going all the way round to the back now I'm here. That's silly,' and put her foot in the door, although Annie and Laura tried to stop her. Mrs Haverill activated the mechanism which closed it from the desk but on meeting the resistance of Carmen's foot it bounced away again. Carmen, for her part, pressed the centre of the plaster rose again and heard the bell inside begin to toll. She pressed and pressed and pressed.

'Let's just go,' said Annie.

'I don't believe this is happening,' said Laura.

Mrs Haverill spoke to Sir Bernard above the ding-donging of the bell.

'You see the material I have to work with?' she demanded. 'The quality of staff here in the back of beyond? What with that and other things it is amazing there is any carpet down at all.'

'Let them in,' said Sir Bernard flatly, and opened the door himself since Mrs Haverill's colour rose alarmingly.

Carmen stepped inside and said, 'I think that was entirely out of order. This is the New World and people are more equal than you'd believe. I am not going to walk half a mile round to the back of a building so you lot can feel better than me.'

Sir Bernard stared at Carmen in admiration while Mrs Haverill said, 'I'm sorry, but you don't have the right attitude for anyone starting work in the hotel industry; you are wasting your time and mine, the lot of you,' and Lady Rowena said, 'Call the police, or are you just going to let that little tart get away with it?' and Carmen said, 'You're all out of turn. We're here by appointment,' to which Lady Rowena responded, 'Good God, school leavers. The whole country's swarming with them.'

'My, my,' said Sir Bernard (a phrase Driver had recently suggested as a mild alternative for 'Fuck me' or 'Jesus wept'), 'there's a lass with a mind of her own. Take her on, Mrs Haverill. Take on all three of them. This is the new young blood this country needs.'

'You're out of your mind,' said Lady Rowena. 'Darling, she's not new, she's as old as the hills.'

Sir Bernard looked again but did not recognise the girl of his dreams. He'd broken his glasses and Driver had taken them in for mending. Now in the days when I had the use of my legs one or two men looked at me like that: that is what unrequited love is all about. You are obviously the girl of their dreams, just as they are the boy of your dreams, it's just they don't remember their dreams and you do. It's a tragedy: so much potential happiness so often wasted by sheer forgetfulness.

'I've changed my mind,' said Carmen. 'I wouldn't work here if you paid me,' but they all knew what she meant. Later, of course, Carmen was to receive the gift of tongues, at least sporadically. 'But if you guys want to, that's up to you.' And she stalked out. She liked to make an exit. Laura and Annie stayed.

Carmen went and sat upon the step and stared moodily into the wreckage all around. The helicopter pilot revved his engines for some reason and sent a dust storm flurrying off towards her, but she took no notice of that.

'Carmen,' said Driver, whose car had approached unseen through the dust, 'by the way. A word of warning to your friend – the pretty one. She'd better be quick getting rid of the baby. There's a soul hanging around, looking for a place. I smelt it as I got out of the car.'

'What does a soul smell like?' asked Carmen, interested through her displeasure.

'Colourless, odourless, tasteless,' said Driver, 'but you do get a whiff of the ozone that goes with them. Pity to see a pretty girl like that mess up her life, don't you think? If she has one child now it'll be three before she's twenty. She's the type. That's another freebie; a piece of advice from someone who knows what he's talking about. When it comes to termination, do it soon, do it now.'

'Bugger off,' said Carmen, I'm sorry to say, and then rather wished she hadn't, for he stopped sniffing and snarled instead, baring perfect teeth, rather too small to be altogether manly. The helicopter tried his rotors again and this time Carmen breathed in dust and spluttered, and when she recovered he'd gone.

Mrs Haverill led Laura and Annie along the upstairs corridors, opening doors to show immaculate bedrooms with an agreeable chintzy, frilly, olde-English air: high mattresses, plump sofas and lavender soap in the blue bathrooms, along with every gift the travelling heart could desire, from plastic shoe horns to presentation folding toothbrushes. Mrs Haverill explained that the rooms were all called after famous English composers, writers, poets, painters and so forth. Sir Bernard was a great patron of the Arts. The Hotel could engage the girls on a casual, part-time basis, no paid holidays or superannuation, for an initial period of sixty days at seventy-five pence the hour. The hours were six in the morning to midday, then two-thirty to seven-thirty at night, with overtime as required at time and a quarter. If the probation period was satisfactory, wages would rise to ninety pence the hour plus productivity bonus and two-week annual holiday, and every second weekend off; hours from midday to eleven pm, overtime at time and a third as required. Meals were free.

To which Annie replied bleakly that she was on a diet, and Laura said she couldn't work on Saturday nights. She never worked on Saturday nights, Woodie wouldn't like it.

Mrs Haverill, who was accustomed to handling young female staff, pretended she hadn't heard. She said Bellamy House expected loyalty and dedication from its staff, a smart appearance and a pleasant manner. If Bellamy House was to be listed as one of the Great World Hotels, as featured in the Economist Diary, which was Sir Bernard's ambition, the staff must do their bit. She would expect them at six-thirty the following Monday. Uniforms could be purchased at the Gaiety Haberdashery, Fenedge, at specially reduced prices.

'I suppose,' she added, 'neither of you is pregnant?'

'Why?' asked Laura.

'Because it is not Sir Bernard's policy to employ pregnant women. Guests hardly like to see swelling tummies under smart uniforms.'
'I'm pregnant,' said Laura, thankfully, and then there was one.

Laura joined Carmen on the step. They walked away together, looked back, and saw Annie waving foolishly out of one of the top windows at them. Already she was wearing a little white cap.
'There's always the chicken factory,' said Laura.
'Never!' said Carmen. 'And you can't anyway: the carcasses are full of oestrogen. You shouldn't handle them, or you'll have a female baby with a beard, or a male one with a bosom.'
'How do you know these things?' asked Laura.
'I read *The Sun*,' said Carmen.

The steel gates, now cured of whatever circuit ailment had afflicted them, opened as Carmen and Annie approached and then slid gracefully together, separating Annie off from her friends.

Heaven knows where Driver had been but as Carmen and Laura left Bellamy House the BMW swept past them, and its exhaust puffed a rude goodbye, a brownish cloud which hung around in the air for a little before seeming to become granulated. The fidgety cloud danced towards them and turned out to be a swarm of bees.

Carmen and Laura began to run: the cloud pursued. Laura's long smooth legs attracted some of the little creatures, Carmen's neck others. The only cover apparent was the Portakabin tucked inside Mr Bliss's health farm for horses, and it was for this they made, squealing, over the cattle grid, up the steps, pushing open the door without ceremony, falling inside, slamming it shut behind them.

Mr Bliss looked up from his ancient typewriter. He was, he told me later, surprised but not offended. Anyone who looks after other people's horses, Mr Bliss says, soon learns to be stoical, not exactly hardened, but at least resigned. Clients will hand over their horses to be cured of asthma, then return them to the very stable whose bedding causes the complaint; explain to them that their child washing down the pony in cold water out of doors on a frosty morning is what gives the poor creature its recurring graveyard cough and they'll react with fury and refuse to pay your bills. Mr Bliss, even as the girls fell into his office, was writing a polite letter to a client who had owned a horse for years and yet needed to be told the difference between hay and straw. The marvel, said Mr Bliss to me, on one of his visits, is not that so many horses are ill, but that so many survive, and flourish, and even appear to like the human race. Mr Bliss's gentle enthusiasms and mild reproaches are endearing – persuasive even to one such as myself – prickly and unlikely ever to go horseriding let alone stroke one of the creatures on its nose, feverish or not.

'Bees,' said Carmen, by way of explanation, picking herself up, brushing herself down, helping Laura up. Mr Bliss went to the door, opened it, looked out.

'I see no bees,' he said. 'Perhaps they've gone on up to the stables. I hope so. A bee sting's good for a horse, especially one with rheumatism. And for mud fever the very best thing.'

'What about if you're pregnant?' asked Laura, rubbing the backs of her legs.

'I only know about horses,' said Mr Bliss, 'but I would have thought very good: a positive life charge for a mare in foal.'

'If she is pregnant she may not be staying that way,' said Carmen plaintively, but Mr Bliss, offering Laura a large tube of his special equine antihistamine ointment (organic, compounded of dock and comfrey), said, 'What's that strange smell? Is it ozone?' So Carmen added, 'but I suppose she'll have to, now.'

'I don't much like being compared to a mare in foal,' said Laura and Mr Bliss apologised, observing that the comparison was not indeed apt, since a mare normally only got into foal after a great deal of deliberation by those in charge of her. He'd left the door open a crack – Mr Bliss seldom shut a door properly, or put a lid back on, or fully closed a drawer, or so Mrs Baker would complain – and a puff of wind scattered his papers, which were many, tattered, and yellowed, throughout the Portakabin. There were bills and summonses amongst them, of course there were. Carmen asked if perhaps Mr Bliss needed an assistant – she would quickly read up on horses – but he said alas, he did not. If they needed jobs, perhaps they should try Little Walsingham. He had an old friend there, a Mr Sallace, who was always looking for suitable people to work for him, and seldom finding them. Just tell Mr

Sallace Mr Bliss had sent them. With some difficulty Mr Bliss located his address book.

'You're sure you don't want an assistant?' asked Carmen.

'Quite sure,' said Mr Bliss. 'Times are hard and getting harder for the equine naturopath. The kind of people who buy horses these days are computer whiz kids and teenage tycoons. They live in penthouses. They put their faith in antibiotics. They believe that their horse ceases to exist when it is not in front of their eyes, and it seldom is after the first rapture of ownership has worn off. But one should not be too surprised: lovers are often like that with one another.'

Little Walsingham! Laura and Carmen were not filled with enthusiasm. They'd been once on a school trip, and found it embarrassing, because Mrs Baker had declaimed from the front of the coach:

> 'As ye came from the holy land
> Of Walsingham,
> Met ye not with my true love
> By the way as ye came?'

and so on as Carmen tried to smoke a cigarette without being seen, Laura slept and Annie practised a finger dressing for her First Aid exam and got the girls behind tangled in bandage.

'I don't know what it is about you girls,' said Mrs Baker as they yawned over the window traceries of the fourteenth-century church at Great Walsingham, failed to see a group of barefoot pilgrims on the road to Little Walsingham, and even one nutter shuffling forward on his knees, or marvel at the proliferation of alleged Places of the Shrine. 'Why do you hate your past?' In the reign of Edward the Confessor, Richeldis, wife of the local Lord of the Manor, dreamt the same dream two nights running – that the Virgin Mary appeared and asked her to build in Walsingham a replica of the House of the Annunciation in Jerusalem, and assured her that a spring of fresh water would appear to mark the spot. The morning after the second dream, the spring began to bubble, the Shrine was built accordingly; Walsingham became known as England's Nazareth, and so great were the number who came to it from all over the world that the Milky Way in the night

sky was for a time known as the Walsingham Way. On and on Mrs
Baker droned. Henry VIII tore down the churches and publicly
burned the Shrine at the time of the Dissolution of the Monas-
teries. It was no bad thing, Mrs Baker declared, that the power
of the land be henceforth invested in the secular authority, not
the religious, but the event upset local opinion very much. Well,
it was bound to, as the whole area's income crumbled along with
Walsingham's spires and grottoes, the pilgrims failed to turn up,
the inns and the hostels closed down, and the prelates, the mer-
chants, the palmers, the pardoners, the necromancers, the sellers
of relics and souvenirs all just went home. Laura, Carmen and
Annie stared that day, at Mrs Baker's behest, at the quaint medieval buildings, the dreary Victorian churches of Walsingham, and
had the sense of a grey place once important now drained of life;
it felt, Carmen complained at the time, like being in an old
people's home. The whole class felt it: they were irritable, noisy
and uncooperative. This wasn't their idea of a day out.

> 'Sinne is where our ladie sate
> Heaven turned is to hell,
> Satan sits where our Lord did swaye,
> Walsingham oh farewell!'

said Mrs Baker over fish and chips at the seafront at Wells-on-Sea,
but the girls were more interested in whether or not she had seen
Carmen smoking. Mrs Baker gave up trying to educate them and
stared moodily out over the flat estuary sea. She wondered why
she bothered. The skuas were dive-bombing the terns. The tide
was out, way, way out, as if even the water had lost interest in so
dispiriting a land. Carmen disappeared, and the whole coachload
of bad-tempered girls had to wait until she was found before they
could set off home. She'd slipped into the seafront palmist's booth.
He told her she'd be a teacher and live in a bungalow, so not only
did she delay the whole party, but she sulked all the way home.
It was not a day that anyone cared to remember.

But on the day of their return to Walsingham, in search of Mr
Sallace and a possible job, the mood of the place had changed. It
was late August after all, and late August is a time for political
coups, for race riots and murders, for prisoners to sit on prison

65

roofs, for troops to move, for tanks to roll, for farmers to burn stubble (if there is nothing more interesting about to raze); the ocean presses closely in on the land, to see what's going on, and slops up and over. It's a season for thunderstorms and lightning strikes; the nose picks up the scent of smoke and cordite everywhere; those who can retreat to country cottages to see the dangerous season out: and the very good prepare to go on pilgrimage to Walsingham to pray for themselves and the rest of the world.

Today the pilgrims were out in number. Queues formed outside the little Anglican Shrine; the services within were non-stop. The incense censers swung all day; candles glittered and guttered; the air was heavy with smoke and scent and sweat, and loud with blessings and Amens. At the new Catholic church just outside the town, altogether airier and more hygienic, the conviction was that here, not there, was the true site of the Holy Shrine. The market square was thronged and noisy. The ritual Protestors shouted on their street corner, declaring the presence of idolatry, demanding that God strike everyone dead but them; street choirs of hymn singers outsung each other; the religious relic shops were doing good business, selling crosses and Madonnas, I ♥ Jesus T-shirts, Walsingham mugs and egg cups, holy pictures, rosaries, Greenpeace posters, Save the Rainforest balloons, special editions of large print Bibles, and so forth, as fast as they could take the money. Good times!

Carmen and Laura found Mr Sallace's workshop in a dark and smelly medieval back alley, cobbled and puddly with God knew what but it stank, led to by a sign saying 'Glossop's Pious Artefacts' and a pointing arrow. The door was small and wooden, as crooked as the wall it was set in. Carmen knocked and an old man flung it open. He was not pleased to see them. He was small, wizened, bad-tempered and as warped in his ancient body as his door was in old oak, but behind him opened out a surprisingly large, light and airy studio; there was a smell of paint and wet plaster in the air, and a sense of people properly and industriously employed, and Carmen and Laura longed to join them.

But Mr Sallace was not impressed by Mr Bliss's name, and said there were no jobs going, would they go away. Carmen had to put her foot in the door again, and say they'd hitched all the way to get there, to which Mr Sallace merely replied he didn't approve of hitching.

'All the way from Fenedge,' said Laura. 'It took for ever.'

At the mention of Fenedge Mr Sallace cheered up and asked if they knew Mavis Horner the Healer. He'd been to her once for arthritis and hadn't had a moment's trouble since. He peered up at them as he spoke, so twisted was his backbone, and on hearing that they were friends of Mavis's daughter let them in, and said he might be able to help after all. He took them over to the trestle tables of the Madonna & Saint section of the studio, and there for the first time Carmen set eyes on Ronnie Cartwright, who, up to his tanned and muscly elbow in plaster, was easing a woman-size Madonna out of her cast. He was twenty-one and had brown curly hair, a nice smile and a straight nose.

'Love at first sight,' said Carmen to Laura later.

Ronnie took Carmen's hand in his while he showed her how to pop blue Madonna eyes into their sockets. He told her he was only doing this kind of work temporarily, that he had ambition, that he was going into marketing, that he meant to be well up the promotion ladder of Safeway in another five years, that Glossop's Pious Artefacts was a lost cause: same blue mantle, same sweet smile, same blue eyes turned to the same heaven. If you didn't diversify, you withered away, though it took five hundred years to do it. If you asked Ronnie, the five hundred years were just about up.

'I thrilled to his touch,' said Carmen on the way home. 'I really did. We are meant for each other.'

'Do shut up,' said Laura. They'd failed to get that job either in the end. Carmen, on trial, had painted the Madonna's eyes mantle-blue, and her mantle eye-blue, and Laura, though painting the toenails the proper pink, had revealed to Mr Sallace that she was pregnant. She was far too young to have a baby, Mr Sallace said, and there was lead in the paint, and he showed them the door. Carmen asked if they could get paid for the two hours' work they'd done for free and he pushed them both out and slammed the door between her and Ronnie. And she hadn't got his number or he hers. She was too proud to go back in and ask for it. They hung around a little to see if Ronnie would come out of his own accord, but he didn't.

On the way home who offered them a lift but Driver? He stopped quite a little way ahead and Carmen had to run fifty yards up to the car window before she realised who it was.

'Lift?' he asked.

'No thanks,' said Carmen.

'Have it your own way,' said Driver, cheerfully enough. 'Suffer if you want. You'll soon come round to my way of thinking. What were you doing at Walsingham? Job-hunting?'

'Yes,' said Carmen. 'But no luck.'

'Well,' he said, 'there wouldn't be, would there? The airline job's still open. You'd look great in the uniform.'

'No,' said Carmen.

'You'd meet some great guys,' he said. 'Your sort of people. Not your average supermarket executive type. Have some ambition, Carmen.'

'You don't let up, do you?' she said.

'No, I don't,' he said.

'True love conquers all,' she said.

'Ho, ho, ho,' he said.

Laura cried out and Carmen looked back to see her flat on her face in the road. A rabbit had run out of the hedge in front of her and tripped her up. Carmen ran back to help her and broke her heel.

'The trouble with bad luck,' said Driver, just before he roared off, 'is that it's catching as measles, and your friends are the first to go down with it.'

'Supposing I lose the baby?' asked Laura.

'You won't,' said Carmen. 'No such luck.'

A kind of minor blight fell over the area. A thunderstorm unleashed itself over the land, flattening such crops as had not yet been harvested; sudden run-off from the roads caused a sewage flowback into a stream leading to the River Wissey, a stretch of which lost enough oxygen to kill a few hundred fish: rain came through the ceiling of Mr Bliss's Portakabin and spoiled his whole drum of girth gall powder, a mixture of kaolin (cheap) and cobwebs collected by local children (extremely expensive): up at Bellamy House a gutter leaked and an entire panelled ceiling, painted before it had properly dried out, collapsed with a crash. Annie, who was just passing, got plaster in her hair and there were five days to go before hair-washing night. I was on my way from the Handicapped Centre to Alison's car, being half lifted, half carried by total strangers, when the famous downpour started: I'm sure it cured my helpers of good deeds for life. But not of course Alison, whose ancient face was lifted to the watery clouds, her thin hair plastered across wrinkled cheeks, her scalp pink and sore-looking where it showed.

'Do your damnedest, God! We won't give in!'

Runs of bad luck

Some people's bad luck is other people's good. Your bad luck when your windscreen shatters: but it's excellent luck for the garage. I spent three hours in a garage yesterday while mechanics replaced Alison's windscreen. I can't just walk away, you see.

Good luck for Audrey that the 'For Sale' sign she has put up outside the house attracts a buyer the very same day. Bad luck for Laura, whose home it is, who's feeling low. The romance of pregnancy is not materialising, only the problems.

Does she love Woodie? How do you know you're in love? Neither Carmen nor Annie is able to tell her, though Annie supposes it to be when it doesn't even occur to you to ask the question.

Good luck that Woodie's come home early from his course to take responsibility for the baby; bad luck that it means he won't get his diploma.

Good and bad luck that Woodie wants to marry her. One evening, Laura faces Woodie and Audrey across the kitchen table. She hopes she can divide and somehow rule.

'If you took the house off the market, Mum,' says Laura, 'you and I could live quietly here with the baby and bring it up together. I'd get a job. We'll manage the mortgage somehow, and Woodie can visit.'

They just stare at her.

'You do mean to help with the baby, Mum?'

'I have to think of myself,' says Audrey. She says it a lot these days. 'It's your baby, not mine.'
Laura feels abandoned. Woodie has an alternative plan. He wants to set up his own business making DIY garden sheds. All he needs is a back garden. If he married Laura, and Audrey lived with them, there'd be no need to sell the house, and she could help with the baby when she felt like it, not otherwise. Because of course Laura would stay home and look after the baby; why have one if you were going to hand it over to someone else?

He was kind, solid, sensible and companionable and Laura agreed to marry him. And whether that was his good luck and her bad or the other way round, who's to say? You can only say of other people what a pity he did this or she did that: but we'll never know how much worse it might have been had they not. At least you're alive to say oh, how I wish I hadn't emigrated. Nature provides itself, through the act of procreation in an endless juggling of chromosomes, through the two that combine to produce the one with infinite examples of supposing-this and supposing-that and seeing it through to the end; but it is not given to individuals to do so interesting a thing – to rewind life back a scene or two, and play it forward a different way. Only writers can do it and they're just guessing.

8

Carmen ran into Mrs Baker in the street just before Christmas. She did it literally. Her father was teaching her to drive. She put her foot on the accelerator, not the brake, and the car shot forward through the Fenedge Pedestrian Precinct, and she knocked over Mrs Baker, who was dressed as Uncle Holly and collecting money for the Rainforests, or the Mexican Earthquake, I forget which: at any rate some good cause in some distant place. I was sitting watching from the Handicapped Centre, wondering why there was never a collection to provide decent official transport for the handicapped here at home, when I saw Carmen run into her. Or perhaps I overstate it. Mrs Baker was scratched on her leg, but only slightly, and though personally I thought she ought to go to the hospital for a tetanus jab, so rusty was Andy's car, she and Carmen went together to the Welcome-In to have a cup of coffee and a mince pie. Andy had turned Carmen out of the car and said he'd die rather than let her drive another yard, and would certainly die if she did: she would have to walk home.

'I told you so,' said Mrs Baker, not smugly but in some distress, on hearing that Annie was still a housemaid at Bellamy House and had failed to get promotion to kitchen work – 'She's just too good at beds,' said Carmen – and that Laura was not just pregnant but engaged, and Carmen without a job. 'I told you girls what would happen if you failed your exams.' But it was strange. Whenever Carmen applied for work, things fell apart. Firms shut up shop as she appeared – Peckhams Poultry had been closed down to clear its premises of salmonella – and personnel officers took against her for no reason.

71

'You are aiming too low,' said Mrs Baker. 'One look at you, Carmen, and they can tell you're only going to stay a week or you're about to plot a takeover, or tell them what to do.'

Mrs Baker asked about boyfriends and Carmen replied as she always did: that she had met the love of her life, a certain Ronnie Cartwright, and was saving herself for him. She even quoted a line about perfect love from *Pelleas and Melisande*, thinking Mrs Baker at least would understand. But Mrs Baker told me later she felt responsible for filling her girls' heads with romantic nonsense when all they were ever going to meet were the local boys. She would campaign to take a number of works off the Set Books list forthwith. Let them be realistic about their chances in the world. Mrs Baker bought another mince pie to console herself and while she was at the counter her eye fell on the local newspaper, and a small advert offering a job for a smart junior at Bellamy Airspace. She took the newspaper over to where Carmen sat beneath the dreadful work of local artists, and Carmen finally called Bellamy Airspace from the telephone box outside the Post Office and asked for an interview.

I watched her from my window. I will swear that when she went in she was pretty enough in her swarthy way, but slightly dumpy, and that when she came out she was beautiful, leggy and bosomy, but repeatedly kicking her feet against the wall as if in a temper.

Carmen called Mrs Baker at home that evening to say she'd got the job. She was to be a receptionist. Her new employers were teaching her elocution and the art of flower arrangement. She was to take courses in make-up and massage. The rest of the time she sat and received parcels and smiled and made clients cups of coffee, and was paid double what she would have got at Peckhams Poultry.
'It sounds,' said Mrs Baker, 'as if they are training you to be a geisha girl.'
'It seems that Sir Bernard Bellamy,' said Carmen, 'likes all his female employees to be truly feminine. Just not pregnant,' she added, remembering Laura.

It was noticeable during the next few months how the luck of Fenedge changed. Peckhams reopened, its salmonella count at last within levels acceptable to the Ministry of Agriculture, Fisheries and Food; the remains of a Roman villa and its splendid tiled floor were discovered not far away, and this attracted visitors with archaeological interests if not much money, so that the many local bed & breakfasts flourished. Sheets which had lain folded in airing cupboards were brought out and aired; egg cups were brought forward from the backs of cupboards, shaken free of dead flies, and washed. Children were made to sit up at table and mind their manners in case paying guests arrived, and they did! Bellamy House brought enough wealthy people into the area to allow a fancy restaurant or so to open up: pubs had themselves refurbished: a Japanese Auto concession was granted to the town, then the launderette bought in a dry-cleaning machine, so you could take your clothes in and collect them on the same day! Hitherto garments had been sent to Kings Lynn and it would be a minimum of five days before they were returned, and the local depot manageress was likely to reject your offering, fingering your cashmere jumper with the egg stain on the front, saying, 'You don't want to waste your money getting that dry-cleaned. Wash it at home. It's perfectly safe.' And you would and it wouldn't be. There was to be a new science wing at Fenedge School for Girls; the place was now designated as a Community Resource Centre and attracted extra funding from the Local Education Authority. Evening classes in upholstery and astrology had started up. A scandal involving royalty hit the headlines and the girls involved turned out to be the daughters of a local vicar, so the media turned up en masse and put Fenedge on the map at last. 'Flirts of Fenedge.' The City Fathers (City, indeed!) had the War Memorial cleaned up, and the flowerbeds replanted. A bus service finally operated, to link Fenedge and neighbouring villages, and the cinema reopened, with a new Dolby stereo sound system, one of the best in the whole country.

It wasn't so much that good things happened as that bad things ceased happening. Or perhaps the Devil was looking the other way: was off stirring things up somewhere else. Bad luck for them. Sir Bernard Bellamy was off too; he had diversified into Scandinavian shipping.

Mavis and Alan suggested to Annie that she lived in at Bellamy House: they thought she'd be better placed for promotion.

'You mean there's no room any more in my bedroom for your office,' was Annie's first reaction. 'That is to say, no room in your office for my bed.'

'You can't stay home for ever,' said Alan, reasonably. 'You're a working girl now. If you'd tried harder and passed your exams and gone to college, it would have been different. But no, you wouldn't listen.'

'I did so listen,' said Annie. 'I listened to Count Capinski, if you remember. It's all his fault.'

'Don't say that name aloud,' said Alan, alarmed. 'Don't even think of him or he might come back.'

Lately Mavis's reputation had soared, recovering from the initial knock it received when Count Capinski first disappeared. For a time her healing powers had seemed to desert her, but now she was back on course, or said to be. Warts vanished and backache went at the touch of her fingers. As Dr Grafton became increasingly eccentric, not just failing to diagnose cancer until too late – which anyone can do – but refusing to prescribe antibiotics or make home visits, and suggesting to patients that wholemeal bread and meditation would cure heart disease, Mavis's laying on of hands seemed more and more acceptable. It was true that you had to pay Mavis and you didn't have to pay Dr Grafton – or only through your taxes – but at least Mavis wasn't judgemental, and didn't equate stress-related ailments – which meant everything which could go wrong with body or mind – with personal sin. Mavis was far more likely to tell you that you were a victim of demonic possession, which could hardly be your fault. You'd just been in the wrong place at the wrong time. So these days she was popular, and was spared much of the putting the living in touch with the dead that she'd been obliged to in the past, if only in order to earn a living. She'd found that exhausting and irritating, if only because the dead had so little of interest to say once they'd been summoned. Now she just laid on hands and felt the healing power channel itself through her, and could see the results.

I had been to Mavis myself, and once again had felt the strange, none-too-pleasant tingling in toes normally unused to sensation. What's more, she had seemed quite inadvertently to have cured a skin condition on the back of my hand, which had never fully healed since I had an allergic reaction to some kind of drip they gave me in Chicago. Dr Grafton had finally agreed to sending further X-rays and CAT scans to Chicago – one could die while the medical profession sorts its etiquette out: their mistrust of one another is only equalled by their mistrust of their patients – and now they started writing to me again. The backbone bypass had worked, they assured me, it was just that it had instantly blocked; the bypass now needed its own angioplasty: they wanted to fill it with miniature balloons which they'd blow up inside the artery to clear it. They'd lately developed a new and better technique to accomplish this, they said on the phone: why didn't I come over? 'We'll get the blood flowing!' they said. 'One way or another, Harriet. We won't be defeated!' But there was something in their tone of voice so like Alison's as she addressed the watery sky and defied God that I was reluctant to accept their offer. I thought I'd just sit there in my window a little longer and observe what was going on, and take time to make up my mind. Perhaps the tingling meant the bypass was clearing the traffic jam in my arteries, of its own accord, without the need for surgical intervention.

But enough of me. There was Annie crying that day into her vegetable soup, feeling abandoned: she mustn't be forgotten: let's return to her predicament.

'She's crying because she's tired,' said Mavis. Mavis had turned vegetarian. 'She's a meat eater. Carnivores exhaust themselves with animal passions.'

'It's nothing to do with being tired,' said Annie. 'It's relief. I've wanted to live in at Bellamy House for ages, but I thought you'd be hurt if I said so. Most people are very nice to me at work, and you get used to the ones that aren't. Even Mrs Haverill being horrid is okay: at least she's taking notice of me. Up here it's all allergies and rheumatics and dead spirits and body bags in the freezer, and everyone trying to be nice when they don't feel like it, and too busy to care about me one bit.'

'You're being unfair,' said Mavis.

'Let her say her piece,' said Alan. 'She'll feel better when she has.'

'Everything I touch up there at Bellamy House is nice,' said Annie. 'It's silky or soft or somehow heavy. Here everything's scratchy, cheap and tinny.'

'It's all good value for money in this house,' said Alan. 'Not a penny wasted.'

'Value for money means ugly,' said Annie, 'and the longer I'm up at Bellamy House and not here the less ugly I turn out to be.'

'You're not ugly, dear,' said Mavis. 'Whatever makes you think a thing like that?'

'The mirror,' said Alan, and laughed before he could stop himself. But that was only habit. The fact was that Annie was looking distinctly better. She'd lost weight and her eyes seemed bigger, even quite large and soulful, and she was sometimes able to wash her hair in one of the guest bathrooms if there was time and it was Mrs Haverill's day off so that it fluffed agreeably around her face instead of lankly hanging. Alan actually apologised for laughing, and it was with the good wishes of her family that Annie packed a trunk, and moved up the hill to be resident staff at Bellamy House. She had a little attic room to herself, and Mrs Haverill let her use up the half-finished circlets of lavender soap from the guest bedrooms, and quite often yesterday's croissants would be served for breakfast, dunked in milk by the chef and heated up briefly in the oven for the staff.

Laura and Woodie got married, quietly, because Audrey was back in hospital and it didn't seem a time for much rejoicing, but there were pretty flowers on the Registrar's table and she had a new dress, the first for ages. Her father Kim did not come. She sent an invitation to the last address she had for him, the minute she knew her mother would be in hospital for the ceremony, but she didn't hear back. She expected he had moved house again. She'd been told by friends that Poppy had lost the baby, so her father need never have left home in the first place, but Woodie helped Laura accept the fact that probably her father had really wanted to go, not just had to go. And that yes, perhaps Kim had indeed thought Kubrick the fish more important than his own daughter. An older generation of men could be like that, said Woodie, especially men young in the sixties, whose brains had been addled by hallucinogenic drugs. But Woodie, said Woodie, was a new man and different. He had feelings and could give voice to them. He spoke to Laura seriously on their wedding night. He knew she hadn't been certain about the wisdom of getting married, but he was convinced they'd done the right thing. He loved her. There wouldn't be much money, but they'd manage. He would make sure Laura's life was rewarding and interesting. They would travel – they could always go camping, even to Europe if she wanted. The great thing about being self-employed as he was, or was about to be, was that the harder you worked the more you earned. Well it must be like that, mustn't it? There was a tremble in his voice and Laura realised that Woodie was as scared of the future as she was, and stopped worrying about whether or not she loved him: it was obvious that she did.

As for Carmen's household, great things were happening there. Raelene had discovered aerobics and the benefits of a low-fat diet: she could bend to pick up the cat dish and wash it; she remembered to buy worm pills for the dog: she served only boiled vegetables, never fried, and sprinkled ground vitamin and mineral supplements into the muesli. Andy and Stephen grumbled but ate what was put in front of them. Raelene, as she lost weight, jumped up and down from her chair to put things straight and wipe surfaces. She couldn't abide dirty clothes: the washing machine and dryer rumbled all day long and into the night too. She planted roses in the garden, even making the hole big enough to spread the roots properly, and adding peat and humus into the sandy soil. She chose a Dortmund climber (*R. Kordesii*) for the north-facing wall (crimson red with a white eye) and *rugosas* (Frau Dagmar Hastrup (pink) and Rosenaie de l'Haij (crimson purple) for the beds in front. Andy, at her request, painted the house, not in colours left over from assorted jobs, but in proper brilliant-white outdoor paint, two coats. Raelene began to answer the phone, instead of just switching it through to the answering machine when it rang, and would even leave Andy a record of calls received and made. She had the van insured and the reverse gear mended, which made proper parking possible. Parking tickets came less frequently.

What brought these changes about? Who's to say? Families sink and rise again. Aerobics and weight loss helped, as did the fact of Carmen's being employed, but Stephen's metamorphosis was probably most responsible. Stephen had pulled himself together, as boys of a certain age sometimes do: he discovered a talent in himself, a capacity for and an interest in science. Dragging a magnet through iron filings had filled him with an enthusiasm for the workings of the natural world. It was his good fortune to have at college an excellent physics teacher whose bad fortune it was to have halitosis so severe that it limited his employment potential. Mr Parker had ended up teaching the dregs of the education system, the unteachables, the alienated, those accustomed to living with smells, their own and others, and rather liking them. Mr Parker's presentation of the engineering problems posed in the supporting of two female breasts of variable size with fabric and wire in one garment further fired Stephen's interest. Tests showed him to have an innate mathematical ability, and before long, via a rather morbid interest in nuclear catastrophe, he was absorbed in the rarefied world of particle physics, and destined, the school thought, for Cambridge.

'We were lucky,' said Mr Parker to the Headmaster in the corridor. 'Sheer fluke that we picked him up. I wonder how many children we lose as we nearly lost Stephen – doomed by our low expectations of them?'
'It wasn't luck,' said the Headmaster. 'The system is devised to pick them out, get them on –' and he hurried off, opening a window on the way. But Mr Parker was given an A level class to teach the following year, and got three pupils to Oxbridge, so it looked as if his luck had changed too.

The notion of 'my son the genius' affected Andy greatly; he had dropped a couple of stone as Raelene stopped frying and now the world seemed full of hope and possibility. He paid his bills, engaged in dialogue with dissatisfied clients, even went over to the Horners and did a couple of days' work in the garage, free of charge. It was true that in error he switched off the big chest freezer, now placed, for some reason, in the back of the garage (what did such a small family want with so big a freezer?) but luckily Alan noticed and turned the power back on.

One day, just before Laura's baby was born, Carmen came back home early – she'd been at her Flower Arrangement and Other Office Skills course in Kings Lynn – to find her parents looking through holiday brochures. Raelene leapt up and took Carmen's coat, brushed it down, and hung it on a padded hanger on the back of the door, and offered her food and drink.

'There's a lovely piece of fish for tea,' she said. 'Grilled with a squeeze of lemon. Only a hundred and sixty calories for six ounces. In the old days,' Raelene said, 'I thought your insides were just a kind of factory: it took in what it needed and chucked the rest away. But apparently the body doesn't know it's a factory. It takes what it gets and gobbles the lot, poisons and all. You have to be so careful what you eat, Carmen.'

But Andy said (he did sometimes resist a little), 'If your dinner's got your number on it it's got your number on it, that's your old dad's theory, Carmen. My, we are looking remarkable today!'

Carmen thought she might one day have to have cosmetic surgery to get the size of her breasts reduced. Clothes did not hang as she liked them to. It was difficult to get going what they called in her Dress Management course 'a line'. Her figure seemed to be variable, as that of other girls was not. She had plucked up her courage and been to Dr Grafton about the state of her nipples, which kept changing shape, colour and size. Could this be skin cancer? He had been scrupulously correct in his examination, but said they looked perfectly in order to him, quite within the ordinary run of nipple, though Carmen might need to use a suction cap when she had a baby, to give the baby something to get hold of. It had, as it happened, turned out to be a day when the aureole was roseate, very pale pink, and the nipple itself hardly prominent at all. She quite liked them like that.

'I know they're in order,' she said to Dr Grafton, 'it's just that they keep changing. They'll be quite different tomorrow. And yesterday they were brown and tough.'

Dr Grafton thought she might be in the grip of a psychosis – to be obsessed by the state of the nipple surely indicated some overwhelming sexual anxiety? – and offered Carmen counselling, but she declined. She said yes, she did have a boyfriend, his name was Ronnie Cartwright, just to get out of the surgery. But it was a relief to know she didn't have skin cancer. She hoped he was right: by all accounts Dr Grafton was so often wrong. Perhaps the condition was hereditary? She asked Raelene, who said Carmen was obviously still growing, and she, Raelene, had read an interesting fact in *The Independent*. (Stephen had started taking *The Sun* to school every morning to his science class, leaving nothing to read over tea, so Raelene had switched to *The Independent*.) Apparently, Raelene said, Marks & Spencer affirmed that the female shape altered to suit fashion. Bodies, in fact, grew into what society desired them to be.

'So?' asked Carmen.

'So well I don't know,' said Raelene. 'But life is full of surprises.'

And thus it turned out to be, the day Raelene took Carmen's coat and hung it up for her – something that had hardly happened since the day Carmen was born, presaging change and indicating guilt.

'Your dad and I have something to tell you, sweetheart,' said Raelene as Carmen toyed with her hundred and sixty calories of pure protein. 'We're going on a world cruise. We may be gone for quite some time. But if you don't see the world now, when will you? The things you regret are the things you don't do, not the things you do do. Right?'

'I suppose so,' said Carmen, doubtfully. It's true to say that no one likes their parents taking off across the world, no matter what they think of those parents. 'What about Stephen? He's still at school. Isn't he too young to leave?'

'He's off to Dounreay,' said Andy. 'Am I proud of that boy!' Stephen looked up from a book called *The Metaphysics of the Quark* and said, 'Day release from Cambridge next year. Work experience this. Forget fission, this is fusion,' and went back to his book.

'So now Stephen's sorted,' said Raelene, 'and finally got his head screwed on the right way, and you're in full-time work, your dad and I are free. And your Auntie Edna will keep an eye on the pair of you. We've put the house up for sale to keep the bank happy. All you have to do is show people round and put them off.'

Carmen thought for a little, then she said, 'But you haven't got the money for a cruise.'

'Oh yes we have,' said Raelene. 'Grandma turned out to have quite a bit in her will. What a surprise! Just enough to blow on a really nice year or so in the sun.'

'I see,' said Carmen.

'So that's settled,' said Raelene in her new bright manner. 'I don't know about not eating pork. Sometimes I really fancy a bacon sandwich.'

Andy said, 'Speaking for myself, doll, bacon's an integral part of my life.' He turned the pages of a brochure. 'Where's the nearest port to the Silk Route? Or is that inland?'

Carmen found herself forgotten. She studied her nails. Yesterday they had been oval; today they seemed almond shape. She had gone from a D cup to a B overnight though, which was a relief. Her parents had stopped noticing. Anyone can get used to anything.

The phone rang. Stephen answered it. It was someone called Bernard for Carmen. Carmen took the phone saying she didn't know anyone called Bernard, and then discovered it was Sir Bernard Bellamy. He wanted her to dine with him that very night. Carmen said she couldn't, she'd already eaten, but then felt suddenly very hungry – what's a hundred and sixty calories to a growing, changing girl? – and said okay. He said he'd send his chauffeur.

'Who was that?' asked Raelene.

'Nobody,' said Carmen shortly. Her breasts felt heavier by the moment. She felt she could never trust anyone again. The world changed too suddenly for her liking. She had survived her childhood by feeling superior to her parents, managed to adjust as they began to occupy the moral high ground: now they were backing out altogether: snatching an already rippling carpet from underneath her feet. She felt like crying.

Andy said, 'Now don't you throw yourself away, Car. Looking the way you do these days, you could catch some rich Arab.'

Raelene said, 'Our Car will marry for love, not money. She's just waiting for Mr Right to come along.'

Carmen said, for what she feared would be the last time, 'If you wanted to call me Car, why did you name me Carmen?'

She went to her room and fell asleep, and woke only when Andy banged upon her door and called, 'Car, it's your date. Funny kind of minicab.'

And I watched from my window as Carmen came down the path between the *rugosas*, the pink and the crimson. I noticed people's legs, particularly, because of the state of my own. Hers were perfect today, lean, long, serviceable. She wore a leather miniskirt at the top of them, covering a tight little bum, just about. My

Aunt Michelle called it 'bum'. I'm sorry. It used to upset my mother if I called it that. 'What *do* I call it then?' I asked once. I knew she didn't like 'bottom', thinking it both imprecise and mealy-mouthed. 'I've no idea,' she said.

Driver got out of the BMW and opened the door for Carmen and Andy said from the step, 'Evening out with the company chauffeur, I see,' to which Carmen replied, 'That's right, Dad. See you later.'

'Mind you do,' said Andy, 'and not too late at that.'

'If I'm not old enough to look after myself,' said Carmen bitterly, 'why are you two going off round the world?'

She couldn't get over it. Abandoned! She snivelled in the back of the car and took no notice of the landscape, though it was a particularly beautiful evening, and even the straight green and brown lines of the beet fields seemed luminous as the low sun struck through them. The sun was sinking red and round, behind stark lightning-struck trees, as if in a rather bad painting.

'Wonderful evening,' said Driver from the front. 'Aren't you thrilled? A date with Sir Bernard. Shouldn't you have dolled yourself up a bit?'

'He can take me as he finds me,' said Carmen. 'And this is my best skirt.'

'That's the spirit,' said Driver. 'I thought perhaps you and I should have a little talk,' and he drove off the road, bump, bump, bump, into a patch of the old woods, and parked the car beneath a particularly gracious oak tree. Though all this part may have been a dream. A flock of birds, those humble sparrows which are so much everywhere that no one watches out for them, rose at once from the branches and left them in peace. A little table stood beneath the tree, spread with a red check tablecloth. Two chairs faced each other. And there they sat, Driver and she. She had a glass of wine in her hand.

'Now I've given you a little on account,' said Driver to Carmen then, 'it's time you did one or two things for me.'

'What have you given me on account?'

'Item, beauty in the eye of the beholder,' said Driver.

'I don't think much of your idea of that,' she said. 'It keeps changing.'

'So does the beholder,' said Driver. 'I could give you Beauty itself if you're not satisfied.'

'So men would look after me in the street?' she sneered. 'They do that already.'

'That's just sexiness,' he said, 'with a dollop of prettiness. Any young girl has that. As it is, it's all worry and anxiety: how do you not get pregnant, how do you best use face shaper, did you remember to shave your legs? Are the tops of your arms over-fleshy? It's too much like hard work getting the right look for the right man at the right moment. But Beauty, the Real Thing, you don't have to do anything about. You just carry it round inside you: it shines out from the middle, nothing to do with you. Protects and perfects as it works. No one worries about hairy legs, and they won't be hairy anyway: your body respects the image you and others have of it. Men try to get to the heart of it through you. They have to possess it, they need to own it. It's like gold: it causes fever.'

'I don't want it,' said Carmen.

'Don't try my patience,' he said. He had high cheek bones. He'd taken off his chauffeur's cap. His hair was glossy. He stared beyond her as he spoke. She found she was glad she didn't want him to look at her. The shoulders of his uniform were square and the fabric was figured with something that had the texture of feather but glinted with metal, as if steel wings were folded beneath. She thought perhaps she had fallen asleep in the back of the car: was she not on her way to a date with Sir Bernard Bellamy, which in itself was dreamlike enough? Dreams within dreams within dreams! Where could you stop? She drank some more wine, and she could feel it run down her throat: that was real enough, essential fuel for the fluttering there inside. She wondered exactly where amongst all that palpated flesh her soul could be: and what was the soul? Was it the organising principle that kept the parts working, or just the difference between life and death? And why did Driver want it, anyway? And would it matter if he had it? Perhaps it affected the cosmos and not her, in which case why bother?

I am putting thoughts into Carmen's mind. All she told Laura, who told me, was that when she took the second sip of wine, she was suddenly conscious of her insides working; she could see herself from the inside out, a collection of organs, throbbing in a not very pleasant but clearly interrelated way, wrapped in skin; she could feel everything her body was doing, from the blood running through her veins into the tips of her toes, to the hairs growing out of her scalp: there was no peace. None of it ever stopped.

Nor would Driver. 'Beauty keeps you young,' he said. 'Next best thing to immortality. The body ages around it, of course, but the thing itself is like a jewel; indestructible. If you have beauty you get to be loved but don't have to do any loving in return. But the real point about beauty is that it gives you power. Beauty is all the power that women ever have. And power is what women want.'

'Mrs Baker wouldn't like to hear you say a thing like that,' said Carmen. 'Mrs Baker says you can get where you want, male or female, if you really want it. It's knowing what you want is the problem.'

Driver laughed in a disagreeable way. Carmen felt he didn't appreciate Mrs Baker as she did.

'Without beauty,' he said, 'women only have the power men let them have.'

'I'll think about it,' said Carmen. 'I promise.' For he was sparking and smoking a bit, like his own engine, overheated.

'So what else have you done for me?'

'Item,' said Driver, in a lordly way, as if he had the whole world under his thumb. 'Good luck all round, for you and your friends.'

Carmen pondered this. It was true that her own life was going well; that Laura had given birth to a baby girl with scarcely a spasm of pain ('My,' said Nurse Phaby, who had also brought Laura into the world, 'you are a lucky girl! You certainly don't take after your mother!'); and that Annie had had the most remarkable stroke of good fortune.

Annie had actually met the man of her dreams while laying a carpet on the attic stairs of Bellamy House. The top floor had finally been opened for guests, in response to popular demand; forget that the increase in the number of guests strained the hotel's kitchens and leisure facilities to the very limit of their capacity, that the water supply was barely adequate to reach the remoter bedrooms, and the staff to guest ratio – what Mrs Haverill referred to as the SGR – moved from one to five to one to ten with no concomitant rise in wages. Annie now worked until seven at night, and did up to eight hours further a week on the Cooperative Task Force, or CTF, the function of which was to undertake odd jobs around the place, thus avoiding the necessity of Mrs Haverill taking on extra staff. Carpet-laying was this week's task. It was Annie's favourite. She loved the tough resilience of the carpet: the brightness of the nails, the sharp quick bang of hammer on head. She loved getting it right. Everyone else was hopeless at it. She had a mouthful of nails: she knelt on one stair, stretched up to the next, sat back on her heels to survey her work. Someone came up to stand behind her. She assumed it was Eddie, her current CTF colleague. She did not bother to look round.

'Hand me the other box of tacks,' she asked, and whoever it was did.

'I'm going to run out of underfelt,' she said. 'There's another roll in the cleaning cupboard next to the Mozart suite.' It was fetched. 'They're so mean in this place,' said Annie. 'They won't buy proper staircarpet underlay. I think the CTF is a con. Mrs Haverill goes on about us pulling together, but what she means is, we pull, Sir Bernard profits and she's in love with Sir Bernard. They're crazy to open up the attic rooms. There are bats up there, and bed bugs in the brass beds. Do you know about bed bugs?' And she described the dreadful things: how they can wake after a hundred years, desiccated by the decades until they look no more than flakes of paper, to creep in the night towards some sudden new source of warmth and damp – that is to say, some sleeping human being, whose only crime is to be warm and damp. The little piece of paper, turning less paperlike every second, creeps towards its victim, and reaching him, her, jabs with its proboscis, injecting both anaesthetic and anti-coagulant so the flesh doesn't hurt or bleed, and no alarm is raised; then peacefully it squats and sucks out human blood until it's no longer papery but bloated, fat and pink. Then, satiated, it crawls away, or scuttles up the curtain, to hide beneath the window pole – oh, bed bugs are cunning! People who're badly bitten sometimes have to be given blood transfusions. Pity the guests, said Annie, in the newly opened attic floor, of Bellamy House, once Sealord Mansion.

All this Annie spoke, and more. And then she looked up and who was standing staring at her but the man of her dreams, not Eddie, who was short and squat and the stuff of nightmares. (It seemed to be either Sir Bernard or Mrs Haverill's quite deliberate policy to staff the hotel with the most presentable females available and the least presentable males. Or perhaps it just is, as research will tell us, that pretty women get employed before plain ones, and physical appearance is not so telling a qualification for employment in the male. Perhaps this accounts for the (to the rational) apparently irrational rejoicing of the world when a baby boy appears from out of the womb and not a baby girl: it just doesn't matter what he looks like, how crooked his nose, how lumpy his figure, how crossed his eyes, how feeble his legs – he will get a job and find a spouse.) The man of Annie's dreams, the tall dark stranger from overseas whom Count Capinski had once promised her, was broad-shouldered, muscular and well fleshed. He had a square jaw, thick dark hair, bright blue eyes, the look of a man slow to anger, too courteous to complain overmuch; the kind of man, in fact, who illustrates the more romantic stories you still sometimes find in women's magazines. What is more, he had an unmarried, questioning, questing glance. 'Let me tell you about the sheep tick one day,' he said. 'Or the lifestyle of the liver fluke. Nothing in the world like the liver fluke.'

'You're not Eddie,' was all Annie could say in her dismay, and she spat tacks from her lips as she spoke. He picked them up with strong working fingers, square-nailed. The nails were not manicured and polished as were those of most of the male guests at Bellamy House: they looked, as nails can, well scrubbed but still ingrained with this and that, in spite of all efforts.

'No, I'm not Eddie,' he said. 'I'm a sheep farmer from New Zealand. I have a room up these stairs, and it has a brass bed, so it's not so much of a buggaroo if I can't get up them because you're in the way.'

And he asked her to have a drink with him after supper; there was no one in this back of beyond to talk to, he said, no one to have a decent conversation with him since he'd left his sheep farm

in the South Island two weeks back to inspect the roe deer of East
Wretham Heath with a view to purchasing. You should never
buy, he said, an animal you hadn't set eyes upon, let alone a
hundred of them, any more than you should marry a girl who
hadn't cooked you dinner. A girl who could lay carpet and talk
about bed bugs wasn't your usual run of Pom, said handsome
Tim McLean, so would she do him the honour of having a
drink? You bet she would! Little Annie Horner, blossoming into
if not quite a beauty, at least something near it, at the sight
of that jaw, those pillars of legs, the sound of the deep – if
slightly nasal, it must be admitted – male voice, and all his
attention focused on her. Was that luck, or was that luck, for
Carmen's friend Annie?

And was that luck, or was that luck, that Laura's baby Rachel
was the most peaceable baby ever, and slept and smiled, and that
Woodie, in spite or perhaps because of his youth, doted upon his
small family, and that Audrey was in remission and could help
Laura with Rachel, so Woodie could make garden sheds in the
back garden, dovetailing joints and smoothing edges with such
beautiful precision that everyone admired them, although each
shed, being a work of art, would take so long to make that few
could buy them if they were costed out right. And Laura insisted
that Woodie cost them out right, including the cost of labour in
the end price. Everyone knew you had to do that. But then one
of Woodie's many aunts died and left him just enough money to
see them through the first year, if they were careful. Woodie's
mother was forty-four when he was born, his father sixty-three.
Now they lived far away and scarcely impinged upon the young
couple's life: more like distant grandparents than parents, content
with a photograph of the baby and a card at Christmas. Was that
luck, or was that luck?

But Carmen said to Driver, 'I don't know so much. I think we
just stopped being unlucky.'
Driver fizzled a bit.
'Item. I've got rid of your parents. They were always going to be
an embarrassment.'
'I love my parents.'
'Too late,' said Driver. 'Many's the time you've wished them dead

in your heart. I'm just sending them off on a world cruise, so be grateful to me. No such thing as a free lunch,' and she was pressed up against an oak tree, pinned against it by his powerful shoulders, and her skirt was up around her waist; well, perhaps it was, perhaps it wasn't. Annie was convinced for a time that everything Carmen said about Driver was not a sexual fantasy but the opposite, an a-sexual fantasy, the truth being that Carmen was having it off with the chauffeur, who was pimping for his employer and cheating on him. But then Annie went through phases of believing the worst about everyone. Laura was never quite so sure. She was content to believe that Carmen just couldn't tell dream from reality.

'Item,' said Driver, pausing. 'All this,' and he put the forest on pause as well, so Carmen could properly appreciate it, or that's what it seemed he did. The moon had risen, somehow, somewhere, unnoticed, only to be stopped now in its course, so that the forest was motionless and all things natural lost their untidiness, their imperfections, and were sealed into neat and tidy pattern: leaves and branches in a complex black tracery, unshifting, interlaced with silver, bathed in the still moon's melancholy light. The moon is always melancholy, if you ask me. Very few understand its motions, or care to, other than astronomers or astrologers, and that's depressing to begin with. Is that a waning or a waxing moon up there? Why is it shining in the dawn sky today, when yesterday you could see it at midnight? Does it matter? Do you care? No. The fact is the moon is all over the place and few of us like it or' can be bothered with it. The sun's uses are at least observable, and what is more you can't look it in the eye without going blind, so it has your respect, but the moon is both random and useless, like a fragment of torn cartilage in a knee joint, causing trouble. It drags large masses of water after it, or so they say, but who believes that in their hearts? All the moon is fit for is to remind us of our place in the universe; it doesn't please me to remember how insignificant and short-lived I am. No way. If the moon decides in its whimsical manner to shine in on Landsfield Crescent, I draw the curtains at once. On one occasion Alison got me to the Handicapped Centre so early, in her anxiety to avoid the non-existent traffic jam of the Fenedge rush hour, that the moon was still vast in the dawn sky, and I had to sit in its light, since the County provides no curtains, and, thinking of Carmen, became full of gloomy prognostications as to what would happen to her and hers if she chose to offend Driver.

'Item,' said Driver, 'not only have I already given you many gifts but there are more yet to come. For example,' he said, 'if I can stop the moon, I can make a moment last for all eternity. Indeed, I can fast-forward and rewind the world, not just put it on pause. Think what that does for sex.'

'I'd rather not,' said Carmen. 'That is disgusting,' for Driver either was or wasn't lunging into her as she leaned against a tree trunk, or else she was sitting ladylike at an ethereal table in a moonlit forest – who could tell? – or was simply sitting in the back of a car, a good girl being driven to a date with a rich man, upset because her parents were leaving home, and was dozing off. Whatever had happened, time had for an instant stopped.

But that's how it is with demon lovers. It's all speculation in retrospect and certain uncertainty thereafter – the blood test for the baby never proves anything definite, or, though you use the very latest tissue-typing techniques to prove or disprove paternity, you can be sure the results will get mixed up in the lab, or even just lost – yet they'll give you a moment of orgasm so piercing it echoes for ever throughout your life. But Carmen had said the wrong thing: denied something she shouldn't have – the moon recommenced its course through the sky, and the dung beetles busied themselves in the rot, the debris and the detritus of the forest, scuttling here, scuttling there, and now Carmen could see only too well that Driver had stopped in a layby used as a public convenience by the many admirers of the old forest. My grandmother used to tell me that in the eyes of the Maker people are eternity's dung beetles: their function to scavenge and salvage what is wholesome out of all things disgusting and nasty, but I don't suppose she knew any better than the next person.

'Do as I say!' snapped Driver in a flurry of sparks, as metal feather scraped on metal feather.

'I'll do as I please,' she said.

Be all that as it may, Carmen was not in a good mood when Driver delivered her to the Trocadero, one of the new smartish restaurants recently put up on the outskirts of town, in classic supermarket style – that is to say, having a central roof peak (thatched in this case) and two long low wings on either side, easy to erect, quicker to dismantle. Inside it was all pinks and crimsons, gold mirrors and little shaded lights, to create an effect that was both hygienic and sexy, smart yet *intime*. It was a favourite place for a rendezvous, for that special occasion, for your son's twenty-first, for a Golden Wedding, or just to say thank you, according to the ads in the local paper. Wives would have had their hair done for the occasion.

'Going somewhere special?' the hair stylist would ask.

'The Trocadero,' the client would boast, and out would come the rollers, the tongs, the backcomb. Everyone knew the Trocadero night-to-remember style. How quickly new customs arise! Carmen just thought Sir Bernard was a cheapskate – though later, looking back in a more kindly fashion, she understood he just wanted to be private, not recognised by all and sundry. He stood up as she followed the waiter in. He was not quite as old as she remembered, but almost.

He took her hand in his. It trembled. He drew her to him for an instant. She rolled her eyes to heaven, not caring whether or not he saw. He let her go. They sat down. The napkins were paper, not even linen.

'Carmen,' said Sir Bernard, and he smiled his crinkly, bright-eyed, famous smile. 'Such a lovely name! I've become something of an opera-goer myself. Do you love opera?'

'No,' she said. 'I was called after Carmen Jones. That's a musical.' She had not yet started on her Music & Art Through History, courtesy of Bellamy Airspace.

Carmen bit the heads off langoustines and spat them out. She had no intention of being nice to Sir Bernard. She just wanted dinner. She didn't see why she couldn't have the one without the other. She was wearing a T-shirt along with her leather skirt. Unfortunately her breasts were at their most tip-tilted, her nipples at their most prominent, and her hair at its shiniest, and the kind of reddish gold it had recently settled down to being. Her perfect white teeth made a neat clean job of the little cooked creatures' heads and her lips made a delicate *moue* as she spat them on to the plate, and Sir Bernard watched entranced and not disgusted. 'So natural,' he said. 'Like the girls I remember when I was a boy. Unspoiled, untamed.'

He talked of love and she talked of Ronnie Cartwright, from which I deduce that her relationship with Driver was indeed purely spiritual, for what was her love for Ronnie but love in the head? Once upon a time his hand had touched her hand, and although that gave great promise of what T. S. Eliot used to call pneumatic bliss (or so my Aunt Nettie told me), that was all.

Sir Bernard talked of concerts and operas, of plays and of having film stars and Nobel Prize winners to dinner, and Carmen said she liked watching television.

He talked of security, of property in her name, of fast cars and furs (furs? He was so old-fashioned!), of her family looked after, of the end of anxiety. She said she wanted to die at thirty. What point in being alive was there after that?

He talked of palazzios and yachts, of holidays abroad, of jet-setting and servants, and she just said, yes, and think of waking up next to you. She was rude, though he still, just about, thought it was charming.

He began to talk about her job at Bellamy Airspace and how her prospects there might improve if she and he were close, and get rather disastrously bad if they were not, and Carmen's eyes narrowed.

He said now I have tested you and I understand why you are different from other girls. You cannot be bought. You hold yourself dear. You are worth the conquest, worth the prize. Will you marry me, my dear?
At which she rose to her feet and spoke in a very loud voice, so all the women with that day's hairdos turned their stiff necks, creasing the make-up they had so carefully worked down to neck-line level, and their menfolk risked the discomfort of their unaccustomed collar and tie and did the same.

'Jesus,' said Carmen, 'that's enough of that. My body's one thing, my life is another. I'm going home.'

'But what about your flambéed apricots?' pleaded Sir Bernard, his hand on his love object's arm, but she shook him off, although the waiter's face, seen through the brandy flames, which flared and threatened to engulf the Trocadero, looked remarkably like Driver's own.

'Feed them to the dogs,' said Carmen, 'and marry one of them.'

And she walked out through the smoke and flame. The entire restaurant was evacuated within minutes; refurbishing work took four months, but Carmen had made her point.

The very next day Tim was summoned back to New Zealand by his mother to cope with an outbreak of liver fluke in his twenty thousand-strong flock; and though he and Annie exchanged addresses and promised to write and phone she knew it was too soon for him to leave – one week more and he'd have asked her to go with him. As it was, she was afraid he would forget her. They hadn't been to bed together. He had wanted to. She had demurred, thinking there was lots of time. And New Zealand was so far away – as far as you can go.

Audrey had a relapse and had to go back to hospital, Baby Rachel got a sticky eye infection and Laura found she was pregnant again and had German measles, and went right off Woodie. And they'd forgotten that the aunt's legacy would be taxed.

As for Carmen, she got a redundancy notice through the post within the week, and had spent one week under the length of time in continual employment which would have earned her cash compensation. That was the day after she'd waved Raelene and Andy off on their Round-the-World-Cruise. They'd only put the house on the market to keep the bank quiet – but they'd left unpaid debts behind them to the value of the property – in the confident expectation that it wouldn't sell. But a buyer turned up at once, and the bank threatened to foreclose if the sale didn't go through.

'Bad luck,' said Mr Prior to Carmen. He remembered her as stunning, but this girl was nothing special. He offered her a job at Peckhams Poultry, and she took it. He was rather sorry about it, all the same.

9

From my bed in the Clinic I can see out over the lakes to the office spires of Chicago. I am on the twelfth floor; there are thirty above me, eleven below. I try to find some significance in this, but fail. I like it here. Years pass. I know the pattern the sky makes: I watch the mists gathering and dispersing on the lake: the changing shades of its green fringes as the sunlight comes and goes: the flux and flow of traffic along the lake road. I hear only the muted average of city noise: all excesses – shrieks, wails, the whispers of plots, the firing of guns, the popping of champagne corks, the squeals of brakes, the revving of engines – are through the double glazing, calmingly evened out to a determined, competent purr. I'd rather be here than in Fenedge, any day, don't think I wouldn't. We all have our ways of getting out.

Surgeons are transplanting neural fibre from some wretched frog into my backbone in the hope of achieving some degree of nerve regeneration. These days they don't have enough to do. Physicians are taking over; invasive surgery is unpopular. Taking heart from my reports of tingling in my toes, these surgeons will not now give up on my legs, though I'm sure I did long ago. They treat me for free – or, look at it another way, though I try not to, being grateful, I allow them to experiment on me free of charge. It would be very interesting if the experiment succeeded, I can see that: it would have all kinds of significance, bring hope to the hopeless, all that. We make jokes about whether I'll start leaping around the room, froglike, or whether I can see undue signs of swallowing in my throat. They are easily entertained, these doctors: the feeblest of jokes and their serious faces light up as if some great gift had been bestowed on them. Then the door closes behind them, and I find myself sad, watching the traffic patterns lace below, wondering what the monstrous sorrow can be: the one which lies at the roots of the universe, so that we're left with such poignant echoes of it in our lives, and have to work it through, so patiently and painfully, aeon after aeon; child grieving for parent, husband for wife, each afflicted with grief for the other, not just the self, which, God knows, is bad enough. What happened once to spoil everything so? I daresay the story of Adam and Eve is not as laughable as most of us sophisticates suppose; perhaps it has the seeds of truth in it. Perhaps once there was indeed a Garden of Eden, and we were turned away from it, and left with what is bound to seem imperfect and spoiled, a disappointment, since we have in our bones, our genes, that glimmer of perfection. But I think it must be the sin and sorrow of gods, not of humankind, which afflicts us, since we find even its mere shadow so intolerable. We have been wrongly accused. Humankind were just dragged in tow like servants, lowly subjects of whichever God turned up, obliged to share his troubles, sop them up. I don't think the belief in one God, not many, was the philosophical advance we were told it was in school: I think it's more tolerable to believe we are suffering whimsically, because once Jupiter or his like erred.

When I got back to Fenedge, having failed to grow sufficient neural fibre to carry commands from my brain to my knees, though I could now tense and relax the muscles in my thighs and repair just a *soupçon* of the wastage of years, I found little had changed. It was as if the place and the people had simply marked time, waiting for my return, for my ongoing observation of them, before doing anything to alter their lives.

Laura had three children, not one, but she hadn't had to *do* anything to achieve that: just lie there with her legs open. It is a great pity that women, being as it were opted into pregnancy by instinct, then have actively to opt out if they don't want to mother a child. It requires great nerve, foresight and endurance so to do – more than Laura possessed. Three babies within four years! But at least she'd learned to drive. In my absence Alison had her driving licence removed: she had put her foot on the accelerator, not the brake once too often, and gone through the window of the public library. She was appealing against the decision, however; she was claiming ageism: others who were worse drivers even than her, she maintained, managed to retain their licences in similar situations. The matter was going to the High Court. Because of her age and status she was entitled to Legal Aid.

So Laura, in the meantime, took on the task of escorting me daily to the Handicapped Centre. Driving the new baby around in the car was one of the few ways, it seemed, of putting the child to sleep, and since Laura could claim a transport allowance, petrol money, for rendering me assistance on the way in to Fenedge and the shops, such as they were, she was happy to do so. So once again I found myself sitting at my window in the Centre, far too many days a week, watching life go by, or not go by. But at least a new batch of nature books had been donated, I assumed from the same source as before.

'So, what's been happening?' I asked Laura, shortly after my return.
'Nothing much,' she replied. Rachel and Caroline flanked the carry cot in the back. They of course had to come too. Our journeys were noisy and sticky and frayed my nerves. Caroline, from the back seat, liked to tangle her fingers in my hair. Laura was looking pretty enough, but stolid, the way girls are when life closes in on them too soon, and she had put on weight. She favoured cotton dresses as being the easier to wash, and woolly cardigans for warmth, and flat shoes for sense.

Woodie had speeded up with the garden sheds, she said, and there was now just enough money to get by on, so she mustn't complain. Audrey had had six operations, but was now in remission, so they had to be grateful. Laura hadn't heard from her father, but so far as she knew he was still with Poppy; that was something. I thought Laura was rather overdoing her Polyanna act and said so. She said somebody round here had to stay cheerful. I remarked that the car was rather full of fumes and could this be good for the children? and Laura said Woodie kept soldering the exhaust system back on to the car but it kept shaking loose. But wasn't she lucky to have such a handyman for a husband?
'Oh yes!' I said.

Annie was still working up at Bellamy House. She had been promoted to Floor Chambermaid and was on an incentive bonus. She had had a desultory boyfriend or so who always broke with her, or she with them; she still corresponded with Tim, the sheep farmer from New Zealand, and this Laura felt spoiled her chances with other boys, or theirs with her. But Carmen was doing really well at Peckhams Poultry: she had been promoted out of the production line and was now a delivery manageress and a union rep.

'Boyfriend?' I asked, and Laura shook her head.

'She's too picky for her own good.'

Laura had this to say to Carmen:

That she'd got to be a bit peculiar: she went to church sometimes. That she didn't care what she looked like any more: that she knew she, Laura, didn't either but she had an excuse and that she, Laura, knew that I, Hattie Upton, pitied her but she, Laura, wasn't to be pitied, honestly: she was happy with Woodie and there was a kind of richness in doing the right thing. (She didn't say that she, Laura, thought I, Hattie Upton, husbandless, childless, sitting in a wheelchair day in, day out, had a nerve to pity her, Laura, who had a husband, children and the use of her legs, but I knew what she was thinking.) And she, Laura, didn't believe in abortion and she'd hate Woodie to have a vasectomy. That Carmen was still a virgin and must be the only one of her age in all East Anglia. That perhaps Carmen had some kind of sexual hang-up.

That sometimes Carmen went with Annie to the disco but only because, Laura feared, Carmen was still hoping to run into the elusive Ronnie Cartwright.

(Carmen was living in a caravan on Mr Bliss's Horse Farm. She had to walk five miles to work every morning and back again. In the height of the season, when Peckhams had their production line running twenty-four hours a day, she would do a twelve-hour day and a seven-day week, on basic hourly rates.)

That if you asked Carmen why she put up with it she said she was the only one on the staff who actually *liked* working at Peckhams, which was why she kept getting promotion.

That Carmen's parents were still away: how they'd gone to New Zealand.

97

Strange, I said, how New Zealand keeps cropping up.
'It's the far ends of the earth,' said Laura. 'They say it's like paradise. The Garden of Eden, still operating. If you want to get out of here, wherever here is, it's the obvious place to go. As far as you can get.'

Sir Bernard? These days he lived in London: Mrs Haverill ran Bellamy House, and Sir Bernard seemed to have lost interest in the hotel. Some kind of planning decision had gone against him. He'd wanted to build a sea wall at Winterton including a marina, but they wouldn't let him because of the wildlife. A kind of hiccough in his upward and onward career. He'd married Lady Rowena in the end. Boring, boring. Sometimes he came down to the Bellamy House Arts Festival – they'd tried doing opera in the grounds à la Glyndebourne, but it hadn't taken off. Nothing happened and nothing took off round here. There was a kind of curse on the neighbourhood, said Laura sadly.

I asked about Driver. Laura said, 'Don't mention him.'
'Why not?' I asked.
'Because if you think of him he turns up,' said Laura. 'It's happened twice to me. I spoke of him once and dreamt of him once and the next day he whizzed past me in the BMW. It was spooky.'
'Did he stop?'
'Of course he didn't stop. What would he stop for? This is the place where nothing happens.'

I thought it was just as well I was back in the area. A period of rest can do no one any harm, but you don't want events just to run out altogether.

A couple of weeks later Laura said to me, 'I told you not to mention Driver, because he did turn up.'

Laura had been standing at the bus stop at the end of Landsfield Crescent with the three children. Rachel had just begun nursery school and Woodie had taken the car to go to an interview with a local cabinet maker who was advertising for a part-time assistant. Audrey was now on liquid foods, which needed to be supplemented by evening primrose oil – a substance not available on the National Health and expensive, so that the household outgoings were finally exceeding its income, no matter how long and hard Woodie worked. Regular employment was beginning to seem the only option open to Woodie – and everyone knew how once you took that path it ran straight, narrow and boringly through to old age, with never a penny to spare or hope of a breakthrough into the world of artist/craftsman. So Laura was feeling dejected enough as she stood and waited for a bus which never came, Rachel on one hand, Caroline on the other, and the baby in the pushchair. All girls. She'd have liked at least one boy. Woodie said why didn't she try again, try for a boy. Was he insane? And the BMW glided to a stop beside her and Driver slithered out. The lines of the car were smooth and glossy; it glittered; it was amazingly clean. And Driver's eyes were bright and blue.

'If it isn't Laura,' he said. 'Would you like a lift?'

'No thanks,' she said. 'The kids would only be sick in the back.'

'True,' he said, wincing.

'Besides,' she said, 'the neighbours would have a fit. What would they say? Getting into a strange man's car.'

She was flirting. She couldn't help it. She was not as lost in domesticity as she thought.

'Don't be so boring,' he said.

'I am boring,' said Laura. 'This is Fenedge, remember.'

'Well,' said Driver, 'don't blame me. I tried to cheer things up and got snubbed for my pains.'

Driver was wearing jodhpurs and a blazer in navy blue with rather a lot of brass buttons all over: so he seemed to be in uniform. His shoulders were square. His hair was glossy and smooth and a little too oily for her taste. She couldn't meet his eyes, and didn't know whether to look above them or below them. She wished she weren't wearing a shapeless cotton dress and a well-washed cardigan. She wished she hadn't eaten so many biscuits with her tea for so long, but how else was she to keep herself cheerful?

'A lovely young woman like you,' said Driver. 'You could have had anyone. Still could, without three children round your neck. Why don't you leave them behind? Forget them, slip into my car and begin a new life.'

'What, just leave them standing at a bus stop?'

'Why not? Someone's bound to look after them. They'll think a flying saucer took you off; they'll never blame you. Your husband would make a good mother: a better mother than an earner any day. Those children are his idea, not yours. He took advantage of you at a weak moment in your life. He shouldn't have done it. If you don't do something, your life is finished.'

'I wouldn't even think of abandoning my children.'

'You've thought of it many times,' said Driver.

'Besides,' said Laura, pretending not to have heard him, 'they might wander off into the road, under the bus. I couldn't possibly.'

'Have it your own way,' said Driver, and got back into the BMW and drove off, and Laura wished for a moment he'd stayed around just a little longer, persuading. She could see her last chance in life retreating, vanishing, a tail light round a corner. Driver was right: if you don't do these things on the spur of the moment you never do them at all.

The bus turned up. Its back doors folded open. The bus conductor stood there on the step. Laura lifted Rachel and Caroline up on to the bus; the conductor did not help her. She took the baby from the pushchair and put it under her arm. The baby started crying. Laura turned to fold the pushchair with one arm and one foot and failed.

'Get a move on,' said the conductor, and then, 'Can't wait about all day,' and replaced first Rachel and then Caroline back on the pavement. They started to grizzle. The conductor rang the bell; the doors began to close.

'There'll be another bus along in a minute,' said the conductor. 'We're late in.'

Laura, looking up from the pushchair, thought for a moment the conductor had Driver's face, but how could it be Driver?

'Like hell there'll be another one along in a minute,' said Laura, as the doors folded to, but she didn't think he heard.

Laura gave up waiting after a further ten minutes and turned back towards home. The second bus passed without stopping. Rachel didn't get to nursery school, and later that day nearly killed Kubrick by picking him up out of his tank to show him to the baby, but fortunately Laura came along in time, so that

Kubrick was merely traumatised, and not dead. She was glad Kim wasn't around to witness it. Woodie didn't get the job. He auditioned for it by turning a chair leg on the spot. The cabinet maker said he was masterly but soo slow.

But one step up from nothing happening is things almost happening.

The next Fenedge almost-event was the moving in of a couple of youths, yobbos or punks, with white faces, ringed flesh, tortured hair, leather jackets with studs and chains, and dirty hands, into the house which had once been the greengrocer's on the corner of the Centre. The owner had had to close due to increased rent and lack of business. The lads, Paul and Tony, forced an entry and set up a squat inside, complete with candles, mess and mantras. The town was fearful of violence and disorder, but the boys turned out to be disappointingly gentle and even helpful – they'd help with my wheelchair of an evening (they were never out of bed in the morning or I daresay they would have lent a hand then as well) – and the landlord – his revenge upon the town – declined to turn them out, so there they stayed; the happening would have drifted from almost-event into non-event, sucked down into the general flatness of the landscape, I daresay, except the whole pattern of the times changed; and before you could say Jack Robinson or 'Thank God Hattie's back in town', events began to erupt, to pile one on top of the other.

Carmen moved into the squat: came in a van on her Thursday afternoon off and took over Tony's room when he moved off to join 'The Travellers' and do the rounds of the summer pop festivals. She brought a bed and bedding, a table, a chair, a mirror; she came over and spoke to me. She said she couldn't go on walking the long distance to work every day from Mr Bliss's caravan. From here in Fenedge she would catch a bus; and the rent she had to pay was marginal. She had been promoted on to the night shift at Peckhams, working as Delivery Supervisor. She had given herself two years to save enough to move out of Fenedge altogether, and she reckoned she could do it in that time, though the cost of living and inflation made saving increasingly difficult.

Peckhams had a new managing director, one Shanty Cotton, who was a great believer in worker participation: she was beginning to get some administrative experience which might stand her in good stead in the wider world. She did not look unhappy: just too sensible and practical for her own good. She wore a headscarf, which I hoped was just because she was moving house, but I feared might have become a way of life. People round Fenedge wrap their heads in scarves a lot: the wind blows hard and long over the waterlands and ears get cold and the mind defensive. I would like to report that Carmen put the squat into instant order, cleaning, sweeping and tidying, wiping the encrusted glass of the windows (although ardent vegetarians, Paul and Tony smoked a great deal – both tobacco and other substances), but I am sorry to say she did not. She was not, she said, 'interested' in housework. She had to worry more than enough about hygiene at Peckhams: she could not be bothered at home. She only had to look at Laura, with her preoccupation with washing and mending, to see where that kind of thinking led.

I enquired about Annie. Annie, I discovered, had that very week received a letter from her Tim McLean, enclosing an Air New Zealand ticket, Club Class, to Wellington, on to Christchurch, and had flown out on the first available flight.
'Well,' I said, 'things are certainly beginning to move,' and Carmen said, 'About time too.'

Tim McLean lived with his parents on a sheep station of twenty-five thousand acres, running some twenty thousand sheep. They were grazed, he wrote to tell Annie, in three mobs on six different blocks for six months at a time. He would explain more when she arrived. The McLean station was most southerly, being in the Southland of South Island, inland from a place called Moeraki, which I was able to look up in the remaindered volumes of *Flora & Fauna Around the World*. The area, I learnt, was called the Scotland of the South, not just because of the Gaelic place names (Karitane? Tutakahikura? Uhimataitai? Scottish? What were they talking about?) but because of its landscape: 'rich, evergreen pastures, in spite of the harsh climate which gives such a short grain-growing season' where the winds blow over a flat, fertile coastal land. I had the feeling Annie was flying to the ends of the earth to a place pretty much like home. Mind you, in East Anglia there were never any moas, those huge flightless birds, now extinct, nor moa hunters, nor the whalers and traders who came, as the skuas come to the terns in the summer, to make the lives of the long-term inhabitants, the Maoris, miserable. The Maoris, who preferred to live in the north by cultivating kumeras or sweet potatoes (Safeway sells them; Alison, when she shopped for me, would always buy them, because once, just once, I said I enjoyed them) down here in Southland, such is the climate, had perforce to become hunters, fishers and gatherers. It is important to remember that in the Southern Hemisphere the further north you go, the warmer it is; the further south, the colder. That their summer is our winter, and our night their day: as if nature were just experimenting, once more, to see what would happen if everything expected was reversed.

Put on your walking boots (serious New Zealand walking boots, well dubbined: no trainers, please) and hike inland, leaving behind the coasts with their abundance of fish, the kanakana, the yellow-eyed flounder, the eel, the koura, the snapper, the dogfish, the mullet, the maitahi (or adult whitebait), the grayling, the upokoroa (though some say all of those have gone now: eaten every one). Pass through the old gold fields, where once grains of actual gold glittered in the black, black sand – for the shores along here are formed from the moraine of the glaciers which once crept down from the Southern Alps to fight and freeze the very sea, but now retreat, retracing their steps, inch by melting inch, season by season, sullenly, leaving a dead, metallic land behind. But further inland a thin fertile soil begins to cover the moraine, and the plains and the foothills are covered by tussock – a short red grass which manages to grow where almost nothing else will. Clamber yet higher, to the steep rocky ridges of Southland, and once again plant life becomes uncommon, though, as they say in the specialist books, full of interest. But what plant was ever not, to those whose preoccupations such things are? Up here, let me tell you, you will come across the tree daisy (*Olearia avicennifolia*), the toetoe (*Cortaderia richardii*) and, if you're lucky, the wine berry (the *coprosina*), the southern rata (or *Metrosideros umbellata*) and the ubiquitous kamaki.

Don't think that down here in Southland you'll find an easy land for anyone to inhabit; the skeletons left behind by the moa hunters show that the earliest settlers led hard lives, bones and joints eroded by digging and paddling, and few lived to be thirty . . .

And to this our Annie is going? This wild wasteland where plant and glacier fight it out? Was this the paradise promised to her by Count Capinski, once upon a time?

Yes, certainly there is birdlife here enough to satisfy the keenest ornithologist – the kapake, the kiwi itself, the weka, the pigeons, the parakeets, the tuis, the korimako or bell bird – but whenever did Annie bird-watch? The bush and the rainforest must be noisier here than anywhere else in New Zealand, but that's not saying much, since the norm is such a profound deep green silence, in which the fall of a leaf can make you jump, and besides Annie is accustomed to the clattering of pans in the Bellamy House kitchen and the whirring of a dozen vacuum cleaners in mid-morning distress, and what noise does a kiwi make anyway? Some even deny that this, the patron bird of New Zealand, the *Apteryx mantelli*, lives down here at all; but Keri Hulme, the Booker Prize winner, has seen one and that's all the evidence I need. The young of the koekoe, or long-tailed cuckoo, are called mimi – and their droppings are sweet and edible. Oh wild and wondrous land! But when will I ever put on laced walking boots, to see these things for myself; though I long to be there, who is there to buy me a ticket? Alison, whose mother is a hundred and four, says that when she comes into her fortune she will take me round the world, but I expect Alison's mother is immortal. And how, in the meantime, will Annie fare? Will she appreciate this wild paradise, by turns deep green, tawny gold and rust red?

I'll tell you how Annie's faring. She's out riding with Tim – not the gentle, formal riding of the few lessons she took with Mr Bliss in anticipation of one day, one day, actually getting to the Land of the Long White Cloud, but the vigorous, impatient riding of those who use horses in the course of their work. Tim is out searching for some twenty missing sheep who may or may not have got into an area known as Saunders Creek, where the terrain is pockmarked by ravines and craters (though you can find the black stilt lurking in the shallow backwaters, so it's worth a visit) where it is not prudent for the McLean sheep, the McLean livelihood, to wander. They will lose their footing, fall, die. The McLeans will lose profit, though of course Tim will also feel for their sorrows. If sheep fall on their backs, and there is no one to rescue them, they just lie there struggling and pathetic, legs help-less and hopeless, until they die of despair, or of thirst, or of the collapse of their lungs, whichever comes first.

'Come with me, sweetie,' Tim said that morning to Annie. She did not mind him calling her sweetie, although it seemed oddly old-fashioned, even condescending; she did not mind anything he did: she did not mind the pain and stiffness consequent upon her getting on a horse. She just went with him. She looked very good in jeans, plaid shirt and her swannie, the universal NZ anorak, a gift from Tim. ('An engagement gift,' he said. Was he joking? Did he mean it? If he did, where was her ring?) The outdoors suited Annie more than ever did the indoors, let alone the frilly bib-apron to which Mrs Haverill had of late doomed all the female staff at Bellamy House, with 'Be Proud of the Spirit of Service' embroid-ered in yellow over everyone's bosom. Annie had not worked her notice out at Bellamy House. 'Come at once' said Tim's letter, so at once she'd gone. Just not turned up at work: left no message; made no apology. Her future called. She'd worried on the flight that so quick a response on her part might be imprudent – wasn't it better to feign indifference in matters of the heart, rather than admit enthusiasm? – but came to the conclusion that since she wasn't the sort to play flirtation games, she'd better not start trying now. It would only go wrong.

She had no difficulty recognising Tim at the airport: she had worried in case she'd dreamt about him so often that the original guest at the Bellamy House Hotel would bear no resemblance to the man in her dreams or the writer of such perceptive and affectionate letters, but it was not the case. All she had to do was shut her eyes briefly, envisage the hero in a teenage comic strip, open them, and there he was: taller and squarer than anyone else in sight, reliable yet tender, his eyes bright and caring and, what is more, directed straight at her, the heroine of her own life; he was at home and at ease in this country as he had not been at Bellamy House. Taller, skinnier, more glamorous girls by far travelled with her, came through Arrivals when she did, girls with high heels, bronzed legs, clearly defined bosoms and smooth arms, but he didn't seem interested in them – what he appreciated, it seemed, was the workaday, the serviceable, the useful. That is to say, Annie wore comfortable clothes – it was only sensible to travel across the world feeling comfortable, not, as Mavis would say, 'gripped about the waist'. Her hair had fallen out of curl; she had spilt Coke down her blue blouse on the journey and where she had attempted to wash it out the colour had bleached; all these things he ignored: he went straight to the heart of her. It was a rewarding yet disconcerting experience. Why me? Why me? Of all the girls in the world? What did I do to deserve this? Is it enough, after all, to simply *be*?

'Oh, Annie,' he said, heartfelt, and that was just about all, or all that was apparently needed. He was not given to talking about his feelings. Sheep, yes; his native land, yes; both could render him lyrical, but in matters of the heart it was what you did, and how you did it, not what you said, that counted. Annie was relieved. She too was rendered awkward by too much emotion. Anyone could safely bring Carmen a rose between their teeth, quite safely throw Laura a surprise birthday party; but Annie found gestures suspicious. It came, she confided to Tim in a letter, from once, when she was sixteen, being embraced by her mother and finding she was looking into Count Capinski's eyes. She'd suffered dreadful anxiety once she'd sent the letter, but a reply came quickly and reassuringly. He expected the event had played into a whole set of already existing fears: no one event could form a whole character, could it? She was surprised that he was both so thoughtful and acute, and so uncondemning or rejecting of her mother's capacity to be two people at once. It was not what you expected from a sheep farmer.

The Glen Trekker Station, which Annie had envisaged as exactly that – some long low clapboarded outback building with a ticket office, long disused – turns out to be a rather grand squat quasi-Georgian mansion, brilliant white against a bright blue sky, standing alone in green lawns behind paling stock fences with pillars and a porch where others had verandahs; it is the only habitation for twenty square miles. There is an elaborate TV aerial on its roof. Annie supposes, rightly, that reception around here will be bad. There are geraniums and nasturtiums in the flowerbeds; green willows droop around a pond. White, blue, green, red: strong colours to an eye accustomed to the misty greys and duns of East Anglia. She feels bolder. Outside the front door stand a Volvo and two Range Rovers. Dogs bark a welcome. Why me, why little me? Without even a fortune to my name? Are you to be Rochester, Tim McLean, to my Jane; am I to control you with the power of my will, my quietness, my virtue? How is it done?

His mother stands at the door, for all the world like an English county lady, of the kind who so intimidate Annie back home: the ones who are so kind and understanding when Annie is on chambermaid duty at Bellamy House but never leave tips. She has neat, brown-to-grey hair, a weatherbeaten face, a lively expression, white and even teeth (they're obviously false; she likes them like that: uncompromising), big competent hands and feet; she has a sensible and profoundly rational air – Count Capinski would never be allowed inside that head, not for one moment. Mrs McLean is old stock: the McLeans are used to running things round here; for centuries they've been telling people what to do. She is the opposite of Mavis, who has somehow to be sneaky to survive.
'We've heard so much about you,' she says. 'Welcome!'

Annie is shown the house – the wide hall with its polished board floors and rag rugs, the Victorian umbrella stand without umbrellas, the parlours leading out of the hall – large square rooms where nobody goes, with antique furniture, family heirlooms, and real paintings by European artists on the walls; everything well dusted and lavender-polished. Flies buzz at the windows; voices echo; shoes squeak. It is very quiet. The real life of the house goes on at the back, Mrs McLean assures Annie – in the kitchen. Who has time to sit down anyway? There is always so much to do. Everyone's hands are always busy. If Mrs McLean has a spare moment she weaves rag rugs. If Mr McLean sits – and he has a bad hip, he sometimes has to – he cleans his guns. As well as keeping the accounts and the stockbooks, buying farm machinery and new animals, supervising the dagging and dipping, the drenching and docking, he trains sheepdogs for shows in his spare time. Marjorie McLean, it becomes apparent, as well as weaving rag rugs, cooks, bakes, sews and bottles fruit with one hand, while publishing the local WI's newsletter with the other. She can mend a leaking gutter, wire a shearing shed, says her son, milk a cow, deliver a baby and a political address, and dress up to be a Top Table Lady at the local dinner dance, without thinking twice about any of it. She makes Annie feel helpless and hopeless by comparison, though at home Annie always seemed more competent than most. Annie has, Annie notices, been put in a bedroom as far as can be from Tim's, and there are no carpets on these upstairs corridors either: it is a very echoey house, one way and another, except for the kitchen, which hums and rumbles with very expensive major kitchen equipment as well as minor – ice-cream mixers, milk-shake makers, automatic lamb feeders, sixties classics and the clock, clock, clock of the loom on which the rag rugs are made. The kitchen needs constant servicing, constant cleaning. It is an enormous room, with many subsidiary rooms off it, in which dogs are groomed, chickens hatched, dough put to rise. Bellamy House was nothing to it. Annie and Tim have not yet slept together, and though he kisses and cuddles her even now, when they are alone, he puts her from him should their embraces become too intense. He has changed. Now it's she who wants to and he seems not to. Why does he delay? Is there something *wrong* with this paragon or is he just thoroughly nice and good, and feels he needs to know her properly first now matters have become serious? And how many years will this take? He is, she notices, reading a book called *The Return of Victorian Courtship: How to Love One Person For Ever.* Is this what it's about? Annie finds that here at the other end of the world there is no one to talk to about these things. She longs for Carmen and Laura, her friends. They'd put everything in some kind of context; explain to her why it's so impossible to get out of Tim a clear answer to a simple question, if only she could formulate the question. Is there some culture block going on here, some traditional New Zealand custom, or is it, as usual, her? Annie sits eating whitebait, whole tiny little pink-white fish, fried in batter, with black pinhead eyes still showing through the coating, wishing she didn't have to, and wondering whether she's meant to be marrying him or whether she's just a friend, no more than that.

Or, as now, she sits on a tussocky hilltop on a horse next to Tim and he calls her sweetie, and she is even suddenly afraid. So far from anyone, in this strange if beautiful land at the far ends of the earth.

'You're brooding, Annie,' said Tim. 'I don't like to see that. No use blaming your mum and dad for what you are.'

Is he using her confidence in the letter against her? Surely not.

'It's a hard life, Annie,' he said, 'here or anywhere. But we don't want anyone saying you're a whingeing pom.'

'What's a pom?'

'You are. Mind you, the kids will be kiwis.'

'So we're having kids.'

'My word yes,' he said. 'Any objection?'

'We'd have to get married first,' said Annie boldly. His horse fidgeted. No one on horseback is ever completely still. He stared into the wind: so frequently having to do it that it seemed to have carved the planes of his face. He was wonderfully handsome.

'Well,' he said, 'you and me know each other by now, and you get on all right with my mum. So I reckon we could take the plunge.'

No one can take this away from me, thought Annie, whatever happens next. Tim McLean's proposed to me. We were on horseback together on a hill somewhere in the world, and this handsome man proposed to me. Do you hear, Carmen, Laura? In the end I was the one to get out of there, the one least likely to succeed; if you could only see me now!

'I reckon we could,' said Annie nonchalantly: her toes curled in her dubbined boots. 'But I think you'd have to ask me properly. You'll have to get off your horse, for one thing.'

He did, which enabled her to get off hers, and ease her aching buttocks.

'You do like sheep?' he asked her. 'You weren't just saying it? Being a station wife is a full-time job. You have to like sheep, and horses.'

She couldn't remember having said she liked sheep. It was not like her to tell so downright a lie: wouldn't she have been more evasive?

'Of course I love sheep,' she said.

'Okay, Annie,' said Tim, 'please will you marry me?'

'Shouldn't we sleep together first?' asked Annie, but he seemed disconcerted, even embarrassed by that, so she added, 'though I can see we could be old-fashioned about this, if we decided.' She didn't want to put him off.

White dots moving on the plain below attracted his attention. 'We'll talk about it all later,' he said. 'Those sheep will be in Saunders Creek if we're not careful,' and he hopped back on his horse, just as two vigorous, handsome, wide-jawed, curly-haired men, Maoris, galloped up and over the ridge on violent, stocky little horses. Tim, by sudden contrast with the other two, seemed almost washed out, too pale, too finely drawn of countenance to be altogether convincing as a leader of men, too indecisive, though still, by virtue of some secret power (perhaps just money in the bank), he was conceded by all to be in charge: he the master, they the station hands.

'Bloody hell, Tim,' called one of them as they thundered past, 'they're heading up Saunders Creek.' Without a further look at Annie, the love of her life set off behind them. The three men hollered and shouted sheep-language – to which the sheep seemed deaf – as the horses, which seemed more hot-headed still than their masters, descended the hill slopes towards the plain. They were having a wonderful time. It will always be like this, thought Annie: a woman in this land, indeed in any land, will be the spare-time pursuit: some necessity will always arise to which she will take second place. Do I care? No. I want him. I'll change him. Just because he was born to sheep, doesn't mean he has to stay with sheep.

At least I assumed that's what Annie thought that day, on horse-back on a hilltop, because that's what women so often think, presented with a man whose perfection is marred by a single fault. For example, he drinks. Or he's a philanderer. Or he gambles. Or he's unemployable. Or he doesn't want children. Or he'd rather look after his sheep than them. I'll change him, whispers the little gnome of wishful thinking who lodges in Everywoman's brain, feeding off True Romance until he grows so fat he pops right out of her head, leaving her sane again; I'll change him. And sometimes she succeeds, though mostly she doesn't.

And meanwhile, back home, Audrey lay in a hospital bed, which was nothing unusual, but this time the sister said she might not be going home again, and Laura and Woodie, checking out her chart when Sister was out of the room, perceived that Audrey was on heavy doses of morphine, which meant that her addiction or otherwise to the drug was irrelevant. It is from such clues that relatives of the very ill come to understand that death is imminent: the word is seldom mentioned, as if the uttering of it brought it nearer, and the whole point of the institution, after all, is the struggle against it, to which all are sacrificed.

'I want to see Kim before I go,' said Audrey.

'No one knows where he is,' said Laura. 'If he knew you were ill I'm sure he'd come.' Though they all knew by then that he wouldn't.

'Tell you what,' said Audrey, 'take a small ad in the newspapers. Say that Kubrick's dangerously ill; that'll flush him out,' and she actually laughed, which was enough to make her catch her breath and, in the catching of it, die. It is something to die laughing, especially if you're Audrey.

Laura and Woodie sat by her bed for some five minutes before they called a nurse. They didn't want anyone to attempt her resuscitation and, to everyone's credit, nobody did. They went together to collect the children from the neighbour who'd offered to look after them. Her name was Angela. She was a single mother, and she lived across the way from Laura, next door to Mavis and Alan, in Landsfield Crescent, in the house which had once been Carmen's. Angela was blonde, buxom and had an easy, amiable nature. More men, in Mavis's phrase, went in her front door than ever came out of it, but her little daughter Effie played and sang up and down the Crescent, and was a good friend of Rachel's; and Angela was a good neighbour, prepared to feed cats and look after children in an emergency. In fact she'd do anything for anyone – 'especially' (Mavis again) 'someone else's husband'.

Woodie went off to the undertaker to arrange the funeral and Laura went through her mother's drawers and cupboards, sorting out the best for Oxfam, the worst for the black rubbish bags. There is something extraordinarily miserable about the intimate possessions of the newly dead: they are denatured, wretched, the energy of their existence suddenly stolen from them; they hang listlessly from hangers, cluster greyly in drawers, overwashed. Laura looked out of the window and saw that the black BMW was parked outside the door, or she thought it was. Or perhaps it was a hearse? She went downstairs and opened the front door, but there was nothing there. It had been a vision, an apparition, a hallucination. It hardly mattered which since it was all in her mind, not in the real world. At least, since Audrey was already dead, a ghostly hearse could not be prophesying her mother's death.

Laura came over to me and wept on my knee for a time and then perked up and said, 'Well, at least Woodie won't have to live with his mother-in-law any more. We'll have the house to ourselves; all ours!' And she snivelled and cheered up a little. 'Only somehow,' she said, 'I only have Woodie and the kids because of Audrey, and now that Audrey isn't there, I feel peculiar about them, as if we're all in the wrong place at the wrong time. What have Woodie and the kids got to do with me, really? How did they come about?'

My toes were tingling; my skirt was damp with her tears. I had not set out in life to become any kind of counsellor, but that is how women trapped in wheelchairs often end up. They can't get away. And the black BMW really was parked outside Laura's door; I could see it, and Angela was leading the four little girls up the street towards it, each one with a nose white and frothy from a Mr Whippy soft ice cream.

'I do wish she wouldn't,' said Laura. 'I try to bring them up sugar-free.'

Driver leant out of his window and said to Angela, 'My, what a lot of little girls! Makes you wonder where all the men are!' and Angela, whose Effie was the result of a long affair with a married man, everyone knew, said, 'They're all married to someone else,' to which Driver replied, 'Well, what the mind doesn't know the heart can't grieve over.'

'What do you want?' said Laura to Driver sharply. She was quite dangerous. The recently bereaved often are: they'll stand no nonsense. The perceived margins between life and death widen: it's

important to stand well back, take no risks. Driver seemed quite
disconcerted by her sharpness.

'Just to say hello to everyone,' he said. 'And to little Rachel,
Caroline and Baby Sara. And of course Effie. I know little Effie
well.'

Little Effie had wide blue eyes and a slender body and she put
her finger in her mouth and smiled at Driver and danced her little
bottom this way and that. She was only five. Too many uncles,
Laura concluded, but at the same time a helpful neighbour was
a helpful neighbour and now Audrey was gone she couldn't afford
to criticise Angela.

'I'm not in the mood for socialising,' she said to Driver, but didn't
wish to give him the satisfaction of knowing why.

'I was really sorry to hear about your mother,' he said, nevertheless.

'How do you know about my mother?' asked Laura. He had been
visiting Mavis, he said, to have a wart on the sole of his foot
treated, and Mavis had just heard from Alan, who was now working at the morgue, collecting bodies from hospitals all over
the county, that Audrey's corpse was amongst those collected.
Morgue provision had recently been rationalised and centralised:
a whole county can collect a lot of corpses in a single day, but
friends and neighbours still get noticed.

'I wonder if you've any news of Carmen?' asked Driver. 'I can't
find her address. I can't somehow sniff it out. I have something
to tell her to her advantage,' but Laura just snapped, 'You needn't
think I'm going to tell you a thing,' and snatched her children
from Angela, and shovelled them inside the front door and then
left them to their own devices and shut herself in her bedroom
and wept. She had to call Angela later and apologise.

'Poor thing,' said Driver kindly to Angela, 'I expect she's upset,'
and Angela said, 'Well, Audrey's well out of it. What had she to
look forward to? Nothing but pain and disappointment.'

'Quite so,' said Driver.

A couple of days later, as I sat consulting my books on the lifestyle
of New Zealand sheep, I watched Laura knock on the door of
what was still known in Fenedge as 'the old greengrocer's'. She
knocked gently, though bravely, since the windows were scrawled
with words such as 'Hate', 'Destroy', 'Destruct', and 'Fuck the

Pigs', and someone had splintered the door by kicking it with a boot with reinforced metal toes. I had watched him do it. One of the resident lads had taken in a white-skinned female waif who apparently did not belong to him, and someone else, a youth from out of town, was after the pair of them. They'd escaped out of the back window and come over the roofs to half jump, half fall to the ground right in front of my window; then they loped off. Without a doubt, Driver was back in town and we were all feeling it. And if Driver was back, would Sir Bernard be far behind?

The door was flung open by a boy with a white face and orange hair who was hung with chains. There were rings in his nose and his ears. Laura looked through to a sodden mess of old blankets, clothes, electrical equipment, squashed cans of lager and graffitied walls. A thin dog came out to sniff up Laura's skirt. She had noticed that since she had children dogs seemed to do this all the time. Or perhaps it was only that now she came in contact with dogs more often than she had in her pre-domestic phase. Who's to say?

The boy first denied that Carmen lived there, then admitted it, or at any rate if she didn't exactly live there, at least that she squatted there, and said she was working nights, she wasn't in. 'Working nights?' asked Laura in alarm, but the lad, who called his dog off and even offered her a cup of tea, explained that she was a wage slave up at Peckhams, and on night work, and it was to Peckhams that Laura proceeded, declining the tea.

These days they take school parties around Peckhams. The chicken works have been in the forefront of the lateral diversification movement in light industry: nowadays one division breeds chickens, lovely little fluffy things: another produces free-range eggs (more or less), smooth, brown and perfect, from these chicks, once grown. The food product facility processes the eggs into 'extruded egg' – yard upon yard of cooked and reconstructed yolk encircled by cooked and reconstructed white, so that when your ham and egg pie is sliced everyone gets a perfect, even, properly presented section of egg in the middle of that slice, never the little unfair end section of white with no yolk you might very well get if you trusted to nature and chance. School children love to see 'long egg' being made, oozing out of the extruding pipes. The great steel drums in the Overall Product Faculty (sic) that churn night and day to meld chicken and herbs and flour properly to make the famous Peckhams Patties are another great favourite: the plop, plop, plop as patty after automated patty falls into its neat little polythene home, ready for freezing, seems to hypnotise. PR, I hear, is thinking of changing the name from Peckhams Poultry to something that smacks rather less of feather and the farmyard, to, perhaps, simply Peckhams Products. Sir Bernard, having diversified into food products, is now a major shareholder of Peckhams Poultry: integral cog in the machine that's the Bellamy Empire. The road beneath your feet, the patty on your plate, the pillow on which you rest your head – Bellamy's, all Bellamy's.

The only part of the process which is off limits to the school children, and not shown in detail in the Info. Pack which so helps them in their essays on the food industry, is the slaughtering sheds, where the birds move gracefully from a state of life to a state of food. With the best will in the world, blood, feathers and entrails get everywhere. The creatures will struggle; it is impossible to have them adequately tranquillised and still keep the food chain free of unwelcome drugs. Whatever's in the hen ends up in the human. There is a big enough problem with oestrogen and the other hormones which, when used in tandem with bright lighting and careful breeding, encourage the eating birds to grow plump and soft, and the laying birds to produce five or even six eggs a day, but can interfere with the fertility of humans.
'Only a happy bird lays eggs,' says Peckhams' PR, but I'm not so sure. My *Enquire Within on Everything* (1789) suggests otherwise: 'If you want to keep a hen laying all winter,' says the author, 'don't let it run with the cock.' But we have other things to worry about beyond the happiness of hens.

At the time we talk about, Peckhams had only just begun its progress into lateral diversification. Shanty Cotton, with his views on worker participation and profit sharing, had only recently taken over as Managing Director. He was not of the new lean managerial classes, not at all. He was a vigorous, portly, handsome, red-faced, cigar-smoking, dandruffy businessman of the old school, though he'd recently learnt a new trick or two, which the Peckhams Board of Directors thought might come in handy. The firm, though already a major employer in Fenedge, at the time I speak of occupied a two-acre site only. Later a couple of acres of old wood were razed to build the Patty Plant. But what's a couple of acres when you consider the plight of the rainforest?

(We've had a further batch of reference books turn up at the Handicapped Centre: these ones are all stamped 'Conservation Library'. One day I will discover who our benefactor is.)

Nevertheless, the Peckhams factory at the time had enough to occupy it to remain active night and day: the appetite for frozen chicken in the nation was keen and getting keener as who but Peckhams under Shanty Cotton led the way in competitive pricing. If you make employees work harder and longer for smaller wages in a time of high unemployment it is not difficult thus to lead the way: you just have to be more ruthless in these matters than the factory next door. The fish finger as the favourite convenience food for children was giving way – as the seas became depleted, and fish scarcer and more expensive – to the crumbed chicken leg. At one end of the plant at the time Laura visited Carmen and set the next set of events rolling, living chickens were delivered, crated up by breeders all over the land to be transported thither by road; at the other, via the slaughtering sheds, frozen chickens, either whole or sectioned, with or without giblets, emerged in packs ready for the refrigerated vans which would distribute the white fibrous flesh throughout the country. Laura found Carmen in a loading bay, at the cold dead birds end rather than the living squawking one, and was grateful for that at least. It is hard to feel sorry for dead fowl – all too easy for one about to die. Carmen was working in a supervisory capacity. You could tell: she had a clipboard and looked pained. Her hair was tied up in a white Peckhams turban. She looked up when Laura approached, and was startled.

'My God,' said Carmen. 'This is no place for a sensitive soul like you. Where are all the kids? You seem kind of half finished without them.'

'They're at home,' said Laura. 'I've got a baby-sitter in.'

'I'm really sorry about your mother,' said Carmen. 'I'm trying to get time off for the funeral, but they're being very sticky. There's a new management. You have to get a chit from the officiating priest to say you're entitled to go. I may just have to be ill and forge a sick note. There's a doctor working here who signs them for twenty-five pence a time. He was struck off years back, but his signature still has that certain something.'

She wasn't quite looking at Laura. She seemed tired and flattened. She ticked off boxes as the forklift trucks moved them from one place to another. She wore gloves and a scarf but still seemed cold.

'So why have you come?' she asked. 'To gloat?'

'Of course I haven't,' said Laura. 'I just thought I'd warn you. Sir Bernard's chauffeur is back in town and looking for you.'

'Is he indeed!' said Carmen, and put down her clipboard and to Laura's dismay sat down on a crate and looked as if she were about to cry.

'Hey, Miss!' shouted a forklift operator, 'you're holding us up.'

The reproach revived her. 'Hygiene problem,' shouted Carmen, on her feet again. Her voice was surprisingly loud. The moon seemed to shake in the sky. She blew a whistle. She clapped her hands. 'Stop the line,' she cried. The moving bands slowed and stopped. Laura thought it was wonderful to have so much power. Motors were switched off; hands went into pockets. Men went for coffee; others stood and chatted. So much for Shanty Cotton.

'Why hygiene problem?' asked Laura.

'Temperature rise is best,' said Carmen. 'No obvious source. Needs a technician. They can't afford the risk of food poisoning. It'll be at least six hours before the lines can get going again. That's six hours more life for a few thousand chickens, and thirty-three men back home to their beds, unexpectedly. There'll be a baby boom nine months from today. Well done, Laura, trust you!'

'But what is it to do with me?'

'I can't talk and work,' said Carmen. 'I'd rather talk.'

'Won't they fire you?' asked Laura.

'They never put two and two together,' said Carmen. 'And if they do I'll just say it's because I'm on my toes and vigilant. Health and Safety's the last scam in the world. Shanty Cotton is a pushover.'

She went away to write a report on a detected brink-of-thaw in one of the bird-plus-giblets crates. These birds, she told Laura, stuffed as they are with a plastic twist containing the giblets of total strangers, are the most prone to inadvertent warming on their journey from point of death to point of sale.

'It all sounds fascinating,' said Laura politely. She was rather shocked.

'I nearly lost a finger through frostbite the other day,' said Carmen. 'See this as natural justice. I am righting wrongs in the only way I know.'

'So what do I say to Driver if he turns up again?' asked Laura. The night shift had closed down: the workers gone home: management had been informed, the technicians roused from their slumber to detect the source of yet further trouble, which Laura knew could only be the result of the way Carmen had just had an assembly line rinsed down with boiling water from the sterilising plant, instead of using cold. Laura drove Carmen back home through the moonlit evening. Angela was baby-sitting. Woodie was at night class, studying Small Business Method and Aims. The moon was yellow and round; the beet fields made flat patterns of silver and black to either side: a chess-board pattern, said Laura. Carmen said it looked like draughts to her; nothing as complicated as chess.

'Tell Driver I give in,' said Carmen. 'Tell him in the end what a girl succumbs to is boredom.' The skin over her finger was peeling where the frost had damaged it. She tore at a shred with her teeth and cried out in pain as it took away flesh as well.

'What's the matter?' asked Laura in alarm. Carmen, whimpering, showed Laura her finger.

'I can't see anything the matter with it,' said Laura, and indeed it seemed perfectly whole and perfect, a flawless finger on a prettily shaped and delicate hand. Carmen stared at the finger too, as if it belonged to a stranger. Laura forgot to steer and drove the car into a ditch at the side of the road, which was at least better than going into one of the poplars which lined it everywhere but exactly here. The ditch had been artificially extended into a pond; it was a habitat of the natterjack toad. A notice, glimmering in the moonlight, indicated the creatures were a protected species. Their mating cries rose to a crescendo as the car splashed nose-down into the ditch; then there was an abrupt silence.

'I am sorry,' said Laura, and got out of the car, knee-deep in muddy water, her long skirt wet and trailing. Carmen was able to get out on to dry land. They left the ditch, and the car and the toads, and began to walk. Carmen's face, profiled, seemed to

Laura to change shape even as they walked: the nose became narrower and longer, the hairline more decisive, the run of chin to ear smoother and cleaner. She said as much to Carmen.

'Just a trick of moonlight,' said her friend, and who should come along behind but Driver in his BMW?

'Had a little accident, I see,' Driver said. 'You go back and stay with the car, Laura. I'll drive Carmen into Fenedge and fetch help.'

And Carmen got into the BMW just like that, and they drove off.

And Laura went back and stayed with the car hour after hour, worrying about the children and hoping Carmen would have the sense to ring home and let them know she was delayed, until she gave up and walked on to Mr Bliss's stables, where she had to rouse him in order to use the phone. A terrible night! She was angry with Carmen; who wouldn't be? She didn't get home until three, and no one had waited up for her. Even Mr Bliss hadn't been particularly friendly. The horses had been restless all night and he'd only just got to sleep.

As for Driver, he said to Carmen in the car, 'Now you know what it's like to be everyone else, no one special. That's what happens if you stand between Driver and his plans for you. Driver has all the time in the world, and you haven't.'

'I liked working there,' said Carmen.

'No, you didn't,' he said. 'A lesson to keep you in order the rest of your life. How to go to work like everyone else, yawn, yawn, short of money like everyone else, no one to talk to, ditto; every path out of here blocked by your circumstances or your own nature. Your own nature being the biggest obstacle of all. Just as well you've accepted my offer.'

'What offer?' asked Carmen but, even more than Tim ever had on the hilltop, Driver seemed to become vague; so much so, it was as if no one were driving the car; just a vague shape, an outline as of a head, only the view out of the car window could be seen right through it, and what a blotchy, patchy version of the moonlit view – as if the moon itself, the source of all light, were covered with mould, splitting its skin as if attacked by the athlete's foot fungi (*tinea pedis*) and its glow accordingly ruptured and disturbed. Poor Carmen!

'Accept the offer,' said Driver, 'and it won't only be you who will prosper. Your friends can have a share of the good times too. Always wise, that. Placate the friends, avert the envy. If you get promotion, find a boyfriend, come into money, always throw a party!' His face was back again: teeth white, gleaming and solid as he smiled; cherubic lips, crimson, dark and full.

'I'll do for them,' said Carmen, 'what I won't do for myself.'

'That's what they all say,' said Driver, 'but it's nonsense. You do it for yourself.'

This, at any rate, is what Laura told me Carmen told her of what went on between Carmen and Driver the night Carmen failed to send a garage out to retrieve Laura's car from the ditch.

'If you believe that,' said Laura, 'you'll believe anything. I prefer to believe he's her ghostly lover: they had it off under an ash tree in the moonlight.' She was still cross. 'What is more,' she went on, and told me how the very next day, what was more, Carmen and Driver were seen together in a boutique in Kings Lynn, the most expensive shop in town – the kind which, when it first opens, makes people hoot with derision at the prices asked, but which seems to flourish nevertheless. Customers are seen going in who have never been seen before, and probably never will be again. County ladies with spaniels at their heels, and women who look as if they might be the mayor, and girls with long legs – and who should be there that day but Carmen, standing shameless in the middle of the shop, stepping out of dingy clothes – the kind favoured by Peckhams staff, wash-and-wearable and never shrinking out of shape because they have no shape to begin with – for all the world as if she hadn't been home all night and needed to get out of them fast. There she stood in bra and pants for all the world to see – but since her figure was so perfect, Witness announced, it was hardly sexy at all, and the whole exercise perfectly decent, for all Driver stood in his navy uniform, braid and navy leather boots, leaning against the counter watching, hand on hip, like a brothel master. Who but Carmen!

Carmen apologised to the assistant, a lanky girl with a superior stoop, short dark hair and no bosom at all, for the state of the clothes she took off, thus without ceremony.

'Junk them,' she said. 'They don't fit anyway.'

Witness described Carmen as long-legged and ravishing: very much a bimbo type. She asked for a size twelve plain black skirt and a plain white blouse, ditto, which surprised Witness, who would have said a ten any day. Carmen said to Driver, 'I'm only here because I don't like upsetting anyone's aesthetic sensibility, even yours.'

Mrs Baker would have been proud of her. Four years in a chicken factory and 'aesthetic sensibility' still came tripping off the tongue. 'I can pay,' said Carmen. 'I have money set aside. If you choose to pay, that's your funeral.'

'Ah, funerals,' said Driver wistfully. 'Few and far between!'

'No one wants to live for ever,' said Carmen, taking the skirt and blouse, the most sensible garments in the shop, into the cubicle and shutting the curtain.

'They might,' murmured Driver. 'The time could come when they just might,' and he sat down on the little plump sofa provided for the purpose, and gazed at the curtain with the foolish, rather endearing expression men have at such times, a mixture of anticipation, anxiety and self-consciousness.

Carmen stepped out of the cubicle. The skirt was too loose at the waist and the blouse far too tight. Fabric stretched between the buttons. Witness reported she went in like a clothes prop and came out like an hourglass.

'God,' said Carmen to Driver, 'you are so old-fashioned!' as the assistant went off to find a size eight skirt and a size fourteen blouse. When she came back she had a red satin dress over her arm as well.

'I just thought –' she said. 'So few girls it would suit –'

The skirt and blouse fitted Carmen just fine if she belted both in, but the red dress fitted really perfectly, if, as Witness remarked, you cared for that kind of thing. It plunged to the waist at the back, curved out at the hip, in at the knee with a kind of red bobbled bounce, and covered the bosom, just, while emphasising a cleavage. It had thin shoulder straps, one of which was ready-made for slipping.

'It's made for you,' said Driver. 'Or shall we say you're made for it? Look at yourself in the mirror.'

Carmen did. She was gratified.

'This is what my dad wanted for me,' she said. 'If my friends could see me now!'

'You only have to say the word,' said Driver, 'and they will.'

'I'll pay for it myself,' said Carmen. 'Though it's madness. Wherever will I wear something like this *to*?'

'Ah,' said Driver. 'That's always the problem. Not the dress, the occasion. But I'm the King of Occasion. Just watch how I step out!'

Carmen paid for the dress herself with her credit card. The assistant had made a mistake. It wasn't in the sale after all. It must have set Carmen back, said Witness, four weeks' wages.

There wasn't a breath of air that night, I remember. The moon had lost its perfect roundness. It was waning. The high tides of yesterday had been very high, but somehow languid. A smooth silky sea had lapped over groins and breakwaters, slipped quietly over the coast road so that the flood signs went up, but no one seemed unduly agitated. The terns bobbed about in the water, unconcerned, looking down at grass instead of sand; and the tide went out as gently as it had come up, leaving a thin coating of silt behind it. Just on occasion the tides of the East Anglian coast behave like this, taking advantage but without rancour, affectionately, as a husband might roll over on to a sleeping wife; the land is possessed by a boredom so profound it can infect even the elements. I couldn't sleep. I sat at my window. Angela had in another uncle for Effie; I could see his shape and hers embracing the other side of the blind. But even that seemed slow and stately, not passionate. I think he was the greengrocer, whom high rents had driven out of Fenedge, but could not be sure. Perhaps I just imagined it.

Then the sky was lit up by more than the moon. Blasts of coloured light crisscrossed the sky: lasers, I presumed – the same, I daresay, as the kind directed into the neural fibres of my backbone, only these weren't a neutral, hygienic, glimmering white, but purples, reds, yellows, mauve – and out of control they raced a whole series of crisscrosses from horizon to horizon. White balloons began to drift overhead; a wind came out of nowhere to flurry them along – I recognised the Bellamy logo – one bobbed down almost to my window. And a burst of music far away, the base notes throbbing, the higher ones hardly heard, echoed over the fields to Landsfield Crescent. Sir Bernard Bellamy was back in residence at Bellamy House. Party time!

And the very next evening, it was said, Carmen and Driver were seen at Bellamy House, dining together. I could envisage the scene. Carmen, in the red satin dress, still believing she can some-how cheat the Devil, that no transaction is valid that depends entirely on bribes and threats. She has, as we know, a sense of natural justice.

Now the red dress, naturally, attracted many stares. The Bellamy House restaurant (four-star) had seen many a stare-worthy dress – the clientele included Australian ice-hockey stars and the wives of Texan ranchers, as well as those espoused to the more boring and conventionally wealthy, whose husbands liked them to dis-play a diamond or two, or a tiara, not to mention their secretaries, or their Other Women, whom they liked to dress down so as not to attract too much attention – but this particular dress, Carmen feared, took the biscuit. She could see it in the face of Mrs Haverill, who flitted in and out of the restaurant, maîtresse d'hôtel, a point of bleak and disapproving reference. And every second she sat there it seemed to get tighter.

No one, mind you, dined more often than they could help in this particular room, no matter how good the chef, or how smooth the service, or how the central chandelier (a million pounds' worth) revolved and played a sparkly tune on the hour every hour, so there was something for everyone to talk about. Those who dined herein felt scratchy and difficult through their meal, and often had indigestion afterwards. The point being that it was in this room that the First Sealord had held his disagreeable orgies, or so Mavis, who had once been here to visit Annie's workplace, claimed. Mavis had shivered and shaken when she'd entered the room, and said a child had died here long ago and was still around, a particularly powerful and angry personality.
'Don't talk such rot, Mum!' said Annie. She'd been on her hands and knees, scouring the floor. There'd been an outbreak of food poisoning, and official fingers had at first pointed to the Bellamy House hollandaise; and though the fingers had very quickly

pointed elsewhere, away from the heart of the Bellamy Empire and not into it, Mrs Haverill was taking no chances. The special operations squad was sent into action to scrub.

'There's more tummy trouble comes from haunting,' said Mavis, 'than ever did from botulism,' and Annie, though scoffing, had scrubbed her way out of the gloomy room as fast as possible. The turning mechanism of the chandelier was switched off out of peak periods: there was not even its wistful tinkling to look forward to.

Tonight the restaurant was three-quarters full, and from Mrs Haverill's looks there would be two diners less if she had her way. 'What's the matter with her?' asked Carmen.

'She's jealous,' said Driver, 'silly old bitch,' but of whom and what she was jealous he did not say.

'Can't you make this dress less tight?' asked Carmen. 'I can hardly breathe.'

'Looks okay to me,' said Driver, 'and since I'm the one paying that's all that matters.'

'You are not so paying,' said Carmen. 'I'm only here because I'm hungry, and I've eaten nothing but fish and chips for years, and I'll pay for myself. I have a credit card. I'm not going to be obligated to you, Mr Driver; don't think I am.'

'Of course you shall pay for yourself,' said Driver soothingly. 'I have nothing up my sleeve.'

He lifted one arm at a time and showed her his sleeves, and she thought for a moment he was right, there was indeed nothing in them. Just black space. But how could that be?

'You've got to learn to trust,' said Driver next. 'There is such a thing as a free lunch, just you wait and see.'

'Yes, but this is dinner,' said Carmen cunningly, though her eyes were so large and bright it was hard to detect cunning in them, or indeed anything but romantic compliance. It is difficult, as she complained to Laura later, to maintain your disagreeable feelings when your facial expressions seem to respond only to cerebral commands of a specifically agreeable nature. 'You're sure Sir Bernard isn't here?'

'Of course he's not,' said Driver, and his eyes were so crinkly and friendly you could hardly tell that he was lying. 'He's abroad. I should know. I'm his driver, his factotum, his *éminence grise*, the whisperer in his ear, his astrologer, his batman, his exercise coach, his nutritionist, his financial advisor, his personal manager. In fact, I am all things a perfect chauffeur is meant to be.'

'His pimp as well,' said Carmen, but she said it so charmingly – she couldn't help it – he didn't take offence. Besides, it was true.

The waiter, Henry, brought a large silver dish of oysters, as ordered by Driver. Carmen made do with melon and Parma ham. The Parma ham was hard and stringy, as it must be meant to be or it wouldn't be served in this state in so many good restaurants. There was a time when I dined in them.

'Do have an oyster,' said Driver to Carmen.

'I'd rather not,' said Carmen, suspecting a trick. If you share an oyster with the Devil, all hell breaks loose.

'I don't know why you're so stroppy with me,' he complained. 'I did so much for you and still you're ungrateful. Didn't I send your parents on an interminable world cruise? Didn't I make your brother a genius? Didn't I try and provide you with a rich and famous husband? What can you possibly hold against me?'

'Three years in a chicken factory,' said Carmen.

'But you told me you liked it,' he replied. Carmen thought perhaps this was what it was like to be married: wouldn't there be perpetual conversations similar to this one, as each tried to persuade the other that they were right and the other was unreasonable? It must be dreadful. Driver quickly ate seven of his ten oysters, tipping the shell between his lips, sucking, swallowing, smacking. She really wanted to try one. She'd never eaten an oyster. If he went on eating at this rate it looked as if she never would. She took one from his plate and squeezed a little lemon on it. It looked disgusting, both flabby and chewy, and amazingly raw, but others seemed to admire them.

'That's the way!' he said. 'Now dislodge its little towbar, and one, two, three, swallow!'

'That felt good,' said Carmen, surprised. 'Even the sea water with it.'

'Nearest thing to sex that isn't,' said Driver, and Carmen was not in a position to argue. What did she know? The oldest virgin in all East Anglia, so far as she could see (which wasn't far: quite a number of us in the Handicapped Centre are without sexual experience, as it happens), but who would think it, in the light of the red dress? She was guilty of the sin of hypocrisy; she could be prosecuted under the Trades Description Act. She was aware of male eyes upon her from all quarters of the room, and not only male, female too.

'More wine?' asked Driver, and poured it without waiting for a reply. She did not drink it. Instead she pushed away the glass, and asked the waiter for the bill. She had to leave in a hurry, she said; yes, they would pay separately. She handed him her credit card. Mrs Haverill came over to ask, quite unpleasantly, if everything was all right, and to observe that Bellamy House did not accept credit cards.

'I'm paying for us both,' said Driver kindly. 'When I've finished my meal. One melon and Parma ham, three glasses of Chablis and one oyster, Mrs Haverill. Not much, but enough! Such a pity she has to go, but she'll keep.'

And off into the night went Carmen, without paying, for she had no cash and Driver would not lend her any, and the waiter Henry offered to, but was sent scurrying back to the kitchens by Mrs Haverill.

These days the grounds of Bellamy House were formal and restrained, their flowers and shrubs flown in from London and arranged in neat rows, lit by orange globes on concrete posts. She was frightened by a voice which seemed to come from all around, not any one point in particular; it was Driver's voice saying something like 'Gotcha!' and laughing, but perhaps it was some night bird she'd never heard about that had taken refuge in these parts – because of the changes in the world temperature all kinds of unheard-of birds now turned up in East Anglia. She could feel the gravel path crunching and tearing at her slim high heels; they'd cost seventy-two pounds – madness in the first place. She thought it was worse than being Snow White in the Night Forest, who had gnarled trees leaning in to leer and tear at her: the trees here in Bellamy Park had been so efficiently lopped and truncated that a far nastier energy was now free to sweep through unhindered. The lights of a car came towards her. She stepped into shadow. It was an old Mercedes 450SL, and at the wheel, driving, was Sir Bernard Bellamy. He was looking good: slimmer, younger, happier, bolder. He was in a hurry. He passed without seeing her.

'Missed me!' said Carmen aloud, in answer to Driver's Gotcha, but no trick of the universe took it up and magnified the sound: it fell helplessly into silence.

In the morning she woke up as usual in the pile of bedding which did for her repose, but when she looked at herself in the greasy mirror propped up on the kitchen table she found her face had remained in its excellent night-out-on-the-town mode, and stretching a leg to observe it, turning her ankle this way and that, she saw that the leg was still long and slim. Her bosom, thank heaven, had shrunk a couple of cup sizes.

A friend of Paul's slept in a drug-induced stupor under the table. She kicked him awake. The new slim feet were tough and service-able. He shambled out into the morning. She called Peckhams' Personnel and said she was ill and wouldn't be in that day. Person-nel said she didn't sound ill to them. Carmen said 'Too bad,' and put the phone down. She went into the room where Paul slept. It was a really smelly room. She threw the windows open so savagely the sash cord broke. She had more strength than she knew. He stirred.

'What's the matter with you?'

'You are,' she said, and started throwing his belongings out of the window – pipe of peace, rusty tins of dope and allied sub-stances, little grinning images and skulls, old greasy jeans, cheap silver earrings, incense, ragged embroidered jackets, condoms, comics . . .

Alison, driving me into the Centre, her licence restored, seeing this scattering of objects out of the greengrocer's window, braked so savagely I hit my head on the windscreen, but never mind that. (The disabled are excused the wearing of seat belts if it's difficult. It's not as it happens in the least difficult for me, but Alison gets offended if I put mine on. She complains I don't trust her.)

Paul stood up. He wore torn jeans and a T-shirt: he seldom took off his day clothes to go to bed, merely his shoes.

'What are you doing?' he asked, hurt and bewildered.

'And you can go too,' said Carmen. 'This is my house.'

'It's our squat,' he protested, 'and I was here first.'

'I'm stronger than you,' she said, and it seemed to be true, for she propelled him easily down the hall, out of the door and into the street, resisting the temptation to lift him with one hand and throw him out of the window, for she thought she might have the strength to do that too. He hobbled for shelter to the Handicapped Centre, where he knew he would find people who understood just how difficult it was to be alive.

A letter came through the door as Carmen stood in the corridor – whose grime and despondency she hadn't noticed till now – wondering what task to undertake next. Perhaps she could make a bonfire in the small backyard and burn all the bedding in the house? Dig a hole and bury the torn plastic bags, the junked takeaway packs, the discarded empties? The envelope was addressed in her mother's handwriting. Carmen thought perhaps she should burn or bury that too, unopened. She had no reason to be grateful to her mother: on the contrary. But she relented and opened it. The envelope contained a cheque for twenty-two thousand pounds; it was made out to Carmen and signed Raelene Wedmore. The letter which came with the cheque asked Carmen to buy her parents a property in Fenedge. She and Andy had won a major tango competition on Blue Line Cruises. She was sending the prize money to Carmen before Andy could book them on yet another cruise to Monte Carlo. 'Your father,' she lamented, 'has developed quite a taste for roulette. I can't stand it. The horses were one thing, but casinos are another. I never know what to wear or where to stand.'

Carmen came over later in the day to ask me if I knew of any houses for sale in Fenedge. I had, it appeared, the reputation of knowing practically everything that went on in the town. I did not enjoy having such a reputation. I do not have a particularly prying or inquisitive nature: I am merely obliged to sit at a window all day. If I don't, people say, 'Wouldn't you like to sit near the window?' and move my chair nearer it without even asking my permission. Sometimes I would be glad just to sit and stare into a dark corner, but that upsets people, so I don't.

I suggested to Carmen that she try asking the greengrocer whether she could buy the premises in which she and her friends had been squatting – 'No friends of mine!' she said – inasmuch as I thought he and his wife would soon be divorcing, and he might be glad of the money. Her eyes quite lit up at the thought – which was remarkable because they were so large and luminous already – and she went off in pursuit of her erstwhile non-landlord. I had no doubt but that the world would fall in with Carmen's plans. A sigh of regret went through the Centre as she left. There was some talk of her likeness to Princess Di over tea and biscuits (donated by the local supermarket – after the sell-by date but not too limp) and it is true that Princess Di looks good and kind as well as beautiful, but there the resemblance ends. To me, Princess Di looks as if some inner grief might presently snap her in two if a whole lot of people aren't careful: that there are tears only an inch or two away from her eyes. Carmen, in the brilliant light of Driver's countenance, had the air that day of someone who would never snap, but bend for ever; who could see no reason why the world should not be as good tomorrow as it was today. Good heavens, how the girl had cheered up!

Laura came to me during the course of the afternoon, having dropped Caroline off for a couple of hours at nursery school. Now, this being the burden of the full-time mother, she had two and a quarter hours to fill in before collecting both Caroline and Rachel from separate educational institutions. To drive all the way home to Landsfield Crescent and back would have been, she said, a waste of petrol money. Barely there, and she'd have to return. She still, of course, had Baby Sara with her, not yet ripe for public education, and Baby Sara was feeling tetchy. Sara had been in a really bad mood, said Laura, sighing, ever since her, Laura's, last spat with Driver. Well, I wasn't in such a good mood either and I told her she was being absurd; no doubt Sara was just teething or bored at being at home all day when her sisters were off in the big world, and Laura unexpectedly said what did I think *she* felt, at home all day while the world went on without her, and then felt obliged to apologise because of course my plight was so much worse than hers, etc . . . And Sara cried louder and the other disabled persons in the room were disturbed and I felt responsible. Fretting babies are, I imagine, even more annoying to the childless than they are to those who are accustomed to them, but I have no doubt Laura felt she was doing us all a favour by thus exposing us to a taste of real family life: Sara's crying seemed the least of her worries and the greatest of ours.

Laura, I am bound to admit, is one of the sweetest people in the world, and this morning I was just not. All my nerves were twitching. My left foot jerked. My mind seemed to lurch in one direction or another, out of control. Laura had had a letter from Annie, which she'd come to report, and I took refuge in the vision of her life in Southland, New Zealand. Other people's lives, if you're me, are often easier to contemplate than your own.

So let's take a look at Annie as she arrives back at the Glen Trekker Station, Tim and the men having abandoned her on the hills overlooking Saunders Creek. Fortunately her horse seems to know the way home, for she's sure she does not. It ambles comfortably, snatching at a rare blade of juicy grass here, a leaf there. Once it even stops to stare at a lizard. Annie is happy to stare at it too. She and the horse, whose name is Tigger, but whose nature seems to be rather more like that of Pooh Bear, develop an easy, almost friendly relationship. Tigger stops outside the back verandah, and silently suggests that she dismount, so she does, and slips the reins on to a ring clearly there for that purpose. Tigger snuffles his contentment. She begins to feel she can cope with this new land. She is quite proud of herself, though her limbs are beginning to stiffen fast.

She goes into the kitchen where pots and pans clatter, and there finds Mrs McLean whipping white of egg into a froth using a wire beater.
'Stiff!' says Annie. 'I think I'll break,' to which Mrs McLean says briskly, 'There's some muscle ointment in the second drawer along of the dresser. Put it on tonight after your bath.'
The ointment is easily found since it smells strongly of eucalyptus of the most powerful, medicinal and unromantic kind. Annie's view of it must show on her face.
'Though we're not the kind,' says Mrs McLean, 'to make a fuss about aches and pains.'
'I don't mean to fuss,' says Annie. 'I just don't like the smell of eucalyptus.'
She fears she is not showing herself as the kind of potential

daughter-in-law Mrs McLean would like, and enquires, to show willing, though she is not in the least interested, 'What are you making?'

'Meringues for tea,' says Mrs McLean. 'The men will come home hungry.'

'You never stop,' says Annie, meaning it as a compliment, but it is not taken as such.

'Of course I never stop,' says Mrs McLean. 'What would I want to stop for? When you stop you're dead. When you and Tim are married' – What? Hold on! You mean we're to be *married*? And everyone knows for sure but me? Oh, Carmen, Laura, where are you now? This surely needs some discussion – 'Jock and I are moving on down to Rongaroa: we're opening up another station there. Only ten thousand head. We're not as young as we were. You'll be glad to be on your own, not with your in-laws. It's only natural. Here, you finish the meringues.'

Annie takes the mixing bowl and whips on, not knowing what else to do. Mrs McLean opens wide the bottom oven of the big cooker, which has been standing open, and there looking out at the world is a small white lamb. Mrs McLean scoops it out and begins to feed the creature milk from a baby's bottle. The lamb looks at her lovingly and with absolute trust. With her free hand Mrs McLean manages to unhook the rope which controls the clothes drying rack suspended from the ceiling, lower it gently, and, with the help of her teeth, manoeuvre one of Tim's shirts off it and on top of the laundry table. Annie marvels.

'Don't overwhip those whites,' says Mrs McLean. 'Best to add the sugar now.' Fortunately the sugar has already been measured out. Wishing she had not ignored the offer of the Bellamy House pastry chef to teach her the arts of cake making – she had longed to learn, but knew his large clammy hand would lay itself somewhere or other on her while she did, and his large belly in the stretched white vest would bump into her, and he had a habit of wiping his nose with his fingers and flinging the product into whatever mixture he was busy at, which made her feel quite ill, so she had declined – she stirred the egg white into the sugar.

'So that's the pommy way!' remarked Mrs McLean. 'Here in Southland we always put the sugar into the white. Still, no reason your way won't work as well!' She was always scrupulously fair.

'Yes,' Mrs McLean went on in her cheerful, positive way, 'Tim always likes a good tea. Are you good at scones? Tim's partial to a good date scone.'

'I expect I could learn,' said Annie. 'To tell you the truth, I don't even know how to make meringues.'

'Didn't your mother teach you?' Mrs McLean seemed surprised. 'We didn't go in much for cake baking.' Annie couldn't recall Mavis ever making a cake. She could see there was something magical about it. You flung these varying powdery and glutinous substances together with some kind of liquid, and lo, the whole melded in the oven and rose into an edible love offering. Annie thought she would practise and become very good at home baking, the best around.

'Well,' said Mrs McLean enigmatically, 'if the young go abroad they marry abroad, and that's the truth of it. But I expect we'd all die of stagnation if they didn't. You did stable the horse, I suppose?'

She took the meringue mixture from Annie, fretted a little over its texture, added a splash of vinegar, and slapped it into perfect shapes on a baking tray and put it in the oven the lamb had just vacated. She gave the oven a wipe out first. The lamb was deemed fit enough to sit in a cardboard box on the windowledge, where it had a good view of what was going on.

'I thought one of the boys would see to the horse,' said Annie.

'Boys? You mean Jack and Ben? They're full-grown men, not boys. You ride a horse, you look after a horse. Rub him down if he needs it, though if it's Tigger he won't. Take him to the stables yourself, and unharness him, and mind you wipe the harness properly, but I'd like you to do the potatoes for the potato cakes first. Jock's partial to potato cakes. Well, you'll do, I daresay. You're handy enough. A bit odd, like most people from abroad, but you can't help that. Jock and I said to each other just last night, well, Annie could just about get her arse in gear if she had to. Tim's made a good choice there, we said. Trust our Tim.'

And she smiled, a really sweet smile, with her perfect teeth, and a face that had never seen face cream but only good honest water, and Annie felt warm and accepted, and that she had come home, and took up the potato peeler.

I went to Audrey's funeral. Alison took me. We were late. The coffin bearers, or whatever they are called, felt obliged – because Alison called out to them so to do, crying aloud that surely the living deserved more attention than the dead – to put down the coffin and help me out of the car. Funerals are like this, I know: anything human and improper that can happen tends to, but one does not like to be the source of the untoward event. No one seemed to mind: people are very good, these days, about what Alison, who likes to be in with the trend, has taken to calling the Otherly Abled.

Laura and Woodie leant into each other, she weeping copiously, he trying not to, the three little girls wailing around them. He was a great prop to these women, I thought: rightly a wood carver, being so naturally and agreeably solid himself. Slow to move, slow to earn, but conscientious and good.

I watched with amazement, as did the many friends and family who clustered outside the chapel waiting for the previous funeral service to conclude (they were running half an hour late), as Audrey's husband – they had after all never been formally divorced – walked towards us up the gravel path that wound from the car park through the Memorial Gardens. He had a beard. He wore jeans and a black T-shirt and sandals. His face was narrow and agreeably haggard. On his arm came a girl who could be none other than Poppy. She was little and lithe and wore a bright blue silk suit through which you could see her nipples. She looked like, and was, the kind of nasty girl men love. The men don't know they're nasty, but other women do. 'Poison Poppy at school and Poison Poppy now,' as Carmen was presently heard to say, but that was when she'd run off with Ronnie Cartwright.

Laura stopped mid-sob as her father came up to her.
'I want you to meet Poppy,' said Kim. 'We're just back from abroad. This is a grim day indeed.' He seemed cheerful enough himself.
'I've already met her,' said Laura. 'We did our O levels together and she cheated.'
'Now, now,' said Kim.

'Don't you now now me,' said Laura. 'This is my mother's funeral. Why have you come?'

'To pay my respects,' said Kim, 'to my wife.'

'Well,' said Laura, 'all I can say is you've left it rather late. This is my husband Woodie, and these are our children. Say hello to your grandfather, kids.'

'He won't like being called Grandfather,' said Poppy, giggling into Woodie's eyes. She could never resist an opportunity.

'You mean,' said Laura, 'you don't want to be called Granny,' and Poppy trilled with fright at the idea and Kim remarked that the passage of time hadn't done much for Laura's nature, which left Laura speechless at the injustice of it all, outraged, for who was to blame for her nature anyway if there was anything wrong with it but Kim? Yet she was overjoyed in spite of herself to see him again. And how was Kubrick, asked Kim: the fish should have another twenty years in him if he'd been properly treated.

The funeral before Audrey's was concluded. Other mourners crunched away; the officiating priest came out to gesture the next uneasy group into the chapel, and the organist played the Dead March rather fast to hurry them all in. Kim stood next to Laura, Woodie and the children. If it hadn't been for Poppy clinging to Kim's other arm it would have made quite an ordinary family pewful.

Alison kept saying, 'Speak up , I can't hear!' in a loud voice. She had just had her eighty-seventh birthday, her mother her hundred and fifth. She and her mother shared a birthday. They had both recently been on television together, in a programme called 'All in the Genes'.

After the funeral, Kim told everyone that Poppy was having a baby.

'I'm terrified for my figure,' said Poppy, staring at Laura's comfortable waist, the hips that these days did so well to sit a baby on.

'That's really nice,' said Woodie. 'A little aunt or uncle for our three!' He felt so defensive of Laura he'd become almost witty.

'We're in very crowded accommodation,' said Kim.

'What he means,' said Poppy, 'is that the Landsfield Crescent house is his now that Audrey's dead. It was in joint names and since you've had the use of it all this time, it's only fair that you move out smartish, because we need somewhere to live.'

'Poppy,' said Kim, 'there was no need to put it quite like that. I was only sounding out the ground.'

'Facts are facts,' said Poppy, 'put them how you like. And the fact is that that house is ours by right.'

Kim smiled goodbye, saying he'd be in touch, and led Poppy off. She was grinning and dancing about and seemed more than pleased with herself. This was a crematorium, so flowers were laid around a named plaque on the stone paving at the back of the chapel. The plaque was made of cardboard. The ashes would be available for collection in due course or could be scattered in the rose garden. The late roses were spectacular.

Laura felt a familiar feeling: a kind of clutching in her lower stomach.

'I'm pregnant,' she said. She always knew almost at once. What she felt, Mavis once told her, was the moment the fertilised egg fixed itself to the side of the uterus, digging in its tiny grappling hooks, securing itself. Now that yet another risk had been overcome – the one of being washed away by the general wombic tides – setting itself in for the next set of battles for life, and the mother registered as pain this moment of triumph.

'I can't be pregnant,' she said. 'I just can't be,' but of course she was.

'I expect it's picked up Granny's soul,' said Rachel, which made Laura feel better.

10

Now it seemed to me that the tides of fortune were in a state of flux, the waters churning and foaming as you can see them do if you take a boat a little way out from shore at just the wrong moment: what a swirling and turmoil there is as the waters going in meet the ones still determined to recede! You have to cling on for dear life.

It was not a good omen for me that the coffin bearers laid down their burden and took me up instead. Wouldn't it have disconcerted you? Wouldn't you, in Laura's phrase, have been spooked?

It was not a good moment for Kim to appear, not good news that he brought: that young Woodie Down and his family had no right, other than custom and practice, to live in Landsfield Crescent. And Poison Poppy was bad news pure and simple.

And yet you can never say, can you, that a pregnancy is bad news, either Poppy's or Laura's. Badly timed, disastrous, inconvenient – misconceived, in fact – and adding to both the world's and the personal burden, as it may well do, still a pregnancy remains good news. You have to cheer the little blighter on, as it digs its teeth in and clings: Well done, you have to say, and mostly feel, to have overcome the million-to-one chance against making it even this far: good on you, mate! Well done! Poppy smirked and Laura tore her hair and waited, seeing that the quality of life she had achieved for Rachel, Caroline and Sara was now in jeopardy, forget Woodie's and her own. *Four?* How would she cope? It is of course a generally accepted rule that the simpler organism must be sacrificed to the pleasure and needs of the more complex. How easily Carmen swallowed her oyster, dislodging its little towbar; how easily the rest of us eat a tuna sandwich; with what equanimity do the rich and powerful not live upon the toil of the poor and powerless. Is the horse not shot to save its owner trouble? How blithely an opera house accepts the tax money of those who love pop: for must not the cultured, the sensitive, the responsive take precedence over the philistine? Even a male medical profession accepts, more or less, that the mental health of the mother comes before the life of a foetus (though why this is not extended to fathers too, I cannot imagine, if there is to be any parity of parenting at all).

In the light of all this, if, when Laura said, 'I'm pregnant,' Woodie replied, 'My God, Laura, you can't be. You have to get rid of it or I quit,' he must surely be forgiven, though it was a long time before Laura did. Forget the foetus, what about Woodie?

One way or another, considering the pattern of the times, I was not surprised to see, on my way home from the funeral, Carmen and Driver standing outside the greengrocer's in animated argument. Alison was so surprised she drove into a bollard outside the Post Office, and as I did not have my seat belt on I went headfirst into the windscreen and woke up in the local hospital. It was as well I did because when they X-rayed me for possible concussion they picked up the shadow of a brain tumour: I was flown back forthwith to Chicago, where no one exactly said that neural fibre was regenerating okay but in the wrong place, though I think that was what was happening. They removed the tumour, and I suspect reimplanted some of it in my lower spine because, when I woke after an eight-hour operation, I was on my face and well bandaged across the lower back. I'd asked them just to get on with it all. I no longer wished to be a well-informed patient. I preferred for the time being just to be a martyr to medical science. But this is not *my* story. I am sorry if it keeps intruding. Let me just say they flew Alison over with me 'to hold my hand' – Good God! Energetic old ladies are adored by everyone, it seems. I was, as it happened, glad enough to have her with me, but they weren't to know that. She is, I suppose, a mother to me, a source of both pleasure and woe: good deeds and bad. She is someone I can blame.

Carmen came to visit me in the Kings Lynn hospital, between the diagnosis of the brain tumour and my transfer to Chicago. I was feeling perfectly well: the tumour, just above the hypothalamus, was causing very little trouble. I asked them to redo the X-rays in case there was some mistake, and they did, but it was no mistake: there it sat in the cerebral cortex – a little knot of neural fibre the size of a marble.

'Hattie,' said Carmen, 'I want to ask you about the soul. Do people have souls?'

Now why does she come and ask me about such a thing? Don't I have troubles enough of my own? Can't she see I'm ill? She has a rather foxy look today – her face thinner than usual, the eyes almond-shaped, so large they seem almost wraparound: yet clearly it's Carmen.

'I know nothing more than you,' I said. 'It's a word, a concept which sums up a person's individuality. The bit of them you think would go on after death if there were such a thing as immortality.'

'Could you lose it, do you think?'

'How would I know?' I was beginning to get a headache. It didn't seem possible that the marble could sit where it was and do no harm at all. 'I suppose you might very well wear it out during your lifetime. Use it up with bad deeds and selfishness, and then, when the time came, you'd just die.'

'If somebody offered to buy it, then the only penalty would be blanking out at the end of your life, not hell or anything like that?'

I didn't think it could be Carmen sitting there. I thought it was probably a nurse after all.

'But why would anyone want to buy it?' I asked.

'Because I am the love of Sir Bernard Bellamy's life,' said Carmen, 'and he's the one who's sold his soul to the Devil, and he's demanding me as his reward. But I don't fancy him one bit and, fortunately, apparently I can't be offered without my consent. And if I'd lost my soul I would easily give that consent. As it is, I won't, no matter what the stick and what the carrot.'

'Good for you,' I said. 'Just take advantage of the carrot, while it lasts.' I noticed that 'By Courtesy of Sir Bernard Bellamy' was engraved on the TV set in the corner, and I assumed my mind was rambling.

'How's work?' I asked, always a safe thing to ask.

'That's going really well,' said Carmen or whoever. 'I've been promoted. I'm Staff Rep. on the Board. Peckhams are moving out of oven birds into egg production.'

'It comes to the same thing in the end,' I said. 'You eat them after they've grown or before they've grown, what's the difference?' and with that wet-blanketing remark I lost consciousness.

I do remember Mavis coming to me waving a card – the official announcement of Annie and Tim's engagement. When the nurse was out of the room she moved my pillows and made me sit up (they like me to lie as flat as possible) while she laid hands on me: thumbs on my temples; little fingers round towards the stem of my neck. She had little white podgy fingers. All Mavis was on the little podgy white side – except for her bright blue pop eyes. She was really pleased about Annie's engagement.

'Those girls,' said Mavis, 'those friends of Annie's. The airs and graces they put on. They never thought Annie would be the one to get out into the big time, but I always knew her day would come. That job up at Bellamy House – she was only marking time.'

I felt the familiar tingle; on this occasion it was in my forehead. I hoped she was doing no harm. I busied myself envisaging Tim and Annie: they were on horseback again; they were surrounded by the tens of thousands of sheep; they rose out of a floor of moving, matted, whitish wool.

'But you promised me you liked sheep,' Tim was complaining.

'I do, I do,' protested Annie. 'But so many of them! I can take them two at a time, even a dozen at a time, but by the thousand, Tim? And everyone of them alive with God knows what kind of ticks and maggots and worms, judging from the conversation over dinner.'

'It's so they don't get eaten alive,' said Tim rather crossly, 'we have the conversations. I expect along with not liking sheep you like rabbits.'

'Well, yes, I do,' said Annie apologetically. There should be nothing but truth, after all, between an affianced couple. He pointed out that the rabbits were letting the lifeblood of New Zealand; that ever since *Watership Down* the public had gone soft on rabbits: these days you had to put down the myxomatosis bug almost in secret.

'I should think so,' said Annie. 'It's disgusting. They sit by the side of the road oozing pus, half paralysed, half blind.'

'That's because they haven't had a big enough dose,' said Tim, and laughed, and she thought he was winding her up, but she couldn't be sure. She knew, because she'd been told so often, that the rabbit and the Labour Government were his family's historical enemies. The Labour Government had taken away farming subsidies, just at the time the European market had squeezed out its customary antipodean imports, so New Zealand had to sell to Iran and become even more unpopular with the US than ever (the nation had declared itself a non-nuclear zone and backed out of the ANZUS pact) until, fortunately, the Gulf War had rendered Iran a friendly power, it being Iraq's enemy – my enemy's enemy being my friend – and now New Zealand was okay again in the family of nations, that is to say, the US, and Anchor butter and Canterbury lamb became the staple diet once again of the British. All this Annie now knew and understood, but still she did not like sheep.

She understood, too, that she'd better keep quiet about Tim having met her laying stair carpet. No one said anything, but she knew if she gave an impression of having come from a County vicarage with bicycles in the hall and dogs sleeping on the smooth lawn, it would go down better with the families thereabouts. There was going to be a helipad built for the wedding, which was to be a big, formal, marquee affair. Annie, it had been decided, was to wear the McLean wedding dress. This had been made in England in 1851, at great expense, for a certain Annie Hardcaster, who was to marry the first Tim McLean in Otago, and shipped out for the wedding. The cost of its making and its shipping had been borne by the McLeans. But the ship carrying the dress had foundered in the South Seas with the loss of many lives. The cargo, however, had been washed up on the islands, some of it still undamaged, and amongst the goods salvaged was the wedding dress. It had reached its destination two years late, by which time the first Annie had died in childbirth, but the dress was in remarkably good condition. It had been worn thereafter by all the McLean brides, or such of them as could get into it. Unfortunately the first Annie McLean, during her short life, though apparently a big strapping girl for her times, came out these days as a size

8–10. The dress was in cream silk, crinoline style and very fancy. They thought it would do just fine for Annie, who had got quite thin.

'Isn't it rather yellow by now?' Annie had asked, but Mrs McLean said no problem: she'd soak it in lemon juice and water and hang it in the sun a little and she'd be apples. And she'd weave Annie a little yellow lace wool jacket – the wool dyed with the yellow liquid that came from boiling up the brown flat pancake lichen that grew on the rocks thereabouts, and then home spun into yarn. The yellow jacket would make the dress seem white by contrast. Annie said she didn't mind buying her own wedding dress, but Mrs McLean said it was a pity not to get the value of the family heirloom.

'So when is the wedding to be?' I asked Mavis. I thought I was feeling better, though I quite wanted to lay my head flat. Mavis said it was only an engagement announcement: Annie had said on the phone, laughing, the wedding itself was going to be a big do somewhere between dagging and docking, drenching and dipping, and as soon as she knew she'd send their tickets. And she'd love to send their air fares to Carmen and Laura, but she didn't like to ask Tim. It was true the McLeans were building a helipad, but there was no money to waste. And I could hear Tim's voice, the voice of the farmer everywhere, for ever at the mercy of the weather, of the seasons, of the Government, facing the ingratitude of the people (those who grow the food are always disliked by those who eat the food: no one likes to be dependent, and everyone feels the necessities of life should come free), saying to Annie exactly that as the sheep milled around them, their little black eyes gleaming and mutinous –

'I can't be expected to ship everyone halfway across the world, Annie. Your parents are one thing, but your friends? Come off it, Annie.' For what new husband in the world wants to encourage the girlfriends, any more than a new wife likes the friends of the old bachelor days? It's the same from Anchorage to Antarctica.

Sister came in and shouted at Mavis because I was sitting up, and my headache came back.

Next to visit me, before Sister banned all visitors, was, of course, Poppy. She had such a pretty, vicious, sulky, sexy, endearing little face, I could see why Kim fancied her and women disliked her. (Being in a wheelchair renders one genderless: I hoped I could be neutral in this matter.) She brought black grapes and ate them nearly all every one, and I was glad when she did, because at least when she opened her mouth to pop one in, with her slightly dirty fingers, it stopped her talking. How she talked! She wanted something from me, of course she did. Amazingly, she wanted my approval: me, lying there betwixt concussion and tumour.

First she complained about Kim. He never made any decisions. It was all left to her. He had seduced her when he was in a position of trust and she was only sixteen, which surely proved he was bad through and through; he'd made her pregnant and broken her relationship with her parents, and stolen her childhood from her. If anyone was guilty of child abuse, said Poppy, it was Kim. Then, what's more, he had lost his job and couldn't support her properly, and kept moaning on about having had to leave his stupid wife and boring daughter, as if it were her fault. She had turned out to be undergoing a phantom pregnancy, which was hardly surprising, considering the time she was having, and he blamed her more than ever. There was no satisfying him. By that time it was too late for her to go back to school or him to his wife, so here she was, tied to an old man, an ageing hippy, with grey beard and toes so horny they hurt her in bed, and he didn't wash enough.

I asked her why in this case she was still with Kim and she looked surprised and said after what he'd done to her it was the least he could do to look after her and support her, no matter what. I've met many women, especially those from working-class backgrounds, who complain bitterly about their husbands from the day they meet them, forget the day they marry them, as a matter of form, and it has nothing at all to do with whether or not they love them, and I supposed Poppy to be one of these. A young doctor came by, looking for a thermometer, and Poppy kind of curled and unfolded towards him in her yellow dress and smiled in a totally welcoming way and when he'd gone said, 'Did you see the way he looked at me? The randy pig!' and went on talking, and I thought perhaps she was something more malevolent after all than the mere product of an environment. And the girls were right to call her Poison Poppy. She'd have lost him his job too if she could have.

She complained that Kim had ruined her life by talking of true love and destiny and that all she'd ended up with was a shabby old car and a little hovel in Kings Lynn, with a man with bad breath who edited guidebooks for a pittance and who had no friends because he was a first-class shit and didn't deserve any. And now – here seemed to be the crux – Kim didn't even have the nerve to face his own daughter and reclaim the house which was rightfully hers, Poppy's, because wasn't she having his baby, and had I any idea what those houses were going to be worth, because of the new bypass and commercial centre Bellamys were about to build, now they had planning permission from the regional board? She happened to know, being a good friend of one of the planners, but I wasn't to mention that to a soul. Three curses on my soul if I mentioned it.

Her eyes flashed when she said that. I felt quite endangered: as if I belonged to a species which would be extinct if Poppy had her way.

'He's still not going to marry me,' said Poison Poppy. 'Even though his wife's dead. He says it's because he doesn't want to upset his precious daughter; now how can that be true? If he loved her so much why did he leave home? He says her problems are his fault. What problems? She's got a husband, her kids, and she's living in my house. I'm the one with the problems.'

It was time for my water. I was allowed water but no food, which was why Poppy was welcome to my grapes, and when Sister came in with my measured six ounces, she moved my visitor on. So Poppy left, still complaining, and looking devastatingly pretty. The marble in my brain, under the impact of her curse – because I most certainly intended to let everyone know Landsfield Crescent was to be central to a major land development scheme – or because Mavis had sat me up, shifted a little that night and I was in and out of consciousness and moved very quickly to Chicago.

11

My first visitor when I was back in my post-operative chair in the window of the Fenedge Handicapped Centre was Laura. She was many months pregnant, and waddled. With every pregnancy her shape became less defined and just somehow bulkier. From the neck down she just spread out in all directions. I was happy to tell her that, though I had suffered, apart from an occasional twitch in one eye and still being in a wheelchair, I had no further ill effects from either concussion, tumour or surgical intervention.

Laura had been distressed for a time, she said, after the funeral, though she was okay now. She hadn't known whom to turn to. I was away; she missed her mother, Woodie was in a bad mood because of the new baby coming; she felt she couldn't see Mrs Baker and confess to yet another child, though Mr Bliss, whom she had seen, had offered her a mixture of rue, fennel and borage to cheer her up – it worked wonders on horses suffering from depression – but she hadn't taken any. She'd finally gone to Carmen to offload her sorrows.

It was evening. Angela from across the way was baby-sitting for the first part of the evening: then Woodie was taking over. Laura did worry a bit about the way Angela kept chatting Woodie up, but she reckoned Angela couldn't help it and no one took her seriously anyway, and she, Laura, just had to talk to someone. It was worth the risk.

She was surprised to find that almost overnight the greengrocer's had been turned from a squat to a desirable residential property in the middle of town: window frames white-painted and a flower basket hanging by a blue front door. Carmen opened the door to her: slate floors gleamed; pot plants flowered; everywhere was tidiness and order. How had so much been achieved in so short a space of time? Did Carmen have some special relationship with the local builders too? She had been promoted at Peckhams, it was said, and rumour had it that that was because of a special relationship with Shanty Cotton, but as Carmen later remarked, 'Any woman who ever gets promotion is supposed to be having it off with the boss. It doesn't mean it's true. Or only if it's Poppy.'

Carmen was in New York business girl mode on the evening Laura visited: her shoulders were padded, her suit of natural linen, her trainers white and *sportif*, her eyes wide and clear, her hair long, reddish and silky, and her features wonderfully regular. It was extraordinary, as Laura remarked to me, how different Carmen could look and still remain the same person – an actress's facility, of course. The look didn't quite fit the house – something artier would have been appropriate, Laura thought. But she had not on that evening been paying much attention to Carmen: she was too preoccupied with her own troubles. Everything but her own self came over blurred, as if she had been wearing glasses which had misted over.

'I went in moaning,' said Laura to me, 'years and years' worth of moan which I had bottled up, and that was the truth of it. Just moaning and complaints. I moaned about my father, who had abandoned me just at the wrong time of my life, and embarrassed me for always by going off with a girl my own age, so I was somehow shy of ever going further than my own front door. I moaned about my mother, who had betrayed me by letting me get married far too young, and couldn't find the energy to stop me, and now had died on me, just when I needed her most. I told Carmen I didn't love my parents, I just hated them. I moaned about Woodie, who made me pregnant and then somehow implied it was nothing to do with him that I was, and how he was a hopeless provider. I moaned about the kids, and how I was expected to give up my own life for them: what about me, Laura asked Carmen, what about me? She was tired of understanding, forgiving and putting herself in other people's shoes: fed up to the back teeth with it, and talking about that she was now having trouble with her wisdom teeth. She didn't want them extracted with anaesthetic because she was pregnant, and certainly didn't want them extracted without – what sort of life was this, anyway?

'Don't shake your finger at me,' said Carmen, backing as Laura advanced. 'Don't rant at me. It's not my fault.'

'I'm not so sure,' said Laura. 'My theory is as your luck improves mine gets worse, and vice versa,' at which she thought Carmen turned pale under the smooth golden tan which looked as if she were just back from the French Mediterranean coast, whose tan is more flattering to the female skin than the tan of most any other place in the world, though no doubt just as bad in terms of ultra-violet rays.

'The only good thing that's happened lately,' Laura said she said to Carmen that day (and this was the first I'd heard of it) 'is that Poppy's baby simply disappeared one day. She went in to have a second scan and the baby which was on the first scan simply wasn't there any more. It happens apparently. The whole lot gets reabsorbed. Cows and sheep and rabbits do it all the time, and just occasionally humans. So at least that took the heat off my own father trying to make his own grandchildren homeless in favour of a misbegotten little sister.'

'Or brother,' said Carmen, and Laura said sadly she'd forgotten people could give birth to boys. And then Laura told me, though it embarrassed her to recall it, she actually fell on her knees and prayed to God for forgiveness for saying such terrible things about Poppy, and having wished a baby out of existence, she was sure she had, and for moaning on about Woodie when she really loved him, and how she wouldn't really be without her children, not for a minute – she was the luckiest person in the world – and she was sorry to burden Carmen in this way, only sometimes she felt there was no one to talk to –

At which point there was a flash of light and smoke from the kitchen and Carmen cried out, 'It's the chip pan' and they ran to the kitchen as one person, and Carmen seemed as surprised as Laura to see Driver standing there over the pan, and the kitchen full of a strange blue light. There was smoking but not burning. 'It's rape seed oil,' said Driver. 'It does this sometimes. A kind of flash fire. Such a pretty colour, rape, isn't it? It brightens up the landscape no end. All that brilliant yellow everywhere.'

'What are you doing here?' Carmen asked Driver. She seemed put out at his presence.

'Cooking our supper,' he said, and he dropped chips into the hot, hot oil. How they sizzled and spat! 'How are you, Laura? How's the new baby?' And the baby gave Laura a great kick in the ribs, and though Carmen begged her to stay, Laura left.

But I had an idea why Driver was back. He had come to collect his dues. You don't get from a squat to a mortgage in three short bounds, from the despatch floor to Staff Rep. on the Board; you don't get your best friend Annie engaged to a romantic hero and a wedding date set; you don't get your legs lengthened an inch from ankle to knee, and two inches from ankle to thigh, without someone coming to claim something, for there is indeed no such thing as a free lunch, or a free dinner either, and Sir Bernard Bellamy was back in town. You could almost hear the earth movers rumbling in the distance, creeping nearer, as he prepared to turn the landscape upside down. And the brave deserve the fair, as the brave will always tell you. The fair, on the whole, just shut up and get deserved. But not Carmen.

12

'All my doing,' said Driver. 'All down to me. Be grateful for your lunch. Give thanks.'

'Not on your nelly,' said Carmen, indicating her pretty house, her worked-upon self. 'All this I got by my own energies, my own efforts, my own skill. Don't tell me I was lucky and try and take the credit, because luck has nothing to do with it.'

'Everything's luck,' no doubt Driver replied, or I would have if I were him. 'Luck who you were born to, luck what country it was in, luck if you're born with cross-eyes or not, luck to be able to make an effort in the first place. Whatever's in the genes is luck, and you'd better face it. Life's all luck, no justice. Luck has everything to do with it, so I have everything to do with it – because the Prince of Darkness is the Prince of Luck. Too bad!' Driver said. 'Just take the money and run! Forget about the ethics. Your fault,' Driver said, 'for wishing me here in the first place; for wanting to get out of Fenedge instead of being content. It's discontent brings Driver to your side, quick as anything! Your fault, Carmen, don't blame me!' Even the Devil, you notice, doesn't want to be blamed. 'And now you have to see it through. If Sir Bernard Bellamy wants you, noblesse oblige, and all that. Manners, if nothing else. Lie down before him and open your legs. Take the money and run.'

'No,' she said. 'And no again.'

'How about if he marries you? Not even if I make it so he never has enough of you; is yours once, then yours for ever? Contrary to the general rule, which is yours once and then never again, because what was had today is forgotten tomorrow.'

'No,' she said. 'And no again.'

'We'll soon see about that!' he said, and there was another flash of blue light and he'd gone, leaving her to eat the chips, which were truly delicious. She poured the fat off to save it for next time, keeping it carefully away from her nice silk shirt, but it went rancid and greenish very quickly, and she threw it out.

And a couple of days later, there Carmen was in Safeway in her position as trainee sales manager (staff), Peckhams, doing her bit to promote her firm, as part of Shanty Cotton's apprenticeship scheme (train more, pay less), when who should come out of the office to show her round but Ronnie Cartwright himself. And he quite took Carmen's breath away: as well he might, being the man of her dreams, as Tim was of Annie's, and hero of the stories she would tell other less eligible men to keep them at a distance: and herself, to explain the oddity of her existence: that is to say, being a pretty girl on her own, unclaimed (or so she said: though Laura and Annie both, as we know, believed a long-term relationship with Sir Bernard Bellamy's chauffeur – who was probably married, which was why it was so secret – kept Carmen from any proper fruitful relationship which would lead to marriage and children).

She'd met Ronnie Cartwright only once, years ago, when he'd laid his hand over hers and taught her how to paint the eyes of the Madonna blue. But she knew at once who he was. Ronnie did not remember her at all, but then her looks had improved no end, though it was a misfortune that she, who never had zits, had that very morning developed one in the worst possible place – on the end of her nose. She had nearly called in sick because of it. 'No doubt about it,' Ronnie was saying, 'chicken's the best business to be in these days. The trend's away from red meat.' They walked in the chill air that rose from the frozen-food cabinets. She looked up at him. He was tall and slim, and fresh-complexioned; he was young, ordinary, kind and cheerful; he had a lot of soft brown hair and soft brown eyes: he was the opposite of Driver, who was the man she knew best in the world, and who was tricksy beyond measure, or why should he respond to her refusal to take Sir Bernard Bellamy on board by suddenly thus producing Ronnie Cartwright?

'These days,' said Ronnie, in his frankly rather flat and monotonous voice, which was nonetheless most attractive to her, for it smacked of stability, continuity (she felt that if Ronnie were in charge of her looks she'd stay the same shape for weeks on end, or even for a whole lifetime) and the sexy pleasures of controlled domesticity – they would have two children, properly spaced, not four in a hurry like Laura; Ronnie would have a job and climb a career ladder, and there would be enough time and routine to give major life events proper attention – not, like Laura, having to cry out that she was pregnant again before her mother's ashes were even cooled – and she, Carmen, would be Ronnie's wife, which was all she had in her heart ever wanted – except every minute the spot on her nose was getting larger, and how could he possibly want her?

'These days,' Ronnie said, 'people just like things pale. They'd rather drink vodka than brandy; white wine outsells red two to one; chicken and fish move faster than beef or lamb. Pork, being in between, pinkish, stays steady. And if you take my advice, young lady' (Was he on the pompous side? Never! Ronnie was without blemish) 'you'll move Peckhams out of battery eggs into free range.'

He waited for her to ask why.

'Why?' she asked, though she knew the answer. She'd told Peck-hams' Board often enough.

'Customers are turning into guilt-stricken carnivores,' said Ron-nie. 'So they worry more and more about the lifestyle of hens. Go for flavour, even if you have to inject it; free range, if you can afford it, barn if you can't.'

'Yes, Mr Cartwright.' He looked at the hen from the profit angle, not the humanitarian, but considering his training what else could he do?

'Please call me Ronnie.' He smiled at her; his teeth were perfect. 'And I'm Carmen.'

'Don't I remember you from somewhere?'

She told him. 'Good Lord,' he said. 'I tried to find you for years. Gave up in the end. You've changed.'

He took her hand and looked for a wedding ring and saw none. 'Not married!' he said. 'Nearly everyone is. Just you and me not.'

'I'm sorry about the spot on my nose,' she said.

He looked rather surprised. It was not, she supposed, the kind of thing you mentioned. She wished she were more like other people. 'It is quite lively,' he acknowledged, 'for a mere zit. Quite lights up the day. What are you doing for dinner tonight?'

So life changed: as quickly as that. But before she could reply there was a commotion somewhere in the store. Loudspeakers asked Mr Cartwright to come to Checkout 8 at once. He smiled, with too much courtesy and not enough regret for Carmen's liking, and departed.

Carmen followed after: she knew who she would see. It was fated. There was Poppy, holding up the line at Checkout 8. She was wearing a white suit and very high heels. Her pretty little mouth moved and moved; her high little voice went on and on.

'It was disgusting, filthy, dirty. I will tell my friends never to come here again. My nerves are in shock. I do not want a simple replacement, I want compensation. I was disgraced in front of my friends. It spoiled an entire dinner party. My dinner guest of honour bit into an after-dinner chocolate and there wasn't a cherry inside, just a horrid little wodge of cat's fur. Or something worse.'

In her hand she held an open box of liqueur chocolates. Half were gone.

'You are holding up the line, miss,' the checkout girl was saying. She'd said it three times already. 'If you are making a complaint, kindly go to the Manager's office.'

'I'll hold up the line if I want to,' said Poppy. 'The public puts up with far too much. They're on my side. Now I'm crying. You've upset me. Cat fur! Or worse!'

Ronnie Cartwright led Poppy off. She was crying. She dabbed her eyes with a tissue, which he provided.

'People are always trying that trick,' said the checkout girl to the line. 'You buy the most expensive box of chocolates in the shop, eat most of it, find something in one of them, or say you do, and bring it back. Then you get another couple of boxes free, and if you're lucky a ten-pound note as well. It's the cash compensation they're after. God, how I hate customers!'

Carmen hovered outside the Manager's office until Ronnie and Poppy came out. Poppy was being brave and dependent. Ronnie was enchanted. He led Poppy to Sweets & Confectionery and gave her two large boxes, crimson velvet with ribbons, from the shelves. Carmen drew nearer; she had her clipboard with her. Ronnie looked through her and past her.

'You're not, I suppose,' she heard him say to Poppy, 'free for dinner tonight?'

Poppy handed him back the boxes as she consulted her pretty little leather diary.

'I have a cancellation,' she said, 'as it happens.'

Carmen drifted off into the Fish section, where there are always few customers, the better to weep unseen. And who should be there but Driver, inspecting a dead lobster?

'They boil them alive, you know,' he remarked. 'Happy?'

'No,' said Carmen.

'It hurts, doesn't it?' said Driver. 'Just think what poor Sir Bernard feels. Men feel rejection as keenly as women. You're not going to feel happy until you do as I say, and neither are your friends, and neither is anyone round here for some time to come.'

And a fuse must have gone somewhere, because there was at that moment a flash of light and a puff of smoke, and Carmen had a kind of spectral vision of the real face of Driver, hoofed, clawed, malevolent and somehow seedy, for a second before he was gone. Then there was a real problem with the frozen fish because the flash had apparently generated a great deal of heat and warning lights on the cabinets were already beginning to spark on and off. Ronnie couldn't continue Carmen's familiarisation tour, he regretted, because of this latest emergency. She slipped away. Poppy had already gone. Carmen caught sight of herself in one of the mirrors in the cosmetic section, and saw that the end of her nose was misshapen and hideous.

It was weeks before the boil – for that is what it was, and it required treatment by antibiotics – had finally subsided and her face was back to normal, that is to say, in general imperfect. None of her clothes fitted her any more. She could no longer get her calf muscles into her slender boots, and her jeans wouldn't fasten around her waist. But at least her bosom didn't bounce when she walked, and no one whistled after her in the street. The flowers in the baskets got some kind of mildew and died, in a sticky mess.

Meanwhile on the other side of the world Annie bunje jumped. Bunje jumping is a sport which originated in New Zealand and is soon to be recognised in the Olympic Games, although it is banned in Britain as too dangerous to attempt. The participant stands on a bridge high over an estuary or river or road with elastic rope tied to specially made boots. He or she then hurls themself into space, and bounces up and down head downwards in the air several times as the rope breaks the fall, before being hauled in, or rescued by boat. The weight of the participant is calculated against the tension in the rope, so that the participant does not continue to dive headfirst into the riverbed or the rope simply snap. The art is to skim the surface and get the hair wet, but not dash out the brains. It was this sport that Tim earnestly required Annie to enjoy with him, and since she loved him and they were engaged, she did.

'But doesn't anyone ever die?' she asked Tim as they kitted up in the Club House.

'Only if they calculate the tensions wrong,' he said.

She hurled herself into space at his bidding, resigned to death. When she stopped bouncing she stared into rapids eighteen inches or so below. She could see the metal in the rocks sparkling beneath the water. She wondered if it was gold. She was rather disappointed when the boat turned up beneath her and she was lowered into it. It was an inelegant process. Tim was in the boat, pleased and proud.

'Did you like that?' he asked anxiously. 'I don't want you to do anything you don't want to do.'

'I loved it,' she said, but she felt that the general splaying of her parts entailed in her rescue, and the way the blood had run into her head, leaving her flushed and swollen, was unfeminine and unromantic. She was not convinced she was what they called in Southland a sporty type. Could she really face so energetic and courageous a life as Tim wished for her? She wanted to be pale and delicate and looked after, not windswept, healthy and strong.

'Good on you,' he said, not noticing her reticence, the politeness in her voice, and that was worst of all. She felt lonely. 'That's my girl!' he said. 'Next weekend we'll go camping.'

'Terrific,' she said, but she dreaded putting on her genderless walking boots once more, and feeling their clodhopping weight, every step suggesting that there was better in life than getting good fresh air into your lungs, which was what Mrs McLean seemed to believe was the highest form of happiness. That, and the achieving of perfection and efficiency in baking, which Annie was on her way to doing. These days she could fling a batch of scones into the oven and they'd come out light and golden every time. She knew which lambs were worth hand-rearing; she knew how to clean the steel knives; she knew how to sand the verandah rails without getting splinters in her hands; she could rub down and stable a horse; she could help Mrs McLean rethread the loom; and still, though there was much talk of the wedding, there was no mention of its actual date. Mrs McLean said to Annie one day, 'I reckon it's time you and Tim shared a room. No point you going pitter-pat down the corridor all night. It wakes Jock and me up: why wear out two beds when you can wear out one?'

Neither Annie nor Tim had in fact been pitter-pattering down the corridor at night. On the contrary, they'd been sleeping the sleep of the exhausted, the virtuous, the genderless, the affianced but not married, though their daytime embraces often these days led them to the brink, though never over the edge, to him inside her. 'Not till we're married,' he'd say. Which was what *How to Love One Person For Ever* suggested, so how could she object?

So after that she and Tim slept together, and Mrs McLean's sister, who had just come to stay, and seemed very like Mrs McLean except she cooked less and played bridge more, occupied Annie's room. Sleeping with Tim was indeed a rich and wonderful experience; and worth waiting for, as he was the first to say: within weeks they had moved from the missionary position in the bed – which was really all either she or he had ever envisaged – to rolling about on the floor in all conceivable patterns of limbs. Every degree in the range of human emotion, it seemed, had its appropriate release in sexual endeavour. They would appear at breakfast exhausted and pallid, leaning into one another, while Mrs McLean fried eggs. Annie was excused cooking breakfast and eating it, but it was only natural that she should wash up. Tim breathed into her neck while she did so, and occasionally took up a dish towel. Mrs McLean's nieces and nephews, staying with their mother, were young persons accustomed to leisure and never helped around the house, which Mrs McLean fretted and frowned about, but what could you do? Mr McLean became more and more taciturn the more people there were about.

One of the nieces said at tea time, 'What became of Wendy, Tim?' A silence fell and there was a kind of nudging around the table. Tim didn't reply. Annie said boldly, 'Who's Wendy? Come on, out with it!' in the way she thought one of them would have done, but no one answered her. Some of Mrs McLean's walnut chutney was produced, and cries of congratulation and amazement created a useful diversion. Tim told her later Wendy was a girl he'd once been engaged to for a short time; she'd gone off with his best friend: if he was a lonely kind of person that was perhaps why. It had made trusting difficult for him, he said. That's why he needed to be sure, before he committed himself: he'd been really and truly up the creek, no two ways about it, for a time.
'You can trust me,' said Annie. 'Completely.'
'Too right!' he said, and smiled his rare, broad, beautiful, endearing smile, and she wondered how this Wendy could have done such a thing: given up Tim for another.

Annie wrote a letter full of such good cheer and frank revelation to Laura, which Laura then showed to Carmen, so that Carmen could only have been relieved. Driver had been making empty threats. Her friends were safe: and Carmen was just having to put up with being herself for a while, and people saying, 'Are you okay, Carmen? You look a bit under the weather,' which really meant they thought she looked terrible. When the gift of beauty is withdrawn, you do. You have lost the art of presenting yourself to best advantage.

As for Laura, she had been astonished shortly after the new baby (Alexandra) was born, when there came a knock on the door at one o'clock in the morning. She was up feeding the baby, and Woodie was up with her. Her pregnancy had disturbed him: but now the baby was here he was attentive and loving once again, and Alexandra, fortunately, was one of those infants who just smile, and feed, and sleep, and glow – the very opposite of Sara, who was a discontented misery from the start, and the reason, no doubt, Woodie had been so against the possibility of having to raise another one like her.

On the doorstep stood Kim. He had a suitcase and no Poppy. It had been snowing lately, and the bare feet in the sandals were blue with cold.

'I've come home at last,' he said. 'I've split up with Poppy. I'll have the spare room. You lot can have the rest; it's the least I can do for you. Well, what do you say?'

Woodie and Laura looked at one another. Alexandra snuggled and rooted at Laura's breast. She covered the baby more closely with her shawl.

'It's up to you,' said Laura to Woodie. 'You're in charge here.'

'It's okay by me if it's okay by you, Laura,' said Woodie.

Kim bounded in – he was never short of energy – and up the stairs to see how Kubrick was.

'Tank's a bit murky,' he called down in his rich voice, waking all the children, who staggered out of their rooms to see what was going on. Sara clambered over the side of her cot, at which she was adept.

'And I can see a patch of white spot,' he accused.

'I keep putting in medication,' said Laura, lying, 'but it never clears up.' Kubrick goggled at Kim through the glass, Laura said to me, as if this was what he had been waiting for for years, but I think she was talking about herself. Father was finally home, repentant, or more or less, and the world was set to rights at last. 'Children,' she said, 'this is Grandad.'

'My name is Kim,' said her father sharply. 'The word Grandad, or worse Gramps, is never to be spoken in my hearing. Remember this is my house.' But Laura could see he was joking, more or less. Rachel and Caroline had to share a room from then on, but that was okay. Since they'd moved Rachel to her own room she'd kept seeing Audrey's ghost by her bed in the night – or claiming she did – though Dr Grafton said it was an attention-seeking device in the light of the arrival of the new baby, and they were to take no notice. All the same, it was as well she was sharing with her sister again. If Kim was back sharing a room with Audrey's ghost, it would serve him right and no doubt keep her contented and quiet. If she couldn't have him living she'd have him dead.

But of course Driver was saving his fire, that was all, making them all feel safe and secure the better to devastate them later. And

Landsfield Crescent itself was feeling the brunt of misfortune. Plans for the new development (badly advertised) had been pinned up in Fenedge Town Hall; a public meeting (ditto), though poorly attended, fulfilled all legal requirements. The file of objections was mysteriously lost, and before you knew it the earth movers were in the beet fields (whose ownership had been silently changing over the last couple of years) and the bypass was being built, and Landsfield Crescent was from time to time showered with a kind of black, grainy, lifeless dust, which effectively blocked any attempt by a growing plant to break out of the earth into sunshine now it was spring. Poor little Sara developed quite nasty asthma, and I was rather happier now to sit in the window of the Handicapped Centre than at my Landsfield Crescent post, and quite looked forward to the hoot of Alison's car in the early mornings. She had had one of those dreadful musical horns installed, which always seems an insult to those braving perforce the perils of the road. What have jokes to do with traffic?

The narrow road between Fenedge and Bellamy House, down which the girls had so often walked, between the fields and the poplar rows, under the arches made by the old trees, past Mr Bliss's stables, was now deemed inadequate for the flow of traffic and was to be widened. To this end, the stables had been compulsorily requisitioned. Mr Bliss had set himself up in Fenedge as a hypnotherapist, using a room in the former library, which had been closed down as the result of Authority spending cuts. I could see the entrance to his consulting room from my window. He was short of clients, which pleased Mavis, if no one else.

'I can heal obesity and smoking perfectly well by the laying on of hands,' she said, 'and there he is, interfering with people's minds. It's unethical!'

However, Mrs Baker, who had put on two stone since her retirement, and was bulky enough to begin with, managed to lose three stone under Mr Bliss's mind control (it was quite exciting to watch her diminishing week by week) and his business gradually began to build. The Pedestrian Precinct was opened to through traffic, for no apparent reason, and construction lorries began to thunder through the very centre of the town. Those who had felt persecuted by its quietness, and groaned about how boring life in Fenedge was, how isolated from the real world, now felt equally persecuted by what they called aural pollution, that is to say, noise, and the way the ground trembled as the juggernauts rumbled by. The metal arms of my wheelchair sometimes trembled so much as they passed I could have sworn they were alive, and a life form not particularly friendly to me, one with which I was in symbiotic connection. (We'd had a delivery of sci-fi paperbacks.) Alison, one of the bravest people I know, it must be admitted, continued to park as if the lorries did not exist, and since their alternative was to stop or to kill her, they stopped, but only just. Then she'd make them climb down from their cabs to assist me out of the car – tough, tattooed, sweaty, infuriated men, who could be surprisingly gentle, but not always. Alison said she'd rather trust a macho man than a new man any day. It was of course embarrassing for me, but still better than watching the way the black dust drifted over Landsfield Crescent.

And still Sir Bernard Bellamy did not appear: his minions worked in his name. Boards announcing 'Bellamy Construction At Work' appeared everywhere. Only Bellamy House stood unaffected by the mayhem all around: its approach was now from the coast road: the Rolls and the Bentleys swept in through a conservation area, and through the colder months special bird-watching parties could be arranged on request through the Porter's desk, complete with hampers, champagne and folding chairs, and cassettes and headphones to give you bird descriptions so vividly you could almost imagine you had seen them: in the early spring the purple sandpiper, the occasional goosander or garganey, and plentiful pink-feet; in March, velvet scoter by the hundred; but the best time of all, the cassette could tell you, would be in October, when the winds have been blowing strongly for days: then the teal, the mallard, the pintail, the shelduck and the eider are out in force, rejoicing in the wildness of the weather. Sometimes even the Mediterranean gull will put in an appearance, though one suspects unwillingly, having been gusted in from warmer parts. And you may catch a glimpse then of the lapwings, still doggedly beating westward (as my *Where to Watch Birds in East Anglia* tells me), their wings barely lifting above the pounding surf. But these ornithological outings aren't too popular with Bellamy House guests, although they're on offer. Most prefer a trip to Newmarket and the horse racing: especially when the Summer Race Course is open. The turf seems a more attractive alternative to sitting along the Wash coast or somewhere in the salt marshes, hoping for a glimpse of a Cory's shearwater, or the rare storm petrel. A pity. I don't get to bird-watch. Alison has a fear of the neuralgia which cold sea winds can bring. I don't suffer from it myself.

13

Peckhams' annual outing to Newmarket fell that year on a particularly fine August day. Only heads of department went, of course, and a few major local customers; other guests were transported in limousines which picked up in Central London, or found their own way to the Race Course. A big marquee had been hired especially for Peckhams; a buffet lunch was to be served: a special in-marquee tote was set up, and the races could be watched on Anglia TV if the spirit or the legs failed. Shanty Cotton had urged everyone to dress up, and the group which gathered in Peckhams' forecourt was, as Carmen described it to me, on the gaudy side. The women wore large hats and bright floral prints, as if for Ascot, and Shanty's tie was more brilliant than his face: scarlet and purple. Only Henrietta Cotton, his gentle, peaceable wife, was dressed in modest grey, and wore a simple straw hat. She looked as if she'd prefer to be working in her garden back home. As for Carmen, she'd woken up that morning with long legs and a small waist, though with her bosom still its ordinary self, so she knew something was up. Perhaps it was just that her suffering for the loss of Ronnie Cartwright was to be stepped up – she had almost forgotten about him, so busy was she at work, making doubly sure she was not demoted, sent back to the factory floor, for Shanty liked to keep everyone on their toes, and at home, arguing with the mortgage company as to whether or not subsidence of the ground beneath her house was her responsibility, the Council's or the mortgage company's insurers. The ownership of property, she began to see, could be an anxious and onerous business. The lorries which passed under her bedroom night and day disturbed her sleep, as well as shaking her house to its foundations. But these things, she understood well enough, had been sent to try her: she would not give way to despair or complaint. And she was looking forward to the trip to Newmarket. Her father

Andy had once taken her to the races before being barred the track, for some reason or another never made clear to her but bitter enough at the time. He'd promised to take her every birthday, but she only went the once, when she was nine. After the arrival of the cheque her parents had fallen silent, apart from a postcard from Monte Carlo, which said nothing about their returning home. Andy's run of gambling good luck still held, apparently.

So here was Shanty, trying to get sixteen people into five Rolls-Royces, all parked in Peckhams' forecourt and holding up a string of Peckhams vans with deliveries or collections to do, and changing his mind faster than he could make it up, in spite of the list in his hand, carefully thought out by his office administrator Janice and approved only the day before yesterday by Shanty himself. But he and Janice had quarrelled yesterday, it seems; she has been demoted to the office administration pool and he no longer trusts her judgement. Office rumour has it that she revealed a boyfriend he didn't know about. And he is probably flustered by the presence of his wife Hen, who always manages to make him feel like a naughty little boy and behave like a bully.

'Pay attention,' says Shanty. 'Let's have a little organisation here, shall we! Four to each car: ladies, take your hats off once you're in place. Nothing worse than a poke in the eye. Henrietta, I want you in the second car with Tony, and Mr and Mrs Snape. Everyone's hat in the boot of car number one, please.' But the ladies decline to be so far removed from their hats, and the chauffeurs have already got out to open the boots when it turns out the hats won't fit in without crushing anyway, so the seating has to be arranged according to size of hat.

'Carmen, not in car number two, after all; you'd better be in car number one with me and Henry and when Ronnie Cartwright has the courtesy to turn up he can be in car number one too.' Carmen's heart lurches. She hasn't known Ronnie is coming. She is wearing a pink confection of a dress she happened to find in Oxfam – it says on the label Zandra Rhodes, but she can hardly believe that – and a white cartwheel hat, and looks, as Mr Snape says when Mrs Snape isn't in earshot, a million dollars. She's glad about the length of her legs, and her feet are comfortable once more in her best shoes, seventy-two pounds' worth, which she hasn't worn since her escape from Bellamy House. And not a zit anywhere in sight! She looks wonderful; a little flouncy and wispy for her own taste, but it seems to suit everyone else okay. Even Shanty, who seems to have gone off her lately, and shuts her up rather cruelly at Board meetings whenever she ventures an opinion on staff morale or the profit-sharing scheme which never materialises, is attentive, and Hen bites her lip a little, so Carmen distances herself from Hen's husband as much as she can. Shanty is feeling the loss of Janice and is looking for a replacement. So much is clear.

Carmen murmurs in defence of Ronnie, 'I suppose major clients are allowed to be late. That's the whole point of being a major client,' and Shanty just smiles and says, 'Discourtesy is discourtesy, no matter what you say, Carmen. And profit is the point, the whole point, and the only point, and don't you forget it, my dear. Remember that and you'll go far. Mr and Mrs Snape, I need you in car two, not three. Philip, what are you doing in car four? This list is hopeless.'

Hen says mildly, 'Couldn't I sit next to you, Shanty? I was so looking forward to today,' and Shanty replies, 'Mr Snape will think you're being rude to him, dear, and please remember this isn't a party, it's a window of opportunity. Mrs Abhill, if you can't manage your hat on your lap there is no point in you getting in next to Philip –' and so on and so forth, until they are all packed in, and still Ronnie Cartwright has not arrived, though there is just the one place vacant next to Carmen in car number one.

Then the BMW nosed in front of the line of waiting vans. Driver was at the wheel. In the back were Ronnie Cartwright and Poppy. Poppy was wearing a smooth green silk suit and a little black pillbox hat with a veil, and looked soignée and well defined: almost as if a black line had been drawn around her to make sure she got proper attention. Driver opened the door for Poppy with a flourish. Out she stepped, with Ronnie close behind her.

'Are we late?' asked Poppy. 'I hope we haven't held people up? Ronnie had a puncture. I told him he would but he wouldn't listen. This nice gentleman passed and gave us a lift. Which car are we in?'

'Oh dear, one extra,' said Shanty.

'Ronnie never goes anywhere without me,' said Poppy. 'Do you, Ronnie? He can't cope. He's hopeless. I even have to do his Head Office reports. Come on, Ronnie, everyone's waiting.'

Shanty said to Carmen, 'Sorry about this, Carmen, we'll have to leave you behind.'

And Carmen had to get out and let Ronnie and Poppy in, and off the procession of cars went, leaving her standing in her Zandra Rhodes dress and the cartwheel hat in the middle of Peckhams Poultry's forecourt.

'Well?' said Driver.

'Well what?' enquired Carmen.

'Would you like a lift to Newmarket?'

'No thanks,' she said.

'If you're still set against Sir Bernard,' said Driver, 'I have one or two others to offer.'

'You mean others you've made promises to you can't keep, for shortage of virgins.'

'Virgins schmirgins,' he said.

Now this conversation comes out of my head, not Carmen's. I can tell you she was pretty stunned, standing there in her gauzy dress, the hot August sun beginning to mount in the sky, and the lines of van and truck drivers hooting and hooting, wanting to offload and load – for their cargoes, living and dead, were beginning to suffer from creeping warmth – but unable to do so until Driver moved his BMW.

'Since you've taken away from me the only man I ever wanted,' said Carmen, stamping her pretty foot, as heroines are meant to do – she found herself doing it in spite of herself: thus rejection, outrage and anger were turned to a mere charming petulance – 'I'll stay single for the rest of my days.'

'We'll see about that,' he said. 'That *is* a nice dress you're wearing.'

'Oxfam,' she said. 'My own money, my own choice!'

'Oh yes,' he said. 'Just happened to be on the rail, never worn, fitting perfectly, twenty-five pence, just the thing for Newmarket. Happens all the time, doesn't it, or is it the Devil's own luck?'

She had to agree it was the Devil's own luck, and got in beside him, if only to stop the van drivers hooting, and to keep Peckhams' production line going, in spite of the absence of managers.

Inside the car everything was dark green, and cool, and quiet, as if she were in the middle of a very, very old wood.

'Where are we going?' she asked.

'Wherever you like,' he said.

'Then take me to Laura's,' she said.

'How boring,' he said, but he changed direction: Traffic lights – as roadworks continued in the area, red lights abounded – always turned green at his approach.

'How about royalty?' asked Driver, and a male hand with a massive gold Gothic ring on its middle finger crept up from behind and laid itself on Carmen's knee. She looked behind her and saw a suave and smiling face, and written on it all the petulance of those born to power. 'Red carpets wherever you go?'

'I'm a republican,' she said, and the hand seemed to melt away.

'I could offer you a diplomat,' said Driver. 'Speaks eight languages.' Carmen turned to see who was sitting behind her and there sat Sergei Moscowitch, whom she had seen many a time on TV, speaking to his tormented nation, though she couldn't remember which one, with his pale intelligent face and dark eyes set in deep sockets, and bags under the eyes the like of which she had never seen. On TV make-up had made little of them. 'And the gift of tongues for you thrown in,' said Driver.

'Everyone speaks English anyway,' said Carmen. 'Why should I bother?' And Sergei vanished, to be replaced by Rollo Hopper from Hollywood, laid back, bronzed, amazingly handsome in a white-toothed, gold-embossed kind of way. And he too she had seen many a time on TV and at the cinema.

'How about Hollywood?' asked Driver. 'You could be a star.'

'It all ends up with drink and drugs,' said Carmen, and she thought she heard Rollo snarl, except there were all three of them now in the back seat, smiling: royalty, the diplomat and the star.

'Forget the judgement of Paris,' said Driver, 'this is the judgement of Carmen. The woman's turn.'

'In that case,' said Carmen, 'I choose none of them.'

There was a flash of light to end all flashes of light and the car door flew open.

'You and your flashes of light!' said Carmen.

'You haven't seen trouble yet,' he said. 'You and your precious friends.'

'Look into my eyes,' she sang, in her newly melodious voice. 'Look into my heart. When I look inside you all I see is the freezer a week after the power's gone off. Everything soggy and rotten and putrid!'

The door slammed behind her, and off Driver roared. Oddly, he was driving a sports coupé – one of those anti-children vehicles in which the back-seat passengers (two's company, three's a crowd) can only sit with their knees to their chin – and how Royalty, Diplomacy and Hollywood could have sat so comfortably there was no explaining.

Carmen marched up the path – there'd been a particularly nasty fall of dust that day as some gentle hill, a rarity in those parts, to windward, had been exploded the quicker to level the ground – and banged on Laura's front door. A cacophony arose inside – the noise of startled and excited children. Laura opened the door. Carmen kicked off her dusty shoes and made for the telephone. Laura tried on the shoes, but her feet were far too wide. She wore a flowered smock, and the baby had been sick down her back.

'I say, Carmen,' Laura said. 'Just look at you! All dressed up and nowhere to go!'

'I want a taxi,' said Carmen to the phone. 'I want it now. Newmarket – yes, Newmarket. Is that a problem? I know it's a long drive. No, I can't go by train. What kind of taxi outfit are you, suggesting people go by train? God,' she said to Laura, 'this place is the pits and getting worse.'

'It's Dullsville,' said Laura sadly. 'Let's-get-out-of-here-ville. Always was. What about me?'

'You just get on changing the nappies, Laura,' said Carmen. 'You wanted kids, you got them. I wanted true love and I see no sign of it arriving . . . Oh, and I don't want a driver who smokes . . . Okay, you win, if he's the only one, so what the hell!'

She gave Laura's address and put the phone down.

'Newmarket!' said Laura, awed.

'It isn't what it was,' said Carmen. 'Anyone can go these

days, even Peckhams. It's all PR. Except I want to go and I mean to go and I'd be on my way now if it wasn't for Poison Poppy.'

'At least she's in your life now,' said Laura, 'not in mine, and just you make sure you keep her there. She ruined my father. She killed my mother.'

'Don't exaggerate. And stop blaming other people.'

But Laura was peering inside Carmen's dress for the label.

'Zandra Rhodes!' she marvelled.

'Oxfam,' disclaimed Carmen.

'You're winding me up,' said Laura. 'So, who paid for it?'

'I did.'

Laura was trying to feed Baby Sara with cereal with one hand and keep Alexandra on the breast with the other, and making a bad job of both.

'Rachel,' said Carmen, 'you're old enough to feed Sara. Help your mother, for God's sake.'

Rachel took the spoon and started delivering mouthfuls into Sara's mouth. Sara, enchanted, stopped wheezing and swallowed obligingly.

'Thank you, Carmen,' said Laura humbly.

'I just can't bear inefficiency,' said Carmen.

'God knows what the fare to Newmarket will be,' said Laura. 'But enough to keep us in disposable nappies for a month.'

– At which point there was a bang on the door. It wasn't the taxi driver but Mavis and Alan, and they were waving a wedding invitation on embossed white paper with silver edging. It named the day, three months hence, of Annie's wedding.

'We won't come in,' said Mavis. 'We know how busy you are. Though time for guests, I see. How nice! The postman delivered yours to us by mistake, but now I've forgotten to bring it over. This one's ours. But what's the odds? You won't be able to go, Laura, all that way – far too expensive. Or you either, I suppose, Carmen. You'll be far too busy. She's sent us return tickets. Club Class, of course. Well, she's in the money now. There's to be a marquee, two hundred and fifty guests.'

'She didn't write?' asked Laura. 'Just the invitation?'

'I don't think she'll be writing to you much from now on,' said Mavis. 'People's ways in life separate. Some reach up to the clouds (she meant Annie), others just drudge along (did she mean

Laura?) and some coil down to the pit (she most certainly meant Carmen). But this we must accept – paths divide.'

Carmen had no time to retort, perhaps fortunately, for at this moment the taxi turned up, hooting his horn, smoking his fag out of the open window, and she had to leave.

Laura, Mavis and Alan watched her go in silence. Mavis said, 'I never thought she was a proper friend for our Annie. She was bound to end up in trouble. What did they expect when they named her? Some people have no imagination.'
Alan said, 'That girl is spoiled goods, there's no mistaking it.'
Mavis said, 'Speak no evil, hear no evil, see no evil, Alan.'
Alan said, 'All I meant was, being spoiled goods, she might not find a husband so easily.'
Laura said, 'Perhaps she doesn't want a husband.'
Mavis said, quite startled, 'Every woman wants a husband, that goes without saying. My surgery's full to overflowing with widows wanting theirs back.'
'Well,' said Laura, 'anyway, if Alan can just find the time, I'd love to have Annie's wedding invitation. It can go on the mantel-piece and I can look at it and dream.'

The date of the wedding, Mavis told me, had finally been settled while Tim and Annie were enjoying a ski-plane ride up the Tas-man Glacier in the Mount Cook district. I could imagine.
'Don't you just love this?' asked Tim. The plane had flown up a wide desolate river valley between icy crags; it seemed to Annie an unnatural place; she had expected the glacier to provide some glittering spectacle of ice facets and frosted spears, the kind of landscape into which Superman in the film threw his learning module to make his crystal palace spring to life, but here was just a creeping valley – creeping backwards, she was told, as the glacier receded – made of blackish ice, a hundred and twenty metres thick, coated with gravel, everything so dead that to be alive seemed the offence. It made you feel too noisy yourself, and the sound of the plane was like the buzz of an insect which pesters you at night.
'I just love this,' she said, and beneath them, as if in response, the great river of ice turned white as they advanced, narrowed,

became frosted, cut by crevasses which were the same blue as the wings of the teal on the estuaries back home, and the crags on the further side came closer, and ahead, towering above, was the Matte Brun peak (3,176 metres).

I know the depth of the ice and the height of the mountains because in the leaflet 'Adventures for the Disabled' ski-plane rides in the Mount Cook (3,764 metres) area are recommended. The invigorating effect of the mountain air and the thrill of the ride will do us good. So they say. Mount Cook's Maori name is Aorangi or Cloud Piercer. Rangi the Sky Father and Papa the Earth Mother brought forth four Children of the Sky, all sons. Aorangi was the eldest; then came Rangiroa (Mount Dampier), Rangirua (Mount Teichelmann) and Rarangi-rua (Mount Silberhorn). The people of the earth live around the feet of what the white man called in his patronising way 'The Southern Alps', and the children of the clouds dwell around their heads or, as Annie discovered, rush straight into their rock walls in aircraft and then, this being the fun of it, bank steeply away with an inch or so to spare so there is nothing to be seen through their camera lens but jagged rock, should they still have their eyes open.

'He's gone mad,' she cried to Tim. 'Stop him!' as the pilot, the plane still juddering from this first manoeuvre, dived headlong into a huge tonnage of snow which seemed to hang by a thread from a vertiginous wall and dislodged it so that it crashed a thousand feet below – she could hear its rumble above the sound of the engine and snow plastered the windscreen so the pilot was blind, but he didn't care: now he was aiming upwards for the sky: he must be, for she was pressed far back in her seat, her mouth folded in against her teeth – but not open sky, oh no, for she could see crags on either side of them as the window cleared, jagged and seamed, so close she could touch them if she could move her arms, which gravity or fear kept pinioned to her sides. Not that she wanted to do either. She thought she passed out for a second or so.

'Don't be a scaredy-cat,' Tim was saying. 'This is a ski-plane ride. The pilot knows what he's doing.'

'Why?' she thought. 'But why is he doing it?'

'The mountain of the Gods,' said Tim. 'These are the thrills of the Gods.' He held her hand. His eyes were very bright; his nostrils were flared. He looked like this sometimes when they made love.

'You okay?' he asked.

'I'm just fine,' she said. Better to die with Tim than live without Tim, and the pilot banked and dived so the wing tips all but caught the jagged ice facets of the glacier and she found herself staring down into the blue-black depths of a crevasse, and she thought, well no, actually I want to live. If I have to live without Tim, still I want to live. An updraft of air caught the plane and tossed it up, out of control, and she screamed before she could say so.

'Lucky that wasn't a downdraft,' said Tim to the pilot, and the pilot laughed.

'You're not nearly so close as you think,' said Tim to Annie. 'No worries. It's a matter of perspective. The mountains are so vast up here metres always look like inches.'

'Oh yes,' she thought. 'Oh yes,' but aloud she said, 'This is a million times better than a rollercoaster!'

Oh yes, thought I, reading my 'Adventures for the Disabled', what's a thrill for some is a nightmare for others. No thanks.

The plane landed on its skis on the névé of the Franz Joseph Glacier: that is to say, the snowy flatlands from whence the glacier is sent creeping to the sea, a frozen river, or drawn back as the supply of snow diminishes. Tim and Annie had their photograph taken by the pilot. She was still trembling but was careful not to touch him so that he didn't notice. Tim kissed her: her lips were steady enough.

'Let's set a date for the wedding,' he said. She felt she had passed the last of the initiation tests. Her credentials for becoming a McLean wife had finally been established. The pilot offered them scones and tea from a hamper. She refused the scones. She was worrying that she might not fit into the McLean wedding dress.

'Tell you what,' said Tim, 'for our honeymoon we'll do a proper transalpine tramp. Up the Fox Glacier, across the Franz Joseph névé, over the Graham Saddle to Mount Cook village. It's eight or nine days. Sometimes ten if the weather's grungy. Mind you, you've got to be fit.'

'How fit?'

'The usual. Jog five kilometres without stopping, humping a

fifteen-kilogram pack for an eight-hour day over rough terrain.'
'I expect I could do that,' she said.
'Well, go into training,' said Tim, 'and make sure. If Mum and
Dad can spare us as long as that. Otherwise we could just go up
to Glencoe for a couple of days. You meet a lot of outdoor types
up there. A real kiwi holiday, that would be. Or we could do the
MacKenzie High Country Walk. Three days of easy walking; not
much to that. Five or six hours a day, with only personal gear to
hump. Or we could do the Arthuis Pass Scramble. You're sure-
footed enough for that by now, I guess.'

On the way back he said, 'You've finally learnt not to whinge,
Annie. I'm really proud of you.'

14

Shall we get back to Carmen's wonderful day at Newmarket? Sun shone, flags waved, crowds thronged, horses paraded, sweated, rolled their eyes and tossed their manes; punters thrilled to victory or were cast down by defeat: millions of pounds changed hands: cheques bounced, bookies yelled, villains slunk, men drank themselves silly in the bar, and women, though there were fewer of them, drank themselves even sillier, and no doubt a lot of sex went on behind bushes or underneath the grandstands; a day at the races is like that – as smooth, sexy and brilliant as the satin of the jockeys' colours. Too drastic for some tastes; excess and risk in the air, and underneath it all the heady suspicion of corruption. Who's paying whom to pull this horse, dope that one? People whisper in each other's ears; talk behind their hands; and small, hunted, thin-faced, weathered, elderly men – stable lads that is, thus dismissively referred to, those with actual working contact with the horses – dodge or doff their caps to everyone in sight. (Servility's bred into them. They are offended by pay rises, so their masters aver. But they would, wouldn't they?) Not poison in the golden goblet of the Borgias any more: just a little nasty something in the bran mash, as friend betrays friend, wife stabs husband, for the sake of the smooth-skinned beasts with the eyelashes and unsafe-looking legs, creatures who can't even speak, can't ever answer back. A horse-owning sheik, they say, has just built a palace for his steed a couple of miles outside Newmarket. The horse lives in marble rooms carpeted with the finest silk rugs: there are gold taps on his bath; he has full air conditioning. He lives better than any human around. But he doesn't have his *freedom*, does he, folks? That's meant to add up to something. He can't leave his palace without help any more than I can leave my wheelchair. And he can't even complain about it the way I can; all he can do is roll his large reproachful eyes.

Down Newmarket way, the fact that the Emperor Caligula declared his horse his successor makes perfect sense to everyone.

An outing to the races has become a favourite PR exercise for many a contemporary firm which wishes to give its client a memorable treat, and stengthen the bonds of trust and gratitude which from time immemorial, etc. have linked vendor to emptor. No doubt the Emperor Nero took the captains of his slave ships to his box at the Arena to watch the gladiators die, and next week beat down their asking price. No doubt the wily Emperor Diocletian, organising his triumph through Rome on the twenty-fifth anniversary of his reign, invited along the suppliers of Roman Purple, with which he was soon to subvert the Senate. (Someone's dropped off twelve copies of Gibbon's *Decline and Fall of the Roman Empire* at the Centre. The print is tiny but the contents are absorbing, which is just as well. I have nothing else to do but read. No one takes me to Newmarket for the day. I have to imagine what's going on: but perhaps it makes a better day out because it's all in the head – who's to say? I'm not.)

The marquee which was Peckhams' for the day took its place in an encampment of others just like it – white canvas elegantly lined with enough tucked and pleated filmy fabric to put one in mind of the princely tents of the Bedouin. There were little gold tables and chairs, and a big TV perched up high to show the races in better detail and at greater length than the human eye could manage – for what do horses do as you press up against the rail but just thunder past; though the approaching and increasing roar of the crowd, reaching its praxis just where you stand, and then passing and fading thereafter, is no doubt excitement enough for some. A temporary tote had been set up in the corner, a booth staffed by two dutifully polite but bored women who had seen better days and better jobs, and a bar where champagne was served free for the first hour. After that you paid for yourself. How everyone drank!

Carmen's taxi driver lost his way several times, so she arrived too late for the free drink, but was not short of offers of champagne from Peckhams' management over lunch. Henrietta Cotton was courteous enough to say how pleased she was that Carmen had

turned up: how bad she'd felt when Carmen had been left behind. 'It's usually me,' she remarked, 'it happens to.'
Shanty just said, 'Glad you could make it, Carmen. Quite an initiative test, what?'

Poppy managed to keep an eye on Ronnie, dragging him away should he drift too near Carmen, while also, on and off, gazing into Shanty Cotton's eyes. Shanty, who was becoming dangerously red in the face, kept chucking her under the chin and saying to Ronnie, 'Wonderful taste you've got, Ronnie,' or 'I'd keep an eye on this one if I were you, Ronnie,' or 'How about coming aboard the Peckhams' ship, Poppy?' while she dimpled and clung. Carmen wondered how anyone could take Poppy seriously, but it seemed men did. While Carmen wore her cartwheel hat and Zandra Rhodes dress she could move only slowly and with dignity. Poppy's pillbox hat was no trouble to Poppy at all. Henrietta sat in a corner under her straw brim and looked sad, but Shanty took no notice.

Driver was not there, but his emissaries were. None other than Prince Leopold stumbled into her as she clung to the rail, cheering, wondering quite what was going on, or which horse was which. He tipped her hat right off, falling to his knees before her the quicker to pick it up, his spaniel eyes adoring, slightly bloodshot, as the eyes of spaniels often are. Royalty on its knees before little Carmen Wedmore of Fenedge, East Anglia!

'A thousand pardons,' begged Prince Leopold, from his knees. 'Kick me, whip me, beat me for my error. I deserve it. I shan't complain. The charm, the grace of your dress: the beauty of your legs!' Carmen moved them closer together: he was staring up them. 'The elegance! Have you escaped perhaps from some royal party somewhere? It is where you rightly belong. Let me introduce myself. Prince Leopold of Croatia, nephew of the rightful monarch, soon to regain his throne. I am the only heir. Open your heart to me and the whole world will open up to you!'

Carmen took her hat and turned her back on him. When she looked over her shoulder he was gone. She went into the Ladies in order to leave her hat there, but someone ran after her with it, so she put it back on and watched a race or so, then returned to the marquee, where all Peckhams and its associates were singing the Whipperpool Song, still moaning on out of a dreadful Sinatra-ridden past:

> 'We're three little lambs who have lost our way,
> Baa-baa-baa –
> Gentlemen songsters out on a spree,
> Doomed from here to eternity –'

'God have mercy on such as we,' said Carmen to Henrietta, who was joining in the singing, in a pitiful attempt not to be a wet blanket. Everyone who was anyone in the Poultry World sang and swayed that day, and swayed and sang, carried away by emotion, regret for time wasted and opportunities lost, and the need to drink to forget. A terrible, wistful, feathery melancholy seized them all.

Someone bumped Carmen's elbow; none other than Rollo Hopper the film star: staring and smiling out of whisky fumes and cigar smoke, and the smell of fried onions from the catering van just outside the marquee: 'Upper Crust Catering'.
'Well, whaddya know,' said Rollo Hopper, 'the girl the whole world's looking for, a star for the remake of *Touch of Evil*. Come with me to Hollywood and perhaps it will be you!'
'And perhaps if I do I'll get every social disease under the sun,' she said, which could hardly be more impolite, and walked away, but he grabbed her arm, with considerable force for a phantom – for such she assumed him to be.
'Leave me alone,' she said.
But he didn't leave her alone. He had his hands down the front of her Zandra Rhodes dress: but not for long, because none other than Ronnie seized him and dragged him away, while Poppy said, 'Don't be so tactless, Ronnie. Can't you see she's enjoying it.'
'God, these Europeans,' said Rollo Hopper, 'so primitive!' and he hit Ronnie backwards into a trestle table carrying petits fours and individual strawberry mousses: Ronnie rallied and punched Rollo, but Rollo got Ronnie's head somehow tucked under his arm and hit him in the eye and then shoved poor stunned Ronnie right into the bar table, so that glasses and bottles broke and women

screamed and the bartender swore and the girl at the tote shut up shop in a hurry, though there were two races yet to go.

'Sorry, darling,' said Rollo Hopper to Carmen, 'no big time on the screen for you. You blew that one!' and loped off, flexing his muscles. Carmen helped Ronnie to his feet but Poppy intervened and led him away to the washroom, saying, 'Darling, you're not very *strong*, are you!', but not before Ronnie had managed to say to Carmen, 'Look, give me a call at my office some time –'

The party broke up. Carmen's décolletage was considered by all to be the cause of the trouble, and perhaps indeed it was. The bodice was ripped in a way that she could not understand, for Rollo Hopper had really hardly got a hold on it. The management limousines departed without her, as they had arrived. She was left standing in the littered desolation, like Ruth amongst the alien corn – alone except for the barman, and the barman when he turned to face her had Driver's eyes and spoke with Driver's voice.

'Come on,' said Driver, 'I don't believe this. Give me a reason. I've offered you two men currently on Vogue's Most Eligible Bachelor list. The third, the diplomat, I did not pursue because I could understand your reluctance: women are vain and whimsical so I can alter their looks at the drop of a hat, but men have their dignity.'

'Oh yeah?' enquired Carmen, as nastily as her lips would allow.

'Well,' said Driver, moderating his initial claim, 'let us say that for various reasons many men tend to like themselves the way they are. But I've tidied up the Prince and the Star no end, so what can be your objection?'

'They're foreign,' said Carmen, for what would Driver understand about love, or why some men have a knack for it, and others don't, and why so many women love men who can do them no good at all? Driver is only ever sympathetic to self-interest. But Carmen had made a mistake: she should not have been flippant.

'Sir Bernard is local,' he said, 'home-grown and local and now you've used up all your excuses.'

He snarled and flashed a little and lightning jumped around the metal support poles of the marquee. Outside the crowds were drifting off home: coaches were being manoeuvred out of parking lots; horses were being shuffled up the ramps of horseboxes, the great majority in disgrace: owners slipped off with the wives of other owners for a quick G&T before the Members' Bar closed. Tomorrow's favourites were changing as the day's results were collated. Some jockeys were on form: some stables performing well: some trainers coming up trumps, others not. Making money is never easy, even if gambling's how you do it.

'Cover yourself up,' said Driver. 'You're a disgrace to your sex.' Carmen made a modesty bodice of discarded betting slips, using the safety pins which attached a floral bouquet to the canvas fabric of the marquee, and covered herself up as best she could. She allowed Driver to take her home. What else could she do? She had to get back somehow. And Driver didn't even have to say, you'll be sorry for this, because she knew she would be. She treasured in her heart what Ronnie had said – 'Give me a call at my office some time' – and hoped that would act as her talisman. In the hour of her most need she could call him up.

Along with *Decline and Fall*, our unknown benefactor had dumped a cardboard box of paperbacks, all romantic fiction, outside the Centre. They stayed outside all night and no one even stole them, as our occupational therapist, a stern feminist, had hoped they would. It rained hard during the night and the volumes, shoddy enough to begin with, were sodden by the time Alison carried them in. It was difficult to separate the pages and so make any consecutive sense of what was written, and some had simply fallen out, and were mixed up with a collection of the torn-out protective tabs of sanitary towels, for some reason also in the box. Well, you have to be grateful for what you get. The tabs are plastic, and hard to dispose of, I know. You can't burn them and it seems unethical to flush them down the loo. I felt, as I sorted through the pages, matching heroine to hero, title to plot, that I was picking over the debris of the world. But most of us live amongst the debris anyway. And what is romance but a tragedy that ends on Saturday night instead of going on to Sunday morning? What's the matter with that? If I lived in a romantic novel some young doctor would come along and first marry me, then cure me: the latter being consequent upon the former. In real life, it would happen the other way round, if at all.

15

I watched Carmen return from Newmarket in the BMW. Driver didn't open the door for her. She seemed angry. She slammed the car door. Driver drove off briskly. Then Carmen's key wouldn't turn in her front door. She stood there for a second or so, apparently puzzled and undecided.

Then the door was opened from inside, and there stood Paul, her original flatmate; his great boots were already shredding her delicate rugs; her window was broken; the front door was peeling and a milk bottle had been broken on the step.
'What are you doing here?' she asked in alarm.
'I live here,' he said.
'You don't,' she said.
'I'm bigger than you,' he said.
'I'll call the police,' said Carmen, but Paul said, 'I'm a friend of your brother and he's asked me to stay, and it's his house as much as yours.'
She had to concede that this was true. It was their parents' house. She had even taken and spent the balance between her mother's cheque and the cost of the house, some three thousand irreplaceable pounds. Carmen went through to her quaint little living room, which still had its shop windows, large and curved, and found it full of cigarette smoke and the smell of beer and Stephen reading *The Sun* with his boots on the white lace cloth she'd thrown over the sofa.
'Hi,' sis,' said Stephen. 'Well, if you've got it, flaunt it!' for her betting-slip modesty vest was dropping. She hitched it up. And there her brother was, already a fixture: he'd been thrown out of college for organising a riot on a local housing estate – not even a political riot but the kind which is a cover-up for a mass exercise in looting. He said he was sick of college anyway; he had lost the

knack of maths; they said it happened sometimes. So he'd come home to think about his future. Driver works fast when he has to: ask anyone.

In Landsfield Crescent everything appeared to be tranquil. Mavis dozed by the TV; Alan fidgeted with a Hornby engine – he had resigned from the ambulance service as Mavis's practice became busier and he now used the garage for his new absorbing hobby, model trains. Angela for once had no visitors and in Laura's house the children were sound asleep, Kubrick goggled drowsily in his tank, and Laura made her father and her husband cups of coffee. She was nothing if not domestic.

Kim said, 'How about me going to the off-licence for a bottle of wine?' to which Woodie replied, 'Not for me, thanks. Once you get into that habit you end up an alcoholic,' and Kim said, 'How about you, Laura?' and she said, 'I'm far too pregnant to drink,' to which Kim replied, 'I feel like putting you two in an old folks' home. I'd go over to see Angela, but I wouldn't want to queer your pitch, Woodie.'

'Angela!' Woodie said, startled, but whether he was startled because Angela's name came out of the blue, or because he didn't want Kim to visit her, it would be hard to say.

'I'll go to the pub instead,' said Kim, and Laura had the same feeling in the pit of her stomach she'd had the day Kim had asked her to feed Kubrick because he, Kim, was leaving home, 'though frankly I think if I went over to Angela I'd be doing everyone a favour.'

And Kim left the house, slamming the door so that Sara woke up with a fright. Laura just sat and stared at Woodie, but Woodie avoided her gaze and went upstairs to put Sara back to sleep, taking a very long time about it. The sensation in the pit of Laura's stomach turned to a pain. The baby was one day overdue.

'I was going to tell you about Angela,' said Woodie, 'but I thought you might take it wrong. Sometimes when you're out gadding about she comes over and keeps me company. She wants me to fit out her van – you know, shelves, sinks and so on. She's going to start a mobile sandwich business. Take it round the development sites. She doesn't just sit about, that one.'

Laura, from experience, felt as if her waters were about to break and went to the bathroom. They did. She mopped everything up and went back to Woodie. 'And Kim came in one day,' Woodie continued his confession, 'while we had our heads together over a drawing and came to the wrong conclusion. It's nothing,' he said. 'There's nothing to it. Your father's a mean old bugger and if he isn't causing trouble he isn't happy. I've got you, Laura, why should I want anyone else?'

She wished he hadn't said that: the answer seemed so obvious. What was she but a baby machine? Who'd want that? Not even Woodie. She hadn't even considered running a mobile sandwich bar; it had never entered her head. Things like that just didn't.

'I think I'd better get to hospital,' she said. 'I have a feeling this is going to be very quick. But Kim's out, so there's no one to baby-sit. I'd better go by taxi.'

Woodie said he'd get Angela to baby-sit, but Laura wept and said no thank you, so Woodie was annoyed with Laura, and in the end Mavis was called in. All the phones in the neighbourhood were out of order (the embryo bypass at the back of Landsfield Crescent wreaked havoc with all mains systems) so they couldn't call an ambulance and Alan insisted on taking Laura and Woodie to the hospital, and going too, not just lending the car, in case she needed delivering on the way. Mavis suffered some kind of frisson while this was going on and when she spoke it was with Count Capinski's voice.

'Dear young lady,' said Mavis/Count – though, God knows, she struggled hard enough to keep him in, clamping her lips shut, but he forced them open – 'with pain and sorrow shalt thou bring forth.' Over and over again he said it, so it was decided Woodie should stay home after all, to look after Mavis, and Laura went to hospital with Alan, who was in a rage about the reappearance of Count Capinski. As Alan rounded the corner of Landsfield Crescent and took, much too fast, the bumpy section where the earth movers had inadvertently taken up a stretch of the Winterton–Fenedge road, and replaced it (after repeated requests) in a cursory manner, Laura saw Angela running towards Woodie and her home and children, and Kim nowhere in sight. It could all hardly have been worse. What was more, Count Capinski, or Mavis, was correct in his/her prophecy.

Meanwhile, in the Land of the Long White Cloud, the serpents which had been uncoiling, ready to strike, hissed and struck and bit. Suspicion and paranoia welled up in Annie: she gave voice to them and in so doing spoiled everything. It may just have been that Annie was so hungry: she had tried on the wedding dress and although Mrs McLean assured her that it fitted beautifully, and was even a little loose on her, Annie could feel it clinging so around her ribs she could hardly breathe in it. The white-to-cream heavy silk fabric had the agreeable patina of age: it spread gracefully over wire hoops; the neck was scooped so low that she couldn't possibly wear a bra: another reason not to eat. 'A McLean bride,' said Mrs McLean, admiring her. 'You've turned into a real beauty since you arrived. That's our Tim, I expect, and some good fresh air and exercise. Don't get too thin, though. Enough's enough.'

But Annie looked in the mirror at a skin hopelessly reddened and toughened by sun and wind and at the muscles she hated to see in her arms and thought well, if that's what the McLeans see as beauty, I certainly don't.

At night Tim would feel her ribs and say Annie, you're getting so sharp I could cut myself, and she'd feel cunning and think he was in the plot to keep her fat, weatherbeaten and ugly.

Carmen and Laura weren't coming to the wedding because they couldn't afford it, and Tim wouldn't pay for their tickets. Yet he could buy a new Landrover, couldn't he, and five hundred more sheep, which turned out to have some kind of blight so the wedding was postponed; luckily her parents had open tickets, the refundable kind. What was more, Tim was now talking of setting up a bunje jumping centre at Arthur's Pass, for when the trekkers, trackers and hikers had a spare moment, and she wondered what was going on: how did he have so much money for everything except her friends' air fare?

It was unfortunate (I am the Lord of Luck, says Driver) that one tea time a batch of scones Annie had whipped up out of a cloud of flour, a flaking of butter, a dash of icy cold water and a drift of salt, etc. had gone into an oven, the fire of which a changing of the wind's direction and the backdraft attendant upon it had simply blown out, so that the oven was cool. By the time the scones were baked they were hard. Annie nearly junked them but decided Mrs McLean so hated waste she had better serve them after all.

'What's this, Annie?' asked Tim, 'a scone or a rock cake?'

'She'll learn,' said Mrs McLean.

'She'd better,' said Tim, and Jock McLean just pushed his to the side of the plate and took one of his wife's jam tarts instead.

'Who's "she"?' enquired Annie. 'The cat's mother or the unpaid help?'

'Don't get your knickers in a twist,' said Tim into the startled silence.

'You might well talk about my knickers,' said Annie, 'since you're in them often enough, and for free.'

They stared at her for a little.

'Now don't take on,' said Mrs McLean, 'just because you made a duff batch of scones. You worked the gluten too much.'

'I did not so,' said Annie, 'work the gluten too much. The southwester started and blew out the oven. Fancy living in a place where the way the wind blows can bugger up an afternoon! At least in the hotel I got paid, and I didn't know what my future was. Now I do. Work and more work, and hanging upside down by your feet if you've got a moment to spare.'

'She's talking about bunje jumping,' said Tim. 'She told me she liked it, but I don't think she did.'

'I am not "she",' said Annie. 'I am your fiancée. At least that's what you tell me, but I think that's just a ruse to keep me here as a servant. I think that's what happened to Wendy. She rumbled you lot. You overworked her to the brink of death, but she got out from under just in time. You talk about this wedding, but it never seems to happen, does it? And you can always get a refund on my parents' tickets if I do a Wendy and scarper. And then you'll be off back to the old country, Tim, to chat up some other girl you find laying a carpet or chopping down a tree, and tell her all about the Land of the Long White Cloud, and she'll fall for it.'

'My,' said Jock McLean, 'that was a long speech.'

'And that's about the longest *you*'ve ever made,' said Annie.

Tim said, 'Once a pommie always a pommie.'

Annie said, 'What does that mean?'

Tim said, 'Whingeing.'

Mrs McLean said, 'You two should keep your tiffs to the bedroom, not upset everyone.'

Jock McLean said, 'I've had enough of this,' and left the room.

Annie threw the scones, or rock cakes, across the room. They bounced. A lamb looked at her curiously and she shrieked.

'You're insane,' said Tim.

Annie said, 'There isn't a girl in this country who'd put up with what I have to. Cheap labour, that's all your fiancées are. I want my wages to date and my ticket home and that's it.'

Tim said, 'Very well then,' and walked out of the room.

Mrs McLean said, 'Now you've upset him too. And me. You have terrible thoughts and I'm glad I don't have to put up with the inside of your head. My son loves you very much, I happen to know, and you've been like a daughter to me, but I think you have insulted us enough and if you go to Jock's office he will write you out a cheque for whatever amount you think is fair.'

'I'm so tired,' said Annie and began to cry but Mrs McLean just shook her head and left the room as well. Really, it could not have been worse.

16

Carmen was crying as well, over her life and times, but at least she had Laura to cry on. Her life was over, Carmen said. All her savings had gone. Her father had finally lost everything in Monte Carlo, and she's had a phone call from Raelene asking for the air fare back home; she'd been demoted at work; she was having to share with Stephen and Paul and the house was a tip, but all this was nothing compared to what had happened between her and Ronnie Cartwright. She'd called him at the office, as he'd suggested, her heart in her mouth, and he'd asked her out to dinner: Poppy was away, Ronnie said, and he got so lonely without her.

Carmen told Laura this while Laura tried to feed Hannah. Laura had such a hard time in labour that the baby had been born, apparently, with a dislocated hip, which had eventually made its presence felt, and was now splinted. Hannah was going to be just fine, but in the meantime there was quite a problem suckling her because of her plaster cast. Laura thought she might have to bottle-feed her instead of breast-feeding and this was really all that occupied her, so she was not fully concentrating on Carmen's problems. Also her husband was indeed outfitting Angela's van, so she supposed his story to be true, but she didn't like the way Woodie kept going over to Angela's to talk about the height of the units, or the depth of the sink, and to help her with the kind of things women on their own – well, some – like to have a man to do. See to the carburettor, a broken window, extract coins from the pump of the washing machine. Not that there could be much to worry about, since Kim now spent whole nights in Angela's house, but it was a bit much to have both father and husband entranced by someone as simple, easy, hopeless, blonde and good-natured as Angela. For all she knew, Kim might pick up some dreadful social disease and pass it on to the children.

But Carmen was not deflected in her tale by Laura's family pre-occupations. To the unmarried and childless, the problems of those with spouse or issue can seem quite peculiar. Carmen, Carmen told Laura, was tired of being a virgin. What was the state, anyway, but just one long non-event? Driver was wrong, she said. There was nothing magic about the virgin state. Virgins had been so popular in Victorian days, and earlier, not because of the man's desire to deflower, despoil and get there first, but simply because if a girl was a virgin he wouldn't pick up a nasty disease. For a time, after the advent of antibiotics, virgins had gone out of favour, and experience and general sexual trickiness were sought after, but Carmen supposed now with AIDS, and no cure, virgins would soon be all the rage again, but she couldn't wait about for that. (She was quoting me, as it happens, from a book written by a man, *The Social Disease in History*. She'd been over chatting to me about this and that.) Laura said men liked virgins because they were all hope, innocence and trust, it was nothing to do with disease, wasn't that why Sir Bernard wanted Carmen? Had Carmen heard lately from Sir Bernard? And Carmen said no, she hadn't heard from Sir Bernard, she didn't want to see Sir Bernard, why should she? And Laura told her why, quoting Count Capinski, who was saying through Mavis's mouth that everyone's luck was bad because Carmen was unnatu-ral, and wouldn't sleep with Sir Bernard. Laura (a) was beginning to believe that this might be true and (b) didn't believe for one minute Carmen was a virgin anyway, so why was she making such a fuss? The baby was now sucking on an empty left breast and grizzling. Laura pulled a back muscle moving her to the other side. Rachel, Caroline and Sara all had terrible head colds, and were in bad moods because they couldn't suck their thumbs and breathe at the same time. All Laura's children had little thin pretty faces and big eyes and very fair hair; all sucked their thumbs, no matter how Laura smeared them with anchovy sauce; and all were charming; but to Carmen they looked like repetitions of a single theme – and she couldn't see why Laura and Woodie kept doing it. But then Carmen was in as distressed and distracted a mood as Laura. She had tried to tempt Ronnie into bed and it

had gone wrong, and now her self-esteem was bruised. When
Laura had calmed down a little Carmen told her how her date
with Ronnie had been.

Ronnie had booked a table at the Trocadero, which was hopeful.
At least he saw it as a special event. She'd worn the rather plain
blouse and skirt she'd bought in the Kings Lynn boutique, since
she didn't want to frighten him off. She was in moderate figure
(she measured herself before she left). 38-25-40 starting from the
ground up, too robust for her taste, but tolerable. She hadn't even
developed boils, a spot, or acne. Over melon (for her: these days
she obviously had to diet) and soup (tomato, for him) he'd spoken
about Poppy, and his love for her.
'She needs someone like me,' he said. 'Someone kind, patient,
gentle, understanding. She's had a hard life, no one really understands. A victim of child abuse. She was seduced by her English
teacher at school. She has psychosexual problems.'
'Poor Poppy,' said Carmen. Ronnie sighed. His lips were
cherubic. His hands were clean, young and smooth. He drank
spritzers – half white wine, half sparkling water.

Over salmon (hers: without hollandaise) and steak au poivre (his:
with garlic butter) he told her that Poppy had abandonment problems, so he hadn't told her he was taking Carmen out to dinner.
But Ronnie felt he ought to make amends for so embarrassing
Carmen at the Newmarket outing: he hoped he hadn't spoiled
anything promising. Carmen assured him there was nothing to
spoil. He said he was glad. Things were beginning to look up,
thought Carmen. Ronnie said that Poppy was staying with her
mother.
'How strange,' said Carmen. 'I thought she was away at a confer-
ence with Shanty Cotton.' Poppy had been taken on by Peckhams
as a trainee manager.
'Oh no,' said Ronnie. 'I'm sure you've got that wrong. Poppy has
no time for older men.' Carmen did not press the matter. Over
black coffee (hers) and deep-filled apple pie and cream (his) he
said, 'You don't mind me talking to you about Poppy, I hope? I
feel you're a sister to me – in a way we have more in common,
you and me, than Poppy and I do – but that's not the way love
works, is it?'

'I suppose not,' she said, cast down, but he was looking into her eyes while he said it, and his eyes were liquid and compelling. Once upon a time Driver had nipped her on the neck, to mark her, or so she had suspected at the time. And it was true that the little wound had never properly healed, so she had become quite accustomed to wearing a plaster on it, sometimes hopefully smearing it with antibiotic ointment from Mr Bliss (Dr Grafton now refusing to prescribe antibiotics altogether), but then the plaster would never stick. Now, as Ronnie looked into her eyes, the wound began to hurt quite badly.

'Is there something wrong?' asked Ronnie.

She opened a couple of top buttons on her blouse to show him the little red patch. His hand gently opened her collar wider.

'How white your skin is,' said Ronnie.

She had assumed, almost hoped, his interest would be medical, but as his hand stroked her neck she could tell that it was sexual. Her wound really was hurting and people were looking. She felt fidgety.

'I think I'll have to go home,' Carmen said. 'It won't let me sit still,' and that was misconstrued too.

'I'll come with you,' said Ronnie, and he had risen and paid the bill and was going home with her, hands and bodies touching whenever possible, without even finishing his apple pie, before she'd really thought about what she was doing. She knew she hadn't wanted it to happen like this: his arm possessively and ungently tucking round hers, hurrying her to bed. She'd wanted him to woo her, persuade her, and then she could gracefully and romantically succumb with a great deal of conversation, and then he would be hers for ever.

'Carmen,' he said in the car, 'I always thought you'd be a great lay,' but again that wasn't what she wanted to hear at all. She wanted true love *and* sex: that was what she was hoping for, after all, had been waiting for all this time.

'No, you haven't,' said Laura, 'because that equals marriage and marriage equals babies, and you don't like babies,' which hurt such parts of Carmen left unhurt for, besides it being untrue, hadn't she helped Laura with her babies since the first whiff of ozone?

But at least Carmen had, finally, got Ronnie Cartwright home, although not in the mood she had anticipated. Stephen's girlfriend Allie was there in Stephen's room, to make things worse – not in the bed; they didn't *have* a bed, just rolling about noisily on the floor with the door open – and the house Carmen had been keeping sweet, clean and inviting for just such an occasion, always with Ronnie in mind, now looked like an airport's whorehouse and smelt of stale beer, cigarettes and sex. Ronnie followed her straight into her bedroom and was just beginning to take off her blouse, tearing at buttons, and she was beginning to help him, and thinking what price Poppy now, this is fine whichever what way, when the telephone by the bed rang and it was of course Poppy, wanting to speak to Ronnie. Poppy had traced her lover through the Trocadero and Directory Enquiries.

'Oh my God, Poppy,' said Ronnie. 'Are you okay? Poor darling . . . yes, I was talking business with Carmen; then she developed this allergy: I had to get her home; yes, of course I'm coming at once: of course I'll meet the train. Poor darling!'

And that had been that. Poppy had had a row with her parents, or so she said, and was on her way home. Ronnie arranged his clothing and left, and she knew from the way he hurried, as she watched from her grimy window, that he was glad to have escaped: whatever madness it was had deserted him: from now on it was all embarrassment.

Now Carmen wept into Laura's shoulder, which Laura could have done without, and spoke words Laura never thought to hear from Carmen's mouth.

'I can't think; I can't work; my life's going to pieces, and all I can do is wait for the phone to ring in case it's him.'

'Why don't you ring him?' asked Laura, irritated.

Woodie came in from the workshop in the garden where he was making up Angela's sandwich counter. The sound of the drill had been bugging Laura all morning.

'I don't want Ronnie to think I'm chasing him.'

'You are,' said Laura shortly. 'Why don't you just give up. He's a creep anyway. Spritzers! Great lays! Whoever says great lays?'

Carmen wept.

'You don't understand him. Ronnie doesn't love Poppy; he loves me in his heart, I know he does. He can have Poppy too, I'll put

up with that, so long as I'm somewhere in his life. Otherwise I'd
rather be dead. Truly, I'd rather die than live without Ronnie.'
'I can't stand this,' said Woodie. 'She's hysterical,' and he slapped
Carmen, who shuddered and came to her senses, or at any rate
had the grace to look startled and confused, vulnerable and large-
eyed as a horse in its maiden race at Newmarket.
'What was I saying?' she asked. 'I can't remember.'
'Love, love, love, you were saying,' said Laura. 'Die, die, die.
You've gone insane. You're bewitched. What's happening round
here?'
At this point the phone rang. Woodie answered it.
'It's your friend Annie,' said Woodie. 'She's at Gatwick and she's
crying and wants someone to pick her up. Who does she think is
going to pay for the petrol?'
'Carmen,' said Laura to her friend, 'you have to sleep with Sir
Bernard Bellamy, because this is getting too much. You are
upsetting the laws of man and nature.'
'No,' said Carmen, 'I won't.'

Meanwhile, Sir Bernard Bellamy's earth movers, their work on
the bypass done, had moved coastward and started filling in the
gravel pits and levelling the sand hills created over aeons by the
slow surges of the Wash. Bellamy Scientific Enterprises had come
up with evidence that as the sea levels rose there could be no
avoiding the harsh fact that land levels had to be raised all
along the north and eastern coasts of the Wash to prevent
inland flooding. Too bad if this disturbed the attractive habitats
that the birds so enjoyed – the salt marshes, tidal reed beds,
brackish and fresh marshes, the willow copses and plantations,
the sandbanks, the shingle pits, the dunes – and would alas
mean the end of the avocet colonies and suchlike ornithological
delights so that the boom of the bittern would never again be
heard on a wild March day: too bad! But at least people could
sleep safe in their beds at night, and not wake to find chairs
floating round their living rooms, and the tide sweeping in
under the door. Since change was, inevitably, in its way, the
Bellamy Advisory Council reasoned that to establish a chain of
yachting marinas – cleverly adapted to cope with high tides and
flooding – would make the whole enterprise self-funding and save
the Government millions. Bellamy Quarries (Mendip branch)

were opening up a new hillside in the south-west and there was now a plentiful and cheap supply of aggregate which was already being railed in for the Fenedge bypass – the ground in these parts was sandy to a great depth, which made the construction of feeder roads comparatively simple (if dusty). It should therefore also be possible to create, as part of the overall coastal development concept, and at minimum cost, a badly needed new airport to serve the needs of the North-East Midlands. While Sir Bernard held conversations at ministerial level about these changes to the landscape, his earth movers just got on with the immediate job of levelling gravel pits and sand dunes. Sir Bernard did not believe in wasting time.

'Forgive the cliché,' he'd say, tapping his broad, strong fingers on his solid oak desk, 'but time is money. Saves it for the community: makes it for the individual. And in these matters of public concern, as the Bellamy Eastern Scheme most certainly is, community and individual interests are as one!' And the bulldozers rolled in, nudging their solid heads into mountains, tossing them high, while everyone tried to figure out the significance of what he said. Sir Bernard was so genial, so charismatic, so engaging, it was hard even for civil servants, least of all ministers, to find fault with him. His eyes seemed to get bluer, not paler, every year: now they were almost as blue as Driver's.

He was sometimes seen for a time with a girl on his arm, not of the bimbo kind but someone well bred, highly educated, often with some notable artistic talent, who could be taken anywhere and fit in, be it to Chequers, the opera or a nightclub, but the relationship never lasted long. Afterwards the one discarded would speak of Sir Bernard fondly and sadly, and with admiration, letting the press know only 'It just didn't work out. I wish him every happiness.' The press liked to speculate as to who would finally win the heart of Prince Bernard (for so they dubbed him), the man who had everything, yet nothing, because he didn't have true love. How lyrical and sentimental the yellow press waxed: this great man, who was saving the whole Eastern Seaboard from destruction while the Government twiddled its thumbs, their unhappy, romantic hero! But that's by the by.

17

In the course of levelling the sand dunes, a certain Jed Foster, a Bellamy skimmer driver (whose sister Sunny was a paraplegic and shared, perforce, my interest in ornithology) perceived a number of what he assumed to be human bones in his sandy load – it is hard to mistake children's skulls. Contrary to custom and practice, he stopped his engine and got out of his cab to take a better look. He had uncovered, it transpired, what could only be an ancient graveyard – lidless lead coffins, skeletons, artefacts, golden crosses, swords wherever he looked. The bodies were lying east–west, which any earth-mover operator knows means the remains are Christian, not pagan (these are usually laid north–south). There were female bodies too – you could tell they'd once been women because strands of long hair still lay around their skulls, and little shiny stones lay in the form of necklaces beside them, the stones being immortal, only the strings that once had linked them succumbing to time. Four of these female bodies, as Jed observed and shuddered, lay eye socket down – which meant they had been executed, for adultery, or witchcraft, or nagging, or whatever female sin at the time seemed unpardonable. The souls of those buried face down are meant never to rise to their Maker.

Jed Foster was working on his own. The western sun was sinking; the terns and the skuas fought it out in the skies above: a single bittern flew over, croaking: an orangey glow struck over the newly turned land and rendered it beautiful. Jed Foster saw gold gleaming, and silver too. As well as bones he now saw shards of pottery: he saw a buckle and a big-bellied figurine, a fragment of leather: a shoe. He was a good man; he resisted the temptation to loot, he picked up nothing. He backed the skimmer off the site, took up sand from elsewhere and, with his great shovel slowly moving, gently dusted the whole area over until it was thinly and decently hidden. Then he went home, washed, changed, and got to a phone box. He thought it unwise to contact his foreman. He would go straight to the top. First he rang Bellamy House and was put through to Mrs Haverill, who said that no one was able to speak to Sir Bernard, who did Jed Foster think he was: Sir Bernard was not in residence anyway: he was very seldom at Bellamy House: why ever did Jed Foster think he would be? Jed persisted and Mrs Haverill grudgingly gave him a London number to call in the morning, saying she doubted anything Jed Foster had to say would be of the slightest interest, let alone advantage, to Sir Bernard. When Jed Foster got home, and had stopped smarting from his conversation with Mrs Haverill, he told his wife what he had discovered. He knew it was something amazing. He had felt awed, he said. Mrs Foster told Miss Foster, my sister in disability.

As the campaign to Save Our Past got going, at first under the leadership of Mrs Baker and Mr Bliss, then under those more professionally experienced, all this became common knowledge. Sunny Foster was a Heritage enthusiast and believed her duty to the past was greater than her duty to her brother's employers, although her sister-in-law did not agree: 'Don't make a *fuss*,' she begged. 'He'll lose his job!' and told everyone everything. It was thanks to Sunny that the first volunteers from Fenedge went out with broom and brush and pan and carefully hand-skimmed sand and soil from the site of the graveyard and the Bronze Age settlement that it served, and the Roman trading estate nearby, and that thereafter half of Fenedge set up camp with folding chairs and thermoses, to guard the site and keep Sir Bernard's diggers at a distance, while the other half of Fenedge tried to egg the bulldozers on.

'What is this sentimental nonsense?' cried the unemployed and homeless of Fenedge, or those about to be so rendered. 'What we want round here is work and housing and medical care, forget the spotted redshank, forget ancient graveyards and the bones of the dead. What about our living ones, our hips that need replacing?' 'Not an inch of this country is not littered with human bones, ancient remains,' said the realists, the rational, and those with vested interests in the development, 'if you dig down just a little. What's so special about this lot? Cranks and lunatics!' 'We don't know,' sighed the lamenteers, 'it just somehow seems wrong; not necessary to dig just here: these graves are a sign that we shouldn't!' But the high tides of the season were so very high at both new and full moons, as the autumnal flights of the shore waders began, that the Eastern Scheme, as it was now called, was well able to claim necessity rather than choice. Dig we must, and dig right here! So what if the black and white oyster catchers would never again stream sedately by, to be overtaken by the swifter bar-tailed godwit and the grey plover; soon all would be forgotten and the yachts of the rich sail sedately by, also a beautiful sight. And who would care, let's face it, except obsessive and depressive people with Adam's apples who had no idea how to run the world? And what came first, the comfort and entertainment of busy humans, or the preservation of an entirely unnecessary and outmoded wildlife? It wasn't even as if you could eat rare birds: they are hopelessly tough. And what was meant by 'rare'? There were thousands of them, millions. Sometimes you couldn't see the land for feathers –

But all these arguments were to come. In the meantime, Jed Foster's call interrupted a conversation between Driver and Sir Bernard. The latter was in melancholy mood. Envisage it, as I do, closing *Decline and Fall*. I read too fast.

'I have everything a man can want,' Sir Bernard said to Driver, 'save the one thing. And that's the one thing you promised me. Everything else I achieved on my own, without you –' Driver stifled a yawn: he had heard all this before from all kinds of people. Any man with sufficient energy, said Sir Bernard, enough brain and guts can make money. If he has enough money he can walk with kings. If he diets he can lose weight: if he exercises he can become strong. If he studies he can learn a language. If he has power, beautiful women will lie down in front of him. What sensible, energetic man needs you, Driver, in other words, Luck Bringer, whispering in his ear? As a short cut to charisma, perhaps – otherwise, what can it profit a man to lose his soul? These days, surely, a man has his life within his own control.

If Jed Foster had approached his task from the east, not the west, the evening sun would have dazzled him; perhaps he would not have caught the glint of human bones. The relics of the sacred site would have been shovelled up and dispersed amidst somersaulting mountains of sand. Had Sir Bernard not been talking along the lines he was, and so irritating Driver, who is to say that the instant's decision, in which Jed Foster turned his wheel left instead of right, would not have gone the other way?

'Where is true love?' asked Sir Bernard of Driver. He was hanging from wall bars in the gym attached to his private suite at the Ritz: he believed this hanging lengthened his spine: something, certainly, had lately made him taller. Even a man's height is under his control.

'I'm working on it,' said Driver grimly.

'There's someone in this world for everyone,' said Sir Bernard. 'My problem is not in being loved; it's in finding someone worth my loving. It's just a question of finding her. And for this, I grant you, a man needs luck.'

'Thanks a million,' said Driver. His lips were quite thin and bloodless, but Sir Bernard was thinking only of the muscles of his upper arms, the stretch in his spine.

'Whatever happened to the girl back home?' asked Sir Bernard, dropping to the floor, lithe and light, his one hundred and seventy-five seconds up. It seemed that Carmen's rejection of him had been erased from his mind. But this often happens: who needs Mephistopheles to misremember the past? Ask any girl who's just met up with an old flame: or man, ditto.

'The one with the tits?' asked Driver.

'That is not how I think of her,' said Sir Bernard. 'It was her soul I responded to.'

'Well,' said Driver, 'as I say, I've been working on it, but she's not easy.'

'I should hope not,' said Sir Bernard, and then, forgetting to whom he was talking, if he was ever quite sure, because of the changing shape of Driver, sometimes evanescent, sometimes in the head, sometimes real and cold and eternal as rock, 'I'm disappointed in you, Driver. All promises and no delivery. If that was how Bellamys carried on, we certainly wouldn't be top of the tree today. Hurry it up, if you please. I've been patient long enough. Now the Eastern Scheme's underway, it's time to think about romance. I need a life partner – a mother for my children. See to it.'

At which the phone rang and it was Jed Foster reporting to the very top the presence of skeletons and artefacts in the Eastern Scheme and asking for guidance.

Sir Bernard ascertained that the site was well enough concealed for the time being and said he'd be down with his driver the following morning to make a decision.

'A lesser man,' observed Sir Bernard to Driver, 'would have said, "Bury the lot and be done with it," but the world needs its visionaries.'

'You mean there might be more profit in an archaeological theme park than a marina?' asked Driver.

Sir Bernard's eyes brightened. He hadn't thought of that.

'We've got to get out of here,' said Laura. 'It's the pits.'

'Dullsville, Arizona,' said Carmen. 'We've got the small-town blues again.'

'At least it's home,' said Annie, and burst into tears. They were in the Welcome-In, opposite what is now the Otherly Abled Centre: catching up, as they said, with one another.

'He was such a pig when it came to it,' said Annie. 'He was taking advantage of me, that was all. I thought he was one man and he turned out to be another. I feel such a fool.'

'You're sure you're not just being paranoid?' asked Carmen.

'Everyone does housework,' said Laura. 'It's part of the bargain.'

'What bargain?'

'Marriage.'

'I wasn't even married,' wailed Annie. There was no reasoning with her. She took her coffee black and refused fudge cake.

I'd watched Annie's return to Landsfield Crescent. Alan and Mavis had been grudging in their welcome.

'We'd have come to meet you,' said Alan, 'but we had to sell the car. Your mother needed clothes for the wedding. All those smart people. And now there isn't even going to be one. Couldn't you have given us more notice? It was inconsiderate of you, Annie. But then consideration was never your strong point.'

'We can put you up on the sofa, Annie,' said Mavis, 'but I can tell you I've just about had enough of lugging your suitcases around.'

Alan said, 'I hope you won't be unpacking them, Annie. There's no spare cupboard space.'

'What happened to my room?'

'Count Capinski's using it for psychic therapy,' said Mavis.

Alan said, 'Annie, you are our daughter. Nothing can change that. But you have to live your own life. You're a big girl now and able to make your own decisions. Laura's only your age and she's got four children. We gave you a good start, but you can't be in our pockets all the time. I have a lot on my plate at the moment. I am changing gauges.'

Annie had a little rest on the sofa to get the feeling of being back home – she was very tired. No one asked her what had gone wrong, or why. Mavis seemed to relent and brought her a cup of tea and a slice of shop cake on a plate. Annie took the tea black and puked at the sight of the cake.

Count Capinski observed out of Mavis's mouth, 'Your daughter has another self inside her, dear lady, not a very nice one. She is trying to starve it out. She is to be congratulated,' so Mavis made no attempt to encourage Annie to eat, and Alan was preoccupied with his trains, and besides she had let them both down in the eyes of the neighbours: this pale thin cuckoo of a girl who they'd somehow given birth to, sent home in disgrace from far across the world. Who would marry her now?

Now Annie, Carmen and Laura sat in the Welcome-In Café beneath the awful paintings of local artists, and bemoaned their fate; how every path they took led them back home again and how strange this destiny was. (It is of course not so strange a fate at all: most people die in more or less the same place as they were born, while struggling to get out of it.) But Annie's return had come like a shower of rain on the desert of their discontent and how it now leapt into life and bloomed; stretching up to heaven like the beanstalk in Jack's morning garden (if you'll forgive the mixing of metaphor) blocking out enough light to bring Driver right to their door, without any of the usual preamble. There he was, his face pressed against the steamy glass of the Welcome-In Café, his sharp nose flattened, his tongue out, his grimace lecherous, a little trail of saliva beneath his chin, and how they jumped!

I jumped too because I noticed that Driver's BMW was parked outside what was soon to be the Otherly Abled Centre, under my window, and the double yellow lines along the kerb had mysteriously disappeared beneath its wheels. Though I thought that might be Alison's doing – it is her trick to go out at night with a pot of grey paint and a paintbrush the better to facilitate the morning's parking. How the rain pelted down! And today the BMW looked particularly sinister – not at all the kind of vehicle driven by a rich man in a hurry, but the kind that carries you off to hell: water streamed off its bonnet, glistening in the fluorescent glow of the neon lights that were attached in far too great a number for safety to the crumbling plaster ceiling of the Centre's Day Room. The building dated, I suppose, from the seventeenth century, and was badly in need of major refurbishment. Rocky on its pins. Better rocky, of course, than not on them at all.

'It's him,' said Laura in panic. 'It's Driver.'
'We were wishing ourselves away again,' said Annie in terror.
Carmen went to the door and tried to throw it open, but it stuck and quivered, being swollen by the rain, so that the limp bleached gingham of the blue and white café curtains shook down dust and dead flies: the gesture was not nearly so dramatic as she would have wished. She tugged again and it opened and there stood Driver steaming beneath his umbrella. Carmen had shrunk an inch or two, or he had grown.
'Voyeur!' she accused him all the same, courage personified, although she trembled. 'Staring through windows! I'll report you to the police.' She had the sense that as she defied him she lengthened and he shrank. He changed his mind and decided to be nice and not strike her dead; at any rate he smiled and his yellow eyes even faded to a quite reasonable blue.
'That's my girl, Carmen,' he said. 'It's only me, Sir Bernard's chauffeur, not some stranger. And a man can look at pretty girls, can't he, without the world coming to an end?' He strolled in and shook himself like a dog, and the raindrops that spattered all around the room burnt little black holes where they fell, as if they were sparks. Not that Eddie, the fat man with glasses who served the coffee, noticed, or not till a week later when he got round to sweeping up. The Welcome-In Café may not be as bad as I

describe. I can only guess. Others go in and enjoy themselves; not
me: no one's going to take me over there.

'So howdie, Laura,' he said. 'Where are the kids? Got a baby-sitter
again? All this gadding about: it'll come to a bad end. Why have
kids if you're not going to look after them?'
Laura opened her mouth to protest, but Annie nudged her quiet.
'And how are you, Annie?' he said. 'Back from abroad, I hear.
Bit of a comedown, isn't it? Bride sent home on the eve of her
wedding? Everyone's talking.'
Tears of humiliation and resentment sprang to Annie's eyes.
'As to little virgin Carmen,' said Driver, 'for virgin read spinster.
The one who no one wants. The one left on the shelf. The one
with a real problem.'
'My mother said,' observed Carmen primly, 'if you can't say
anything nice don't say anything at all,' at which he snarled and
rumbled a little and then said, 'Your mother never said anything
like that, Carmen. I know your mother well, and if you're like a
daughter to me now you know why,' and while Carmen gaped he
pressed home his advantage, saying, 'Sir Bernard asked me to ask
you, Carmen, if you'd have the goodness to dine with him in the
next week or so.'
'No,' said Carmen.
'Why not?' He stamped his foot, or pawed with his hoof, or was
it just that a very large grey truck rumbled by? In any case the
ground shook.
'I don't like his messenger,' said Carmen. 'Coming in here
steaming –'
'Carmen,' said Laura, 'just a dinner – please!'
And Annie said plaintively, 'We've been so unlucky, Carmen.'
Carmen turned to look quite savagely at Laura, and at Annie.
Driver laughed and said, 'Only a fool has friends. You'll change
your mind, you'll see. I'll be back for you a fortnight today.'
Carmen said, 'I'd rather die,' and someone came in to ask if
Driver could move the BMW because it was blocking the road.
He left the Welcome-In obligingly, as if he were just an ordinary
chauffeur in a rather military-style uniform. He moved his BMW
from outside my window: the truck driver, who had been
manoeuvring to get by, inch by inch, and failed, moved into
reverse gear instead of into first and backed through the window

at which I sat, bending metal, shattering glass. I had just time to get out of my wheelchair and away, before the truck driver, in his panic, engaged the tipping mechanism and delivered an entire load of what turned out to be balsawood blocks into the room. The wood was so light that no one was hurt. That was fortunate, as everyone said, but I felt it was a matter of degree. Far more fortunate for it not to have happened in the first place. What surprised everyone most, however – the handicapped (as we used to call ourselves, as if human beings were engaged in some kind of race) are more accustomed than most to putting up with circumstances suddenly beyond their control – was that as the lorry crashed through I had got out of my wheelchair and run across the room. I couldn't repeat the action, though of course I tried. But it had happened, and been witnessed. Dr Grafton denied its possibility and said it was a group hallucination: in fact my chair had been at the back of the room, away from the window, but then he would say that, wouldn't he? Dr Grafton was convinced that I had earned my disability by having undergone an abortion in my youth. (Well, that is to say, the baby underwent it, not me.) I rashly mentioned the event to him as part of my medical history on first coming to Landsfield Crescent and joining his panel of patients.

'Well, there you are,' he'd said. 'That's what it's all about, then.' Dr Grafton didn't approve of abortion, and felt that the Otherly Abled should just sit or lie quiet and put up with whatever card fate had dealt them. Dr Grafton, in other words, was what used to be called a fatalist; not a good thing, if you ask me, for a doctor to be. But he was the only one around who could write prescriptions which released drugs from the chemist, if he could be so persuaded, and he did at least take an interest.

18

It was a month before the Centre was reopened under its new title, the The Otherly Abled Resource Centre. There was much dispute between the insurance companies and the Council as to who was to pay for what in the general refurbishment of the Centre, and even some suggestion that the disabled should be left to fend for themselves and the building reopened as a tourist information centre to service Sir Bernard's new Eastern Coastline Development, but in the end reasonable funds were made available. The Centre was reopened, its exterior unchanged but renovated to suit the conservationists, its interior intelligently converted to provide proper ramps for wheelchairs, a kitchen fitted out to suit our needs and a physiotherapy room. There was a heated pool in the garden and easy access to the back door for dropping off and even parking. The Mobile Library came twice a week and we now had an ever-changing supply of recently published books, and read what we wanted to, not what we were obliged to, and were bored as a result. And I knew all these things to be a blessing, but nevertheless many of us lamented the gritty energies of the haphazard past, when we had so much to complain about: it is very boring to have bureaucracy as an ally; it is more fun to have it as an enemy. But this is not my story. I will go back to Laura, Annie and Carmen, and what transpired in my absence from the Centre. The tale goes as follows:

'You'll see,' the Devil had said to Carmen, 'you'll soon change your mind,' and it was certainly true that domestic matters, bad enough already, took a turn for the worse.

Carmen went home to find her parents in residence and herself, like Annie, relegated to the sofa in the living room.

'Dark, pokey little place, this,' said Raelene. 'From what you wrote, I thought it was going to be something special. And filthy! Couldn't you have got something better with the money? Well, we'll just have to make the best of it. Your dad and I have had enough of travels. We're home for good, you'll be glad to hear. How about a cup of tea, Carmen? We're parched.'

She had a leg in plaster – it seemed she'd had a very nasty break, tumbling down one of those steep flights of steps used to disembark passengers from aircraft if there isn't space in the bays. She'd just been unlucky, they said: nothing inherently dangerous in the steps: millions used them daily without disaster. No, it hadn't hurt much: she'd had a drink or two on the flight. It did mean she'd have to be waited on. And what was a daughter for but to help her old mother in the hour of her need?

'Mum,' said Carmen, 'I suppose Andy *is* my father?'

Raelene turned pink, then white, and said of course he was; who'd been talking out of turn? She refused to say any more, on the grounds that it wasn't fair to Andy, who'd always been a good father to her, so that Carmen felt she'd somehow pulled a carpet out from under her own, Carmen's, feet. Her whole existence, she now understood, rested on so shaky and shifting a foundation it was hardly surprising her body kept changing shape in its attempt to keep its balance. She might be anyone's, she could see, from the Devil's child to the milkman's, and had always known it in her heart. If she pressed Raelene, she would just be told that Raelene had no idea at all who her father was; she'd been conceived in an alley at the back of a pub somewhere, by-product of fun with a stranger, and she didn't want confirmation of it. So she dropped the subject.

Andy and Stephen sat drinking beer in front of the telly and working out betting systems. At least Andy had got rid of Paul. He wanted no punks in his house, he said. Idle layabouts, the lot of them.

And not only was home invaded: the trouble spread to work as well. Carmen went to Mr Snape, the Personnel Manager, as she did from time to time to ask for the morning off to go to the dentist, though what she intended to do was to go round to Laura's to cheer her up. Mr Snape looked embarrassed and said that dental and medical appointments must henceforth be made outside working hours; otherwise proper confirmation in the form of a letter would be required, and adequate notice of intent would have to be given.

'Since when?' asked Carmen, and who but Poppy should step out of the shadows to say, 'Since I went on the management team, Miss Wedmore. You will, I imagine, already have noticed some changes. Peckhams is now a slim, efficient, cost-effective organisation. We are about to announce staff cuts at ten per cent of total levels; we will achieve this wherever possible by natural wastage, but there will inevitably be some compulsory redundancies as Peckhams moves to face the recession and falling markets. Times are hard. We may even go on to short-time.'

'But we've just announced a twelve-million pound profit,' said Carmen. 'I thought we were doing so well!'

'I'm glad you have the concept of "we",' said Poppy. 'Peckhams expects loyalty from its staff, and does its best to deserve it. The profit-share principle has proved unworkable, alas; that is to be withdrawn in favour of achievement-related bonus incentives, and the presence of staff members on the Board is no longer deemed necessary: the numbers were proving cumbersome. The smaller the management team, the more efficient.'

'You mean no more outings to Newmarket for me,' said Carmen, and Poppy smiled, but her eyes were remarkably cold and hard. 'I think when you say that,' said Poppy, 'you go straight to the heart of Peckhams' problems, don't you think so, Mr Snape? Too many employees out for themselves, grabbing what they can get, not working for the greater good.'

Poppy was having an affair with Shanty Cotton. Everyone knew. She had been seen advancing on him, little frilly skirt up to her waist, wearing no knickers, in his office after hours: while he backed away, crimson in the face, terrified but helpless. A cleaner had barged in on them and reported the incident to the whole works canteen, and might not have been believed had she not been fired that very week for negligently performing her duties and putting product hygiene at risk. Everyone knew she was the best and most responsible of all the cleaners. Carmen tried to persuade her to sue for unjustifiable dismissal but she refused. 'I know when I'm beaten,' she said. 'That young woman is the Devil's spawn, and if I were you,' she added, 'I'd get out too. She's got it in for you. I've overheard a thing or two.' Which only made Carmen the more determined to stay; the more determined to face and surmount whatever further problems Driver had in store for her. For the more she thought about Sir Bernard – and she did think about him, studying his face in the newspaper or on the TV screen, for the Eastern Scheme was attracting a great deal of media attention – the less willing she felt to oblige Sir Bernard, enemy of her native heath, let alone Driver. If it was her fate to remain loveless all her life – she had no doubt but that Driver kept suitors at bay – so be it. She had rashly kept company with Driver, shared an oyster and a conversation or so with him, accepted car rides here and there and he had eaten a little way into her soul; she could only hope that given time it would repair itself.

Sir Bernard had been down to the ancient graveyard and pro- nounced it worthless.
'Just a mess, isn't it?' he said. 'Neglected, rubbish soil! Nothing grows. The sooner the hard core's down the better. We're not going to be plagued by protestors, are we, Driver? Sacred sites, ancestor worship, the conservation hysteria of the middle classes?'
'Not if they don't know about it,' observed Driver.
Sir Bernard looked at him a little sharply, and said he had no wish to infringe any regulations, he meant to play this by the book, he hoped Driver was aware of this. He didn't want too many short cuts taken.
'Look,' said Driver, 'let me put it like this. The professional pro- testors won't have a leg to stand on. We have excellent lawyers, who specialise in working within the law. Ordinary people round here need and want these developments. Shouldn't we get out of here? From the look of it, this was just some kind of plague pit.'

They retired to the BMW. The wind whistled and moaned in from the sea and slung sand into Sir Bernard's eyes.
'I have no one to talk to, Driver,' he said. 'No one who really cares for me.'
'You have me,' said Driver. 'I look after you.'
'Only because it's in your interests,' said Sir Bernard. 'I need a woman I can love, not just a woman who loves me. Where is Carmen? Why do I have to wait so long?'

'Carmen's on ice,' said Driver. 'Wait and see. Only a few days left to go.'

The BMW drove off and Sir Bernard's minions gathered the teams together and said it was henceforth a firing offence for anyone to hold up work because of 'remains'. Jed Foster felt wholly unappreciated and indeed insulted and told his wife, who told his sister, who was in treatment with Mr Bliss for her smoking problem. Mr Bliss was now enjoying a relationship with Mrs Baker – that is to say he and she 'were an item' – and he told her, and by the next evening the protest groups were out in the sand dunes with posters, cameras and pet archaeologists, and collecting names for a petition to the Ministry of the Environment outside Fenedge Post Office. The Devil never has it all his own way. Not quite.

Carmen, thwarted in her dentist excuse, simply got Stephen to call Mr Snape the next morning and say she was ill, and took the bus out to Landsfield Crescent to see Laura, who described herself as alone in the house, although all four children, for once, were with her. But to a depressed mother children are no company. Rachel and Caroline were off school (it was closed for the day to facilitate a teacher refresher course); Sara had stuck a coin up her nose the evening before and had spent much of the night in hospital with Laura, and the baby, now resentful of her plastered hip joint, was grizzling. Laura had been crying. She was accustomed to having Woodie in the garden workshop, available to come and help her with the children whenever emergencies arose. But now Woodie had rented an old warehouse in Fenedge, where there was more space and less distraction, without a thought of her, Laura, left at home.

'They're his children as well as mine,' complained Laura. 'He seems to forget that.'

'He has to earn,' said Carmen, defensive of Woodie, for she was a worker herself and understood what it meant, though Laura did not.

'Take his side,' said Laura, 'that's right. Along with everything else.'

'What do you mean,' asked Carmen, 'by everything else? I've risked being fired to see how you are, and how you are is like this. It isn't nice at all.'

'It's all your fault,' said Laura, 'that things aren't nice. When they bury you, I hope it's face down.'

Carmen had to sit down to recover from this. Laura cried and said she was sorry. It was just that Kim was a hopeless baby-sitter and she wished he'd gone away and stayed away and never come back. It was thanks to him that Sara had stuck a coin up her nose. Kim had started saying he wanted the house to himself, and he drank too much; what if he took it into his head to throw Woodie and her and the family out? If there was a Woodie to throw out. On her way back from the hospital she'd called in at his new workshop to surprise him and found him there with Angela, kissing. They hadn't seen her. She'd slipped away. She didn't want any advice from Carmen, because it was bound to be bad. What should she do? She had four children to think about, and they needed their father, she couldn't think about herself.

Then the phone rang. It was Mavis for Laura, to say Annie had been taken into hospital. Annie had something called anorexia and she was in intensive care, and asking for her friends, though, as the Count/Mavis added, no one could say Carmen and Laura had been very supportive friends. Mavis went on to trace back Annie's troubles from the time she'd failed her exams due to keeping the company of these alleged friends. Mavis was upset. 'It makes you wonder,' said Mavis, 'why you ever have children. All that work, all that orange juice, all the sacrifices, and still it turns out badly,' and she slammed the phone down.

Carmen and Laura had a brief discussion as to who should look after the kids so they could go off to the hospital. Laura refused to ask Angela, though Carmen thought she should, and since I was sitting across the road waiting for the Centre to reopen, and Alison was visiting me, all four were lugged over, grizzling and snivelling. It was, they assured me, an emergency. It wouldn't happen again.

'That girl,' said Alison after they'd left, 'was far too young to get married and is far too young to be in charge of anything, let alone anyone. There should be a law to protect people from themselves. Poor little mites, left in the care of a cripple and a crone –' As soon as their mother had left the room and was no longer a witness to their distress, they stopped grizzling. They fiddled with the controls of my chair instead. Alison then stood on her head to entertain them. The sight of her upside-down face, around which her full skirts fell, displaying her skinny legs and her white inter-lock bloomers, started them crying again. Standing on her head was Alison's party trick. Her mother had stopped doing it at ninety. Her daughter, it seemed, meant to outdo her. Alison was so light – in fact, barely six stone – it was not the problem it would have been for someone fifty years her junior, as I am. I am still not too old to have babies myself – not quite. My problem is not merely the biological clock, but how to regain the use of my legs and find an agreeable and useful father for my potential children before it's too late. I can see these problems might be insurmountable. I was twenty-three when complications following a bodged pregnancy termination required emergency invasive surgery, and a wasp bit the knife-wielding hand mid-stroke, and a section of my neural fibre was inadvertently severed. So you understand why I am preoccupied with concepts of 'lucky' and 'unlucky', and the ethical links which join them. 'Lucky' to be alive, 'unlucky' to be paralysed; 'deserving it', as Dr Grafton would say. But deserving what? The luck or the unluck? Forget it.

Laura and Carmen arrived at the hospital to find Annie indeed in the intensive care ward, Mavis and Alan at her side. A drip fed into her veins; she was linked up by wires to an ECG machine. Another measured her blood pressure, tightening around her stick-like arm every few minutes or so. Her chest was bare the better to service the machine, but she, once so plump, now had no bosom at all to speak of, so no one bothered to make her decent. 'That blood pressure's too low, doctor,' said Alan.

'I am well aware of that, sir,' said the doctor.

'That pulse is too slow,' said Alan. 'I know about these things.'

'So do I,' said the doctor shortly.

'We don't want her having any of your pills,' said Mavis. 'They kill more people than they cure. Healing is a matter for the spirit, not the body.'

'Just allow me to get on with it in my own way,' said the doctor, 'if you please,' and then to Mavis, 'How long has this been going on?'

'I've no idea,' said Mavis. 'She's been out of the country.'

'It's a cry for help,' said Alan, 'that's what it is.'
'But didn't you notice her getting *thin*?' the doctor asked.

'I want Tim,' said Annie to Carmen and Laura. 'Tell Tim I love him. I haven't heard from him, nothing. No phone call, no apology, nothing.'
'I thought she hated him,' whispered Laura to Carmen.
'It was only a lovers' spat plus air fare,' whispered Carmen.
'Don't make jokes,' said Laura, but Annie had smiled and a little pink came into her cheeks: and her systolic blood pressure was up two points next time the machine hummed and squeezed her arm.
'Get me Tim,' commanded Annie, and closed her eyes, exhausted.
'Well,' said the doctor, who was of the new holistic school, 'people can die of broken hearts as well as anything else.'
'She might *die*?' asked Carmen, to whom this had not occurred.
The doctor just shrugged and went off in response to some other emergency, and Carmen hoped he was being like this to keep Alan and Mavis in their place, but could not be sure.

Count Capinski spoke from Mavis's mouth. He said, 'The omens are bad. There is a Jonah amongst us. She must sacrifice herself or be the sacrifice,' and then Mavis clamped her mouth shut and opened it again to say in her own voice, 'You girls are so selfish and so preoccupied you didn't even notice your own friend had galloping anorexia.'
Alan said, 'Fair's fair, Mavis, we didn't notice either, what with one thing and another.'
– to which Mavis replied, 'You mean your toy trains,' and Alan said, 'I meant that man you make me share your bed with.'
Annie opened her eyes and said, 'Home Sweet Home, goodbye' and closed them again, and a nurse came along to change the drip and shooed the lot of them out.

When Carmen left the hospital she was crying.
'Well?' asked Laura.
'Okay,' said Carmen. 'I give in. I'll sleep with Sir Bernard. Anything.'

On the way home Carmen passed Mr Bliss outside the Post Office. He was collecting names for the petition organised by the 'Stop the Sacrilege' section of the 'Save Our Past' group. The protest movement had split, within days, into factions, which, while not overtly hostile to one another, had trouble getting along. New Agers felt antagonistic to the Christian groups, who were complaining about the desecration of Christian remains but ignoring the pagans: archaeologists did not wish to offend the developers more than they could help: the respectable Heritage people did not wish to be involved with the only just respectable Green Peace party, which, along with the SPB (Society for the Protection of Birdlife), wanted the wildlife parks preserved, or with Friends of the Earth, who objected on principle to marinas; but all agreed in this: that they did not want Sir Bernard's earth movers to roll on another cog, that here was an area of public concern, and all were prepared to lie down, indeed almost looking forward to lying down, in front of the giant machines. After that, any coincidence of ambition stopped, and argument began.

'These nutters can't put a stop to the whole Eastern Scheme, can they?' asked Sir Bernard. He'd never known anything like it. Every environmental organisation in the country seemed to be turning out and *The Sun*'s headline yesterday had run 'Bellamy Boobs'. He hadn't liked that.

'I doubt it,' said Driver. 'Too busy cutting each other's throats, as per usual. What we need is some big PR stunt.'

'I need a new girlfriend,' said Sir Bernard. 'Get me Carmen.'

'Okay, okay,' said Driver. 'What will you give for her?'

'Anything,' said Sir Bernard.

'Done,' said Driver.

'And clean up those headlines while you're about it,' said Sir Bernard.

'No problem,' said Driver, or at least I could only assume from the next day's headlines – 'Stand Up To 'Em, Bernie!' – that their conversation had gone thus. Some subeditor may have been bribed, of course, but I don't like to believe that: I would rather conceive of a conversation of cosmic intent.

Yet here was Mr Bliss battling on, stopping passers-by in the face of the inevitability of defeat, ignoring his own sore feet. It was an

October day and very windy. Carmen's hair, which was growing longer and redder by the minute, whipped around her face. Mrs Baker, sitting at her folding table, on her folding chair, had a hard time keeping leaflets and questionnaires from flying around the square. The public was obstinate this morning: they trusted no one: they were on Bernie's side: they didn't want to be laughed at in the popular papers.

'What we need round here is jobs and houses,' said one passer-by, 'not meddlers like you.' And the next said, 'I hope you have a licence: you're causing an obstruction: I'll report you for this.' After that a number said, in effect, 'What's good for Sir Bernard is good for Fenedge,' and others, 'There's only old bones up there. Dead for ages. So what?' and the librarian, who should have been sympathetic, refused to sign, saying, 'There's more than enough talk about ghosts and curses in this town. Don't say you're infected too, Mr Bliss, Mrs Baker.' It was depressing.

Then Carmen came by and luck changed. 'Keep at it!' said the passers-by, queuing up to sign. 'This is our town, not theirs. A crying shame what they're doing up there,' or 'The little people against the big company! Good for you!' or 'Hopeless, but let's give it a try.' Eddie from the Welcome-In came over with free cups of tea. 'Had enough of these lorries,' he said. 'It's time to act. Someone in the disabled place could have been killed. Supposing it had been bricks not balsa?' A languid wasp, the last of the season, struggled in a cup of tea. Mr Bliss rescued it with one of the leaflets. This one read 'Bellamy's Triumph is Britain's Shame'.

'Good morning, Carmen,' said Mr Bliss, looking up from his task. 'How goes it? Like the hair! What is it? Henna?'
Carmen looked at her reflection in the glass of the Post Office window and said, 'Yes, I'm a redhead,' because she could see she was. She'd started the morning mouse.
'Mrs Baker,' asked Carmen, 'you remember the Faust legend? All that stuff about Mephistopheles?'
'Yes, I do,' said Mrs Baker, 'and so would you if you'd paid any attention to me at school. It's a terrible thing for me to sit here and watch the young women of this town, whom I am meant to

have educated, get into the state they are, especially you, Carmen. Helpless and hopeless.'

'Why didn't Faust ask to stay immortal, and cheat the Devil that way?'

'Because Mephistopheles had set the goal posts: that is to say a trap. If ever Faust wished the day would never end, on that day he would die.'

'You mean he wasn't allowed to put life on Pause: stop it at the dirty bits?' Andy and Stephen were for ever doing that. Pressing the Pause button on the video remote control: moving the picture frame by frame. Girls with spread legs in the 18 Certificate: was that flicker of flesh what they thought it was? Usually it was.

'Nothing to do with dirty bits,' said Mrs Baker tartly. 'Goethe's Faust was engaged in earthworks: moving mountains and so forth. Employing an army of workers: irrigating dust bowls, making the desert bloom: putting right what God had neglected to do. I even remember you doing an essay on it. You got the one A you ever got.'

'Sometimes Annie and Laura and I used to steal Antoinette Ridley's essays and copy bits out of them,' said Carmen. 'Perhaps it was one of those.'

'You three were the reason I gave up teaching. Why do you want to know about Faust?'

'No real reason.'

'It's quite cheering,' said Mrs Baker, 'that you're interested, and can still get your tongue round the word Mephistopheles. I might even go back into teaching once Mr Bliss and I are married.'

A puff of wind caught up the leaflets on her table and rearranged them. 'Despoliation Rampant!', 'The Vandals of Waterland!', 'Stop the Sacrilege!'

'I brought in a dress for Oxfam,' said Mrs Baker. 'You can have it if you like. Nineteen forty something. I wore it only the once to a dance. I think it might do for you.' She had it rolled up in a plastic bag beneath the table. 'Mind you, I was an altogether different shape from you,' she said, 'when I was a girl. We used to go in more at the waist and out at the hip, but I expect you can alter it.'

Carmen shook it out. It was white taffeta, scooped low at the neck, oddly bridal in effect.

'I expect I'll fit it,' she said sadly, 'by the time I come to wear it.'

'It'll need steaming out,' said Mrs Baker. 'Perhaps your mother will do it for you?'

'I can do it myself,' said Carmen. 'I'm a big girl now.'

In the letter box Carmen found a letter from Mr Snape at Peckhams. It had been delivered by hand. By her continued absences from her place of work, it declared, Carmen had broken the terms of her contract. She was hereby relinquished: let go. This too seemed a deliverance.

Carmen called the hospital and Staff Nurse told her that Annie was off the critical list but still dangerously ill.

'Tell her she's going to be okay,' said Carmen; she had hoped to hear of a miraculous recovery; she was disappointed not to.

'We don't take messages,' said Staff Nurse. 'This isn't any old ward, this is Intensive Care. We're too busy.'

'Just tell her,' said Carmen.

'But it mightn't be true,' said Staff Nurse, and Carmen recognised the voice. It was Antoinette Ridley, of course, who had been at school with Carmen, passed all her exams and clearly been passing them ever since. 'Anyway,' said Staff Nurse, 'we have a lot of people in here who really do need attention.'

'So does Annie,' protested Carmen.

'Anorexia!' jeered Staff Nurse. 'A self-inflicted disease. I've no patience with it,' and put down the phone, and it was clear to Carmen that no-one was really out of the woods yet. Driver was holding Annie as a hostage to good fortune. Antoinette Ridley was famous for drowning her sister's pet guinea pig because it had chewed a hole in her best jumper. Antoinette had not been popular: she was too clever and seldom smiled.

Carmen went into the bathroom and tried on what had once been Mrs Baker's best dress. She hoped Driver would turn up soon.

'Moulds itself to your figure!' said Raelene, coming in to find some aspirin, though in truth Carmen's figure seemed to be moulding itself to the dress. 'I've never seen you wear white. Mind you don't drop anything down it. And whatever have you done to your hair?'

Carmen felt quite comforted. There were advantages to having her parents home again. It is better to be nagged than forgotten.

She put her arms round Raelene, who was surprised but pleased. They seldom touched.

'You've changed,' said Raelene. 'You used to be so prickly. We should go away more often, your dad and me. That chauffeur fellow was round again this afternoon asking for you. He said he'd call back at seven. I'm sure I've seen him somewhere before.'

And she puzzled about it a little and then seemed to come to a worrying conclusion. Since her leg had been in plaster, and she'd had nothing to do but eat, she'd put on at least a stone. Her flowered blouse strained over her bosom.

'Carmen,' she said, 'I don't want you to have anything to do with that man. For all you know he's a close relation.'

'You mean he's my father?'

'Of course I don't mean he's your father. He's much too young. Your father's my age or older. He has to be. I was only sixteen when it happened.'

'You mean he's my half-brother?'

'I'm saying no more,' said Raelene. 'Just there is a resemblance.'

It occurred to Carmen that if her unknown father had been in the habit of fathering children, any number of young men in Fenedge might be her close relation, her half-brother, but she supposed that was the same for any young woman, any place, any time. You just had to take your genetic chances.

'Right little cuckoo in the nest,' said Raelene. 'You never fitted and it was no one's fault but my own.'

She wept a little into Carmen's shoulder, so Carmen took off the dress, put her jeans and bomber jacket back on and went downstairs to make her mother a cup of tea. It is never nice to discover you are not who you thought you were, but it has its compensations. She felt more charitably towards her father and towards Stephen, knowing they were only half the responsibility they had been, and fetched them cans of lager quite happily when they shouted through to the kitchen for them. Let them go to hell their own way: she was three quarters there already; who was she to protest? 'Sugar?' she asked Raelene, preparing to spoon it in, but Raelene said no, she'd have a sweetener, she was going on a diet.

On her way home from the hospital, Carmen had put her hand in her jeans pocket and found a ten-pound note there. On impulse she'd gone into Boots and spent it on cosmetics; the expensive kind, not tested on animals. Her face would have to live up to Mrs Baker's dress. But Boots must have given her someone else's bag because now when she opened it up in the kitchen she found it to be full of even more expensive creams, and essences and perfumes, as well as a far fancier brand of make-up than she'd dream of using; and a little black beaded bag – a free offer, but not too bad – inside which was what could only be a packet of condoms.

She thought she'd call the whole thing off it was so vulgar and just go to the cinema instead and not be there at all when Driver turned up, but on her way to the door she heard Raelene telling Andy to shut up, Mavis was on the phone, and Mavis had been to the hospital and Staff Nurse had said Annie was back on the critical list, and this was the worst day of Mavis's life.
'Might be the worst day of Annie's life,' said Stephen, who had a keen ear for parental insensibility if nothing else.
'Not to mention the last,' said Andy, and they both laughed.

There was nothing for it. She went back upstairs to fill the grimy bath – except someone seemed to have cleaned it lately – with appropriate essences, which were so oily that when she was in the bath drops of water slipped and slid off her skin as she lifted her arm to look at it: a long slim arm to match the legs. Her muscle tone was good, she noticed. Sell your soul to the Devil and never have to do aerobics again! The Devil was all short cuts: he did a good editing job on your life. In fact what he was really good at, Carmen decided, was turning people into the video of their life. He left out all the boring bits. When your soul was sold you would no longer have to live in real time; you would not have to cut your nails unless it was of dramatic import, or ever go to the toilet again (unless there was someone lurking there, to make it a good scene). You could open a teach yourself book and close it in the next frame, having learnt everything in it. She could tell Laura was good, so very far from losing her soul, because of all the slow, boring things she had to do, and do without any capacity to fast-forward, just plodding daily through nappies and baby food. She wondered if she, Carmen, would soon be able to rewind – replay lovemaking, pause at orgasm for ever; or would it be the newest technology, so it could switch itself to Play again after so many minutes on Pause, for fear of damaging the tape, just wobble and sparkle and begin again? But you could slow-rewind from time to time, if you were careful never to get to the end of the tape and so let yourself in for automatic fast rewind, which was presumably what happened when you were drowning and your life flashed before your eyes. You could stay young for ever, presumably by playing only the first section of the tape: and you wouldn't end up bored, because you could constantly re-edit events to make them more satisfactory. The thing was not to press the Eject tab inadvertently. Then Driver would step forward and retrieve the cassette of your life: claiming not just world rights in it but universal rights, rights throughout the universe, for all infinity (terms used in the contract I, Harriet, had to sign for Paramount when they were making the film of the life of the famous surgeon whose hand slipped when he was operating near my spine. They were buying me out of the film, not into it, not unreasonably. I used the three thousand dollars they paid me to buy my wheelchair). Then Driver would just stack the cassette in his video tidy along with all the others. All the world a screenplay, and all the men and women in it bit part players, and free will just a minimal chance of rewriting your own lines if the Director didn't notice. Driver as Director: Mephistopheles become Videostopheles.

Carmen stepped out of her bath. She was used to Radox Herbal Salts in the water. She suspected that whatever was in the expensive green globs of liquid from the gold bottle discovered in her shopping bag was making her mind work faster than usual. It was not altogether pleasant: as if a million little sparks were making connections. She thought perhaps it was a side effect, something inadvertent: she didn't think Driver had planned it: if you thought too much, what use would you be to a man like Sir Bernard? He wanted presumably what she could see now in the bathroom mirror, toothpaste-spattered as it was: a person, a female, settled down into a Madonna body, only with a stupid, pretty face – wide-set eyes, high forehead and bruised mouth, and a Michael Jackson look about the eyebrow, and a Dallas hairstyle, and nails which even as she looked were turning from crimson-painted to palest pink. She did not think she could respect or admire a man who could only love a girl like her, but that was not the point. If she did not do what was expected of her, if she did not agree to take her proper place, lie down in front of him, be the missing jigsaw piece that made sense of the puzzle, the wind would blow so thick with sand through Fenedge that it would blot out the sun altogether. She had been called to the Devil's safe house and had to go. The towel on the back of the door was clean and dry. Oh yes, her lucky day: everyone's lucky day, even Annie's. That it might be Annie's good luck to die, her bad luck to live, was too hard to contemplate.

She put on lipstick and eye colour since it was there. She put on the dress, which made more sense of her face; or perhaps it was the cosmetics which did that. She took up the black bead bag, which would never have been her choice, and looked really stupid with the white dress, and went downstairs. It was five to seven. She had not been watching the clock. She suspected time had adjusted itself to her. As she went downstairs she heard Stephen say to Andy, 'But we've just had this programme. Those cops were singing that song half an hour ago, I'll swear it.' They did not see Carmen pass. She had lost her visibility: perhaps it went with her singularity, and now she was to be like everyone else. She opened the door. There was no BMW.

The phone rang in the hall. Carmen went back inside. It was Laura. She said she'd taken matters into her own hands. She'd rung Tim in Southland, New Zealand. Mrs McLean had answered the phone: Laura reported the conversation to me the next day. I had to wait: since Annie's return, I was further down her list of confidantes.

'Mrs McLean,' said Laura, 'I don't know what your son is playing at, but my friend Annie is dying for love of him. Can I speak to Tim?'

'Men have died and worms have eaten them,' said Mrs McLean surprisingly, 'but not for love. And in the meantime our sheep are being eaten alive by a new kind of worm too and Tim's seeing to them. So you can't speak to him: he's drenching.'

'Tell him to stop drenching and get over here to Annie at once,' said Laura.

'I might at that,' said Mrs McLean, even more surprisingly. 'He's miserable without her. Come to think of it, we all are. She made a lovely scone, when she put her mind to it. Whatever got into her? Was she ill?'

'Yes, she was,' said Laura. 'She was anorexic.'

There was a short silence, into which the waves of distance squeaked as the breathing of the two women bounced up to satellites and back again and the oceans that divided them washed over an earth somersaulting through space.

'You can get like that,' said Mrs McLean, 'if you do too much baking. It happened to my sister. Now she's fit for nothing but to play bridge. Is Annie bad?'

'Yes,' said Laura. 'She might die,' and she began to cry.

'Whinge, whinge,' said Mrs McLean, not unkindly. 'All you pommy girls, always crying. I'll see what I can do. No worries.'

Woodie had come in as she put the phone down and said it was a good thing they only knew people in Fenedge: if Laura wasn't gadding about she was on the phone. The bill was atrocious.

'I actually gave him a piece of my mind,' said Laura to Carmen on the phone. 'I don't know what got into me.'

Laura said she'd been calling the other side of the world and would do the same thing again if Woodie went on whingeing, and keep the phone off the hook all night, what was more. What was Woodie playing at? All Woodie did these days was moan and groan and find fault. Why was he trying to put her, Laura, into the wrong? What was he doing so wrong that she, Laura, had to be worse than him, Woodie, in Woodie's mind? Well? Woodie looked quite shocked. Was it Angela? And Woodie needn't open his mouth to say she, Laura, was (a) jealous, (b) insane, because she, Laura, knew what was going on, and she, Laura, was fed up. If Woodie didn't stop it at once she was walking out and leaving the children for him to look after, and Angela too. See how Angela's sandwich business went if she was up to her armpits in kids.

'You wouldn't, would you?' asked Woodie, impressed, and he was the old Woodie, marvelling at her, looking at her as if he were part of her, but that she was the best part. She hadn't noticed that Woodie had of late stopped doing that; only now, when it began again, did she feel the lack of it.

'I would,' she said. 'Well, I might.'

'It wasn't really anything,' said Woodie. 'Angela's just like that. She has a good heart, and if you're alone in the room with her it just seems so natural.'

'Then don't be alone with her ever again,' said Laura, 'or I'll cut off what matters with the carving knife.'

'I wouldn't want to lose that,' he said. 'Or you. You were so busy with the kids I didn't think you'd notice. I'm sorry. It's stopped anyway. She likes older men, really. Whenever she was with me she talked about Kim.'

Laura said she didn't want to know. She would take time to get over it but she supposed she would. She'd have to: what choice did she have?

All this Laura said into the phone while Carmen stood on first one high white satin heel, then the other. Raelene had lent her the shoes in which she had won the tango competition with Andy. Lucky shoes, she said.

'So that's my news,' said Laura. 'I just had to tell you. It's better and worse. Better because it's in the open, worse because now I have to get over it. How's Sir Bernard?'

'I'm seeing him tonight,' said Carmen.

'About time too,' said Laura, without even asking what Carmen was wearing, so preoccupied was she with herself. 'Woodie wants to take me out to dinner, but I've been so upset and my eyes are too puffy. But I feel kind of washed out and purified.'

'I'm glad,' said Carmen. The BMW was outside: Driver sounded the horn.

Alison was detaching me from my chair and into her car as the BMW drew up: always a difficult task – made by Alison to look so very difficult that passers-by would stop and help. Today Alison all but dropped me. I squeaked in alarm and Driver came over to help. His arms were strong. He looked at me as men seldom looked at me; as if anything were possible. He said nothing. He smiled: did what he had to, and returned to his car, leaving me quite breathless with desire, a sensation I have tried to train myself out of: better to be deaf to the speech of the space between the legs than to hear it, if the brain is in no position to relieve the body's residual clamouring, stop its nagging.

'I hate the way men patronise women,' said Alison. 'Who asked him for help anyway?'

Carmen came out of the house, radiant in white, and I mean that: it was a trick of the light, of course.

'That girl's got an aura,' said Alison. 'Eighty-seven years in the world and I've never seen an aura. Now I have. A white one too, very special. But isn't that Carmen?'

'Yes,' I said.

'Every town has its bad girl,' said Alison, 'but they don't usually have auras. Fenedge is looking up.'

Her mother saw auras, said Alison to me on the way home. She'd sometimes pretended to do so herself, as a child, just to keep up, but it had never been true. An aura was a kind of light like a halo which shimmered around people, if only you had eyes to see. Sensitive people, as her mother was, could see them; the problem had clearly been that Alison just wasn't sensitive. Auras came in different shades, depending upon the mood of the person wearing them and the beauty and feeling tone of that person's soul, and white was the most spiritual and the most transcendent of the lot. Alison was glad she had finally seen one, and a white one too. Her mother had never seen a white aura; she'd complained about it: now her eyesight was so bad she never would. The incident had upset Alison. When she stopped talking about auras, she was silent all the way home. I think she was crying. It is upsetting when the old cry: there seems to be so little time for things ever to come right for them. I cried too. I had, through Carmen, cast Driver as Mephistopheles, or Videostopheles, Satan of the new fictional world so many people lived in, or tried to, but only because I fancied him, this swaggering young man in uniform and breeches, and could never have him; never have anyone. I might as well be dead. I had gone to Chicago hoping never to come back, except in a coffin. A bad night for Alison, a bad night for me. The crone and the cripple, weeping into pillows for things that might have been and never would be now.

19

We will cheer ourselves up with Carmen's sacrificial, soul-searing night out with Sir Bernard. The BMW took the old Fenedge–Winterton road, now widened and kerbstoned: the former beet fields were home to a new mixed housing and light industrial estate, prettily enough done in Disney style. The old trees had been bulldozed away to make room for filling stations and builders' yards: and square office blocks, housing insurance agencies and banks, dry-cleaners and launderettes; there were TV aerials and satellite bowls everywhere.

'It's horrible what they've done round here,' said Carmen.

'You'll come to like it,' said Driver. 'You'll enjoy seeing people well housed and well serviced; you'll know they're happy and not likely to start revolutions. You won't have to look at it anyway. You'll be up there in Bellamy House. The rich have the best views.'

And he turned left and up the new private road to Bellamy House; here the developments stopped abruptly, and they were going through the old forest; branches meeting overhead, as if everything was as it always had been, and there was enough room in the world for everyone; and only the glitter of metal on the occasional treetop suggested a security system and alarms to keep out those not entitled to admire the serenity of nature. They reached the steel gates of Bellamy House itself: the BMW activated a response; they were admitted. The gardens were formal and tranquil: the moon was full, though Carmen could have sworn it had been new only yesterday. She did not suppose Driver could actually control the phases of the moon, but it was clear that he could control her perception of them. If he wanted her to see full, she would see full, and that was that. No wonder the First Sealord had had an observatory built, and installed a telescope, the better to define, measure, record and catalogue and by scientific method achieve a world not totally vulnerable to the vagaries of human perception. And now the telescope had gone, and the observatory been turned into guest bedrooms, it should have surprised no one that the moon could wax and wane out of turn, and what was seen or felt, sniffed or heard be taken as true enough.

The bed bugs on the observatory level had resisted all attempts to eradicate them: they lodged between the plastic skins that had been stitched between the old curving lead window frames to take the weight of the plaster, and no amount of pumping in insecticide seemed able to stop the creatures creeping out at night to bite the guests. These were the cheaper, attic rooms, it is true, but it was still not good for any hotel's reputation to have even the economy-class guests wake up in the morning quite drastically spotted by red weals and white lumps. (Bed bugs have been known to bleed a child to death.) Word gets round.

But down in the restaurant area the staff had other preoccupations that evening than moonlight and bed bugs. Mrs Haverill was making their lives miserable, the more so because Sir Bernard and a Miss Wedmore were to dine that night. She was giving Henry, the waiter whom Carmen had encountered at the Trocadero, but who had moved to Bellamy House, where, though wages were lower, tips were allegedly higher, a particularly hard time. 'Henry,' said Mrs Haverill as Henry passed with a tray heavy with glassware, sent back by her for polishing three times, 'one moment, if you please. This is Bellamy House, not the caff you have been accustomed to. You do not go up to guests in the bar and say "whaddya want?". You say, American style, "Good evening, and how are *you* today? My name is George and I am here to serve you." Will you repeat that?'
'My name isn't George, it's Henry.'
'Your name is what I say it is, young man. And how are *you* today – the emphasis is always on the "you", to make the customer feel special. It's friendly and yet respectful. Personalised staff–customer contact is the pillarstone of the Bellamy Empire, and if it doesn't suit you, you find work elsewhere.'
'Good evening, and how are *you* today?' said Henry. 'My name is George and I am here to serve you.' That said, Henry was

permitted to put his tray down. His biceps bulged and ached. He wished he had not left the Trocadero, whose policy it was never to rehire those who had once left its employ.

Mrs Haverill opened the door to Carmen. Mrs Haverill wore black. Her jaw was set square, as the jaw of one who had had to endure many things: her eyes were mean, as the eyes of one who meant to endure no more. Carmen felt as if perhaps she was the last straw. She wished she had a dark anonymous coat to cover up the white dress, but none had appeared upon the scene. Driver had either not thought of it, or decided against one. She felt conspicuous and alone, and supposed this was the lot of the bad girl. Good girls got escorted.

'You'll be the girl for Sir Bernard,' said Mrs Haverill bleakly, and began the walk up the winding stair to the balcony level and the first-floor suites. Carmen followed, as she supposed she was meant to do, and then stopped.

'Mrs Haverill,' she said to Mrs Haverill's back. Mrs Haverill continued upwards. Carmen tapped her on the shoulder. Mrs Haverill jumped as if stung – she was not accustomed to human touch, it seemed – and turned to face her. 'You know my name perfectly well,' she said. 'Why don't you use it?'

'You're interchangeable,' said Mrs Haverill. 'That's why. And I hope you're not thinking of dining with Sir Bernard in public in that dress.'

'What's wrong with it?'

'It's white,' said Mrs Haverill. 'It is an insult to the brides of this country. Well, some of us work and some of us get by.' And she continued up the stairs, Carmen following after. Carmen wondered if, when her soul was gone, she could have Driver strike Mrs Haverill dumb: but perhaps when your soul was gone it wouldn't seem important – you'd just be impervious to insult: not suffer and smart under humiliation, because you'd ceased to be conscious of it. Driver would not have to alter the world for her sake: just rewrite her nature, for the benefit of the one, the disadvantage of the other. Easy peasy.

Sir Bernard's suite was large, ugly, grand and rich with deep red leather. A pair of stag's antlers loomed over a carved wooden fireplace. There were dark oil paintings on the walls: large ones,

gilt-framed, crowded with deep cliffs, chasms, stormy skies, tossing dark green foliage, and clusters of what looked like fireflies,
silvery, gleaming against the black crags.
'Well?' he asked. 'Like it? It's just been refurbished.'
'Love the paintings,' she said. 'Hate the room.'

Sir Bernard stood beneath the antlers, nursing a glass of sparkling
water. He wore a black dinner jacket and black bow tie, so
Carmen could hardly make any judgement of him at all: he
seemed to be someone in an old film. If she touched him her hand
might go right through the screen. Or perhaps he was a hologram.
He was taller and thinner than she remembered: he might well
have a star part in this film – be the villain himself. The old Sir
Bernard, pre-Driver, would have had to make do with one of
the bumptious minor baddies clustering round the Mafia boss.
Perhaps this was all Driver offered – to promote you first from a
non-speaking to speaking part, then from supporting actor to lead,
from lead to world star.

Carmen could see, looking through the open door to the bedroom,
a wide double bed with a dark red quilt, heavy crimson and gold
tapestry curtains hung at the windows, caught back by a tassel.
Perhaps those newly rich and famous always harked back to the
grandeur of the Victorian past, in the same way as men who
officially change sex and become women seem to like to go back
to the fifties and wear twinset and pearls and sensible shoes. They
choose what to them seems respectable, safe and boring, likely to
last for ever.

Sir Bernard and Mrs Haverill, who seemed inclined to hover, for
which Carmen was grateful, were having an altercation about
whether Sir Bernard and his friend were to dine in the main
restaurant or have a side table in the Bistro. Sir Bernard preferred
the latter since he thought Carmen would find it less stuffy there:
Mrs Haverill was determined they should dine where she had
decided, that is to say, in the main dining room. There would be
fewer witnesses, she suggested. Or perhaps Sir Bernard would
prefer to cancel and a waiter should just bring up a tray with
champagne and two glasses. Bellamy House had recently bought
in some very reasonably priced champagne for just such occasions.

'Look, Mrs Haverill,' said Sir Bernard, surprisingly patient, 'if I want to be seen dining with Miss Wedmore behind a potted plant, I will.'

Carmen looked more closely at the paintings and discovered that the fireflies were in fact faeries, with gossamer wings, dancing in the wind, regardless of the apparent danger of being battered to death against rocky crags.

Mrs Haverill left. Sir Bernard remarked, 'I keep trying to fire that woman but I never quite manage. This place runs at such a profit, I relent at the last moment. She is famous for her awfulness. There are a whole lot of customers out there, it seems, who love nothing more than to be bullied and insulted. And I'm always surprised at how low the staff turnover is. So you like the paintings? A treasure trove of Martins turned up in someone's attic. I stepped in before the Tate and got the lot for three million. A bargain. I suppose you identify with the faeries. Your white dress, this dark room –'
'I hope I'm more substantial than that,' said Carmen. She could see herself in the mirror behind the dreadful wall candelabra. Her face had changed between the front door and Sir Bernard's room. Her eyes were deeper set. She thought she looked more interesting and rather less pretty, and was quite pleased with herself.

Sir Bernard said how he'd looked forward to meeting Carmen again. Their last encounter had gone badly. He'd been in a state: just broken up with Lady Rowena, the interior designer. His contract with her firm continued, however, perforce. Sometimes he thought they were taking their revenge. He was much better at controlling men than he was women. Look at Mrs Haverill . . . was he babbling on? He was nervous. He wished he could have a drink to steady him up, but he no longer drank, well hardly ever. Would Carmen care for a glass of Chablis? He'd open a bottle.

Carmen would. He did. His hand touched hers when he gave her the glass. He was no hologram: his skin against hers was dry and warm. She understood that he was real.

He suggested they go down to dinner. Carmen said really it wasn't necessary. He said sadly, 'I see. You want to get it over.' She denied it. Sir Bernard said, 'One of the problems of being a new man, made over in some more desirable image, is that matters take on a new significance. A year or so back, a pretty girl who knew what to expect, a glass of wine, a closed door – there'd have been only one outcome, but now I'm a serious person. I wish that I were not. I can see this is going to be difficult.'

Carmen said, 'Being made over, becoming a new woman, works the other way for me. What price virginity now, say I? How can you know the world and its ways if you know nothing about yourself, let alone the other sex?'

Sir Bernard was awed by the notion that she really was a virgin: in his experience girls were just sewn up. He had assumed Driver was exaggerating.

Carmen said, 'There's no virtue in it. I see it as neurosis. I'm just not normal. One of those women the fertility clinic won't inseminate. There's something wrong with them, everyone agrees.'

But the conversation was becoming clinical, too rational for comfort, or so Sir Bernard complained. Carmen could see that her new self, if it were to please, would have to work hard not at being bright and entertaining, but at being low-key and a little dull, or it might offend. She found herself wishing to please Sir Bernard and that was strange. She thought she caught a glimpse of Driver's eyes looking at her out of the candelabra mirror but could not be sure. Sir Bernard's will prevailed and they went down to dinner in the main restaurant. Mrs Haverill's bleak face was split by a smile. The waiter came up to them and said, 'Good evening. And how are *you* today? My name is George and I am here to serve you.'

Carmen said, 'You are not so George, you are Henry.'

Henry said, 'Mrs Haverill says I have to be George or I'll lose my job,' which was not of course exactly what had been said, but what George felt to be the case.

Sir Bernard said, 'Well, that's it. Mrs Haverill goes. She makes a nonsense of everything and this restaurant is stuffy beyond belief,' and he made a note to remind himself of it. It was true that it was the eyes of the elderly only which were fixed on Carmen, and there was no one present vigorous or powerful enough to be worth the impressing. It was a disappointment. Carmen too felt it. Sir Bernard and she talked courteously about various matters – the short-sightedness of those trying to hold up the Eastern Scheme, with which Carmen found herself agreeing; whether or not Carmen liked opera: it was Sir Bernard's passion, though not yet Carmen's, in spite of her name (honestly: *opera*, in Fenedge!) but got no further than the hors d'oeuvres – melon and Parma ham for Sir Bernard, avocado and cassis sauce for Carmen – before she dropped a little cassis on her bodice.

'It is very oppressive in this restaurant,' said Sir Bernard. 'It's said to be haunted. There are too many dead eyes looking at us, and now you have spoiled your dress. We had better go upstairs and put cold water on it before it stains for life. That is what my mother used to do.'

She had not thought of him having a mother. They talked about her on the way upstairs. Of course he had loved his mother, very much, but she had not loved him. She had done her duty by him, no more. A religious woman who hated her husband, she and the cold east wind blowing in from the North Sea had made his childhood miserable: had defeated his brothers but had rendered him the more expansive, the more ambitious. Since he couldn't rule her he'd rule the world. He's always known it.

The bathroom was a big chilly room, with marble bath and basin and an ugly swan carved in white stone from which the water flowed. She took off her dress and handed it to Sir Bernard. He put one towel beneath the stain and dabbed at it expertly with another, which he wetted beneath the tap.

Driver had not bothered to provide underwear, so she was wearing, as usual, a pair of Raelene's knickers and a bra done up with a safety pin. She wished now she had done better. She was not so much sluttish in her choice of undergarments as taking proper precautions against unexpected shape change, but how was Sir Bernard to know this? Though he was more likely to believe her than anyone else she knew. He handed her a towelling dressing gown from behind the door, without looking at her properly. She thought perhaps all the girls on his arm had been for show only. She did not wish to think so.

'It's very difficult,' he complained, waving at the bed in the next room, 'getting from here to there.'

Carmen said she could get into bed and turn off the light and he could undress in the bathroom and come through. He thought that would be a good idea. He said she must not construe his dithering as lack of enthusiasm. She said she would not.

I only have Carmen's word for all this. By the time the episode had passed through her imagination and mine, the account of it may not much resemble any actual event, let alone any characters living or dead, as they are described in that cowardly denial on the screen before the film begins, which nobody ever reads.

Carmen took off what she was wearing and arranged herself neatly in the bed. The sheets were white cotton: the kind no doubt his mother favoured. She could see herself in a long swing mirror. Her hair was longer than she remembered, and a darker red than before; her breasts were above the sheet. She didn't like them at all: there was a pronounced curve upwards from the ribcage to the nipple; they were immodest. She looked again at her face in the mirror and Driver looked back at her. She shrieked and covered her breasts with the sheet. It is a terrible and shocking thing to look in a mirror and see someone else's reflection.

'Don't make such a fuss,' said Driver. 'I'm your father, after all. And those are my breasts, not yours. They're sensational. I must say I can hardly forgive you for your underwear, but I suppose you're here and that's the main thing. It's been quite a battle.'

'How's Annie?' asked Carmen.

'All depends,' said Driver, 'on what happens next. I want no screaming rape, meaning I can't do this, I won't do that, all the stupid things girls say. I want a happy, cheerful, secure and satisfied Sir Bernard delivered back to me in the morning, and then I'll see about Annie's breakfast.'

'Mind you do,' said Carmen, and hopped out of bed and threw a tartan rug over the mirror. His voice ranted on a little and then gave up. She put on the white towelling robe and sat on the end of the bed. Sir Bernard came in from the bathroom. He wore a red silk dressing gown with a black Chinese motif. His shins were hairy and his feet were bare. His toes were long.

'You're not making this easy,' he said.

'No, I'm not,' she said. 'This is your responsibility, not mine.'

'The thing is, let's face it,' he said, 'it's impossible.' He sat on the end of the bed beside her. 'In the days when I drank, it was no problem. I lurched drunkenly forward and the woman fell drunkenly backward. But once you've told them about your mother her shadow hangs over you and spoils the fun.'

'I don't know how it's done either,' said Carmen, 'that's always been my problem. Why I'm in the state I am now. My friends have no trouble.'

'When you're actually presented,' Sir Bernard complained, 'with what you've specified, the kind of thing you say you want on the Dating Agency form – slim, red-headed, intelligent, cultured girl with tip-tilted breasts – it's all too much. You're terrified it might go wrong.'

'Tall, slim, handsome executive type, non-smoker, non-drinker, sensitive –' said Carmen. 'I thought I meant Ronnie Cartwright, but I see now it could be you.'

He lay a tentative hand upon her knee: it remained tentative. He withdrew it. They sat side by side, companionably, but without touching.

'All the same,' he said. 'It seems a pity. I do so hate to waste an opportunity. By my not wasting opportunities the Bellamy Empire has grown big. But not, alas, in this case, the Emperor.'

He said he thought his initial instinct had been right. He needed to marry her. In the quiet familial bed there would be no trouble. He would be as potent as the next man, probably more so. What did Carmen say? He would be honoured if she married him. They would wait until their wedding night for this kind of thing. If she would forgive the cliché, he wanted all of her, not some of her.

Carmen told me she thought of Annie, and of Peckhams, and of life ever after in Dullsville, Tennessee, and of Laura's children for ever snivelling into their paper hankies; and she thought she could redecorate Sir Bernard's suite and cheer him up, and she thought she might make up to him where his mother had failed, and she thought how perhaps when she'd said Ronnie Cartwright she'd always meant Sir Bernard anyway: and she thought no girl in her right mind would refuse such an offer: what was twenty years' difference in age anyway: if there was no sex it might be just as well, and there might be: he was just behaving as a gentleman should. And while she was thinking, Sir Bernard spoke: 'My millions would be at your disposal. I'll get on with developing the world, keeping the wheels turning; you get on with saving the whale, the ozone layer and the rainforest. So long as you don't interfere with my long-term plans, do what you like.'

'Done,' said Carmen.

'Carmen,' said Sir Bernard, 'don't tell Driver about this turn of events. If there's anything he hates it's anti-climax.'

'Done,' said Carmen.

They kissed on it, politely but lovingly, warm moist lips (hers) against warm dry ones (his). They slept in their dressing gowns, side by side.

In the morning the helicopter came early for Sir Bernard, but before he left he rang his PR agent and told him to arrange a wedding; as soon as possible, to oil the troubled Eastern Scheme waters.

When he had left, Carmen took the tartan rug from the mirror. Driver's face leered out of it. His breath misted the glass, which was peculiar.

'How was that?' he asked.

'He's killing as many birds as possible with one stone,' said Carmen. 'We're getting married with maximum PR.'

'I told you it would work out fine,' said Driver, delighted.

'I suppose it was you who gave him the gift of infinite virility,' said Carmen, and yawned and stretched with every appearance of languor.

'He didn't ask for it,' said Driver. 'He said he never had any problems in that respect. I'm glad to know he made it without me.'

'Indeed he did,' said Carmen. 'Now will you please go and see to Annie?'

Whether or not Carmen's tale was true, whether or not the night spent with Sir Bernard was as chaste as she said – and what we were hearing was just another example of Carmen's capacity for blocking out her own sexuality; in other words, downright lies –

the fates seemed to take her compliance with male authority, her willingness to submit to Sir Bernard, as good enough for them, and Annie ate, and was restored.

Staff Nurse approached Annie that morning as she lay white-faced in Intensive Care, wired up to all kinds of monitors and drips, none of which seemed to do her any good. Her blood pressure was low, her pulse slow: she hadn't spoken for days.

Said Staff Nurse, hand on hip, 'I don't know why this hospital wastes its energy on people who'd rather be dead. If I had my way there'd be no treatment whatsoever for anyone with cigarette-, sex- or diet-related diseases.'

A flash of anger lit up Annie's eyes. Her pulse took a little leap on its monitor.

'No point in offering you breakfast,' said Staff Nurse. 'You'd only turn up your nose. Anyway, it's all gone.'

Annie sat up; the monitors went haywire, alarms went off, quietly, so as not to alarm the patients.

'I'm entitled to breakfast,' she said. 'You're paid to provide me with it, so do it.' Mrs Haverill could not have done better. Staff Nurse fetched it; Annie ate, not much, but just enough to move her off the critical list.

When Tim arrived two days later, he found Annie sitting up in bed, sipping hot chocolate.

'Oh, Annie,' said Tim.

'Oh, Tim,' said Annie.

'I'll stay home and watch TV with you,' said Tim, 'if that's what you want.'

'I'll go out and bunje jump with you,' said Annie, 'if that's what you want –'

And so forth and so on until the need to fix a rapid wedding date was re-established.

'Isn't it drenching time?' asked Annie. 'You shouldn't have left the sheep. It was irresponsible. Laura had no business dragging you all the way over here.'

'I'll pay her fare over,' said Tim, 'and that of any of your friends you care to name.'

'We can't afford to waste money like that,' said Annie. 'Where would it stop? I have an excellent recipe for apricot chutney; your mother will love it: let's get home as soon as possible. And we're not going Club Class, we're going ordinary, like anyone else.'

20

The local evening papers were the first to run the news of the Bellamy–Wedmore engagement. The headlines were big enough, but respectful. 'Local Girl Makes Good' and 'Peckhams Employee to Marry Boss'. The national media, who picked it up the next day, took off with excitement. 'The Baron To Marry Bimbo,' cried *The Sun*, which was scarcely fair. 'Frozen Chicken Girl Wins Tycoon's Heart.' 'Say goodbye to hope, girls: he's snaffled!' and so forth.

Stephen went out and bought all the papers.
'Now how did she swing that one?' asked Andy.
'I always knew she had it in her,' said Raelene.
Stephen guffawed, and offended them.
'You'll have to get a job, Stephen,' said Andy. 'Can't hang about here for ever.'
'You do,' observed Stephen.
'I suppose it's time I stirred myself,' said Andy. 'Can't let our Carmen down. She won't want layabouts in the family now. And how about you cleaning this house up a bit, Raelene?'
'How about you doing it for a change?' said Raelene, so swiftly and sharply that to her astonishment Stephen actually got up and started picking up lager cans and putting them in the bin. Andy contemplated a full-length photograph of Carmen, which took up all of Page 4, and said, 'Personally, I always thought our Car could make it to Page 3 if she tried. But Lady Bellamy isn't bad. I'm proud of her.' He started wiping down the front door, in preparation for the arrival of the media.

Henrietta and Shanty Cotton studied the photograph as they ate breakfast.
'Fancy that,' said Henrietta. 'Carmen Wedmore of all people.'

Isn't that just lovely? Except I'm afraid it will keep the Sacred Site out of the headlines for a while.'

'That'll be what Sir Bernard has in mind,' said Shanty Cotton. He was eating muesli with skimmed milk. He had stopped eating bacon and eggs for breakfast and was not looking so red in the face.

'I'm sure it's true love,' said Henrietta, and Shanty Cotton was ashamed of himself. Poppy would never have said anything so sweet and trusting. He decided that Poppy was not a good person to have in his life. He would get rid of her before Henrietta found out. Not that he was normally averse to Henrietta finding out – it kept her on her toes – and he felt ashamed of this too.

He leant across the table and squeezed her hand and her face turned pink with pleasure. It was a wonderful thing to be able to do for another human being, and so simply. To turn Poppy pink with pleasure a man had to exhaust himself, and eat muesli.

Kim saw the photograph and said to Woodie and Laura, 'They've air-brushed it.'

'They have not,' said Laura.

'If I say anything you contradict it,' said Kim. 'I've had about enough of it. Why can't you be more like Angela? Now there's a woman to be getting on with.'

'Then you just get on with her,' said Laura and got up and put on her coat.

'Where are you going?' asked Woodie and Kim in unison. They liked her to stay in one place, she had found, and do nothing unpredictable.

'I'm going to see Angela,' said Laura.

'You can't do that,' said Woodie and Kim in unison.

'I can,' she said, and she did.

'I think,' said Laura to Angela, 'the best thing is for Kim to move in with you to save you from yourself. Then Woodie and I will have the house to ourselves.'

'Would I have to cook for him?' asked Angela. She seemed to have the mental age of a child of nine.

'Yes, you would,' said Laura. 'And you and he can baby-sit for

Woodie and me, so long as you're never alone with Woodie in a room again.'

'All right,' said Angela placidly. 'Kim's quite old, but I don't mind.'

'Move me out and move me on,' said Kim, when he heard. 'I don't mind. I deserve it. You keep the house. I'm a black plastic bag man, at heart. Always was: what do I need with a house? All I need is someone else's nice warm bed and no responsibility. What about Kubrick?'

'Take Kubrick with you,' said Laura. 'Look after him yourself.'

And after that there was no more trouble between Woodie and Laura. She came to me to ask for my views on sterilisation, and I said I didn't advise it, though what did I know? Woodie had a vasectomy instead and, though that always smacks to me of self-punishment, I daresay he thought he needed punishing. But I believe it was the reversible kind. Whoever knows what's going to happen next?

The photograph of Carmen presented itself to Alan and Mavis, newsprint blowing in the wind, rattling through the sky, landing at their feet. They had seen it before but naturally studied it again.

'She isn't wearing a bra,' said Mavis. 'I'll swear she isn't. Our Annie would never be photographed like that.'

'Our Annie is doing all right for herself,' said Alan. 'She's found true love and that's more important than marrying money.'

They were up at the construction site; sitting by the side of an oblong hole in the ground, where a skeleton in a lead coffin had been discovered. Whoever it had been was over six feet tall without the skull, which was missing. Archaeologists had put the bones in a plastic bag and labelled them: they'd taken photographs of the coffin and carted that away as well.

'I call it grave-robbing,' said Mavis to one of them: a tough young man with a red beard, who was removing the pegs in the ground that had distinguished Bronze Age from the rest. They had lost interest in this part of the site: the pegs were needed elsewhere: they were in short supply. Someone had turned up an elaborate tiled Roman paving, in good order.

'That's no grave,' he said, kicking sand into it to prove his point. 'Once everything's gone it's a hole in the ground.'

'Not to the spirit which laid in it,' said Mavis, her pale eyes rolling a little, as if Count Capinski were coming back. He hadn't been around for a while, not since Annie had risen from her sickbed and walked. Mavis and Alan had held hands while they walked up to the site.

The archaeologist moved on, complaining of the number of gawpers and gapers who not only made it hard for the contractors to get on with their work, but in their ignorance trampled scientific evidence underfoot. There was a lot to be done – the bulldozers were due to roll. Yes, yes, there was plenty of time to do the job properly. People made such a fuss. They were sentimental.

'I don't think it's sentimental,' said Mavis when he'd gone. 'I think if a body's three thousand years old or three days old it deserves the same respect. Not to be put in a plastic bag and dumped on a shelf in some college somewhere so someone can get a degree.'

She and Alan sat for a little beside the hole in the ground, out of respect for the dead, and contemplated mortality, and the fact that the University Archaeology Unit, which was doing a study of the site, was employed by Bellamy Enterprises, and no doubt wished to be employed again. The unit of whichever university accomplished the most work in the least time for the minimum pay, and kept the public at bay, and never held up the development schedule, and fulfilled the letter of the law – which insisted that ancient sites, once discovered, were at least minimally investigated – was the unit which survived to work again.

'Six feet tall and without a skull,' said Mavis. 'I wonder who he was, or what happened,' and she shivered. 'Whatever it was, it wasn't nice. I can feel it.'

The sky above them was yellow-streaked and sulphurous. Birds flew overhead: to Mavis and Alan they were nameless: though Mavis knew a raven when she saw one – which she never liked to do, particularly in the gardens of her patients, since they were birds of ill omen. If she did catch sight of a raven she'd get the family to call in Dr Grafton at once, just to be on the safe side. She could feel a breath on her neck. Perhaps it was the wind, perhaps it was something else. She could hear the whispers of distress around: a vast uneasiness rising from the earth.

'Funny place, this,' said Alan. 'Never seen anything like it, betwixt

233

and between,' and indeed it was a melancholy place, spoiled as a landscape, but not yet hard-cored, concreted, put to human use. The Eastern Scheme was in temporary abeyance as injunctions were received and fought by the Bellamy lawyers, who expected a satisfactory outcome. The press, as Sir Bernard had anticipated, had stopped nagging about the rights and wrongs of the development. Its readers, only cursorily concerned with such matters, were far more interested in the Wedding of the Year, and what special qualifications Carmen could possibly have thus to entrap the untrappable Sir Bernard. They could unearth no previous boyfriends, which was in itself suspicious, though Poppy gave an interview in which she let slip that in her opinion Carmen had got promotion by sleeping with her boss, and then gained access to Sir Bernard by sleeping with his chauffeur. This sent the press belting round to Shanty Cotton's home, but the Cottons were on a second honeymoon. Sir Bernard's driver was on a bodyguard course somewhere in Switzerland and could not be found. *The Sun* came to the conclusion, welcome to its readers, that Carmen was a virgin; although features about the new celibacy fell on stony ground. To be a virgin, they quickly realised, was to be pure when all around were impure, and that was interesting. Celibacy, which implied no one was at it anyway, was a bore.

Old newspapers whipped around Mavis and Alan as the wind rose. Someone had fetched them in for packing human remains and artefacts, no doubt, and then forgotten them.

'Tell you what, Alan,' said Mavis, 'I think we'd better get the Church in to do an exorcism.'

'Can't you do it?' he asked, surprised.

'I'd rather it was someone official,' she said, and felt better at once. The wind which whirled the newsprint took another layer of sand off the dunes which Jed Foster had already skimmed with his skimming machine. (Jed Foster had lost his job, for reasons quite unconnected with his disclosures about the site, or so it was said.) Mavis and Alan got sand up their nostrils, and between their teeth, and when Alan had a bath that night there was sand in his belly button. Mavis took a bath with him, since the Count was not around. She said she felt he'd finally died, poor old man, of cold and disease in his dungeon somewhere long ago. It was rare for the spirits of the living to travel, said Mavis, and out of their own time, but it sometimes happened, at least according to her books. She hoped she'd made his last days easier. She was pleased, Mavis said, to have Alan to herself again, now that Annie was finally off their hands. The bath was quite a squeeze, since neither of them was as slim as they used to be.

Alan said, 'Well, I'm glad you finally decided three's a crowd.'

Mavis said, 'I told you that years ago, when you made me have Annie.'

That at least is how I imagine the scene. At Mavis's instigation the local bishop was asked by the protestors if he was willing to perform some kind of religious ceremony over the graves and, to many people's surprise, he agreed. It could not be exorcism, he said, because there was no real evidence of hauntings, only at Mavis's say-so, but a service of reconciliation was perfectly in order. And that too is how it happened that Count Capinski never made another appearance, and Mavis closed up her healing shop. Dr Grafton, suddenly busy, took on a young assistant, who had more faith in what were known locally as 'doctors' drugs' than did his employer, and those who believed in them chose to see the younger man. The medical needs of the neighbourhood were at least adequately served at last.

Those who looked beyond the headlines as the Bellamy romance broke would have seen a brief paragraph announcing the death of one of the oldest women in the country, that of Alison's mother, whose heart had simply stopped beating in her sleep. 'Fancy having to wait,' said Alison after the funeral, which she made me attend, 'to be eighty-seven before you're free of your mother and can be your true self!'

She said she thought now at last she was allowed to give up and be old. She stood on her head for the last time. She ceremoniously tore up her driving licence. She would have to look after herself from now on, she told me. She thought she would look for some kind of sheltered accommodation. I would have to visit her, from now on. I said that might be difficult. She said the least I could do was make the effort.

The County agreed to ferry me by ambulance to and from the Otherly Abled Centre in Fenedge, since the new back entrance allowed their vehicles proper access. The town had taken on a new lease of life – it didn't exactly bustle, but it had certainly become busier – as a result, I suspect, of the arrival of the media to examine the life and times of Carmen Wedmore and discover how exactly it is that poor girl catches rich man. The pubs filled up: even Angela's sandwich van made some kind of profit. Trade begets trade. The greengrocer was sufficiently heartened to buy back his shop from Raelene and Andy, for whom Sir Bernard purchased a house in Landsfield Crescent, where they said they'd always felt most at home, and Fenedge was gratified once more by the sight of oranges and apples, pears and plums and a nice healthy cauliflower or two in its otherwise grey and frankly lifeless centre.

My daily ambulance rides were comfortable enough but, after my adventures with Alison, boring. One evening, desperate for diversion, I took it upon myself to visit Alison in the old people's home whither she had, following her mother's death, almost instantly departed. Mr Bliss's stables had changed hands once or twice and were now Restawhile and home for twenty elderly residents. 'Rest a while till what?' Alison asked bitterly, even as she put her possessions up for sale and moved in. 'The grave?' But it was her choice to be there. I left in my chair at five-thirty in the evening, for a journey that I knew would take more than an hour and exhaust me. It did. It rained a little. I was uncomfortably damp beneath my layers of plastic. The new kerbstones installed on what I remembered as halfway between country track and country road jolted my spine badly as my wheels encountered them. The light was bad, worse than I had anticipated. I had brought a torch, and needed it. But then the skies cleared: and there was the moon, rising and full. I realised I was on the road towards the Devil's safe house, and that I had been rash in attempting the journey. I half expected to see hordes of vampire bats swooping towards me, but of course that was nonsense. Sea-lord Mansion had long been Bellamy House and helicopters, if anything, now took the place of the vampires. But I could hear the sound of the natterjacks, or thought I could, and that was eerie – the sound of a busy, alien life still managing to hold on somewhere between bank and launderette. A fox crossed the road in front of me, with what might have been a chicken in its mouth.

He stopped and stared with red eyes – I shone my torch at him: in artificial light animals always seem to have red eyes – and then trotted on: his mouth impolitely full. There were no cars on the road: it was just as well. It is bad enough for the motorist to be held up by cyclists, far worse to have to crawl along behind a plastic-clad woman in a wheelchair. But as the moon rose higher my fear dissolved. Good and bad, I saw, were made even in the same light: the star – or was it a planet? Venus perhaps? The library service did not normally carry books on popular astronomy, but I could always ask – which kept the moon company kept me company too. To live in the world was not to be lonely: it was an insult to it to be bored: a privilege to exist at all, even without the use of legs. I turned into Mr Bliss's stables, as everyone still called the place – forget Restawhile – and made my way up the lane where once Laura and Carmen had run on a hot summer afternoon, terrified by a swarm of bees. I found the front door in the dark – no one had bothered to install an outdoor light – and reached forward for the bell and reached so far I simply fell out of my chair, and hit my side a crack on the metal boot-scraper, and rolled on my back, and lay there, contorted and in agony, calling out but unheard until Alison, who naturally liked to make herself useful wherever she was, opened the front door to put the milk bottles out. (In fact the milkman no longer called, for the local dairy had ceased its delivery service, and the bottles had to be fetched in from the step again, but no one had the heart to tell Alison so. She was born, I imagine, with the knack of creating extra work for others, and remained so until the end of her days. Perhaps it was sheer amazement at what she had created that kept her mother alive for so long.)

Be that as it may, Doctor Grafton was sent for: the general opinion being that I had slipped a disc. His young assistant came instead, rolled me over on to my face, and gave me a sharp, precise crack with the side of his hand in the small of my back. Now I don't know what happened. Perhaps the paralysis was indeed hysterical; perhaps the Chicago neural graft had finally done its work; perhaps some disc in my backbone, which had been causing the trouble, was released: perhaps the benefit which flowed from Carmen's assent to her own female nature flowed into me as well – though what feminist would want to hear that? At any rate, feeling and the capacity for movement came back into my legs. It was some months before I was, as it were, fully operational and was able, as they say, to take my place in normal society – though personally I think we were more normal in the Otherly Abled Centre than many outside it.

21

But I must tell you what happened up on the dunes on the evening of the Reconciliation Service. In my mind it was the same evening that I recovered the use of my legs: the same moon shone upon us all, but that's how I like to remember it, not how it was. It makes a better story. Let us say it was because the whole town and many of the Bellamy House guests were up in the sand dunes, chomping their way through the gravel pits, frightening the waders away, that the roads were so empty that night and events turned out for me the way they did. (Had I arrived later at Mr Bliss's stables, Dr Grafton and not his assistant might have turned up and matters been very different, but who is to say?)

Sir Bernard, his fiancée Carmen and their driver turned up at Bellamy House during the course of that afternoon. Red carpets awaited them. They had been on a pre-honeymoon in the Bahamas to escape the press. Carmen was tanned, and had a very large diamond ring upon her finger. The first thing she did on her arrival was to take a taxi to Landsfield Crescent to see Laura and Annie. Annie was back from New Zealand, buying her trousseau. She had decided against wearing the McLean wedding dress: she was having a new one made: the fabric woven specially by one of the few remaining mills in the North of England – the very same firm which had made the original. Having discovered just how much money there was in the McLean bank accounts, she had no fear of spending it, and since her will was now stronger than Mrs McLean's – 'One brush with death and she's off, just like my sister,' mourned the latter – had no trouble extracting all the funds she needed from the family.

Annie and Laura were gratified that Carmen had come to visit them: they'd thought perhaps she'd grown too grand. It was tea time. Caroline and Sara watched TV as they ate. Laura spoon-fed little Alexandra, now at last out of her plaster cast.

'It's like feeding birds,' she complained. 'Cheep cheep cheep, they go, and call you back if ever you try to get away. Don't believe marriage is any kind of happy ending. It's the beginning of trouble. I should never have done it. Why can't you take my example as a warning?'

But Annie fingered a swatch of ivory silk fabric and Carmen turned her ring so it caught the light: they knew well enough they'd let Mrs Baker down, they said, but it had always been on the cards that they would. Annie said she had the responsibility of twenty thousand sheep, didn't that add up to something? Carmen said she was already organising private funding for climatological research with relation to the ozone layer, was not that some kind of excuse? Alexandra hiccoughed and regurgitated a great deal of bland porridge and Laura gritted her teeth.

'Fenedge girls grow rich,' she said. 'So what?'

There was a hoot from outside. It was Driver in the BMW.

'So he's still around,' said Laura. 'How's your soul, Carmen?'

'Just fine,' she said.

The front door bell rang, and Carmen opened it to Driver. His uniform was silvery grey, and glinted like the inside of a plover's wings.

'You must come at once,' he said, 'the mumbo jumbo's about to start. Anyone who's anyone is up at the site, except you three. The protestors are going nuts, the camera crews are out, the Bishop's setting up, and there are millions at stake. Will Sir Bernard be allowed to proceed or will he not? Will the East Coast be saved from flooding, or will the conservationists win the day and drown the human race? Lover boy wants you up there, Carmen, on the double, so get your arse in gear.'

'I do what I please,' she said.

'No you don't,' said Driver. 'Today's favourite can get to be tomorrow's hag. Skinny shanks! Remember I own your soul.'

'You'd better go up with him, Carmen,' said Laura. 'I'll get Kim to baby-sit and Annie and I'll come up together.'

The three of them looked at Driver as if they had other plans for Carmen's soul than that he should claim it so easily, and he sparked a bit and snarled; it was just like the old days.

Now there are varying accounts of this event. All agree that the site had been hard-cored, that is to say spread with aggregate and rolled to provide a flat, dark grey, dead surface, empty of all animal or plant life. The walls of the Roman villa had been flattened, its tiled floors had disintegrated, the holes in the ground that had once been graves were forgotten for ever, the Druid well was obliterated: all had been mished and mashed together to help create this useful and universal flatness. Only the spirits breathing and sighing in the restless air made everyone uneasy. The sun was setting; the moon was rising. The evening was glowing in yellows and oranges, not just pinks and reds, as evenings in this part of the world occasionally do when the winds from the east are about to change, and veer to the north, bringing the wild weather, blowing in the sea birds – the teal, the mallard, the pintail, the shelduck, the eider, the occasional Mediterranean gull, the lapwing. But they'd just take one look and be off again.

Ranged on the top of the sand dunes were seven earth-moving machines: they were bright yellow themselves, like children's toys on a massive scale. It was clear they were waiting, poised, for the ceremony to finish, to swoop and begin trenching the hard core for the installation of the pre-stressed metal rods that would provide the base of an automated dock for ocean-going yachts, or so the press had been told. You could tell the machines were impatient. They fidgeted; their long arms hovering and shifting slightly from time to time.

On the slopes beneath the machinery stood the grey-suited executives of the Bellamy Empire, and the planning officials, and the Mayor of Fenedge and his team. They were not in sympathy with this event: respect for Church and State required them to be there, and with solemn faces, though in their hearts all thought it was mumbo jumbo.

Facing them on the other slope stood the protestors, a dishevelled lot, truculent and badly organised, their banners tawdry and hopeless. They'd lost. The Eastern Scheme proceeded. As a sop they'd been given a reconciliation service, offered by a Church which had lain down in front of big business, not the bulldozers, which had failed in its capacity for indignation. The Bellamy

House guests, clambering over the ridge from the direction of the gravel pits, made their way to the other slope, where they felt more at home.

In the centre of the hard core stood a small trestle table, white-clothed. A couple of battery-run electric candles flanked a jam jar full of flowers. Late roses from someone's garden: some pretty bracken. The evening wind sighed and lamented.

Sir Bernard and Carmen were down on the hard core next to the Bishop's table. A couple of selected newspaper men, a single camera team and one radio reporter were with them, permitted to take advantage of the photo opportunity. The others, out of respect for the Church, were kept back by Sir Bernard's security teams – Laura and Annie kept Carmen company. Driver parked nearby: he sat in the BMW, as if sulking.

The Bishop had the back of his 2CV open. He'd parked with the protestors. He was youngish and good-looking. He was wearing jeans and a sweater. He took out his robes and put them on. Mavis hovered around to help him; she wanted to adjust the flaps of heavy cream fabric that hung from his shoulders. His assisting clergy tried to edge her away, but she ignored them. The Bishop took his shepherd's crook from the back seat – it would not fit in the boot – and walked towards his table. There was scattered applause from the crowd, a Godless lot who saw this as mere spectacle, although impressive. A gust of cold wind rebuked them.

'Pathetic,' said Driver to the radio reporter, lowering his window to do so. 'A service of reconciliation. What for? There's nothing here that lives or grows. Not any more.'
'Can I record this?' asked the reporter.
'No,' said Driver, and the window slid up, nearly snapping off the reporter's nose.

'Don't lower the seas,' said Sir Bernard to the TV man. 'Raise the land. Save the world and line the pocket! What this planet needs is one strong, good man, one man so immensely rich, immensely powerful, immensely wise, that all consent to his will.

One man held back neither by electorate, nor Church, nor fear of
failure, sustained by love –'

'Can I record this?'

'Certainly,' said Sir Bernard.

'Bernie,' said Carmen, 'do be careful. You're getting a little
carried away. It isn't safe.'

'Don't be a wet blanket, Car,' said Sir Bernard. 'This is a wonderful day. Wonderful! Glorious! A day of triumph! Second only to
our wedding day. And there being no more diversity of power,
peace and justice shall prevail throughout the world.'

'Attaboy!' remarked Driver. He had got out of his car and was
egging Sir Bernard on. He was grinning. It was not a pretty sight.
'You tell 'em!'

'As there is one God in heaven,' Sir Bernard told them, 'so shall
there be his equivalent here on Earth.'

Driver's eyes were unnaturally bright. The TV man wondered if
both were high on cocaine. It was more than likely. He had his
camera whirring.

'I suppose we'll never know now,' remarked the press man, 'just
what treasures lie beneath our feet.'

'The site is safely sealed over,' put in Driver, since Sir Bernard
looked blank, 'for future generations, when new and more precise
archaeological techniques have been developed. We are doing
both the past and the future a service, as well as making the
present prosperous.'

The wind got up a little. The crowd on the left sang 'For All the
Saints': a scattered sound, but brave. Unbelievers joined in. Sir
Bernard had a walkie-talkie in his hand. He liked to be directly
involved. The contractor's voice crackled through it. 'Shall I keep
back the machines, Sir Bernard, or shall we just go on? This
delay's costing a thousand a machine an hour. The men are
already on overtime.'

'Keep 'em back,' said Sir Bernard, 'till this charade is over.'

The contractor's voice came through the radio speakers in the
cabs of the earth-mover team. 'Anyone else turns up any old
bones, they join Jed Foster in the dole queue. Understood?'

It was unfortunate that his voice came through the public address
system as well as in the cabs, but fortunate that the Bishop's voice
overlapped his.

'In the name of the Father, the Son, and the Holy Ghost, let us remember that in the distant past others like us walked to this very spot, in the same spirit as we do today, to lay their dead to rest, give thanks for their lives, and commend them to God, in the sure and certain hope of the Resurrection to eternal life through Jesus Christ our Lord –'

Driver guffawed, but the Bishop's voice was rich and convincing and no one joined him in his derision. The Bishop held up his arm as if to hold back the bulldozers: a small, white, defiant figure centred in a black wasteland; he was Canute failing to hold back the waves of progress, but he was magnificent. A sigh ran round the living crowd, and subsumed the sighing of the dead. Mavis later swore she saw their spirits streaming off towards the west: white, like liquid gossamer, released, leaving the place which had held them captive for so long.

'Man does not live by bread alone and woe to them that do not understand it – those who deny that Christ is within them,' said the Bishop to the elements, and to all those who had ears to hear, and heard.

'Eternal God,' he said, and the sound carried out to sea, 'who holds all souls in life: shed forth, we pray, upon your whole Church in paradise the bright beam of your light and heavenly comfort –'

Driver yawned but yawned alone.

'– so that at last our dead brethren enter into the fullness of eternal.joy, through Jesus Christ our Lord, Amen.'

'That's got to be that,' said the contractor, more publicly than he knew. 'Back to work. Stand by to fire charges.'

Many of the crowd took to their heels. The table was hastily folded. Even the Bishop retreated. Laura and Annie clung together but wouldn't abandon the action: they felt they saw too little of it.

'What fools people are,' cried Sir Bernard. 'You offer them progress, they choose superstition.' He held Carmen fast to his arm. She couldn't have run if she'd wanted to. A whistle blew: birds wheeled into the air. Stones and dust flew all around them. The stones missed; the dust fell on everyone except Driver, who stayed shiny black and magnificent, proud as a raven perching next to a flock of raggedy, rusty crows. Sir Bernard ignored it all.

'Let God himself,' cried Sir Bernard, 'marvel at man's audacity. We will change the course of the rivers, we will reshape the mountains, we will reform our coasts – we will make the very globe bend to our will.'

'Come off it, Bernie,' begged Carmen. 'What are you doing really? Spoiling a few acres, unsettling a few birds. Don't say these things. It's dangerous.'

'The valleys exult,' cried Sir Bernard. 'Leviathan bows down. Like a worm I crept from the soil. Colossus-like I stride the earth –'

'He's flipped,' said Laura. 'You can't marry a madman, Carmen.'

'Leave now,' begged Annie, but Carmen just said 'I love him' and wouldn't be moved, not even when another explosion showered them with debris. They could see on the rim of the site the crowds melting, cars departing. The sun was sinking fast.

Sir Bernard left the group and scrambled to the top of a dune, the better to appreciate control of the landscape. He flung his arm to the sky.

'See how the God approaches, a raging fire behind, a furious storm before. Let all heaven and earth be my witness: may my valleys be for ever full: the silver and the golden bowl intact for ever: this is the day of man's creation, man's victory over God – may this day last for ever!'

Now I bodge this together from many people's accounts. I was not present. All agree that the Bishop's service was inspirational, and that Sir Bernard stood on the edge of the site and raved, and that Carmen swore she loved him and seemed to mean it. Mavis says that she saw the sun rise again in the west and make its way back across the sky as if reality were in rewind, but she was the only one to do so.

All agree that Sir Bernard clutched his heart and had some kind of seizure – that he fell to the ground and rolled down the slope and lay there as if dead, as another explosion sent rock and debris flying and all for a second stood stunned. Some confirm that Driver said something bizarre, like 'Jam today was what he wanted: he couldn't wait for jam tomorrow, but tomorrow always comes,' and that his voice was louder and stronger than it ought to have been, but probably because he had his radio system switched on and it was coming over the loudspeakers. It is clear that Carmen called out for an ambulance and Driver gloated and said, 'Too late for all that resuscitation rubbish now. His soul is on its way to me: I feel its approach, I tingle, I tingle,' and jerked about like Elvis Presley, and that Sir Bernard too twitched quite a bit before lying still.

And only Laura claims that with the last explosion she, Annie and Carmen found themselves in blackness, surrounded by a ring of flames, and that Sir Bernard's body lay at their feet, that Driver, in a black-to-grey outfit suitable for the Lord of the Ravens, all metal feathers and broad shoulders, faced them and that his eyes were pools of fire; and that she was brave enough to tell him what nobody but her truly believed, or Driver could conceive of – that Carmen's relationship with Sir Bernard was platonic, that she was still a virgin, that the tears Carmen wept over Sir Bernard's body were virgin's tears, and so she had cheated him, and kept her soul, and so had Sir Bernard. I don't believe all that. I think that's just the fantasy of a girl who's at it all the time, does not take proper contraceptive precautions, and has four children as a result.

Annie reports a ring of flame and blackness and Driver speaking in Mavis's voice and saying, 'Run to the ends of the earth, run as far as you like, I'm still your mum: you'll never get away,' and in Alan's voice saying, 'Starve yourself to death, there's no escape; you're half your mum and half your dad, for ever and ever, that's it,' which left her shaken and upset.
And that Driver then took on Audrey's face to moan and groan at Laura and gabble about original sin and how she was her father's daughter and no amount of motherhood would cleanse her: and that when back in his own body, he capered about, baa-ing like a sheep and jeering at her, Annie, and prodding Carmen with a cloven hoof in a shiny leather shoe and telling her to stop praying to God because God was out to lunch and he was in charge: and how Carmen's tears turned into diamonds as they fell upon Sir Bernard, and enraged him further. 'Little Miss Frigid!' yelled Driver. 'I'm your dad and don't you forget it; every girl's

dad, the spice in your life, the fork to your knife –' and then he
was talking to himself, first with Raelene's face, then with Andy's.
Raelene was weeping and wailing about rape, and Andy saying
she'd been asking for it.

He began to sound so ridiculous, so over the top, that she, Annie,
began to laugh, and Laura laughed too. That calmed Driver. He
said to Carmen, in a perfectly reasonable voice, 'Shall we have a
little self-interest here, Carmen? A young girl like you married to
an old man like him. I'm off and he'll fall to pieces without me:
he'll blow farts; his breath will stink; he'll wear slippers and his
trousers rolled. Bored? You'll die! Five years on and you'll look
into someone else's eyes, as sure as rotten eggs are rotten eggs,
and I'll be looking out of them. I'll have your soul in the end.
You were born for me and me alone.'
'I love him,' said Carmen.
'Then let me have both your souls,' he pleaded, 'for my cassette
shelf –' – now why, Annie wanted me to tell her, was Driver
suddenly talking about cassettes? – 'then the two of you can be
together, side by side, incorporated and consumed, for all
eternity.'
'No,' said Carmen. 'I'd rather live in real time.'
'Boring, boring, boring,' he shrieked and with a smell of singeing
feathers he was gone, along with the ring of flame.
Bizarre, said Annie, but that's what I recall.

But I dismiss this too as Annie's fantasy; for all her staunch
everydayness, I think she had indeed inherited some of Mavis's
capacity to read minds, though she always fought against it. She
projected into Driver's mouth all the things she knew but would
rather not, and had picked out of people's minds details she had
no right to. And perhaps there was some slight hallucinogen in
the air, from the heather that the contractor's explosions had fired,
because Laura had been affected too.

When reality re-established itself, nevertheless, Driver and the
BMW were gone, simply gone, and the ambulance was there, and
Sir Bernard was sitting up, his head on Carmen's shoulder. The
ambulance driver said, 'I could have sworn he was a goner,' and
had to sit down himself.

Sir Bernard said, 'Carmen, I have a shocking headache. What's going on?'

'You were stunned by a rock, I think,' said Carmen. 'But you're okay now.'

'What was I saying? I seem to remember becoming quite excited. I'm too old for this kind of caper.'

'I expect you are,' said Carmen.

'You'll have to keep my slippers warmed,' he said. 'Time to rest on my laurels.'

'It is, my darling,' she said, and her eyes seemed to slip sideways, but Driver was gone: she had chosen.

'Remind me to fire the driver,' said Sir Bernard to Carmen as they helped him into the ambulance. 'If I can fire Mrs Haverill, I can fire him too. He really gets above himself. I'm perfectly capable of driving myself.'

'Of course you are, Bernie,' said Carmen, clambering in after him.

And the ambulance doors shut, and off Sir Bernard and Carmen drove into their future, and the contractor's bulldozers roared down, Annie and Laura fled, and the great Eastern Scheme was underway once more.

22

Many of us, including me, though I had to use a stick, managed to cross the world to get to Annie's wedding, which was a triumph, under brilliant skies, of helipads, marquees, Pavlova cakes and wonderful New Zealand wine. The white Chardonnay is superb: golden in the bottle, nectar to the tongue. The bride was slim, not bony, and sucked barley sugars before and after the ceremony. Her father gave her away: her mother wore a pink dress which became her very much, but was too like the one Mrs McLean was wearing for comfort. It was Mrs McLean who changed, into a pleasant blue outfit. Mavis and Alan were seriously contemplating a move to New Zealand. Mavis loved the bush – so quiet, dark and sinister, unspoiled. Laura and Woodie came with all the children – they too thought they'd stay, if the Government would have them. A wonderful place to bring up kids; and the pace of life would suit Woodie. Sir Bernard paid for their tickets: whatever Carmen asked, it seemed, he did. In the end they had been married secretly in the Bahamas – Sir Bernard had quite gone off PR since his accident – and presumably the wedding night went okay; at any rate Carmen was now pregnant. Annie was not sure whether she wanted children, though Tim said he'd like a little brood of kiwis some time. They went off to the Franz Joseph Glacier for their honeymoon. The returning party slept off the excitement and the Chardonnay while night turned to day, and day to night, with extraordinary rapidity outside the aircraft window. I kept the blind open, though I was meant to keep it down for the film, the better to see the Southern Cross, and the strange starry constellations of the other hemisphere. Cassiopeia, Betelgeuse, the Red Dwarf. I was not sure whether I would have time to study the stars and learn their names, now that I had to take my place in normal society. My disability allowance had ceased. I would have to find a job, or write a novel: something.

I would like to report that the Devil's safe house burnt down: was razed to the ground as some desperate member of staff, out of control since the departure of Mrs Haverill, attempted to burn out the bed bugs. But it would not be true. Bellamy House still stands, and makes a decent profit, and nothing exciting or scandalous or remarkable seems to happen there. But then nothing exciting ever happens in Fenedge these days. A tradition has grown up that you must never insult the town aloud, or hope too vehemently to escape it, in case the Devil happens to be flying by, and overhears, and all hell breaks loose.

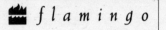
flamingo

Flamingo is a quality imprint publishing both fiction and non-fiction. Below are some recent titles.

Fiction
- [ ] The Things They Carried *Tim O'Brien* £4.99
- [ ] Matilda's Mistake *Anne Oakley* £4.99
- [ ] Acts of Worship *Yukio Mishima* £4.99
- [ ] My Cousin, My Gastroenterologist *Mark Leyner* £4.99
- [ ] Escapes *Joy Williams* £4.99
- [ ] The Dust Roads of Monferrato *Rosetta Loy* £4.99
- [ ] The Last Trump of Avram Blok *Simon Louvish* £4.99
- [ ] Captain Vinegar's Commission *Philip Glazebrook* £4.99
- [ ] Gate at the End of the World *Philip Glazebrook* £4.99
- [ ] Ordinary Love *Jane Smiley* £4.99

Non-fiction
- [ ] A Stranger in Tibet *Scott Berry* £4.99
- [ ] The Quantum Self *Danah Zohar* £4.99
- [ ] Ford Madox Ford *Alan Judd* £6.99
- [ ] C. S. Lewis *A. N. Wilson* £5.99
- [ ] Meatless Days *Sara Suleri* £4.99
- [ ] Finding Connections *P. J. Kavanagh* £4.99
- [ ] Shadows Round the Moon *Roy Heath* £4.99
- [ ] Sweet Summer *Bebe Moore Campbell* £4.99

You can buy Flamingo paperbacks at your local bookshop or newsagent. Or you can order them from Fontana Paperbacks, Cash Sales Department, Box 29, Douglas, Isle of Man. Please send a cheque, postal or money order (not currency) worth the purchase price plus 22p per book (or plus 22p per book if outside the UK).

NAME (Block letters)_____

ADDRESS_____

_____